More Praise for *Deep in the Shade of Paradise* . . .

"A magical gumbo of quirky characters . . . this bodacious piece of work [is] one of the great bargains in our overpriced world. Buy it and rejoice at your good fortune."

—*The Dallas Morning News*

"An outrageous tale of gothic proportions . . . The spirit of this book is just so bighearted, it's nearly impossible for the reader not to get swept along."

—*The Boston Globe*

"Highly entertaining."

—*Tampa Tribune-Times*

"A funny, wise, and tenderhearted novel."

—*The Charlotte Observer*

John Dufresne is the award-winning author of *Louisiana Power & Light* and *Love Warps the Mind a Little* (available in Plume editions), both of which were named *New York Times* Notable Books. He teaches at Florida International University and lives with his family in Dania Beach, Florida.

Deep in the Shade of

PARADiSE

by JOHN DUFRESNE

A PLUME BOOK

PLUME
Published by the Penguin Group
Penguin Putnam Inc., 375 Hudson Street, New York, New York 10014, U.S.A.
Penguin Books Ltd, 80 Strand, London WC2R 0RL, England
Penguin Books Australia Ltd, 250 Camberwell Road, Camberwell, Victoria 3124, Australia
Penguin Books Canada Ltd, 10 Alcorn Avenue, Toronto, Ontario, Canada M4V 3B2
Penguin Books (N.Z.) Ltd, Cnr Rosedale and Airborne Roads, Albany, Auckland 1310, New Zealand

Penguin Books Ltd, Registered Offices: Harmondsworth, Middlesex, England

Published by Plume, a member of Penguin Putnam Inc. This is an authorized reprint of a
hardcover edition published by W. W. Norton. For information address W. W. Norton &
Company, Inc., 500 Fifth Avenue, New York, New York 10110.

First Plume Printing, February 2003
10 9 8 7 6 5 4 3 2 1

Ⓟ REGISTERED TRADEMARK—MARCA REGISTRADA

The Library of Congress has catalogued the W. W. Norton edition as follows:

Dufresne, John.
Deep in the shade of paradise / by John Dufresne.
p.   cm.
ISBN 0-393-02020-7 (hc.)
ISBN 0-452-28406-6 (pbk.)
1. Plantation life—Fiction. 2. Louisiana—Fiction.
3. Weddings—Fiction. I. Title.

PS3554.U325 D44 2002
813'.54—dc21   2001044487

Printed in the United States of America

Original hardcover design by Judith Stagnitto Abbate/Abbate Design

FOR CINDY

What do we know but that we face
One another in this place?

—WILLIAM BUTLER YEATS

Contents

Acknowledgments

Thanks to Tristan, from whom Boudou grew, for putting up with my absences, and to Jill Bialosky and Dick McDonough for suffering my indulgences. And as always, to the family: Lefty, Doris, Paula, Mark, and Dee Dee.

If a man could pass through Paradise in a dream, and have a flower presented to him as a pledge that his soul had really been there, and if he found that flower in his hand when he awoke—Aye, and what then?

—SAMUEL TAYLOR COLERIDGE

The Loudermilks
(from Alvin Lee's Bible)

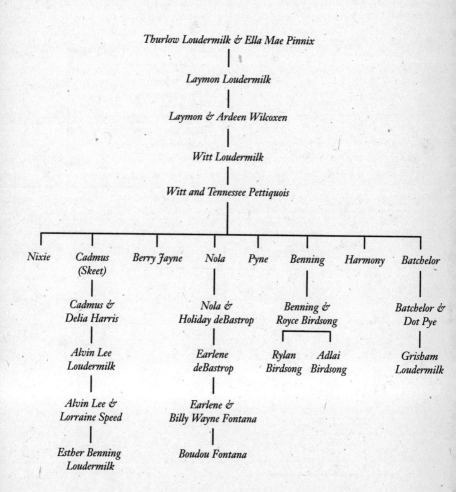

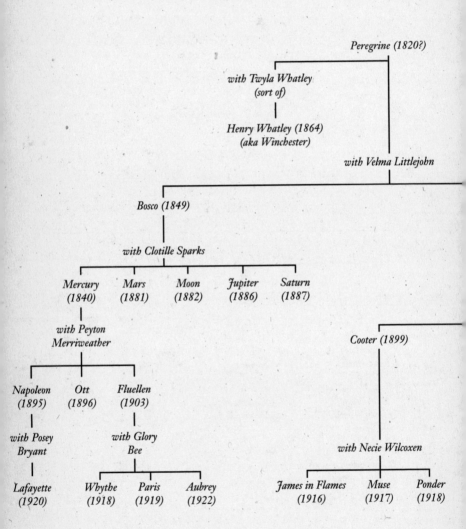

Family Tree of the Documented Fontanas
As Near As Grayson Berard Can Figure It.

(Dates Approximate in Some Cases.)

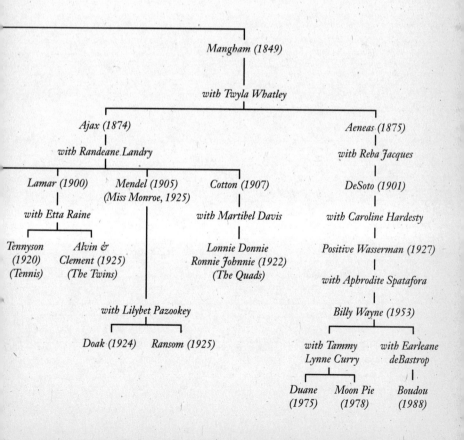

Mangham (1849)

with Twyla Whatley

Ajax (1874)

with Randeane Landry

Aeneas (1875)

with Reba Jacques

Lamar (1900)

with Etta Raine

Mendel (1905)
(Miss Monroe, 1925)

Cotton (1907)

with Martibel Davis

DeSoto (1901)

with Caroline Hardesty

Tennyson
(1920)
(Tennis)

Alvin &
Clement (1925)
(The Twins)

Lonnie Donnie
Ronnie Johnnie (1922)
(The Quads)

Positive Wasserman (1927)

with Aphrodite Spatafora

with Lilybet Pazookey

Doak (1924)   Ransom (1925)

Billy Wayne (1953)

with Tammy
Lynne Curry

with Earleane
deBastrop

Duane
(1975)

Moon Pie
(1978)

Boudou
(1988)

Deep in the Shade of

PARAD*i*SE

Prologue

If I write it down, then I don't have
to remember it. I write to forget.

—BOUDOU FONTANA

Earlene Fontana did not name her baby Willie Fox or George Jones. She named him Bergeron Boudeleaux deBastrop Fontana, and she calls him Boudou, rhymes with *Who do?* And, naturally, we've kept our eyes on this final Fontana. He's got all his physical parts. He's a handsome boy, in fact. Reddish hair, dark brown eyes, freckles. He's got all his mental apparatus as well, and then some. He can taste sounds, smell words, things like that. When Boudou was six, he could put together a five-hundred-piece jigsaw puzzle in two minutes. There are no cloudy days for Boudou, but there is the day the cumulonimbus clouds in the southeast blew up into the shape of a sleeping armadillo. And he can tell you that that day was a Tuesday, September 24, or whatever. And he can tell you what he ate for breakfast that day and how it tasted. He can tell you what was playing at the cineplex, and if he happened to have read the business page of the *News-Star* while eating his grits, he could repeat every quote from the New York Stock Exchange. Some folks here in Monroe think, Well, that's it, then, isn't it? That's the Fontana curse, that reckless memory. Others of us think, How can recollection do a person harm?

In case you were not around for our earlier story concerning the ill-fated Fontana clan, you need to know a bit of what we have chronicled: that ever since the sudden appearance in the Delta of Peregrine, the first Fontana, in 1840, the family has suffered a magnificent history of mischance, misfortune, miscarriage, misadventure, and ruination in Ouachita Parish. Now, granted, some families will swim the occasional woeful lap in the gene pool (like the Hippolytes over to Solomon Alley, who had the several hydrocephalic babies in a row), but what has befallen our Fontanas surpasses understanding. For generations, nothing but illness, depravity, reckless and fatal bravado, improbable accident, all manner of tragedy— natural, manufactured, and, some contend, divinely inspired—has visited the children of Peregrine. Clever Fontana, dim Fontana, graceful or clumsy or sorry-assed or enterprising Fontana—no difference—all of them star-crossed, doomed. Like these:

Ajax. When Le Terre des Leperaux opened in Carville in 1894 to treat what we've come to call Hansen's Disease, hospital administrators decided it prudent to have the patients delivered on river barges at night. Ajax was the pilot in charge of the operation, and, as fate would have it, he fell in love with a member of his cargo, a delicate young woman from east Tennessee named Birdie Rodale, who was in the early stages of infection. Ajax, charmed by her delightful and self-deprecating wit and keen intelligence, convinced himself that beauty was skin deep, that love did not enter through the eye, but through the heart. However, as Birdie's disease progressed, as her nose collapsed, as she lost the blinking reflex, developed corneal ulcers—her eyes now dollops of glazed meringue on her nodulous and swollen face—as her hands curled and her toes blackened, Ajax found himself repulsed by her and sickened by his own repulsion.

Unable to face Birdie or to face his own ugly and abhorrent behavior, Ajax filled a croker sack with stones, tied the sack to his waist, and stepped off the barge into the Mississippi.

Alvin and *Clement* were identical twins and were in love with each other. Yes, in every way. Early one summer evening, after inspecting the mulberry trees in their garden, after cocktails on the veranda, the gentlemen climbed to the roof of the Layton Castle, held hands, and leaped. They landed face down in the oyster-shell drive. Clement, unfortunately, lived, lived to be ninety-five, and ended his days counting cockroaches on the ward ceiling at the North Louisiana Hospital for Mental Diseases.

Doak loved persimmons. He was eighteen when it happened, bald, chunky, and wearing thick, wire-framed spectacles. Doak shinnied his way out a persimmon branch, reached for a ripe persimmon, heard a crack, grabbed the fruit just as the branch split and dropped him onto the spear point of a wrought-iron fence below, impaling him through the gut. They found Doak with his eyes opened, the spectacles dangling from one ear, his lips puckered, the persimmon half eaten.

Wythe died when he swung the butt of his rifle at Faxon Mendinghall's coon dog and shot himself in the face. *Ransom* treated his luxuriant hair with camellia honey and egg yolk one evening and then made the mistake of setting his sleeping bag beside a fire ant mound. *James in Flames* got his name when a carnival fire-eater he was standing too close to swallowed a bit of fuel or accelerant or something and then belched, spraying James with fire. Luckily James got stopped, dropped, and rolled by the bearded lady and the pinhead. He died two years later while grouse hunting out by Cheniere Break. He got the bright idea of flushing the birds with dynamite. He lit the fuse and tossed the tube toward the thicket. His bluetick, Blaze, fetched it and chased after James in Flames till he caught up with him, and they both exploded.

And so on and on. And we're not only talking unusual deaths here. The Fontanas have been the sickest and the most executed white family in the history of Louisiana. Why? we ask. Why such relentless catastrophe in one family? And here's the thing: We will not accept an answer like "Just 'acause" or "No reason." We won't accept the premise that nothing is responsible for something. Life may, now and again, seem implausible, but our understanding of it is not. Nothing is random. Everything connects. Not chaos, incongruity, and agitation, but design, significance, and harmony, thank you very much.

And so in trying to understand the seemingly incomprehensible Fontana experience, we come to rely on theories which resonate with our particular awareness of this world, like the aforementioned theory of the curse (an idea supported by our mainline Christians—as you will hear) or of tremendously bad karma (by our New Agers, who sometimes confuse coincidence with cosmology) or of genetic mutation (by our medical community—homeopaths excepted [and which is really a variation of the bad-seed theory posited by our Holy Rollers]) or of improper diet (our nutritionists, both at the Ouachita Parish Family Health Center and Wellness Clinic and at the mall) or of simple perversity (our atheist)—well, there's no end to it. You all, of course, are free to believe whatever you wish to believe (if you honestly believe that you're free of your syntax and your vocabulary). Anyway, it's not important what we all make of the Fontana calamities, but what Boudou makes of them. His two half-brothers, Duane and Moon Pie, came to early and violent ends, and their daddy, Boudou's daddy, Billy Wayne, died on the very day Boudou was conceived. What's the boy to think? His momma told him you only find what you're looking for. If you're looking for a curse, well then, you'll sure enough find you a curse.

Boudou, though, seems unlikely to tumble into the same contemplative black hole that swallowed his daddy. He prefers doing to considering. On a given day, you could find Boudou down to the Ouachita slough hunting for spear points or traipsing along the river, or he might be grappling for catfish in the bayou or gigging frogs in the Bottom. He might be teaching himself how to juggle, might be lassoing a fence post or doing magic tricks for the regulars over to the Zodiac Car Wash. He doesn't seem susceptible to a curse, and we do have our fingers crossed because we all love that child to death.

Since we last spoke about the Fontanas, the world has changed some. Scientists have discovered elements in the universe that can be in two places at the same time and that something can come from nothing: a *virtual proton*. And this: a pulse of light that passes through a transparent chamber filled with "specially prepared" cesium gas appears to be pushed to speeds three hundred times the speed of light, so fast that the pulse exits the chamber before it enters! Time travel—that's where we're heading, or where we've been.

Cicero Wittlief had these findings in mind when he spoke up at the February meeting of the Great Books Club (Wittgenstein's *Philosophical Investigations*) at the Ouachita Public Library. He said these apparent paradoxes in the universe were nothing more than God's letting us know He can do anything He pleases. Light's a wave one day, a particle the next. Gravity's an attraction one day, a feature of curved space/time the next. The universe is steady one day, expanding the next. First there are five planets, then nine. Science is all the time trying to keep pace with God's whimsy. Bobby Sistrunk wondered was God maybe bored or unhappy.

Margaret Grimes stared across the seminar table at Royal Landry, asked him what he was smiling at, did he think creation was funny or something? Just thinking, Royal said, how some of us are looking for order and validation. We want to believe in an immortal being who made all that we apprehend and all that we imagine, who is outside of time and space, who is All-powerful, All-Good, All-This and All-That, who is the formless, matterless creator of form and matter, who is the generator and the repository of every atom and quark, and this absolute being, who is the essence of existence, and the existence of essence, knows us intimately, and furthermore, He likes us, loves us, watches over little us.

Ted Muto stared at the Van Veckhoven twins, at Cindy's left ear, at Sandy's bangs, damp and forked. Margaret leaned forward, elbows on the table. Let's say, she said, that the universe is a novel. When you close it, do the characters still exist? Ted said, Did they ever?

Shug Johnson, who seemed to be off in a world of his own most of the session, spoke up. He said, We're like stars, like galaxies, like clusters of galaxies. We're not where you think we are. Shug coughed, wiped his lips with a hanky, apologized. Even when we look at each other, he said, we're looking into the past.

And then Chiquita Deal snuck a look at her watch. She said, We need to talk about our retreat up to Lake Moliere. And everyone took out an appointment calendar, and, well, we'll leave them to it.

And what else is new? Well, our Northeast Louisiana University became the University of Louisiana–Monroe, and our utility company, Louisiana Power & Light, has gone regional and renamed itself Entergy. The lesson this teaches us, we suppose, is that you should not be allowed to play with words until you respect them. And we need to tell you about Shiver-de-Freeze. Monroyans discovered the area that would become Shiver-de-Freeze shortly before the War Between the States. They were drawn here by the healing waters of Lake Moliere, then presumed to be bottomless, by the abundant fish in the Louisiana River, and by the chalky, tasty blue clay dirt and the stands of wild pecan trees in the river's flood plain. Archaeological evidence suggests that aboriginals wandered here from Poverty Point and bathed in the not-so-malarial waters of the river nearly three thousand years ago when Lake Moliere was still a bend in the river and at about the time that Greek armies laid siege to the walled city of Troy. A thousand years later, the Cole Creek Indians, we think it was, built an earthen mound now called Mount of Olives, over a crematory. Later, the Ouachita Indians used the area for hunting and fishing, but considered it sacred land and would not defile the place with settlement.

And so the first houses were not built here until after the aforementioned war, when certain prosperous citizens of Monroe, those who had turned a tidy profit amid the recent upheaval, men like Breard Toulon, Birl Dooley, and James Spatafora, decided they would build themselves summer homes by the lake, just these few miles outside of town. This is about the time that the nomadic Fontana tribe showed up, pitched camp along the bayou that would take the family name, and engaged in subsistence trapping and fishing. The Fontanas stayed put until they noticed the first crew of gandy dancers laying track for the Bastrop & Monroe Railroad, at which time they drifted away in the direction of the Tensas wilderness.

Shiver-de-Freeze, by the way, is a corruption of the French *cheval de frise*, or "horse of Friesland," because it was the Frisians who first employed a defensive appliance of war, a device fashioned of pieces of timber twelve feet long with six sides into which were driven a great number of wooden pins about six feet long, crossing one another, and having the ends armed with iron points. Built to check cavalry charges. Then it became the name for any line of spikes or barbed wire fixed on the top of a railing, a method of construction used by Breard Toulon to build his corral, the first permanent structure along the Louisiana River.

Now, the reason you won't find Shiver-de-Freeze on most state maps is that it's a political subdivision of Monroe, a satellite ward, if you will, a kind of Monroe-in-exile, a place apart. One time it was called "the colony," then "the territory." Later folks called it "the precinct" or "Uptown" or "the island." If you have the official Ouachita Parish Department of Transportation and Development map, you could see the unidentified boot-shaped white polygon in the green Cities Service area. Up by the old natural gas fields, just west of Highway 139. That's it. That's Shiver-de-Freeze. Appended to Monroe, but with a distinct cultural, natural, and social identity. Shiver has a modicum of self-rule and an annual town meeting at which all of the town's 375 residents and property owners get their say, including the six deaf-mute Engrams whose private sign language no one else can understand.

There's always at least two stories, the one you set out to tell and the one you discover along the way; the one you know about, the one you don't. The intentional and the actual, you could say. (Take the New Testament, for example. Maybe it's the story of a God who became a man. Or maybe it's the story of a man who thought he was a god.) And maybe our intentions are not as significant as our discoveries. Maybe what you hear is more important than what we say. At any rate, welcome (or welcome back) to northeast Louisiana and thanks for coming by to listen to our story.

The Woman Shall Answer:

I WiLL

In the Bible, sexual intercourse is called
knowing, *and it's not called that by accident.*

—ALVIN LEE LOUDERMILK

This is the story of a wedding, a wedding that's also a reunion and a farewell, that's also—well, we'll get to all of that in time. First off, though, you should meet the espoused: Grisham and Ariane.

Grisham Loudermilk, groom-to-be, who was twenty-six, and who had recently passed the Louisiana Bar Exam, and who would begin working for the firm of Davis, Orum, Swearingen, Verlander, Loomis, and Street in Lafayette when the honeymoon (a week in Gatlinburg, Lord help us!) was over, was sitting at a table in a saloon called Gator's with a young woman he'd seen here before but had only just met. The single-carat wedding ring he'd picked up at Zale's was in its snappy suede box in the inside breast pocket of his suit jacket. The jacket was slung over the back of his chair. His tie was loose, his collar unbuttoned, his bottom lip was glistening as it does when he is being glib and charming.

Grisham was leaving for Shiver-de-Freeze in the morning. He'd be driving up with his best man, Duane Prisock. Grisham was telling this young woman, Miranda Ferry, a joke about a Jew, a WASP, and a Cajun. After this drink he would suggest they retire to some more intimate spot, and she'd agree. Women adored Grisham Loudermilk, were disarmed by his cornflower-blue eyes, his dimples, his arresting smile. They sensed that he appreciated women, defined himself in terms of them. Grisham himself found this amusing, this perception that he was better than he was, more sensitive, understanding, and considerate.

Grisham reached to Miranda's face, touched a strand of her coppery hair, and tucked it behind her ear. She blushed, smiled, shifted in her chair. She wanted to close her eyes. She took his hand, turned it over, ran her fingernail along his love line. She looked at Grisham, then back at the two children she saw there in his palm.

Ariane Thevenot, bride-to-be, was packing for the wedding, for the honeymoon, for her move to the new split-level across town. Would her clothes even fit in those tiny closets? She called Grisham one more time. Her entire life was changing, and her fiancé would not answer his goddam telephone. She was breaking out in hives. Wouldn't that be nice! And her mother was no help at all. She was downstairs in the parlor entertaining Father Pat McDermott (of the hot sauce McDermotts), fawning all over him like she does. Ariane could never figure that. For one thing, he's so fat it takes two people to see him. He was down there now, flexing his table muscle, cupping a snifter of cognac in one hand, holding a cigar in the other, conducting the Acadian Pops Orchestra on the stereo like he was the high and the mighty. All those McDermotts thought they were something on a stick. What would she do if Grisham swelled up like Father Pat one day? She got this all-too-vivid picture of herself on top of an engorged and naked Grisham, and all she could think of was a dung beetle rolling home its booty.

What's gotten into her? Ariane scolded herself for her sacrilegious thoughts about the right reverend. If she could only get rid of this headache. But Father Pat was so patronizing and so always there at her house—still she had to be pleasant, at least through the wedding. He was going to perform the ceremony, after all. Felt like someone heated an ice pick in oil, stabbed the point into that little indentation in the socket bone between her eyelid and eyebrow, and then plunged the shank into her brain.

Ariane looked at her bed and saw herself at seven years old, snuggled under the covers with her doll Annie, right after her daddy dropped dead at Rivard's Seafood Restaurant—got this demented smile on his face, grabbed hold of the tablecloth, yanked it down with him when he fell, covering himself with crawfish shells. At first Ariane thought he was joking like he does, and she jumped on his belly, called him a silly bobo. Ariane saw her young self fingering a tuft of chenille on the bedspread, closing her eyes so tight the black turned green, and willing her daddy back to life. If she could just pray hard enough, if she were good enough, pretty enough, sweet enough, why then her daddy would be back home when she woke up, back sitting at the kitchen table, eating his andouille and eggs, sipping his chicory coffee, reading from the *Daily Racing Form* with his lucky pencil, the one she'd bought for him at the Immaculate Heart of Mary Church Bazaar. He'd tweak her nose, say, Ariane, honey, here's a little filly named Daddy's Best Gal that I'm going to bet just for you. He'd kiss Ariane on the forehead. Yes. But he never was back at the table, never did plant that kiss. Ariane heard the stereo fade downstairs, the telephone chirp. Maybe it was Grisham.

Miranda lived in a silver Airstream trailer at the Pinedale Mobile Home Court. Looks like a lunch box, Grisham thought. Miranda lifted a corner of her coco doormat and picked up her house key. She told Grisham how she'd driven her home here from Orange, Texas, where she was from. Uncle Phil and Aunt Loretta gave her the trailer—a 1963 Trade Wind model.

Grisham had never been in a trailer before. Wait'll he tells Duane about this. Grisham Loudermilk, Esquire, fooling with a trailer tramp. Miranda left him sitting at the fold-down kitchen table while she freshened up in the lav. Grisham heard the water running, the squirt and crackle of soap in Miranda's hands. He could hear someone, somewhere in the park, practicing scales on a cornet. He'd never seen a kitchen quite like this one. If you could call this little space a kitchen. Someone, probably Phil and Loretta, had glued travel stickers all over the cabinet doors. On one of them a cowboy rides a bridled jackrabbit. A drive-thru redwood tree; a stegosaurus in Port Orford, Oregon; a face on a barroom floor in Central City, Colorado, altitude 8,500 feet. And this: *You Don't Know Beans Until You Come to Boston, Mass.* There was a china dinner plate with Dwight and Mamie Eisenhower's picture on it hanging over the stove. Miranda's salt and pepper shakers were Rhett Butler (salt) and Scarlett O'Hara (pepper). Miranda yelled to Grisham that there was beer in the icebox. He got up. Who calls a fridge an icebox anymore? Grisham took a can of Pearl out of the little fridge. He popped the tab and drank. He read the magnetic poem on the refrigerator door:

rusted whispers of peach

the underfluff of our
elaborate apparatus
sleep
the boil of after
the crush of water when
the raw moon heaves

He shook his head. *Underfluff? Exhibit A, Your Honor. The literary evidence will show that the defendant is incapable of understanding the nature of the charges being brought against her.* He reads a newspaper article taped to the door. A woman told police she still loved her boyfriend, Lonnie Bouvier, even though he shot her five times for not picking up dog food at the grocery.

When the rain began, Grisham had to ask Miranda to speak up. She just smiled, kissed his shoulder, climbed over him and off the bed. Grisham wondered about someone who would choose to live like this, no television, no pets, alone, without a porch or a yard or an attic or a foundation. Live in a house with wheels. And how could you sleep with this noise, or think even? And then the fragrance of the sheets got his attention. Smelled like damp dirt, clay. He gathered Miranda's pillow to his face, inhaled the fizz and chalk of her—like tilled soil, humus. He remembered his mother's housekeeper, Florence, at the sink eating laundry starch.

Grisham looked at Miranda, the light from the open refrigerator splashing on her naked body. She waved to him, asked if he was hungry. What? Do you want something to eat? she yelled, and she mimed eating with a spoon. And just then the rain softened, the windows went blue with lightning. What are you making? She told him, Soup on the rocks. He said he'd have a beer. Grisham located his underwear and trousers and put them on, put his shirt on. He joined Miranda.

She opened a can of beef broth and poured it into a glass of ice cubes. She tapped in a drop of lemon juice concentrate. She raised her glass to Grisham. Cheers!

"Do you always eat like this?"

"I usually get dressed."

"I mean . . . what else do you eat?"

"French fries and ice cream. Cottage cheese and applesauce. Froot Loops and Hi-C."

Grisham couldn't tell if she was serious.

Miranda wiped broth from her chin with her fingers. She looked at Grisham. She said, "Good fish gets dull, but sex is always fun."

"Excuse me?"

"Something an Amazon tribesman said in this documentary I saw in anthropology class."

"You want to be an anthropologist?"

"That would be nice."

"What do you do?"

"Work on a poultry farm over to Carencro." Miranda told Grisham she sexes chicks, grades them, debeaks and vaccinates them. She catches them, too, feeds them, castrates the cockerels. A little bit of everything.

Grisham tried to picture testicles on a little bird.

"You got to open them up a bit. Get in there with a heated knife and forceps."

He watched Miranda drink her soup and thought how odd this was. Here he was in a cramped kitchen with a naked woman in a house that moves, and the woman was smiling at him, and he wondered what someone watching this scene would make of it all, would think of him, and it was all so strange that he was certain this had happened before, and if he turned and looked over his left shoulder he'd see a glass vase filled with fondue forks. And he did, and there was. A stainless steel bouquet. And he knew that Miranda was about to speak, and he recognized each one of her words in the moment before it was pronounced.

"I want to live in the desert someday," she said.

It was like he was reading his lines. "Why do you want to live in the desert?"

"To live in the desert."

Grisham was trying to figure it out. Usually this sensation lasted only a few seconds. He didn't know Miranda. Things don't happen twice.

She said, "Are you okay?"

Suddenly Grisham was certain that he was dreaming all this, that he was still in Miranda's bed, and this revelation unburdened him. Miranda was telling him something about how living in a mobile home kept you focused on the future because you had no space to store your past. He smiled. He couldn't help it. She was so cute. He looked at the tops of her ears, at her shoulders, at the hollow of her throat. He let himself imagine what life might be like with Miranda. Unpredictable certainly. Portable. Spontaneous. He saw the two of them sitting in the cab of a pickup, hauling the Airstream down some empty Interstate. Roy Orbison on the radio maybe. And whenever they feel frisky, they pull off the exit, find a campground, and hop in the sack. But what if an axle snapped in West Texas? What then? Grisham didn't want to live in the desert. What's the point of living somewhere else? It was nearly ten, and Grisham wondered why he was still here, why he hadn't called Ariane. She'd be worried. He looked at the telephone on the coffee table. She'd be livid. He looked at his suit jacket on the back of the chair.

Miranda said, "You can leave, you know. I don't expect anything." Someday she hoped she'd have a lover who'd behave as elegantly when he left as at any other time, who wouldn't twitch, check his watch, fall silent, who would tell her again what he had whispered to her earlier. She could love a man who took his leave with grace and goodwill.

Yesterday had been Ariane's last day at Lamy Lumber Brokers after five years at the same desk, and her friends Deirdre, Maryellen, and Lulu took her out for bourbon sours and buffalo wings at Bannisters, gave her a stuffed white autograph-dachshund that everyone in the office signed, even people she didn't really know, like the guys in shipping, and even Mr. Warren Lamy himself. Lulu wrote: *Aloha! from Horneylulu (because I like to get* leied, *ha ha!).* She told Ariane she wrote the inscription after everyone else had done theirs so that Chuck Drinkwater, the perv in sales, wouldn't get his nasty hopes up. I draw the line at married men, Lulu said. That means Grisham's safe. And they all laughed.

In her room, Ariane folded a silk camisole and arranged it in her overnight bag. She hated that she wouldn't be at work anymore, wouldn't get to gab with Mrs. Broussard about recipes, wouldn't gossip on break with Ramona and Grace, wouldn't find out how the romance between Ed Hall and Lourdes Perez turned out. This was the creepiest thing about life—you got to know people and then they were gone. You went to the same schools with your friends for twelve years. You came to rely on certain rhythms, on ritual conversations. You knew where you stood. You had nothing to prove. And then they told you it was over, and *snap!* the world changed. Who were you now?

Yesterday she hadn't let anyone see, but she did, she cried at her desk, at the water cooler, in the file room. She gave her *Far Side* calendar to Maryellen. Maryellen said, Cheer up, girl, we'll still be buds—this is only our job. But, of course, it was more than a job; it was a world, and Ariane was no longer a part of it. And she was forgetting already, forgetting the brand of copier they used, the color of the storage cabinets.

Ariane wished she were one of the adventurous people who find exhilaration in change, who embrace the new, cultivate the unexpected, accumulate friends. As soon as Ariane got close to anyone, she began to wonder how the friendship would end. She pictured herself saying goodbye on the telephone or at the airport or in a funeral parlor. Was this why she was getting married? For something permanent? Or the illusion of something permanent?

Ariane looked at the photo she had tucked into the frame of the vanity mirror. She and Grisham on the deck of the *Delta Princess*. Grisham looked like a little boy—bangs in his eyes, a droopy smile, like he was saying he's in your hands now and he hopes you won't hurt him. Ariane loved Grisham. Of course, she had also loved other boys. J. C. Ludy in junior high. He gave her up for baseball. It was nearly ten and Grisham still hadn't called. She was tired. She lay on the bed, closed her eyes, listened to the peal of thunder. J. C. had owned a bait shop by the Vermilion River until about a month ago. He bought all his worms, crickets, and minnows with a Mastercard. The interest was more than his markup. So now he wanted to be a television fisherman.

After J. C. there was James Hughes, a shy boy with warts on his hands who took her to church dances and to the movies. She dated Blanton Gilman right through high school, but then he went off to Hammond to college, and that was that. Ariane's mother called it— Blanton's off studying bachelorhood is what. Boys like a girl with a little something upstairs, she told Ariane.

Ariane was almost asleep now. She found herself thinking about—imagining, really—the Loudermilk place up in Shiver-de-

Freeze, where she had never been. It was her wedding day, and everyone was out in the backyard, and everything was just saturated with color and sharply defined. Brilliant sunshine, live oaks dripping with moss. The leaves so green they were red. She was taking her vows. Father Pat nodded. She said, With my body I thee worship. Whoops. She had to start over. Father Pat cleared his throat, spit into a handkerchief, put the hanky up the sleeve of his cassock. The assembled guests all smiled. Ariane blushed, began again. I, Ariane, take thee, Grisham, to be my bedded husband. And then Grisham pulled a ring the size of a dinner plate out of his pocket.

Ariane wanted to open her eyes but didn't have the will or the energy. Her reverie had a life of its own. Now everyone at the wedding decided to go swimming in the lake, clothes and all—so the leeches can't fasten to your skin. Of course, leeches can go right up under a wedding dress, someone said. Ariane heard her mother and the priest downstairs, laughing like loons. She was grateful to be saved from bloodsuckers.

Father Away

Your daddy's only curse was
believing he was cursed.

—EARLENE FONTANA

Boudou yelled good-night to his momma. He chounsed his pillow, snuggled under the covers, switched on the lamp, and opened his daddy's Bible. He read the inscription on the flyleaf: *To Billy Wayne Fontana, Soldier of Christ. From Sister Helen.* He turned to Job and pulled out the snapshot he kept there. Billy Wayne's standing alongside his LP&L bucket truck, wearing his utility belt, work boots, jeans, and a white T-shirt. His thumbs are hooked into the belt, and he's squinting at the photographer. Boudou somehow understood what Billy Wayne was thinking: My real life's not the one I'm leading. And then Boudou saw what his daddy saw: Earlene with a camera in front of her face. And behind Earlene their brick duplex on Concordia. There's a plastic Mexican and burro on the lawn, a crawfish chimney by the drainage ditch. Boudou shut his eyes, slipped into drowsy dreams, half in, half out of sleep, and his daddy is still there. Boudou asks him, "Why did you want to be a priest?"

"I wanted to be a saint, I guess."

And then they're sitting at the levee, looking down at the brown waters of the Ouachita. The *Delta Princess* is docked at the landing. "So why didn't you become a priest like you wanted to be?"

"I met your momma."

"Well, I guess you didn't want it very much."

"I loved her."

"You left her."

"I blamed her."

"For what?"

"For stopping me from doing what I was supposed to do."

"What was that?"

"Ending the Fontana line—no offense—and the curse for good and all."

Boudou hears the raspy *quark!* of a night heron, sees it wading along the shore, watches it spear a minnow. In one way Boudou was bored with these dreams—hypnagogic hallucinations, Dr. McDonough called them—because he and his daddy always seemed to be having the same conversation. Dr. McDonough told Boudou that he, Boudou, was angry with his father and that's why Billy Wayne kept returning—he wanted to be forgiven. But Boudou didn't feel angry. He'd seen anger often enough to recognize it. Anger was someone screaming bloody murder, or someone being silent. Funny what anger will do to a body that it's trying to escape: make you stamp your feet, slam cabinet doors, punch your fist into a wall. That's what Varden does. Boudou says, "Daddy, what's going to happen to me, do you think?"

Billy Wayne puts his arm around Boudou, pulls him close. "You're going to save us all."

"How?"

"You'll find the way."

Boudou imagines himself at night in the swamp, the fog so thick he can't see his hand in front of his face. He knows it's miles to home and he can only take teeny steps, but he can make the whole trip that way. "She's doing fine, you know."

"Who's that?"

"Your other wife. She married Russell Sikes, owns the Out of Body Travel Agency in Louisville. Seen her at the Piggly Wiggly pushing a baby girl in a buggy." A man in a bass boat fishes in the thickets. Looks like he snagged his line.

Billy Wayne says, "Regret eats the soul."

Dr. McDonough told Boudou to come right out and forgive Billy Wayne the next time they "spoke." But Boudou didn't think any child had the right to say that.

And then Boudou slipped from fantasy to dream, and in the dream he has lost his way, and Billy Wayne tells him, You won't find it by looking inside. You got to look out at the world. That's where the way is, where salvation is. And in the dream Boudou opens the night table drawer to put the Bible away, and when he does, he sees the drawer is crammed with tiny wriggling fish, all slapping their sleek, silver bodies against each other so that it sounds like rain in the trees.

Starlight Lit My Lonesomeness

*If you ever leave me, Earlene, I'll
light myself on fire outside your front
door. That's how much I love you.*

—VARDEN ROEBUCK

Earlene Fontana wrote, *I'm staying with you till the last dog dies.* She said the final word out loud, tapped her foot. She thought *size, lies, lives, rise, ties.* She put down her pen, massaged her hand. Then she remembered film. Need film for the wedding. She got up from the table, stretched, yawned, went to the fridge, and wrote *film* on the shopping list. Anything else? *Batteries.* She caught her reflection in the window. Not bad for two in the morning. If people could just see her like this—backlit, silhouetted, distant—if they didn't look real close, well, they might think she was as pretty as she used to be.

Earlene stepped outside for a breath of air. What she got was the reek of the paper mill across the river. Starry sky, moonless night. She listened to the trill of the chorus frogs. This morning as she lay in bed half awake, she remembered her best friend from third grade, Brenna Watts, saw the two of them walking past the shameless boys who loitered outside Womack's Grocery, heard the boys make that smutty sound, pursing their lips, sucking their teeth. Clay Trotter, who's dead now of leukemia, said how he loved the taste of bayou trash and laughed with his redneck friends, like he wasn't some kind of trash his own self.

Earlene was eight then, nine maybe. Brenna moved away in fourth grade. To Rhode Island. Earlene looked up at the Northern Cross, wondered what Brenna might be doing now, and if they were to meet again, would they disappoint each other. She thought how that vulgar incident was light-years ago and yet she was still angry with those boys, and hurt that Brenna never tried to contact her. *Light-years* made them sound like they had been years without significance or heft or burden. Why that image this morning?

Earlene went back into her kitchen, latched the screen door. She walked down the hall to Boudou's room, checked on him, took the Bible off his chest, raised the sheet up to his shoulders. Yes, this time Earlene has her son, so it doesn't hurt so much. But how had she allowed such a thing to happen again? First, her husband Billy Wayne left her for another woman. Now Varden has left her for his own little world. Yes, Varden's back there now, asleep in their bed, but he's gone from her all the same.

When Billy Wayne left Earlene, he told her he didn't love her. A lie. Earlene knew that. She knew Billy Wayne wanted love to beatify him, and when he found himself unhappy or restless, he lost his faith in his love for her. But Earlene could feel that love now. And there's their darling child Boudou as proof. Loving Billy Wayne had not been easy—like trying to gather light. Still, if he hadn't died . . .

Back at the table, Earlene sat, stared at her writing tablet. *With you always; love is the bind that ties.* She read her two lines, replaced the semicolon with a dash. Varden said he loved Earlene, said it all up and down the street. But Earlene couldn't feel it. He was forever declaring his devotion to and dependence on Earlene. Not only isn't that love, it's not even flattering. When she finished writing this song, she'd show the lyrics to Varden, see if he recognized himself.

Well, darling, I hope you realize / I'm with you till the last dog dies. / You know love is the bind that ties.

Earlene met Varden at a recording session in Shreveport. Varden Roebuck and the Buckaroos were rehearsing one of Earlene's songs for their first album. Boudou—he was just six then—said he didn't much like Varden's shiny, purple voice. Earlene liked it fine. When they were first dating, Varden was a fervent lover, enthusiastic and grateful. It seemed he couldn't get enough of Earlene, and, to be honest, that worried her. So much attention, so much ecstasy, she didn't feel she deserved.

And now Varden had all but stopped making love to Earlene. Unless she threw herself at him. These days his idea of sex was to lie there and be caressed, massaged, manipulated. Even this was exciting to Earlene, if a bit predictable and unembellished. He'd have a night every once in a while where he'd seem to be his own self again, but more often he was too tired or his back was out. I'm tuckered, Earlene, he'd say, and maybe he'd kiss her cheek if he felt guilty, pull the covers up, turn away, shut his eyes, leave Earlene to her book.

Earlene became aware of the birds singing, welcoming the first cyan light of dawn. She'd been up all night and had three lines to show for it. Lines she wasn't even sure she liked. She went to the sink and splashed cold water on her face, used a dish towel to dry it. She looked at her reflection, turned her head to the left, the right. She mussed her hair, feathered her bangs. If I tell him he doesn't want to make love anymore, he denies it. He says we made love three days ago when it was really a week ago. As if three days isn't my point anyway. Well, at least I can write about it.

"Write about what?"

"Jesus, Boudou, you scared the life out of me. Was I talking out loud?"

"Did you know the echidna doesn't dream?"

"What are you doing out of bed?"

"I heard you talking." He yawned, folded his hands on the top of his head. "Anyway it's six."

Earlene held out her arms. Boudou walked to her. They hugged. Earlene kissed his forehead. "The *what* doesn't dream?"

"Echidna. An Australian anteater."

Earlene let Boudou go. She filled the kettle with water, put it on the stove to heat. Boudou stood there in his boxers and stared out the window.

"Sit, I'll make you some cocoa."

Boudou sat cross-legged on the bench and tried to read where his mother's handwriting had carved itself into the soft pine table-top. He turned his head to catch the light. He could make out *hold-it smiles*. He thought about the school photographer, Mr. Gallipeau, and about Mr. Gallipeau's thick, glossy lips and the threads of saliva that connect his top and bottom lips when he says, "Cheese!" or "Sit still, Mr. Wiggles!"

Earlene said, "You were talking in your sleep."

"I was awake. I was pretending that my dad was with me and we were talking."

"What about?"

When Boudou told his momma about the conversation he'd had, okay, *imagined*, with Billy Wayne, she said she didn't think Billy Wayne would have said what he did about sainthood. He might have thought it, but he would not have expressed it. That would have been unsaintly, after all. Boudou said, "He's changed some since you knew him. He's more outspoken now."

Earlene turned down the flame under the water. She put the cocoa on the table, told Boudou he didn't need to spoon sugar into it. It was sweet enough already. Just like he was.

"Was the Fontana curse that killed him, wasn't it?"

"Was snakes. You know that. And I don't want to hear any talk about curses." Earlene sat, took the Visine out of her robe pocket, tapped a couple of drops in each eye.

"Why do people always talk about the Fontana curse, then?"

Earlene sat by Boudou. "See, it's people can't understand how things keep going wrong with the Fontanas. They want an explanation. They don't want to hear about chance, won't believe in luck or anything so unreasonable, uncontrollable. They need cause and effect. So they borrow this notion of a curse from the Bible, the sins of the father visited upon the children and whatnot."

" 'Even until his tenth generation shall his descendants not enter into the congregation of the Lord.' "

"And I suppose that makes them happy. Boudou, if there ever was such a thing as a curse, you could lick it." She kissed him on the forehead. "Tell me something new. And then we got to get moving. We're leaving for Shiver-de-Freeze this morning."

Boudou sipped his cocoa, looked at the ceiling where a coffeepot explosion years ago had left a stain in the shape of either Holland or a balding man with a prominent chin, depending on which eye you closed to look at it. He said, "You know how the universe is expanding faster and faster and will just keep going. Everything's rushing away from everything else. So someday everything will be so far apart that for all practical purposes, nothing will exist except emptiness."

Earlene shook her head. "Go take your shower."

"Cat bath."

"Shower."

"If you fell into a black hole and looked back, you would see the future flash before your eyes, but you wouldn't be able to tell anyone about it."

"Stop stalling."

"Do you think that's what death is like—being in a place where you can know the future? Where everything has already happened?"

"Except your shower."

"Should I wake Varden?"

"He's not coming."

"Adlai's going to be there, right?"

"Adlai, Royce, Benning, Alvin Lee, Grisham. Everyone. The whole family. Now get a move on."

Boudou headed down the hall.

Earlene poured herself a cup of coffee. She opened a cabinet door and looked at the photo taped there of her and Billy Wayne on their honeymoon at Cementland. Not an honest-to-goodness honeymoon, of course, just the local attraction they visited the weekend after they married. They're standing by a stegosaurus that looked more like a bony-plated snail than any kind of dinosaur. Billy Wayne's got his arm around her waist, and he's smiling to beat the band. George Binwaddie took the photo. That may have been the happiest day of her life. Billy Wayne couldn't hardly take his hands off her. They were never more than three feet from one another. She looked into the Polaroid camera that afternoon and saw a brilliant future laid out for herself and her friends. And now George is dead. So's Billy Wayne. So's Fox. It wasn't the world she'd been planning on. Billy Wayne used to quote Pascal, who said life was a prison from which every day people were taken away to be executed. Earlene couldn't keep this lovelessness up much longer. She'd leave Varden and find someone else. Or not. Live alone without the abrasions of unmet expectations that have left her raw.

Earlene carried her coffee outside, sat on the steps. Why does she need love from a man when she has her friends to love, her family, her boy? One thing men have always brought with them is trouble. Marzell Swan. Billy Wayne Fontana, Royal Landry, Varden Roebuck. Trouble and sorrow. Maybe this is what happens when you've decided to move on—you grieve for your life, for all you've missed, all you've lost. One day she might even miss Varden.

Earlene opened her notebook and made a new list, *SILENT THINGS: The wind without grass or shrubs or sand or trees. The lies you tell yourself. Ants. The flight of a barn owl. Time that you ignore. A stalking cat. The space between musical notes. A blush. Lemon on the tongue. A falling body. Enfleurage. The moment when a cell divides, and—*

"Your turn for the shower," Boudou said.

Boudou stood inside the door, his face mushed against the screen, water dripping down his face. "You know what your new banana shampoo smells like?"

"Did you use the nail brush? Let me see your nails."

"Like triangles, sparkly, spinning triangles."

"Oh, Boudou, give your brain a rest."

Scrambled I

And God said He was not the author of confusion.
That's what He said. Whispered it in my ear.

—DURWOOD TULLIVER

Adlai Birdsong was busy at the stove, seeing to it the eggs were bright-eyed and the bacon limber. Adlai was twenty-one and cared for his aging parents and for Avondale, the family farm. Most of the tillable land now was rented out to neighbors. He heard the pipes clang and the water shut off in the shower. He thought about how this here bacon connected him to Donnie Carr over to the meat department at Saterfiel's Dixie Dandy. Right this minute, Adlai figured, Donnie was probably kissing Anniece Pate good morning. Adlai had courted Anniece in high school, even declared his undying love for her in writing on the Flandreau water tower. He painted, *My love, my dove, my undefiled.* A mistake, it turned out. Anniece would have nothing to do with him. Still, even now, when Adlai thought of Anniece, which was often, he felt a rush of pleasant warmth at his neck and shoulders, and his eyes would close. More than anything, Adlai would like to be in love and in marriage. Who you are, he thought, depends on whom you love.

He didn't notice his daddy Royce traipse into the kitchen wearing only his pajama top and his cordovan slippers. Royce said good-morning and kissed his wife Benning on top of her head. When he sat and felt the tacky vinyl on his bottom, Royce made the face he makes when he eats a pomegranate. He said, "I did it again." Benning patted the back of his hand. Royce marched off to his room to put on his trousers, if he could find them, and his robe. The robe, he knew, was on the bed-thing, the what's-it, the bedpost. At least it was there once.

"Did you get the Rambler serviced, Adlai?" Benning said.

Adlai dropped yesterday's bread into the bacon grease and stepped back as it splattered. "Kebo Haley looked to it yesterday afternoon. And I fetched Daddy's medication. Got your evening dress Martinized. The car's all packed."

Adlai turned on the radio so his mother could listen to Brother Durwood Tulliver's syndicated *Holy Minute* program ". . . brought to you in Flandreau as a public service by radio station KSON and the Half-Moon Full Gospel Church, your unairified house of worship on Old Monroe Road."

"Oh, Brother Jesus!" Durwood Tulliver screamed. "You're a blind-eye opener! Yes, you are! You're a deaf-ear unplugger, a lung purifier, a gimpy-leg stiffener! You're a tumor-shrinker, Lord, an artery-unclogger! You're a heart-stiller, a soul-stirrer! You're a dead-raiser, a corpse-invigorator! You're a mind-sharpener, Lord Jesus-uh!"

Benning said, "Amen!"

Adlai pulled out the chair for his daddy. Royce smiled and sat. He touched the knife, the fork, the spoon, in turn, with his pointing finger. He stared at his napkin. "The painters were in the bedroom till three in the morning working on the sash and trim. Your mother slept right through it."

Adlai shook the napkin out of its fold and tucked an edge into the collar of Royce's pajama shirt. "You dreamed that, Daddy."

Brother Durwood said, "My nephew Bowie was eight years old when he had his lovely blue eye poked out, had it ripped and tore open while he was playing David and Goliath with Randy Ottnot's boy. When that little Ottnot seen what he done he commenced to screaming like a banshee. Bowie, though, he's as calm as pudding. He's holding his hands up to that ex-eye, cupping the juices and the spongy bits in his palm, and he says to the Ottnot, Don't cry, Junior. Jesus will give me back my eyesight. Praise God. And did He do it? Yes, He did it! Made that scrambled eye better than it ever was."

Adlai served breakfast, switched off the radio, sat. Benning said grace. Royce said, Eggs. Adlai said, Just the way you like them. Royce saw his face upside down on the back of the spoon, wondered how the face got tumbled in the air like that between his nose and the table.

Benning said, "We've got so much work to do before the wedding."

(Just so you know, Grisham was Benning's nephew—her late, younger brother Batchelor's boy—and he's Earlene's cousin, Earlene being a Loudermilk on her mama's side [Nola Loudermilk deBastrop was Benning's baby sister].)

Adlai reassured her, "We've got all week and Earlene will be there to help." Grisham's wedding was a reminder to Adlai of what was missing in his own life. He wanted what his cousin was about to receive: devotion and embrace, intimacy and tenderness, the love of a woman until death. Adlai considered the river of happiness, how he was wading in shallow water, up to his knees in cheerfulness, but what he desired was to drown in exultation. Such was Adlai's hunger for romance. He wanted a woman he could not live without, a woman blessed with enthusiasm, a woman with an exhilarating smile, who was witty and surprising and unconcerned with rectitude.

But where in Flandreau would he find such a woman? Most of the girls he had gone to Flandreau High School with—the accessible objects of his desire—were already married or either had moved to Shreveport or Monroe, or were, like Anniece Pate, otherwise engaged. And for now, and for as long as his parents needed him, Adlai was attached to Flandreau. But no woman had ever told Adlai that she loved him, and he feared none ever would.

Royce said, "We were knee-deep in September the year of the grasshopper plague." And he looked at his coffee. "Those big grasshoppers. Yellow ones."

"I'll just clean up and we'll get going," Adlai said.

"Aunt Merdelle said this was the end of the world coming, which was true enough for her brother Buck, my daddy. A cloud of hoppers descended along Millhaven Road and put out a grass fire, they were so thick."

Adlai cleared away Royce's plate.

Royce said, "My uncles laid out Daddy's corpse on a wooden board between two chairs in the parlor. They put a tub of ice and sawdust under the board. My job was to pick the ice into small chunks and put the chunks on Daddy's neck and inside his shirt. Cousin Mercidean kept the bottle flies from landing on the corpse."

Benning said, "This will be the first time we've had a family gathering up at the house since—well, since Rylan was alive."

The Eye Cannot See Itself

THE SUBJECT OF RECEPTION

Light is an agency
by which an object
of regard
arouses
the observer's eye.

—poem written on a napkin and found
by WINSOME POON at the Tolerance Street
Bar-b-que Res'rant ("Bring a Change of Clothes!")

Whenthe Rambler let out a sudden and piercing screech (Like a freight train's brakes, Benning said; Royce said, Like two milk bottles rubbed together; Adlai thought, Baby, caterwaul, howler monkey, a thousand fingernails sliding down a blackboard, and the whine of Dr. Cullipher's high-speed drill and the sound you might make if that diamond-burr drill bit were to puncture the enamel of your lateral incisor, drive through the dentine, pierce the odontoblast, enter the pulp chamber, and stab the throbbing nerve) and then began to overheat, Adlai eased the car onto the gravel bed of the rest area and parked. He helped Royce out the backseat and led him to the stone picnic table.

Benning remarked at how this was a lovely spot for lunch, spider lilies in the drainage ditch, blue-eyed grass and red irises along the roadside, and a view through the oaks and kudzu to the site where, in the last century, stood the prosperous community of Forksville. According to the state historical marker that Benning read, the Mount Zion Cemetery, burial ground for the McClendons and Faulks, would be yonder, just past the orange trash barrel.

So while Adlai walked a quarter mile to the Bayou Bedding Barn to phone Kebo Haley, Benning fetched the food hamper out the car and set the table. The blue tablecloth featured a fanciful yellow map of Louisiana with a drawing of cotton plants and oil derricks and steamboats and other economic icons. She smoothed the wrinkles from the state, set the bowl of corn pudding on Shreveport, the thermos of iced tea on Opelousas, the fried chicken and beet salad in the Gulf, the cheese biscuits on Ponchatoula. Royce snuffled. Benning lifted the tinfoil from the angel pie and peeked at the deflated meringue. Oh, well.

Royce said, "Smells like rain."

"That's almond you smell." Benning stood behind her husband and rested a cloth bib on his chest. She drew its arms around his neck and fastened the Velcro closure. She squeezed his shoulder. "The sun's out, darling."

He said, "I'm getting wet."

"Just your imagination."

Royce shut his eyes, put his arms on his head. "No picnic today."

"Sugar, it's not raining, not even an intsy bit."

"Run to the barn!" he said. And then Royce saw himself take the woman's elbow and lift her to her feet, and they both felt the deafening concussion of thunder, and he told her to just leave the food, and they were off across the field, soaked and laughing, slipping in the mud, running, and still the barn seemed far away, and Royce hoped they'd never gain its shelter, that they would, instead, always be holding hands like this, stumbling, giddy with fear and delight, happily battered by the elements, soaked to the skin by the wanton rain, pleased indeed with this their great fortune, to be together through the long and furious storm.

Benning said, "What are you smiling about?"

"I was with my wife. We—"

"I'm your wife."

Royce looked at Benning. She wondered what he saw.

Royce said, "You're my wife *now*."

"I'm your only wife. Ever."

Royce looked at the tablecloth, at the bass leaping out of Toledo Bend Reservoir, wiped his face with the bib. "Here comes the boy."

After lunch, Adlai collected the paper dishes, the chicken bones and gristle, and carried it all to the trash bucket. He noticed the several canted headstones through the tangle of brush, stepped through the bed of tickseed and wild violet, and knelt by the stones. *She Never Turned a Stranger from Her Door.* Mary Faulk never did. *1801–1839. The McClendons—a people sturdy as the oak, stalwart as the pine, gentle as the brook, and enduring as the hills.* And imbued with a delightful sense of irony, Adlai thought, and nostalgia for a more bucolic and temperate dwelling place. And this couplet above the last home of Alice McClendon:

> *Regard this grave you stand above*
> *This earthen bed as cold as love.*

What treachery was it that spoiled her life? *As cold as love.* What seditious heart so vanquished Alice that she immortalized her bitter regret in stone? Adlai ran his fingers across the whiskery lichen on the crown of the stone, imagined this Alice in her best dress. It's indigo, ankle-length with a belted waist, gathered sleeves. She's standing now in the back of the pew of the Forksville Temperance Church, staring at a page in her prayer book. Her black felt hat is garlanded with satin rosettes and banded with crimson velvet ribbon. She's not crying. Adlai stands at the back of the church. He sees an owl nestled on a rafter. And he can see Alice, see the lace handkerchief in her left hand. The preacher's theme today is *From This Day Forward*. He talks about marriage as a social contract, a community obligation, a sacred and civic duty. He tells the couple before him and the assembled congregation that you, Mary Margaret Mangan, and you, Charles Otis Faulk, are about to pass from dalliance and infatuation to commitment and devotion.

Adlai realizes that Alice is here this morning to witness the annihilation of her hopes and to cleanse her battered self in humiliation. Her special friend, Mr. Faulk, has taken another, but Alice is still in love and cannot make herself out of it. Adlai hears the creak of a bench, a cough—of what? he wonders: impatience? annoyance? Someone laughs quietly. Someone else calls his name.

"Adlai?" Benning said. "Did you pack your daddy's memory sack?"

Adlai fetched the sack from the car and delivered it to Benning at the picnic table. The sack was Benning's idea, her way of enabling Royce to cart along his past, a way to keep remembrance and identity portable, tangible, and evocative. She fashioned the sack from a failed cotton dress that she'd worn the day she walked to Pate's Pharmacy and asked young Tyler what she could do for a boy who could not move his head.

Adlai loosened the drawstring and slid the sack's contents onto the table: the gold-plated Elgin watch with a pigskin strap; the burgundy pearl Parker fountain pen with its silver clip in the shape of an arrow; the black and white photo bordered in white—the picture is Rylan, the brother Adlai never knew, at ten, riding a fenderless bicycle on a dirt road, shoeless, hatless, shirtless; the letter, folded into a square and enclosed in a plastic sleeve—the letter, Adlai knew, written by his great-great-great-uncle Starkey Birdsong to his sweetheart during the siege of Vicksburg, written but never posted,[*] the tarnished skeleton key; the Zippo lighter featuring the logo of

---

[*] This digression and other items of possible passing interest are noted with an asterisk and can be found in the Appendix.

the Krewe of Atreus; the silver Confederate half dollar, dated 1861; Royce's Louisiana driver's license, due to expire in six months; the wisteria sachet; and the Boy Scout whistle.

Benning picked up the photograph and held it for Royce to examine. "Here's Rylan."

Royce said, "He's awfully small."

Just then Kebo Haley pulled into the rest area in his wrecker. He stepped out of the truck, took a new fan belt from around his neck, and told Adlai, "Let's take a look, Ad."

Kebo apologized for not changing the belt yesterday when he saw how shiny it was getting. No excuse.

Adlai said he should have studied auto mechanics at school, and then he could have taken care of a little problem like this.

Kebo sucked his teeth. He said, "You have to have an instinct for the four-stroke engine. You have to understand the beauty and simplicity." He handed Adlai the screwdriver, bent over and reached for something below the motor housing. He stood up, spoke to the engine. "I can't tell you how embarrassed I am about this fan belt."

When he finished, Kebo sat with the family and tried to pay Royce for the inconvenience his oversight had caused. Royce told him, We don't want your money. Benning put Royce's totems back in the sack. Adlai asked Kebo would he like a chunk of angel pie.

"Go on, taste of it," Benning said.

Kebo nodded. "I don't know but what I'll try a sliver. Cut that half in two for me, Adlai."

Adlai said, "Last time I had angel pie I dreamed that night the air got a skin and you could poke at it and see the dark inside."

"I've been divorced from the former Mrs. Haley for twenty years now, and I still dream about her every night practically." Kebo put down his fork, wiped his mouth with his fingers. "And that means I end up thinking about her every day. She could be dead for all I know."

Benning said, "Earlene's little boy Boudou remembers everything at all. They're studying him over to UL–M. Got a brain like a blotter, they say."

Royce said, "Sometimes you can remember *what* happened, but other times you can only remember *that* it happened."

For just a minute, we'd like to intrude here to let you know about the state of memory research going on over to UL–M's Lamkin-Baker Institute for the Study of Memory. It seems that our traditional understanding of memory as the faculty of retaining and recalling past experience isn't quite accurate. Memory is a reexperiencing of that past event. It's not that you remember someone playing the piano, but that you sit there and hear the melody again. Well, that's one theory they're working on.

A few of the researchers are convinced that memory and imagination are essentially the same process, although they don't necessarily result in the identical product. The significant problem here is that the operations may, and normally do, contaminate each other. This insight has defense attorneys all over the parish delirious with anticipation. If memory is by its nature blessedly corrupt, then you can bundle all your eyewitness accounts in a burlap sack and drop them off the DeSiard Street bridge. Am I right about that, Your Honor? The adulteration of memory by imagination might explain these radiant-light, near-death narratives and past-life regressions and all that. That's what Dr. Johnny Paul 't Hooft, director of the institute, had to say on the *Good Morning, Ark-La-Miss* television show a while ago. And that's what ignited the academic feud between the institute and the university's Center for Applied Parapsychology. A furious Professor Bonnie Darling (she's neither, according to some of her staff) of CAP phoned the show and sounded off, calling Dr. 't Hooft's remarks typically rationalist, predictably male, and disappointingly occidental.

And probably we should be thinking *memories*—plural. There's long-term memory and short-term memory, episodic memory, factual memory, memory for skills, spatial memory, emotional memory, linguistic memory. And what about memory that hides the past from our consciousness? What do we name that? Inaccessible memory? And why is it that we forget?

And then there's what's being called the narrative theory of memory, which imagines a life as a succession of impressions (Is it me or is it hot in here?), concepts (Eternity), images, desires, puzzles, emotions, expectations, recollections—all of that without the experience of a simultaneous, unifying framework for this succession. A life, then, is a chronological sequence of events. But chronology isn't meaning. It's memory that provides the missing framework, gives structure and coherence to our lives. Memory is our plot, our story, our reason, our sense, our future. Without it, we are nothing.

All of which carries us back to Royce Birdsong. His past is leaking away, and he's losing himself, losing his sense of profluence—the idea that he's going somewhere, not just wandering, lost in a desert of disremembrance. He'll become, he fears, a person without self, a form without content. There are days when he isn't certain his experiences are his own, days when he can respond but not think. There are still clear days when he can see himself, other days when the *I* is closed, and he is blind.

Royce said, "Kebo Haley, what brings you out this way?"

"A fan belt, sir."

Royce tried to picture it, an ovulating fan—no, that's the wrong word. The fan that turns and has the silver grillwork.

"What's that you got?" Adlai said.

Benning said, "Photograph of Grisham and his young lady." She handed the picture to Kebo.

Kebo smiled. "Grisham hasn't changed a bit." He passed the photo to Adlai.

Actually Grisham's hairline seemed higher, or was it just that he was combing his hair straight back? And his face was fuller. "This is Ariane?" Adlai said. "She's beautiful." No, this is beyond beauty,

Adlai thought. This face is like the idea of beauty, the source of light. Adlai's ears were ringing.

Benning said, "Adlai, are you all right?"

Adlai tilted the picture toward Kebo. "Isn't she just incredible-looking?"

"Not the most flattering pose, really. Looks like she was surprised by the flash."

Adlai wondered was there ever beauty more luminous, more celestial than this. Is there a love chemical or something? He said, "I wonder why she's marrying Grisham."

Kebo said he hoped it was for love. And then he excused himself. "Air up that left front tire, Adlai. You might could have a slow leak."

The Black & Lovely Gro.

*A lavish of people got no time for
their space and no space for their time.*

—DELANO 6SMITH

Delano 6smith (big *6*, little *s*) sat on a red plastic milk crate outside the Black & Lovely Grocery, drinking malt liquor from a can, fiddling with his luckball—a little do-fotchet made of cloth and clay—and thinking about dreambodies, which are what we are before we're born and after we die ("the articulation of oblivion," the philosophically minded might say), and which are the usual subject of his paintings. Delano's dreambodies are as actual as wind or fragrance, but they are not sensitive to the difficult forces that affect our living bodies, like gravity, electricity, time, and love.

Purvis Cheniere's Black & Lovely Grocery sold—still sells— comestibles, sundries, live bait, fresh meat, and liquor, and served a light meal at its couple of tables: tamales, fried dills, and whatever fish Purvis had dragged out of Lake Moliere the night before. The store sits just west of the Bridge of Sighs on Rue Royale, the gravel road that leads from town to the lake. The building itself had become Delano's canvas, so to speak. He'd illustrated its clapboard walls with vivid, inspirited murals, which had attracted the attention of art dealers from New York, Berlin, and Montgomery. One gallery owner from New Orleans, precious little thing, who wanted to know Delano's astrological sign right off (he told her the Ocelot, and she took a step back) offered to buy the building from Purvis. She laid her checkbook on the candy counter, clicked her ballpoint. Purvis said, Thank you kindly, sweetheart, but no, thank you. Now, can I make you a plate of fried gar with ketchup and mustard?

Delano got written up in the *Times-Picayune* and in our own weekly, *The Vindicator*, where there was a photo of him in his paint-dappled blue jumpsuit. He'd sold some smaller pieces, done on cedar roof shingles, to the Morris Museum in Augusta, Georgia, which he never planned to visit because that's where the masters play golf, and golf is the black hole of imagination, the emptiest passion.

Shiver-de-Freeze, by the way, is home to a number of untrained artists, all prolific, passionate, and visionary. Some folks allow that this blessed circumstance may be due to the quality of light here. Shiver-de-Freeze exists in a meteorological anomaly called a "blue hole." It receives much less rain than the rest of Ouachita Parish, and the rain that does fall, falls mostly at night or just past dawn. Days are robust and luminous. The arriving sunlight is unfiltered and substantial. Like varnish on wood, it brings out the grain, blemish, and luster of each enlightened object.

Carrie Dangerfield works with straw and mud, and shapes nightmarish scenes of West African gods. Her pieces are especially valuable because they deteriorate, and, as we know, only what does not last is of lasting value. One Night Standiford designs two-by-one-inch plywood obituary "cards" out of crushed glass. We've got folks making masks out of plastic milk jugs, building fountains out of used cars, and turning tubeless TVs into historical dioramas.

But we were talking about Delano's murals. On the east side, the river side, of the Black & Lovely was a depiction of Captain Fihiol and his men encountering the natives of what's now Shiver-de-Freeze for the first time. The Indians are all waist-deep in the river and smiling. The title frames the painting: *The Belongers Welcome the Edible Ones to Their Home.* The west mural shows a fanciful forest looming up behind a rustic chapel and is called *The Trees Speak and Wait to Be Heard.* On the backside there's *Robert Johnson Walking His Hellhound Down Jesuses' Passway.* Dog's got both eyes on one side of his head, teeth like a saw blade, tail like a scythe.

Delano used acrylics to paint the plate-glass windows out front. One window recorded the present, the other the future. The current events window featured a recent highway tragedy: *On Quasimodo Sunday D'Andre Brown Drives His Ranchero to Jubilee.* The window to the future was blank, and that's what had Delano thinking about dreambodies. What exactly Delano saw there in his mind was a barefooted woman in a bone-white nightgown type of deal, and she had wings of white mesh and pleated organdy and floated over Tohu Bohu Swamp in the milky moonlight. Honeysuckle wound through her iron-gray hair. Just then an automobile, a purple one, drove into Delano's vision, its tires crackling on the oyster-shell, and parked in front of the grocery. Two doors slammed—the evident world asserting itself once again. He shifted his waffled butt, scratched his patchy white beard, watched the mother and son approach.

Delano knew he'd never seen this red-haired boy in his life, but realized he knew him just the same. The mother wore jeans and a sleeveless white blouse. The boy had a diamond in his left ear, wore short-pants overalls and a gray T-shirt. Delano nodded to the child. The boy smiled. His momma smiled. Delano said, "Fontana."

Earlene and Boudou stopped. Earlene put her hand on the screen door latch. Delano introduced himself. He pointed to the signature on the mural. "D/6, that's me. You the memory boy."

Boudou said, "How do you know me?"

"Knowed your kin. Knowed Lafayette when he started up his First Seasonal Church of the Second Deluge. I was just a peeper then, not more than five or six, but I remember all those white folks out on their ark on the river, waiting for Jesus the Rain to flood the sinful Delta. Knowed Ronnie, Lonnie, Johnnie, and Donnie, too.

Blowed theirselfs up at Camp Polk. Knowed Fluellen, too.* You favor your daddy."

"You knew him?"

"Was in all the papers. Pictures and anything." Delano sipped his malt liquor. "Be seeing you around?"

"We're going to Cousin Grisham's wedding."

While Delano chatted with Boudou and Earlene outside the Black & Lovely, inside, Benning, Royce, and Adlai sat at the table near the purple martin gourds and the elaborate multi-storied bird-houses—one of them, in fact, a faithful enough model of the French Colonial Loudermilk manse, Paradise, with its upstairs gallery, brick columns, outside staircases, the dual-pitched, hipped roof, the three gabled dormers out front, the central chimney—sipping their coffee while Purvis filled their considerable grocery order. (Shiver-de-Freeze is, by the way, the purple martin capital of the world, and most children here grow up thinking that the song goes, "For purple martin's majesty . . .") Adlai set Royce's watch back a half hour to Southern Daylight Time and slipped the watch into the pocket of Royce's flannel slacks.

Benning said, "The last time the family was all together here, Adlai, you were about ten."

Adlai said he remembered being here, but couldn't remember anything about it.

"These days Alvin Lee takes care of Paradise." Benning leaned toward her husband. "Royce, how you feeling?"

Royce lifted his shoulders, breathed deeply. "Drunker than who shot John."

Adlai opened *The Vindicator*, read about the parish Adopt-a-Highway program and how the Lesbian Visibility Project had agreed to tend a mile of Faith Street, south of town. There was an article entitled "How to Precipitate Money." Another called for a return of the three-pronged fork. This Sunday's sermon at the Church of the Day of Wrath at Hand will be, *You Think God's Just Setting There on His Bohunkus?* And there was a photograph of former Shiverene Radley Smallpiece being released from Angola State Prison in his wheelchair.

Adlai said, "Listen to this." He spread the newspaper on the table, smoothed it, and read a personals ad: "SWM, 50ish, into holistic wellness, dolphin consciousness, karma, past-life regression therapy, crystals, pyramids, ESP, spiritual growth, vision quest, UFOs, Rolfing, channeling, reincarnation, psychic awareness, Feng Shui, spiritual healing, deep-tissue massage, animal and angelic communication, macrobiotics, kundalini yoga, Marian apparitions, aromatherapy, Area 51, automatic handwriting, Carl Jung, foo fighters, and the Internet, seeks SM, 38–50, into same, for psychic stimulation and possible romance. Must be non-smoker, cat-fancier. Write to paper at Box 202."

Purvis said, "Sounds like Macky Ptak. Works for Pug Wolfe over to Curl Up and Dye."

Earlene held the screen door open for Boudou. They stepped inside. Boudou smelled the thick and ropy aroma of deep-fried fish. Lard will do that, erode the angles of even the freshest, pointiest fish. Earlene recognized the voice she heard. "Aunt Benning."

"Lordy, look who's here, Royce. Earlene and little Boudou. I swan, he's as tall as autumn cotton."

Earlene kissed her aunt, uncle, and cousin. Benning gave Boudou a hug. Earlene and Boudou pulled chairs up to the table. Purvis carried over a tray of iced teas. They all gabbed about the coming wedding.

Benning said, "Adlai's doing all the cooking. Earlene, you and I can see the house gets cleaned and aired. There's flowers, photographer . . . I don't know what all else."

Royce said, "And, Rylan, you'll clean out the attic with me."

Benning said, "Sugar, this here's Boudou."

Royce said, "I know that."

Boudou said he loved attics. And then while Adlai told Earlene everything that had and hadn't happened to him since the Anniece Pate romance, Benning watched Royce scratch his ear and wondered what life will soon be like without him, tried to imagine herself alone in bed, alone in the sitting room with her book, tried to imagine the unbearable silence that Royce's stilled voice would leave—the echo of insensibility. Then she stopped herself. This is life, after all, and this is how it goes. Isn't this what she has known all along? Isn't this the separation we prepare for all our lives? She heard Adlai say he brought along his violin and maybe he and Earlene could play her songs out on the veranda. Benning couldn't help it. She wondered what her life would have been like had she married Carver Staples. Pretty boy, Carver. Slate-gray eyes. Went off to Harvard. Now she'd be a bank president's wife. And Rylan would not have died.

Earlene told Adlai he'd be the next getting married. He said, I wish. Benning thought, He does? Adlai pictured a wife, this time a woman with thick light brown hair, loosely tied back. She's not wearing makeup as far as he can tell. She *is* wearing a man's white Oxford shirt, a black skirt, black ankle socks and white running shoes. She's got these smile lines on her right cheek. Dark eyes. And she's wearing a silk tie, loose at the collar. In fact, Adlai realized, she's the waitress he spoke with over to Vicksburg at the Bacchus Grille. He didn't know her name. Sometimes they'll tell you. Hi, I'm Ricki, and I'll be your server this evening. Sometimes a waitress'll wear a name tag: *Veronica*. Or she'll write on the back of the ticket: *Thanks* (or *Thanx*), *Brigette*. Otherwise you're at her mercy. You can't just ask a waitress her name because that would sound like you were coming on to her even though it shouldn't, and she would assume you were just another one of the boorish pick-up boys, and she would never, ever be able to see you as a sober and adoring husband. And Adlai kept thinking about all that while he helped Purvis and Boudou load the groceries into the Rambler and continued when he sat down again at the table. He snuck a peek at the Grisham and Ariane photo, held his thumb over Grisham's face. The girl of his fantasy was no match for Ariane.

Benning thought she might should go ahead and schedule an appointment for Royce with Dr. Fell while they were here. She asked Purvis for the doctor's number.

"Doc Fell's run off."

"Says which?"

Purvis told them how the town should have known something was up when Doc began closing the office for long weekends. He bought himself a new Jeep, a red one. New suits. You think you know a person. Purvis shook his head. Dr. Fell started wearing contact lenses, got his teeth bleached, dyed his hair. Looked like he had a crow sitting on his head. Got the fat sucked out of his hips and his breasts. Then he ran off with an HMO from Ruston. Told us he was sorry, but managed care was his destiny.

"So we got a new doctor. Parnell Broadway. Office is in his rent house on Felicity."

Boudou thought about how a word like *felicity* worked because all the colors of the letters blended so nicely—you could get stuck on a lovely word like that, watching the colors shimmer and float like fireworks, feeling its warmth wash over you like heated syrup, and not hear anything else the speaker said.

Benning helped Royce to the bathroom. Earlene looked at the cans of yellow cling peaches, Oregon blackberries, at the boxes of Swan's Down cake mixes, the Holsum bread, Little Debbie snack cakes. She looked at the meat counter—the butcher paper dispenser, the cone of twine. Whenever she visited Shiver-de-Freeze, Earlene found the Black & Lovely unchanged, and she was happy about that. It meant she still belonged and was welcomed. The same pressed tin ceiling. The same festive spirals of fly paper overhead. The same plank floorboards, the big old National cash register, the ice cream freezer with its bandage of duct tape, the burlap sacks of rice and red beans, the bushel baskets stuffed with greens and squashes. Earlene knew that if she looked over to the candy counter just now, she'd see her barefoot eight-year-old self, bangs in her eyes, mud on her knees, pointing at the horehound drops, taking one from Purvis in exchange for the penny, thanking him, telling her friend Althea they could share sucks till the drop disappeared.

She was eight and she was Early—that's what her grandma called her then, Early deBastrop. What everyone called her. *Early deBastrop, early to rise, makes a girl healthy, happy, and wise.* That was the summer she came here with Grandma to get away from all the commotion that boiled up at home when Aunt Eunice went to the sheriff about what Uncle Danny did to her baby and Uncle Danny shot himself in the eye with a .22 pistol and his brain ended up all over the bathroom walls, so that Grandma would discover a desiccated booger of gray matter on the Venetian blind a month later and would sob and say, It ain't fair I should have to clean up after someone else's abomination.

Earlene saw Early loitering by the screen door, hushing Althea, spying on the grown-ups—the men at one table, ladies at the other. The men in their overalls talked about the price of this, the cost of that, and seemed as solemn as soap and dull as dishwater. But Early listened to Nathene Butts and Jinx Miller, who smoked Old Golds and talked about movie stars and knew so much about the actors' loves and pet peeves and favorite foods that the actors could have been the ladies' own-born cousins or something. And then she heard Purvis tell Boudou to get himself a stick of blow gum, why don't you. She felt encumbered by the years, like she had grown up all at once, all in this place. She excused herself, asked Purvis could she use the phone in his office. She said, Boudou, I don't want you eating a lot of sugar. One piece! He took three. Two for later.

Adlai heard a squeak and looked up to see Delano begin his window painting. What appeared was a horizontal person floating in the middle of the pane. Unconnected to the world. Except that if you looked beyond the skin of glass, beyond Delano, you saw that this body was in the sky, just above the live oaks across Rue Royale. Delano painted the gown white and then the bare feet so white the gown went gray. It's a woman for sure, they figured. Delano drew the outline of the head. He stepped back, knocked an ash from his cigarette.

Adlai pointed out how the flying lady's left is really her right. Like a mirror. We're like inside the painting. I see what you're saying, Boudou said.

Earlene said, "Pick up, Varden, I know you're there. Well all right, then. I want you gone when we get back home." She heard the squeal of the interrupted answering machine.

Varden said, "Earlene, what's this?"

"I don't even know why you're with me."

"Because you're mine."

"We're finished."

"No, we're not."

A Presence Hungry to

REVeAL *Itself*

It's the nothing that makes us something;
it's what we miss that hits the mark.

—7UP JINGLE

A. Where We Store Our Memories.   Royce knocked his forehead on a rafter. He wondered if he'd remember to duck on his way out. The air in the attic was thick, wooly almost, moist, sweet with mildew and rot. Royce and Boudou inspected the contents of an old zinc scrub tub: a Maid-Rite brass washboard, a bacon hanger, a hog scraper, a pair of wire egg baskets, a 25-inch butcher saw. Royce sucked in the moldy air, trying to catch a breath to ballast his dizzy brain. He coughed. His eyes itched. He sat on the edge of an old sheet-covered davenette, took off his suit jacket, wiped his face and neck with a handkerchief. Boudou unfurled a braided rug—looked like it was made of old shirts maybe—and sat on it at Royce's feet.

He sneezed. Boudou couldn't wait to open the old steamer trunk. He ran his fingers along its crystallized metal finish. The sort of chest a pirate might bury.

Royce told Boudou this didn't seem to be one of his good days. He noticed a pile of woven baskets beside the treadle sewing machine, made a mental note to take them downstairs later, knew he'd forget, wondered why he bothered. To prove he's not a loony, that's why. "Some days I can see clearly—the details, the colors, all in focus. Some days the world is gray and blurred, and if something doesn't move, I can't see it. Sometimes I'm in the light, sometimes in the shadow."

"Me, too. My senses are all scrambled."

"How so?"

"I see colors of sounds, shapes of smells, pictures of numbers."

"Like number *one* is a flagpole; *five* is down and around and a hat on top?"

"*One* is a man who lives alone, wears overalls and a straw Stetson. *Eighty-two* is a white feather quill. *One thousand two hundred and fifty-six* is the man in the overalls and his four brothers are having friends over to a party. There's a pig roasting on a spit in the yard, a raggedy black dog under the porch."*

"How do you do that?"

"You can do the same. You can close your eyes and see, right? Or look at a book and see marks and lines, dots, squiggles, but hear a voice. Put your hands on the wall you can feel them talking downstairs. If you see someone eat a lemon, you taste its sourness, you pucker up. You taste with your eyes."

Royce rubbed his aching knees and stretched his legs. "Growing old is for the birds, Boudou. It's the goddamest surprise." Royce took the memory sack out of his jacket pocket. "I'll tell you a story." He took a small cardboard box from the sack and opened it. He showed Boudou a butterfly pinned to a bed of cotton. The butterfly was black, with clouds of blue and small cream spots and chevrons on the rim of its wings.

He said, "Once upon a time at the King Cotton Ball . . . 1951, I think. Was at the Scottish Rite Temple in Monroe. Champagne and

Chateaubriand. China, crystal, silver, and liveried waiters. Cully Oxendine and the Louisiana Power & Light Orchestra. Benning and I sat with the Spurgeons and the . . . fellow owned a department store and his wife. Denholm, was it? Anyway, after the meal, the orchestra played the 'Union, Justice, and Confidence Waltz' and released thousands of these here swallowtails from an enormous silk chrysalis attached to the wall behind the orchestra, and all the celebrants' breath was taken away, and we stopped dancing and applauded this magnificent sight, these delicate celestial creatures rising like shimmering embers to the vaulted ceiling. They swooped, drifted, stalled, rose, flitted. And then the band swung into Raymond Scott's 'Reckless Night on Board an Ocean Liner,' and Benning told me it looked like the sky was falling. Before the song was finished, the butterflies had begun to tire. Or lose their desire, perhaps. They had, of course, no field of Queen Anne's lace to fly to. Some of them dropped into glasses of wine and drowned. Clusters of them clung to taffeta gowns, which agitated some of the highstrung ladies. Others gathered on the hems of tablecloths or lighted on the draperies, as if summoned there by the brocade flowers. Pretty soon desperate swallowtails were caught up in coiffures. Cully had the orchestra play louder to drown out the wails, the sobs, the epithets of disgust. When people made for the exits, they slipped on the slick carpet of twittering corpses, and when the doors were flung open and then abandoned, a pack of street dogs ambled in and began to paw at and then chew the butterflies. And then the dogs took sick."

Royce tilted the box to the light. He told Boudou, "This fellow here collapsed onto a vinegar cruet. I carried him home in a champagne glass. That's where he died."

Boudou told Royce that when he was younger, like six, he was briefly afraid of soap bubbles. One night he was taking a bubble bath, making a bubble beard and a bubble mustache, and Earlene was in the bathroom, drinking coffee and reading to him from Stephen Hawking's book about time, and when Boudou said he didn't get it about all these universes, Earlene told him to imagine that the bathtub was everything that is. Well, okay, he could do that—so long as he dismissed the pesky notion that the tub had to reside *in* something. Earlene said that each bubble is like a universe, and the entirety of existence is like a foam of universes, and that little crackle and hiss you hear is the noise of universes losing their tension and bursting out of being. Boudou realized you could never tell by looking which soap bubble was about to pop, and he figured that at any second our own universe could explode, and there would be nothing left in its place, and no one around to even remember that it had ever been.

Boudou told Royce about the first thing he ever saw—a white tennis shoe. He was two; he was on the living room floor. Earlene was somewhere talking to someone or something. Suddenly he knew he was part of the world of that shoe and that his mother saw him in the same way that he saw the shoe, and if he crawled around it, it changed shape, and if he got close, so he could smell it, the shoe grew larger, the room disappeared.

Royce said, "Let's take a look in the chest, shall we?"

What they discovered was a century's worth of military uniforms, from butternut to khaki, all pressed and folded and ready to wear. You could be a private or a colonel or anything in between, depending on the conflict in which you'd like to be engaged. In other trunks they found evening clothes and work clothes, boots, capes, dusters, and hats, all kinds of hats: nightcaps and stocking caps, Panamas, felts, cowboy hats, bowlers, derbies, beavers, coonskin, straws, and tams. Boudou looked at Royce and smiled. "Who do you want to be?"

B. The Treason of Images.   Adlai stared at the brown and white orchid above July on the Lazarus Funeral Home calendar. *Dionysus "Dion" Lazarus, Licensed Bereavement Counselor. Visit us at Prudence and Thanatos, near the Social Ocean.* He stared at the blossom until it became a dog. And then it was an orchid again. Adlai heard the phone ring and Earlene answer. He heard her tell Varden if he wanted to talk, he should carry his sorry ass up here and talk. The name of the orchid. *Paphiopedilum.* He heard Earlene say, Well, that's your decision, Varden. I'm not going to discuss this on the phone.

Adlai thought how last year at this time he would have been over to Anniece's house with Anniece's dad, Tyler. The two of them would be cooking supper for three, hoping Anniece would join them, knowing she wouldn't. Stuffed mallard, sweet potatoes, scalloped cabbage. Knowing she was over to Donnie Carr's and the two of them'd probably be ordering some nasty takeout. Later, Adlai would bring the leftovers by Donnie's single-wide. Anniece would scrunch up on the sofa, tug her T-shirt down her thighs, and roll her eyes. Adlai heard Earlene tell Varden, You're always embarrassed when we're alone.

A month ago today Royce called Adlai from Ruston to say he couldn't remember the way to drive home. Adlai directed him. Royce called two hours later from Choudrant. "I know where I am," he said. "And I know where you are. I can't get my bearings. I'm in a parking lot, and I can't get out. I can see the street, Adlai, but I can't drive to it." Adlai told Royce to hang on, he'd have Kebo drive him out there.

And then last week at this time . . . at four-thirty. Well, he was sitting on the glider in the backyard reading that new book on the Fontanas. Reading about the Eugenics Society.* Funny how so much had happened since last week that it seemed as long ago as last year. And last month seemed both impossibly distant and uncomfortably immediate. The past keeps expanding; the future keeps shrinking.

Adlai had been playing this game for as long as he could remember, lining up parallel days as if they were photographs in a slide show. What fascinated him was how their succession made no sense. You could look at any moment in your life and see that it did not predict what followed and did not reflect what came before. Here you are at the Law School mixer, doing the watusi with the Queen of Theta Chi, and the two of you are so enraptured you forget there's anyone else in the gym. Right then you both decide that "Don't Hang Up" is *your song*. You tell Claudette you love her. She weeps on your shoulder. And here you are twenty years later, and you're living in Frostburg, Maryland, where you manage Hoffman's Nursery. Your wife, Lexie, a local girl, works the counter at the Princess Restaurant to earn the extra cash you need to send the kids to St. Michael's and to spend that week next summer at Rehoboth Beach. You've never been happier.

Adlai sometimes imagined snapshots of his brilliant future: he and his wife—her back's to the camera—planting peas in the garden; he and Kebo outside Dee Dee's Diner, Kebo's waving to Dee Dee and Adlai's pushing a baby carriage. Adlai felt like a writer must feel who knows how he wants his story to end, and he's not above manipulating his people to make that happen.

(By the way, this is not meant as a jab at our own beloved drudge. Our author prefers beginnings to endings and likes to say there are no resolutions: people go on with their lives. He also says that the event is not the thing that matters. Well, maybe not for him, but you and we know better. This perfunctory disregard for incident is precisely why authors have narrators and editors.)

What was it Shakespeare said about love? "Brief as lightning in the collied night." Well, you could say the same about your life, Adlai figured. A flash of light in the darkness. And you weren't even sure what you saw or if there was anything to see. With that in mind, Adlai knew there was no time to waste, that regret was the cruelest cut.

When Earlene walked into the kitchen, she found Adlai writing messages on Post-It notes. For Royce, he said. She read one: *What you eat is inside.* For the fridge? she said. Bananas, Adlai said. Earlene wondered if Royce might not be insulted by the notes. I won't mention who they're for, Adlai said. He wrote a bold *NO!* for the knife drawer.

Earlene made coffee. She told Adlai he was lucky, all these literals in the kitchen would save Post-Its and time. The aluminum canisters labeled *Coffee, Tea, Sugar, Flour.* The red and white plastic roll-top bread box labeled *Bread.* The spice rack and spices, the cookie jar, the recipe file box, the Caloric range. You wonder why the manufacturers thought they had to explain. Adlai said, No one puts cookies in the cookie jar. Earlene opened the fridge. "It says *Milk* on the milk bottle. What could you confuse with milk?" Just below the freezer, a drawer labeled *Meat Keeper*. On the bottom, two drawers labeled *Humidrawer*. Ah, a figure of speech. Another compartment said *Dairy*. But, of course, it was no dairy at all, just a cheese closet.

"It's not the name. It's the function that confuses Royce," Adlai said. "Like he'd know what an umbrella is called. He might not know what to do with it."

Earlene poured coffee for the two of them and sat down at the table across from Adlai.

Adlai said he knew this woman once, who's dead now, who kept olive oil in the creamer, cream in the sugar bowl, sugar in the coffee can, coffee in a fruit bowl, fruit in the bread box, and bread in the oven.

The phone rang. They heard Benning answer, ask whoever it was where they were at. Adlai said, "She used to cover the fruit bowl—with the coffee in it—used to cover it with a vinyl bowl mantle that looked like a shower cap." Adlai stirred his coffee. He smiled. "Leona Veach. That was the lady's name."

Benning walked in, got a coffee mug, filled it, and sat down at the table. "Alvin Lee and his wives are downtown shopping. Be back directly."

C. Heavenly. Boudou and Royce sat on the veranda wearing baggy one-piece woolen bathing suits and straw boaters. Royce had a pencil in his mouth which he regarded as a cigar. He said, "What was your name again, son?"

"Avery, Commodore. Avery Kitchen."

"And your intentions toward my daughter?"

"Honorable, sir, I assure you."

Royce took the pencil from his mouth. "And I suppose you'll expect to work for the family's dreamboat line?"

"*Steamboat*, sir. Yes, well—"

"Tush, tush!"

Boudou looked out at the lake. "I can't help but admire the vista here at Belvedere, Commodore."

Royce excused himself, said he, if not the Commodore, needed a nap. Boudou promised to keep an eye on things. He watched a row-boat glide across the black water. At first it looked like two girls rowing the boat, both sitting in the rowing thwart, staring backward at where they had been, moving toward what they cannot see. Then it looked like one girl. Two arms, two legs. Boudou wiped the lenses of his spyglasses with the hem of his shirt. He looked again, focused. They must be sitting so close together you can't tell where the one of them ends and the other begins. But why would they choose to row with one arm each? The boat is slipping south on the oxbow, to the dock, he supposed, at the last house there.

Over to the Shiver-de-Freeze Museum of Social and Natural History, in the Pioneer Room, is a framed, hand-drawn map of this area as it was in 1871. The map was sketched by Bink Loudermilk and shows what is no doubt the Fontana camp on the bayou, although Bink has it labeled *Fontina*. And he calls the bayou Indigo Bayou. The lake, where he marked the site of his home, he calls Lake Asphaltitis. He built his house on the west side of the east-bending crescent of the lake at the midpoint in the arc. Bink died of yellow fever in 1874. Died out there on the veranda, shivering on a straw mat, soaked in his own sweat and urine, skin tough and cracked as old cheese, and babbling about that which is empty and formless. His last coherent words, according to his cook, Comfort Douglass, were, "What is the question again?"

And now Boudou stood not two feet and 125 years away from the deathbed, watching a pair of bright blue damselflies curled in a mating wheel on the lid of an old milk can. Watching them through the binoculars, seeing the lacy wings like leaded glass, the black humps of eyes. And then he lifted the glasses and looked across the lake at Tohu Bohu Swamp, the dark and jungled, the allegedly trackless impenetrable home to alligators, snapping turtles, fishing bats, and fritillary crawfish, the domain, they say, of red-eyed loup-garou, the werewolf, who is insatiable, savage, and cunning. Boudou scanned the moss-draped cypresses, saw one tree clouded with egrets. And then he heard a billowy red gunshot, saw thousands of birds lift as one off the canopy of trees like the chime off a bell.

The actual shot came from the north, from near the Black &

Lovely. What Boudou saw was a man in a wheelchair below the bridge near the lakeshore. The man wore a brown felt hat and a brown jacket and a white shirt. He held the pistol to his right cheek like a girlfriend's hand. As Boudou watched, the man pointed the gun straight over his head. If he shot now the bullet would come right down into his hat. The man leveled his arm, aimed into the swamp, and fired. He hit a tree at fifty yards or so and sent bark flying. If he's trying to kill loup-garou, he's crazy. Bullets pass right through a werewolf. Boudou looked for the boat but couldn't find it. He did see two men in the backyard of the house next door, men he recognized from the Ouachita Public Library. The Great Books guys. He waved to them, but the men seemed caught up in an argument.

Boudou focused on the gunman again, who was now wheeling himself back toward the bridge. The circling birds were settling into their dense roost. A blood-red automobile, a fancy one, passed over the bridge and onto the dusty Rue Royale. Boudou knew who this was. Oh, boy! he thought. He ran to the French doors, opened them. Earlene, Benning, and Adlai turned to him. Earlene said, "You shooting off caps out there?"

Boudou said, "Here comes Heavenly!"

Unspeakable Joy

It was fine with my parents that when Brother Loudermilk would visit on Tuesday evenings we would cleave unto one another. Why mother even cooked chicken and saw that my sheets were clean. And Alvin Lee, His left hand was under my head, and his right hand doth embrace me. *He was a perfect flowing stream; he was a thunderbolt.*

—OUIDA SNEAD (LOUDERMILK),
interview in the Monroe *News-Star*

Alvin Lee Loudermilk, Benning's nephew, Earlene, Grisham, and Adlai's cousin, made quite a name for himself over to Morehouse Parish, enjoyed, as it were, a brief season of celebrity—infamy, some have said—before returning home to Shiver-de-Freeze and becoming, once again, the caretaker of Paradise. Alvin Lee had founded his own church in Mer Rouge—the Fire Baptized Evangelical Temple of the King—and that's where his troubles began. It may be that Alvin Lee did not understand that religions are commercial and political enterprises as sure as they are moral ones. Alvin Lee's defenders will tell you that he was persecuted and ostracized for preaching to the impoverished, the disenfranchised, the dangerous, for broadening their moral options, and for recruiting souls from the corporate religions with the passion and power of his eloquent witness unto the Lord. All chin music, his detractors will say. Alvin Lee's transgressions were mighty, were plentiful, were immoral, were illegal.

Alvin Lee's congregation were a visually beguiling crew. To explain, we need to return briefly to the late summer of 1970, when three young entrepreneurs, Gypsy, Princess, and January, drove into Mer Rouge in a Volkswagen microbus with the curious idea of dragging northeast Louisiana into the Age of Aquarius. They opened a clothing store down on Broad Street, called it Carnaby Street, which didn't make sense to anyone. They were friendly enough, but they talked funny. Might have been from Illinois or California or England. Who knew? They seemed to enjoy marijuana as much as our farmers did. But no one bought their clothes. You just can't work a field in hip huggers. Wear sandals, your ankles will swell up with chigger bites.

They decided to promote their business and enliven the parish's cultural life by holding a music festival out near the Colliston place by Bayou Bonne Idée. It'll be like Woodstock, Gypsy said. It'll put Mer Rouge on the map. We've already got bands lined up to play, January told the Town Council. Crispian St. Peters, the Grass Roots, Sonny and the Sunliners, and maybe, if we play our cards right, if you gentlemen can help us out financially here, the Rolling Stones. Mayor Blaine said, "You ask Ferlin Husky?"

Well, a few days after the meeting, our trio vanished from Mer Rouge, leaving behind the rent bill, all their stock and hardware fixtures, a stack of comic books, and dozens of eight-track tapes. And so the former Carnaby Street stayed vacant for twenty-five years until Alvin Lee rented it from Blaine Realty to use as his church. And he was wise enough not to toss out the clothing with the shelving units, the comic books, the counters, and the bong. Alvin Lee began his missionary work among the unaffiliated, the apathetic, the listless, and the indolent, some would say, residents of Mer Rouge.

Humanists, backsliders, agnostics, sinners. He visited the mobile homes scattered along Highway 165, spoke with patrons of the Gin Pleasure Spot, Mr. D's Cypress Lounge, Tick Creek Landing, and the D'Arbonne Street Social Club, preached to the ladies and children at Denzel Purdy's Washeteria. Alvin Lee had something to offer his converts other than the Word of God, other than eternal salvation, other than sobriety, hope, meaning, and compassion, other than an edifying social milieu. He had to offer what no other church in Morehouse Parish had. Alvin Lee had all them Carnaby Street glad rags.

Now, you couldn't tell a Southern Baptist from a Methodist to look at them. You couldn't tell a Methodist from a Presbyterian from a Holy Roller from a Catholic. But you sure could tell a Templar of the King, as they called themselves, from all the rest. The Church of Sartorial Anachronism and Shameful Flamboyance is what the Reverend Wally Butts called Alvin Lee's storefront house of worship. The Reverend Butts condemned the congregation's vanity and ostentation, its wardrobe pride. He said, right from the pulpit, that he found something iniquitous and feminine about men in silk, don't y'all? Amen, the congregation said. And they said, Stay right there, Brother Butts! Stay right there!

Pastor Burg Jones at African Methodist Episcopal raised his hands to heaven, rolled his eyes back in his head, swayed his mighty body, said, We living now in a bominstic, modernistic, hand-shaking, drug-taking, jaw-jiving world today, Lord have mercy, and these flashy, trashy spawn of Satan over to the alleged evangelical church are polluting the mystical body of Jees-us-uh! And the reverend commenced to pounding his beefy thighs, and the veins at his forehead swelled and pulsed with the rush of the blood of indignation, and he called upon the Lord to smite the tricked-out, prinked-up infidels, the polyester peacocks and bell-bottomed babes over there on Broad Street. And the congregation responded with *Amen*s and *Praise God*s and the reverend's neck bellowed out like the vocal pouch on a bullfrog, and he talked about how the Lord's house has no rooms in it for doxies and coxcombs, for mannequins and popinjays, for the beaus and belles of vanity. No, it does not! And the rev-

erend tossed off his suit jacket and loosened his tie and wiped his
steamy face with a hanky and he said, The Lord's heavenly train
don't carry no dandies, no dungaree dolls, no fops, no voluptuaries.
And the Elder Jones so exercised himself, going on as he did, rebuk-
ing the tie-dyed banty cocks, scolding the bedizened strumpets, cas-
tigating the patchoulied lords and ladies of decadence and style, that
he dropped to his knees and shattered his tiny patellas. And in his
remarkable pain, he screamed that the chic shall not be comforted,
that they who hunger and thirst after splendid raiments shall be
emptied, that we cannot eat the bread of life off a fashion plate. And
then he fell forward onto his enormous face and released the clot in
his neck somewheres and sent that glob of plaque coursing to his
heretofore dextrous brain, where it burst a capillary and sizzled a
bundle of neurons and an important few synapses and whatnot in his
frontal and temporal lobes. And now the reverend speaks continu-
ally in tongues and stares longingly at the beautiful vision always just
an inch or two, it would seem, above his head.

Meanwhile, if you were driving past Sonics you might have to
look twice at the carhop to make sure he wasn't Sammy Davis, Jr., in
a leather Nehru jacket, love beads, and medallions carrying an order of
chili dogs to a red Chevy pickup. Outside the Hit and Run Food
Mart you would have seen a few gentlemen—deacons of the temple—loitering out front in velour suits, silk shirts, wide, op-art ties,
floppy hats, and plastic shoes, listening to Marvin Gaye or Fontilla
Bass blasting from a portable eight-track player. Or down at the
Coffee Shoppe Named Desire, you would have seen young moth-
ers in granny dresses, lace-up boots, paisley scarves, sipping coffee,
discussing how to remove a barbecue sauce stain from a fringed
suede vest.

Alvin Lee's congregation was small but highly visible. Yet, as we
said, he did have to leave town, abandon his ministry. It wasn't that
he had pretty much sanctified Elvis Presley, although that did ruffle
some ecclesiastical feathers. Alvin Lee explained about that at the
trial, how, yes, he did have a plaster bust of Elvis on the altar, and,
yes, said hand-painted bust had been a bourbon decanter in a previous incarnation. Elvis did have something to tell us about burning

love, did he not? About loving tender, loving true. About not being cruel. And about suspicious minds and like that. And then Alvin Lee told the judge, jury, attorneys, and spectators present the *Parable of the Two Elvises*, how the brilliant child was born into poverty and anonymity, and how, behold the singer went forth to sing, how he rose to become like unto James Dean, full of grace and beauty, vitality and talent, and how this triumphant and pious country singer was reduced into profligacy and wound up like unto Evel Knievel, becaped, becollered, befuddled, his once-empty pockets now stuffed with Super Anahist nasal spray and Feenamint laxative gum, his once growling stomach purring now with a surfeit of banana pudding and sauerkraut, his honeyed voice gone to gruel. Yet it was not the glorification of Elvis that drove Alvin Lee from Mer Rouge. Nor the somewhat alarming ramifications of his devotion, such as when he electrified the courtroom with, some would say, a dark and dubious revelation, one that sent a row of Baptist spectators wailing out of the courtroom. Alvin Lee was explaining to his attorney Rance Usrey that, no, he did not believe, as many do, that Elvis is alive and lurking around fast food restaurants and truck stops. He did not believe that Elvis has risen from the dead, but he knew that a part of him is alive.

"His spirit, you mean?" Rance Usrey said.

"No, sir. I mean his very cells. A section of Elvis's colon, about as big as a testicle, is being held over in a Memphis hospital. Frozen."

"Why?"

"So they can clone him. That's what all this Scottish sheep business is about. It's not about more mutton, more wool. It's about Elvis and Jesus."

Rance wondered why in blazes he took this case anyway. Why was he a lawyer at all? He never wanted to be a lawyer. He'd just have to tell his wife tonight that's all. Emma, he'll say, honey, I have to quit. I'll call Jack on Sunday, meet him out at the club. We'll talk. I'll tell him my heart's not in it anymore. I'll stay on till he finds someone else. And Rance saw Emma right then in front of his eyes. Emma's on the sofa, listening to him, her legs tucked under her. He sees that her eyes are glistening. She's gripping a melon-colored Kleenex in her hand; now she's smoothing it out. It matches her blouse. He touches the tear in the corner of her left eye. She smiles, looks at her hands. God, he loves her so much he can hardly believe it sometimes. He'd like to be with her now instead of in the courtroom. He'd draw the living room curtain, put on a Mozart's Violin Sonata in C, *Andante Sostenudo*, pour two glasses of Pedro Ximénez sherry, touch her knee. She might ask him, What will you do now, dear? He'll say, Maybe I'll work with the Bastrop Community Theater. I've always wanted to act. I could teach at the community college. I'll write a book—

"Counselor," the judge said.

Rance snapped out of it, excused himself. "I'm fine, Your Honor. A little dizzy spell." Rance turned to Alvin Lee. "So, Reverend Loudermilk, you say it's about Jesus?"

"It is."

Rance turned to the jury, made eye contact with the foreman, then with the lady in the second row who tended to drift off to sleep. He said, looking at the panel, but addressing his client, "Would you explain, Reverend?" Rance smiled, touched his fingers on the rail of the jury box. He had the audience in his hands. He dropped his gaze, humbly.

Alvin Lee asked if he might be anecdotal for just a second. The judge wondered if he should call a sidebar, give himself a moment to collect his thoughts, get a clarification of that word *anecdotal*. He looked at his watch, a gesture that could be interpreted as both contemplative and decisive. "Proceed," he said.

Alvin Lee said, "I was over to a snake-handling church in Claiborne Parish. The one where the boy died who drank the battery acid."

Rance said, "Why would anyone drink battery acid?"

"You hear the word of God, and God anoints you and tells you to drink the acid."

"How do you know it's God talking?"

"My sheep know my voice, and a stranger they'll not follow. The voice of Jesus numbs your head and arms all the way to your toes. You are under the power, and you feel light all over like you're floating, like that, yes, like an angel."

"Isn't that risky?" Rance said.

Judge Flowers said, "Gentlemen, you digress."

Alvin Lee apologized, said he had a fierce habit of digressing. When he was a boy . . . He apologized again. He said he'd seen box full of snakes over to that Holiness Church of God in Jesus' Name. The preacher there, Jesse Simms, reached in among the snakes and drew out a three-foot-long snakeskin, called it an "unabridged desquamation." Had the whole skin, nostril to button.

Rance said, "You were going to tell us how this sheep and Mr. Presley were connected to Jesus."

Alvin Lee said, "The prepuce."

"The who?"

"What Jesus left behind, him being a Jewish boy and all. His desquamation. You see, the temple priests saved the foreskin of Jesus, immersed it in olive oil in a sealed amphora." Alvin Lee explained how Mary gave the amphora to the Apostle John, whom everyone suspected was her favorite all along, how John took it to Malta, how an angel brought it to Charlemagne, the papists carried it off to Rome, how it then got good and lost, got captured by the Nazis, rescued by Her Majesty's Secret Service, how it was kept in a monastery on the Isle of Mull until eighteen months ago when it was shipped to a biotechnology firm in Berne, Switzerland, where it now sits in a bath of liquid nitrogen, awaiting the moment when science catches up with faith and the cells of our Savior can be cloned, how during our very lifetimes, the world will welcome the second virgin birth of Jesus Christ. Praise God.

All of which left the Baptists, as we said, wailing and stumbling past the bailiff, the jurors trembling, the millennialists among the spectators smiling, the court stenographer hyperventilating, and Judge Flowers tapping his gavel and calling for a brief recess. But that wasn't why Alvin Lee had to leave Mer Rouge neither. And it was not that he owned a Solo Flex bodybuilding apparatus. It was not that he wore black suits, black boots, sunglasses, blousy white silk shirts. People will tolerate simple vanity in a man, especially a preacher—that's kind of his job, isn't it?

What got Alvin Lee eventually in dutch with the town, what got him into the courtroom, on trial, was his marriages. Not the fact that he had married twice, but the fact that the marriages were simultaneous. People were not even upset that Ouida Snead was only eighteen at the time, barely out of baton twirling camp. Alvin Lee told his congregation, David had five hundred wives, Solomon, one thousand. I ain't half the man they were. And the words of the prophet are these: *He* can remarry and remarry and remarry. *He* can. *She* cannot. I did not make these rules, brothers and sisters. A barn-yard of hens needs just the one rooster; a herd of cattle, one bull; a pride of lions, one king. Who is it says you cannot love two people? Jesus does not say that. Jesus says, Love one another. Jesus says, This do and thou shalt live.

Ouida's uncle, Billy Gibson, football coach for the Eagle's Nest High School Soldiers of Christ, himself a deepwater Baptist, was who blew the whistle on Alvin Lee, got the IRS and then the legal system involved. Got the press all hot and bothered. Some folks said Billy was jealous that his favorite niece's attentions were directed elsewhere, that Ouida was more than just the apple of Billy's eye, that he went after her, the razor-tongued said, not as an ox to the slaughter, but as a fed horse in the morning, neighing after his sis-ter's daughter.

Uncle Billy called the IRS and summoned an investigator to town. He met with the investigator at dusk in the Whammo Burger parking lot, claimed Alvin Lee's temple was no kind of church at all. He said it was a science fiction scam like the what-do-you-call-it? Like your Scientology. It's worse. It's a joke, a fraud, a cult, a tax-dodge, Mr. . . . what did you say your name was?

The investigator said he thought all churches were frauds and cults, and every one of them ought to be paying property and income taxes. Could wipe out the national debt in the blink of an eye, feed the starving, clothe the naked, shelter the homeless, not just here but all over the world. Turned out the investigator, J. Howard Gengerelly, was from Long Island, New York, and so didn't understand about Jesus quite the way we do down here, didn't reckon how Christ haunts our homes, how His sacrificial blood courses in our rivers, how His death shadows our days. Mr. Gengerelly did wonder out loud how a high school football coach at private school could be driving such a fine four-wheel-drive vehicle.

The bigamy charge was more difficult to ignore. At least for District Attorney Hollis Mabry, who was up for reelection and whose campaign had been recently damaged by the unsavory revelation that he had served his wife with divorce papers as she lay in the hospital undergoing chemotherapy for breast cancer. Both of Alvin Lee's wives testified at the trial. Lorraine, his wife of twenty-six years, said, "I believe in the Lord. If the Lord lays on Alvin Lee's heart to have another wife, that's the Lord. Alvin Lee can get him another." Ouida said, "When the man asks the woman to marry him, when she accepts his proposal, right then and there they are married in the eyes of God."

For his part, when he took the stand, Alvin Lee said, "Whatever I believe, I ought to be able to practice it. Ain't this America? No matter what it is, I got a right. We ought to be able to believe what we want to believe. If you can't practice what you believe, why believe it?"

Well, Alvin Lee never legally married Ouida Snead. Theirs was an eyes-of-God-only marriage. Therefore, no bigamy. Therefore, what are we all doing here? Case dismissed, and I'll see you boys in my chambers, Judge Flowers said, meaning Misters Gibson and Mabry.

People's suspicions about Uncle Billy's motivation were incorrect if the grim and scandalous evidence of his untimely death is any indication. A week after the trial, Billy Gibson was found hanging by his neck, suspended by a rope attached to the raised shovel of his John Deere JD410 diesel-powered backhoe tractor. The engine was still idling when Emory Dean, Billy's friend and assistant coach, found Billy in the barn. Billy was hitched by a cloth safety harness wrapped around his neck. Autoerotic asphyxiation, the medical examiners called it. Not so rare a thing as you might hope.

Billy had fallen in love with his tractor. Had photos of it all over his bedroom walls. Wrote love letters to it, which Sheriff Jimmie Hall found in a chest of drawers and burned immediately. Some things, he said, are not even decent for evidence. Billy was naked in the end except for a pair of knee-high nylons and red high heels.

Most of the details were kept out of the paper, but word leaks out. When the Eagle's Nest football team met West Carroll Christian Academy that following Friday night over in Goodwill, West Carroll's *Scourge of Islam* Marching Band formed a tractor at midfield and broke into a syncopated rendition of "My Funny Valentine." Poor Emory was in tears on the sideline. He wondered what poisoned love could drive a man to such dreadful intimacy. He gazed upon the band, the cheering crowd, and asked, Is God among us or not?

The way then was clear for Alvin Lee to remain in Mer Rouge and watch his young church prosper in grace and in prestige. But now he felt he was driven into the wilderness, a land of drought and of the shadow of death, an uncreated country. And he was drunk with doubt. This marriage to Ouida had not been his finest idea. Yes, he loved two women—that was the simplest and loveliest of things. But he was no longer sure he could live with both. And he could not send Ouida away. And he understood that it would be effortless to love all women. He realized this every time he stood in the pulpit and looked out onto the congregation and caught the rapturous gazes of the trembling, perspiring women being slain just then in the spirit. Yes, the ministry is an aphrodisiac. *Can a man take fire in his bosom, and his clothes not be burned?* A strut across the stage with a Bible in hand is still a strut. Alvin Lee determined, if he could, to avoid the near occasion of sin, determined not to allow the needy Christian sisters to take him with their eyelids. He resigned his office, vacated his pulpit. He sat with Lorraine and Ouida in the kitchen of their rented mobile home and discussed their future. Lorraine said her future was with Alvin Lee, and that's all she would say. This was when Ouida put down her nail file and shared her dream. She told Alvin Lee and Lorraine that she wanted to be a cosmologist when she grew up. She's always loved fixing people's hair.

Alvin Lee asked if they wouldn't mind returning with him to Shiver-de-Freeze, where Alvin Lee could check with Pug Wolfe did she have a vacant chair in her beauty shop for Ouida. Ouida said she'd enjoy to. Well then, for the near future they would live in Shiver-de-Freeze, where Alvin Lee would be able to gather himself, relax, imagine a bountiful and untroubled future, await the arrival of his baby, Lorraine being flourished with child. And now that Grisham had decided to marry, Alvin Lee found himself back in the bosom of his family. Well, he would soon as he parked the car and hustled on into the kitchen.

Plots Are for Graveyards*

If any lady not yet past her Grand Climacterick, of
a comfortable Fortune in her own Disposal, is
desirous of spending the remainder of her Life with
a tolerably handsome Fellow of Great Parts, about
five feet six inches, she may hear of such a one to
her Mind by inquiring at the Theatre Coffee
House for Mr. F., a Sophister of Cambridge.

—AD IN AN EIGHTEENTH
CENTURY NEWSPAPER

Since nothing in the world is trivial to storytellers, since there is nothing that does not require their attention, since any object or idea can become the focus of the storyteller's curiosity, and since it is the storyteller's job to see the world in an unhabitual way, to apprehend what is there, not what's supposed to be there, and since most of what absorbs a storyteller is what others neglect to see, and since storytellers by nature are collectors of irrelevant and inconsiderable information and are in the habit of making impulsive and intuitive connections between the world and memory, between the *here and now* and the *there and then*, and since a story is not a logical construct, but is instead arbitrary, opportunistic, whimsical, unpredictable if inevitable, then it would seem that digression will be inescapable, significant, and illuminating.

What is a digression, after all, but an aside, an apostrophe, a parenthesis (or, as so often in our case, double dashes), not a defect in control, as some—those who mistake indication for intrusion—have said, not bombast, slackness, diffusion, tautology. Logic is one way of thinking; story is another. Logic thinks with ideas; story with people. Logic simplifies and eliminates: story complicates and includes. Logic is clarity that informs; story is the chaos that clarifies. Logic is the god you know; story the devil you don't. Both may carry you to wisdom and revelation, but, ah, the journey! You can drive from New York to Miami on I-95. Or you can go by way of Bemidji and Tolstoy and Tonapah and Monroe. Digression is the choice of journey over destination. You can blaze a trail or follow one. What if wily Odysseus had gone straight home from Troy? Where would Western Civilization be? Here in Shiver-de-Freeze, Pete Maravich Elementary School has adopted a motto that seems appropriate to mention here: *Process Is Our Most Important Product.*

Digression is one way that the teller of the story invites you to include your own past, your wonder, your values in the life of the story, by suggesting that it is both necessary and beneficial to pause, to reflect, to allow the image on the page or in the voice to fire across the synapse to eye or ear and trigger a nexus of associations, memories, and emotions. Like this: When you sat there in the attic with Royce and Boudou, you may have remembered a similar visit you took as a child to your grandmother's attic, recalled how hot it was up there, how carefully you had to step, how the insulation lay unrolled and exposed, how the roof slanted, and how you ducked under beams. You may have remembered the camphoric smell of mothballs, and with that smell would have come all the details of the airy cave: the old porcelain sink, the garment bags hanging from exposed nails, the dusty Depression glass dinnerware stacked beside

the folded boxes from C. T. Scherer's Department Store, the photograph albums stored in the steel trunk.

And even as you read the next sentence—about Royce noticing
the woven baskets—you are back in your grandmother's attic looking at photographs of people you don't know, ladies in floral print
dresses, wearing feathered and veiled hats; men with cigarettes, lean-
ing against automobiles, thumbs through their belt loops; an empty
railroad depot, the tracks heading away to a landscape of bare trees,
the rail yard littered with handcarts and piles of sooty snow, and you
hear your mother calling you to lunch, but you are curious about
this missing snapshot, the four triangular corner mounts forming a
dark rectangle. Who removed the photo from the album and why?
And who is the purloined ghost? And at that moment you realize
that secrets lie all around you, that the world is so much larger than
you had imagined, and that you are a part of it, and that this is a
world of loss, and that all of these people whose names are penned
on the borders of the photographs, whose smiles and shadows have
been preserved, these people named Eustache and Marie, Walter,
Pamille, Theona, Grace, Emma, Cousin Butchie, Big Fred, Little
Fred, that all of them were tillers in the garden where the flower of
you now blooms.

So digression is not part of the logical development of the plot.
Its importance lies in thematic relevance, in emotion, understanding, tone. And here we have a moment where you can write your
own digression. (Royce and Benning are napping; Alvin Lee and
Adlai are scrubbing floors upstairs; Earlene's writing in her room—a
list of *Things That Stop You in Your Tracks*; the wives are shelling
beans in the kitchen; Boudou's sitting in a pecan tree.) Ready?

This is a digression about love. Our story, after all, is about love
and marriage. Well, what about love? Love ennobles. Love hurts.
Love nourishes. Love enslaves. Love is the opposite of indifference.
Love abides and love vanishes. Love enthralls and love alerts. Love
illumines our path. Love robs us blind. That's a start, at least. Your
turn now. Pick up your pen. Use the blank page opposite—it's yours.
You are not defacing the book, you are completing it. So please
write—allow yourself to become susceptible here and later to the

nuances and the assault of love. The page is not going anywhere unless you want it to. Write small, think expansively. (Feel free to use extra pages if necessary and fold them into the book.)

Okay. Recall your first love. Write his name. Write it here:

Now say it out loud. Try to remember her clearly: the eyes, cheekbones, earlobes, the hollow below the throat. Remember the emotions of the romance. Don't forget that passion and love include anger, pain, and pity. Try to remember your own compulsive and odd behavior. Your world and its priorities were changing. Recall the agony of the silent phone. These were remarkable days when your imagination controlled your involuntary bodily functions, when the thought of her would set your heart pounding, though so little of the blood reached your dizzy head. You would stumble over your own feet when you saw him. You imagined this loved one watched your every move.

Recall your big date—the first one, the senior prom, whatever. The first night that popped into your head is probably the right one. Write about the date in loving detail, from the time you left your house until the moment you separated at the door. (You *will* need the extra paper.) Remember the touches, the smiles, the caresses. Remember her smell—Ambush, lilacs, Ivory soap, gardenias, Prell. What did you talk about? And what did he say that surprised you? Was there a song that the two of you heard that night, and do you remember the lyrics? Describe what the two of you wore. Where are you? What are the sounds around you? The smells? The tastes? Write about everything you can remember. Then write about what you don't remember.

What is it like remembering all of this now? Do you feel a sense of loss and sadness? Or is it a pleasant recollection? A sense of loss is

perhaps inevitable since one of the losses is your youth, your inno-
cence, and all that they stand for. Do you think of your first love
often these days? Do you wonder if she still thinks of you? Do you
want to find him? Bring all of the emotions you've just unearthed to
the reading of the novel.

For extra credit, or for kickstarting your own story, continue
writing. Imagine that you married this first love. You did not break
up because he went off to college and found someone else. You
stayed together, even though some days you felt trapped and
doomed to mediocrity. Imagine your life with her now. Picture your
house, your apartment. Look around at your things, at hers. Walk
into every room and out into the yard. You can smell supper cooking, hear music on the stereo. Who lives here? Do you have children? Pets? Now it's morning and you're driving to work—where do
you work?—and you realize that something is missing in your life.
It's what keeps you up at night. It's what you need before you die.
Write about that.

Here's your page.

(If you like what you've written and want a reader, send it to the author at *johnny bob13@hotmail.com* or by post in care of the publisher. Who knows, maybe he'll collect them in an anthology.)

B ut digressions do take time, and in an effort to pick up the pace a bit, we offer **a summary of Chapter 10,** which would have been called *The Marriage of True Minds*. In it we fooled with the notion of the various connubial enterprises in progress. Grisham and Ariane's upcoming nuptials, of course, and how that was not unlike the wedding of our attention to the lives of Adlai, Earlene, Boudou, and the others, and not unlike the marriage of imaginations—ours and yours—that results in the experience of the story. We talked about how every narrator's intention is to charm, allure, seduce, and otherwise arouse the reader's interest, how every story should be a prolonged and pleasurable intercourse.

Here's what you missed: Grisham and Duane stop at the Red Bird Café for breakfast before the drive up to Shiver-de-Freeze. It's

clear that Duane admires the hell out of Grisham's escapade with—
What did you say her name was, Grish? Then the two of them drive
out to the trailer park and spy on the Airstream. The scene of
the crime, Duane calls it. Grisham thinks he sees a shadow pass by
the window. He wonders if Miranda has made the bed yet, tidied the
kitchen table, erased his presence. Duane looks at Grisham, at the
Airstream. He puts his head back and laughs.

They stop for lunch at Shea's Lounge in Urania. Oyster po'boys
and brews. While they're playing darts, Ariane drives past the
lounge in the backseat of Father Pat's Lincoln Town Car. She's
thinking that her mother (who finally gets the dignity of her name—
it's Mélia) ought not to be massaging Father Pat's beefy neck like
that. And how long can the two of them go on talking about the
price of things? God! An oak church pulpit costs $1,200. A sliver of
the True Cross would cost $9,000 if you could sell relics, which you
can't. A portable confession booth, three feet by three feet and seven
feet high: $600. Ariane remembers when she used to be happy and
alert all of the time. Now she's so inside herself and resentful. Used
to notice everything, how the swirls in flow blue china made pictures
if you squinched your eyes a little, how some people squat just
before they sit, how ant lions leave that perfect circle in sand. Now it
seems like what she notices is only what irritates her. She used to
feel calm, tender, attached. Now she feels brittle, unsettled, dis-
tanced. She doesn't know why she feels that way. She doesn't want to
feel that way anymore. She counts seventeen Holsteins in the pasture to her left.

When they cross the Bridge of Sighs it's almost midnight and
Father Pat wonders if they've lost the right road. He stops the car.
Ariane sees an old man painting waves around a floating woman on a
store window. He's painting by lantern light. A man in a wheelchair,
wearing a leopard fur hat, sits by, watching him. Mélia shouts to the
men, Yoohoo, she says, is this the road to Paradise?

Now it's six a.m., and back in Carencro, Miranda stands in the
chicken yard, holding four Dorkings in either hand. She's got them
by the legs, their shanks between her fingers. She thinks how they'll

be dead by the end of the day. She feels the jerks and tugs of their struggle. They flap madly, lunge, twist. Her arms are not her own, she thinks. She thinks if she could raise her arms over her head, if she could just manage this, if she could show these furious fowl the sky above, then maybe they would carry her away.

The Amorist

Love is not seen except by blindness, not possessed except by absence, not understood except by fools.

—UNDERWOOD ABDELNOUR,
THE LECTURE MAN*

A dlai had been awake most of the night. Sometime near one o'clock he'd heard the bride and her entourage arrive. Earlene and Alvin Lee, who had stayed up reminiscing, settled the guests into their rooms. The bride's bedroom was down the hall from his own on the second floor. He listened to Ariane's voice. She had one of those honeyed susurrant voices that soothed like the pressure of hands or wind or warmth.

He drifted to sleep and dreamed he was at Joey's Fleur-de-lis listening to a country-punk band called Linoleum Blownapart. He sat with Anniece and Donnie, who knew all the words to "Jiggle the Handle." Even in the dream, while Donnie sang the line about the wax in his candle, Adlai wondered if he'd be dreaming about Anniece for the rest of his life.

And then he was startled awake by thunder. He rolled over in bed, closed his eyes, thought about supper, how Ouida smelled all the food before she ate it and wouldn't touch the turnip greens or okra. Royce had stirred his coffee faster and faster until he stirred the cup right off the table. Lorraine talked about how when she was poor as Job's cat one time, the Lord saw to it she got food stamps. It was like the loaves and fishes, she said. They was always more stamps in her cookie jar. And then she shared her favorite Bible verse, Romans 8:36. *For thy sake we are killed all the day long; we are accounted as sheep to the slaughter.* She said, I eat that verse. I drink it. I sleep it. I breathe it. Lorraine's baby is due any day now.

And then Adlai watched himself sleep. He was in bed and so were his thoughts, but the watcher in him disengaged, sat on the chair by the window and looked on, saw the back of his own head, the flattened hair, the red skin lines of the wrinkled sheets. In bed, he thought about the pain he felt in his chest—strained muscle or heart attack? He'd never sleep now.

Adlai went to the kitchen, brewed coffee. He poured milk into a ceramic cow creamer. Adlai went out to the veranda, leaned back against the kitchen door. He liked being up before anyone else. Even as a crib baby, he'd awaken at first light and watch the ceiling brighten, the cabbage roses bloom on the wallpaper, wait to be fetched by his momma. Lightning illuminated the lake, the swamp, the eastern sky, the unfamiliar Lincoln Town Car in the drive, the upturned rowboat on the lawn. Adlai counted. *One Louisiana . . . two Louisiana . . . three . . .* He heard the thunder, reckoned the storm was now seven miles away. He saw the lights of the Black & Lovely.

Back in the kitchen he read a piece in yesterday's paper about a couple who killed each other in a duel in their own living room while their children watched TV in the den. The kids were still watching cartoons when the neighbor arrived with the police. Adlai poured himself a coffee, thought about how objects have attitudes: the humble coffee mug, the dutiful fan, the petulant telephone, the tenacious fridge. He noticed a couple of old books on the fridge.

Problems of Love and Marriage by Barbara Fairfax and *Deharbe's Small Catechism*, published 1882. He took the catechism to the agreeable table and looked out the honest window at the first drops of rain. He thought he heard the squeak of an upstairs floorboard. He listened to the music of the storm, the rustle of leaves, the thunder. Adlai sensed a presence behind him. Perhaps a displacement of air caused by the entrance of the intruder had swirled toward him and tickled the hair at his neck. Adlai turned, and as he did, lightning flashed through the house. He beheld Ariane: her dark eyes; pronounced cheekbones; her brown hair short, straight, burnished; her smile. This was the most placid, lovely, and graceful countenance he had ever seen. She wore a tan blouse, dungarees. She was shoeless.

"You must be Adlai," she said.

"You're Ariane."

Adlai stood, pulled a chair away from the table for Ariane. She thanked him and sat. He poured a cup of coffee, handed her the little cow, and watched her lighten the coffee. He was transfixed. Love enters your life in only this way—unexpectedly and suddenly while the rest of the world goes about its business, ignorant of your blessing.

Ariane said, "What are you reading?"

He held up the opened book. His eyes itched. He sneezed. Old books, old mold, mildew, dust mites—millions of them eating, defecating, crawling through their planet of wood pulp, shedding their armored skins, and all of it, larvae and fecal matter included, ballooning toward his face on the current of air generated by the turning of a page.

"Have you seen Grisham at all?"

This time when the lightning flashed, the electricity went out, the lights went dark, the clock stopped, the refrigerator's motor shuddered and wheezed to a silence. Adlai heard the whisper of Ariane's breath and then a report of thunder. He realized his heart was beating quickly and resolutely. He heard a hum—like the buzz of a high-tension power line or the buzz of existence—in his head. He felt both tense and relaxed. He would have said something, but then the power and the light returned, the refrigerator motor clicked and whined into operation.

What a bad idea this is—getting a crush on your cousin's betrothed. He looked at the step-on-the-pedal trash can by the broom closet, then at the floral dishes on a shelf over the sink. He said, "I've got to scoot over to the Black & Lovely, fetch us some cheese for the grits. Maybe some catfish for the eggs."

"I'll go with you."

"It's pouring out."

They draped their heads and shoulders with Adlai's jacket and walked into the driving rain. Ariane thought maybe they should walk backward, but the dirt road was muddy, rutted, and just now teeming with bullfrogs, many of them mating in frantic little clusters. One frog, his forearms swollen, his vocal sac inflated, tried to climb a cypress tree or either knock it over. Another had the twittering legs of a smaller frog sticking out of its mouth. Adlai wanted to pay attention to all this amphibious unpleasantness, but every nerve in his body was alert to his left arm and how it touched Ariane just above his elbow and at the back of his wrist. And his body, despite Adlai's better judgment, despite his notions of civility and decency, was conspiring to brush against Ariane's hip or thigh, her hair, her cheek, her anything.

Ariane said, "Who do you suppose that is?"

Adlai saw a wheelchair, the back of a head above the seat back, ball cap on the head.

Ariane said, "Appears he's stuck."

Adlai nodded to the gentleman, said hello, noticed the back wheels which were sunk in mud above the push rims. He introduced himself and Ariane, said, "We'll have you free in a jiffy."

The man nodded, said his name was Radley Smallpiece and he was mighty grateful. Adlai took hold of the handles, got his foot on the tipping lever, and shoved. Ariane tugged on the arm. Radley rocked his torso, watched Adlai through the rearview mirror attached to the arm, said, "I have no pleasure in the death of the wicked." The wheel gained purchase, and the chair came loose of the muck. Radley said, "If you all could carry me to the tarminated road, I would appreciate it." Adlai and Ariane covered themselves with the jacket and pushed. Adlai thought what an odd little family they must look like, the drenched couple out for a stroll with their ponderous baby. Radley sang, "Savior, Like a Shepherd Lead Us," and Ariane sang along with the chorus. When they reached the pavement outside the Black & Lovely, Radley said, "This'll drill, children. Drill just fine, thank you."

Because Delano 6smith had covered the window with a drop-cloth to protect his painting from the storm, it was darker inside the store than usual. Purvis stood shaving at the sink behind the counter. Adlai introduced Ariane.

"She's here to marry my cousin Grisham."

Purvis wiped shaving cream off his face with a towel. He walked around the counter and shook Ariane's hand. "Is that so?"

Ariane smiled. "Pleased to meet you."

Ariane and Adlai took turns wiping their hair dry by the wood-stove. Adlai asked Purvis did he have some cheese.

Purvis said he did, astonishing cheese, in fact. "Sharp as a serpent's tooth, sweet as reconciliation. I got a Natchitoches cheddar make you forget about heaven and hell, make you love yourself and who you're with." Purvis explained how the milk and the rennet come from a heard of Belted Galloways on a little farm near Chopin. "These cattle," he said, "were grazed in a new grass meadow. Year ago last spring. At the first bloom of wildflowers. So what you got is the fragrance of ground orchids and asters and the perfume of star grass."

"We need to get some of that," Adlai said. "A pound."

Purvis said he hadn't gone out in the storm to run his trotlines. No catfish this morning. "Later when it fairs off some, I'll get out there."

Ariane examined a display of canning tools.

Adlai said, "We just met Radley Smallpiece."

"Old boy's wound so tight he don't cast. I like him, though."

Ariane tried to imagine what the syringelike deal she was fooling with could be.

Purvis said that Radley used to live in town, had a wife and all, one of the Heartline girls. She ran off with a long-haul trucker. Radley took to drink. Purvis told Ariane she was holding a cherry pitter and told Adlai that Radley's just been released from prison. He kilt the fella what kilt Seal Boy.*

"Think he's dangerous?"

"Only to himself. No one much cared for Seal Boy. The Chameleon just pulled the trigger for the ones who done it, and they're in jail. His family, I mean. But carny people are clannish and they want to appear to be executing justice. So they called Radley."

On the way back to Paradise, in the now-misting rain, Ariane tore open the butcher paper and broke off a corner of the Natchitoches cheddar. She took a bite and stopped. She smiled and fed a piece to Adlai.

He said, "My God, it's like tasting a string quartet or something."

Adlai wondered would this cheese ever taste as good as it did right now. Had he, in fact, made up how delicious it was? Or was it the electrically charged air, the ozone, the small rain, the gentle light, Ariane's galvanizing presence that had rendered the taste and the moment pure and timeless? He said, "Ariane, I hope you won't take this in the wrong way. If anything should happen to you, you know, with Grisham or anything, well, I'll be here."

Ariane smiled, stepped away, cocked her head. "That's sweet, Adlai, but nothing's going to happen."

"I just figured if I didn't tell you, I'd lose my chance. I mean, for all I know you're being coerced into this—"

"I love Grisham, Adlai. You're funny."

They heard the bleat of a horn and turned. "Speak of the devil," Ariane said. She rewrapped the cheese. "He's with Duane."

The car stopped. Grisham rolled the window and stuck his head out. "Don't you two have enough sense to come in out the rain?"

As he opened the door for Ariane, Adlai wondered if he always breathed like this, lifting his shoulders, drawing the air deep into his lungs. He said hello to Grisham with a voice he didn't recognize. He shook Duane's hand. He watched water drip off Ariane's chin, noticed how when she talked the tip of her nose moved up and down.

Talking in Circles

Sadness is everyone's secret.

—EARLENE FONTANA

Royce and Boudou sat side by side on the rowing thwart of the rowboat *The Golden Pastime*, on Lake Moliere. Only Boudou was rowing, and so they were traveling in a tight circle, and that didn't bother either of them. Royce wore a fedora and a trench coat over his pajamas. As they circled, a breeze drifted them south toward the dock at the next house. Boudou told Royce that he would be Royce's memory if he wanted him to. Royce said, "Wouldn't our lives get all mixed up?" Boudou said remembering for him was as easy as picking lint off a cotton wagon. "Whatever you tell me, I'll remember, so you won't need to bother with it, and you can just concentrate on getting better."

Royce said, "You'd hate to think this that the climax of your life was barreness, was hollow at its center, exhausted, depleted, that the whole struggle has been for nothing." Royce drew his hand along the shaft of the oar. "Memory is the fire of our life, but my mind is a paper sack."

Boudou said, "I'm real happy to be here. Are you?"

"Yes, I believe I am, Boudou."

"I've never been to a wedding before. I think I'll dye my hair blue. Match my suit."

"I expect you momma might pitch a fit over that one."

Boudou said, "Tell me something you remember." He levered his oar on the oarlock. The squeaking stopped. He watched water skate along the edge of the blade, assemble itself into a column, pour off the paddle into the black lake. He heard the voices of girls, it sounded like, coming from shore, from over by the bramble thicket.

One girl's voice sang, "*A*, my name is Alice, my sister's name is Kate."

Another voice said, "When one of us is tardy, the other one is late."

Royce said, "Rylan's death. That poor baby was so sick and afraid." Royce took off his hat, ran his hand through his hair. "It hurt me just to breathe, to see how this was killing Benning. I was lonely, hopeless, desperate. That's when I learned what it is to be a human being."

Boudou looked up at Royce. He squinted an eye. Royce's white hair seemed to turn dark in the light.

Royce looked at his hat, said, "Who am I supposed to be again?"

"Royce Bogart, Private Eye."

"The worst that can happen is the death of a child. You never get over that devastation—you never really go on from there. Not as the whole person you were."

One girl's voice sang, "*B*, my name is Bigsley, my sister is one, too."

Another girl's voice sang, "Singular or plural, we are still both *you*."

"Mr. Royce, did you know my daddy?"

"I met him one time when he and your momma paid a visit."

"What was he like?"

Royce made a fist and tapped it on his chin. "My only picture of Billy Wayne is him standing in our field looking up into a live oak. That's all. Looking at what, I can't fathom. At mistletoe maybe. Just standing still with his hands tucked into his back pockets." Royce looked around the boat. "Maybe we should go on in, Boudou."

Earlene and Alvin Lee sat in Adirondack chairs on the lawn, both of them staring down at the pair in the boat and at the sun shimmering off the lake. To look at them lounging there, you might think here's a long-married couple, content to be near each other, at ease with silence. Intimate and deferential. Alvin Lee crossed his left leg over his right, scratched his ankle. Earlene held her coffee cup in both hands. She closed her eyes. She thought about *THINGS THAT TAKE YOUR BREATH AWAY*: *When your lover holds your head in his hands and kisses your forehead first, your lips, your right eye, your left eye; a sharp blow to the stomach; the accident of your existence; undeserved kindness; in the bedroom, on the bedclothes, the lingering scent of one who is gone; the shame of loss.*

Alvin Lee considered the imminent arrival of his child. Soon there would be another person on earth. A miracle, yes. One that Jesus Himself never did perform. And Alvin Lee wondered, Why is that? If you think about it, a baby beats water from wine hands down. From what we know, it looks like Jesus was a virgin. Alvin Lee wasn't judging what he thought of as the Lord's puzzling continence. Heaven knows, every man has his peculiarities. Jesus might have been shy, afraid even. Alvin Lee had seen many a torch extinguished by the warm wind of womanhood. Jesus might have been stuck-up. Or maybe He was too proud to do something so simple that any of the rest of us could manage it. Anyone can create a human being, He was saying. But can any of you die and then come on back? Jesus is the God with the human brain, after all. He's entitled to his frailties.

When Alvin Lee excused himself for asking, but inquired anyway about this Varden Roebuck he'd been hearing so much about, Earlene told him how that particular adventure was over—at least so far as the romance was concerned. Varden himself might be harder to get rid of, like a wine stain or the stench of tomcat.

Alvin Lee said he was sorry to hear that. Earlene said he needn't be. She said she hadn't walked away from love but from convenience. "I'm better off alone. My history with men has been abysmal, and I'm beginning to think it might not be the men."

"You'll find someone else."

The boat meanwhile had drifted closer to the dock of the house where the Great Books Club was holding its annual retreat. Margaret Grimes and Shug Johnson sat at the kitchen table eating. Margaret complained that the poached eggs were too hard.* Shug asked Royal Landry to pass the salt if he would. The three of them were arguing about Pascal's Wager. That's what drove Ted Muto back to his room before he'd finished his Postum. Ted never understood why anyone would waste a skinny minute worrying about eternity when there was so much to occupy our minds right here. Like beauty, passion, food, the Van Veckhoven sisters.

"The spirit of finesse," Shug said. "Intuition. God is to be felt by the heart and not known by reason. Reason, my friends, can only lead to atheism or agnosticism."

Margaret pointed her knife at Shug's chest. "So what's your point? Should we just stop thinking? What do you trust, your head or your heart?"

"Depends what's at stake."

"This isn't the Middle Ages, Shug."

"If I believe in God, and God doesn't exist, I've lost nothing. But if I don't believe and God does exist, well . . ."

Margaret would have said something about loss—of dignity, time, energy. She would have mentioned the integrity of reason, the eminence of the scientific method. And she slid the plate away from herself to do so, but she was preempted by Royal's theatrically intrusive and alarmingly loose cough. She told him he ought to have that looked at. That's a churchyard cough.

Royal said, "If there is a God, and He knows you don't believe in Him in your heart or your mind, but only because you're playing the odds, is that going to get you into heaven?"

That's when Bobby Sistrunk walked in with an empty plastic cereal bowl and asked were there any more Fruity Pebbles.

Back in Paradise, Lorraine eased her pregnant self into the Queen Anne chair in the sitting room. She asked Benning where Mélia and her priest were off to so early. Ouida lifted Lorraine's legs onto the ottoman and took a seat beside Benning on the sofa. Benning said they'd gone to town to St. Collette's so Father could say Mass. "So how is it you all three ended up married?"

Ouida said, "Alvin Lee first noticed me when I was Queen of Vacation Bible School and he was preaching on the Song of Solomon, and he called me up to the front of the tent and asked could I sing a hymn to Jesus Christ, my personal Lord and Savior, and I reckoned I could and I sang acapulco—you know, without music—sang 'The Solid Rock.' "

Lorraine said, "When I first saw Alvin Lee look on Ouida with those eyes, well, I was mad as a snake at haying. I fell to pieces and was brought to the psychopathic ward at the Bastrop Community Hospital. I say I was agitated—I was bad hurt—but I never did cry, not once. Doctor they had up there told me why don't you cry instead of holding all the pain inside. Sounded to me like Satan talking.

"And then the Lord spoke to me. He come on the television there in my semi-private room. Miss Liszt in the other bed, she said all's she saw was the little fellow on *Fantasy Island*. Course Lammy Liszt would not see God on account of she's Episcopalian. And the televised Lord said, Lorraine, darling, let me be your psychiatrist. And I was cured."

Benning said, "And now you all are having a baby. I sure am looking forward to dandling that child." And then she turned on the radio, and the three women listened to Durwood Tulliver's *Holy Minute* show. The reverend asked the ladies this morning to put their hands onto the radio as a point of contact and to pray with him. He needed guidance. Yes, he did, dear Lord. He needed to find the true path through the wilderness of civilization. Amen. Amen, the ladies said.

Brother Durwood said, "I want to be just like Paul, the deformed little wanderer from Tarsus. Yes, I do. I want to be Your broadaxe, Lord. I want to be Your infantry, Your bazooka. I want to be Your speed cop who pulls over the mighty violators. I want to be Your magistrate who sentences blasphemers to life in hell without parole. Jesus, Lord, I am Your whistle-blower, Your anointed finger-man. I'll point them out to You, Jesus, the robust boys and the flashy girl all primped up for churchgoing, strutting down Your aisle, dear Jesus, like they's in some fashion show. How do I know this, brothers and sisters? 'Cause I got me a search warrant from God to know their hearts, and their hearts are defiled with treachery and lechery. They would shatter our solar system with their fornications and sodomies and bestialities. We are doomed, brothers and sisters. Thank Our Lord Jesus Christ with me now. Thank Him that this world is not our home. Praise God, Amen."

At the kitchen table Grisham told Adlai, Ariane, and Duane the story about the man from Opelousas who was so scared of somebody coming after him that he slept with a pistol on the nightstand. One night the phone rang and startled the man, and he reached over, picked up the pistol, put it to his ear, and squeezed the trigger.

"Well, that's real cheery," Ariane said.

Grisham said he'd like to think that just as the unfortunate suicide opened his mouth to say hello, just as he was wondering who could be calling with bad news—it's always bad news at three a.m.—he awoke just enough to realize what was happening—how foolish this was, how ludicrous this would look to the neighbors, to the guys at the shop, to the bowling team, how his trying to protect himself resulted in his killing himself—such grim irony—but just maybe, he thought and hoped, maybe the gun isn't loaded. Did I forget to load it? But before he could discern an answer, everything went blank.

"Twenty-two caliber," Grisham said. "And the epilogue is that the cops checked out the phone call. Was a wrong number. Some drunk up late was trying to reach his ex."

All Adlai could think about was that bullet, that brain, how the destruction and death might have seemed instantaneous, but was not. Even before the bullet exited the barrel, gas from the firing would have shot under the skin and expanded against the bone, causing the skin to split like a starburst, like the casing on an over-boiled hot dog. That would have happened first. The bullet itself would have made short work of the epidermis, the hair follicles, the sebaceous glands, the arteries, and all that superficial business, before it burst through the skull and into the temporal lobe and began tunneling through the cerebrum, separating gray matter from gray matter, mangling speech, silencing hearing, obliterating consciousness, destroying memory, stacking tissue in front of it, sending shock waves ahead to the left hemisphere, trailing a confusion of hemorrhages, and then burrowing into the white matter, into and out of the corpus callosum, back into white and gray matter before reaching the skull plate where it ricocheted and came to rest in its spongy bed near the optic chiasma. At which moment did the shooter die?

"Adlai, are you all right?" Ariane said.

"I'm fine."

Duane said he read a book about people who died and came back to life. What happens, apparently, is you go through a long, dark tunnel and then you see this brilliant light.

Ariane said, " If they come back, Duane, then they weren't gone. Death's terminal. It's not a swoon or faint."

Duane said, "Well, Jesus came back from the dead."

Adlai said, "If Jesus had been embalmed, we wouldn't be celebrating Easter."

Grisham announced that he and Duane had to head into Monroe to pick up their tuxedos, would anyone like to tag along?

"If you want me to go, I'll go," Ariane said.

Adlai was beginning to understand what Boudou meant about sounds producing physical responses. Ariane's voice gave him goose bumps.

"Of course I want you to come," Grisham said. "If you want to come."

In the yard, Earlene closed her eyes and felt the sun on her face. Earlene felt like a cat sometimes. Used to be she'd want to rub her cheek against the edge of a man, bury her head in his neck, insinuate her length against his, ram her head against his leg. Now she was happy with this puddle of sun. "I wish we didn't have to leave, wish we could all just stay and live here together."

"Wouldn't that be great."

"What do you think of Grisham's bride?"

"I try not to think of other women. I've got two of my own."

Earlene thought, *Double wives, troubled lives*. Maybe a song in that. "Is that a problem?"

"Becoming one."

(*G*od is the name we give for the reason we're here.* And here *we* are between chapters, letting life interrupt, and that's the sentence that occurs to us. [Shug Johnson said it, and we'll get back to him in a moment.] And this from Jean-Jacques Rousseau: "I have suffered too much in this life not to expect another." How are these two notions connected? [Everything can be connected.]

And what does our author do between chapters? He eliminates chapters, crosses out paragraphs, cuts lines, like this one that he thought was so clever: *Love is the gravity that settles chaos.* And all the while he's reminding himself what he heard Margaret Grimes say at a Great Books meeting [*Jude the Obscure*]: Any text includes that which it excludes.

And what is it *you* do between chapters? Stretch your legs perhaps? Pour another tumbler of iced tea? Maybe you try to remember what you're supposed to pick up on the way home: milk [low-fat], bread [light rye], vinegar [balsamic], chocolate [you deserve it]. Chapters end so you can catch up on [what's been called] the real world. That and so you can close your eyes and stare at Ariane, see in her countenance what Adlai sees. So you can rummage around in the Loudermilk kitchen, open the fridge, the cabinets, the junk drawer, check the notes on the calendar. So you can wonder what's going to happen.

Maybe you think about a friend, a family member with Alzheimer's, and you can't get that person's image out of Royce's story. Or you wonder what's Boudou's sun sign [Cancer]. Maybe you think, So here I am in Shiver-de-Freeze, and I haven't seen much of the town. Well, you'll be visiting Dispersed of Judah Cemetery and the Social Ocean directly. And if you haven't peeked already, we can tell you the next chapter's a long one, and maybe you don't have the time right now—your subway stop's coming up or you just have to get some sleep. Don't feel compelled to push ahead. Maybe you do have time for a quick philosophy joke.* Before you flip ahead to the Appendix, however:

Back to God for a minute. God is what is invoked; an object of adoration; the initiator; the singularity; the essence of all that is; actuality; the source of Time; the end of Time; the Omniconfident, All-Inscrutable, All-Insensate, All-Dispassionate, Ultradevastating, Impervious and Imperturbable, Omnicomplacent, Absolute and Guileless One; the autobiographical author of the universe.

And what then is this object, *the universe*? What is this object, *God*? How did they begin? And where? Where is this absolute elsewhere, this unknowable territory where what would become lay dormant in nothing? And why the universe? Why God? Why anything at all? If God is the reason for us, what is the reason for God? Is God merely the projection of our shameless expectations, and is that what Rousseau knew?

We may not know what Rousseau had in mind, but we do know what Shug Johnson thought about such cosmological questions because he delivered a paper at a Great Books meeting entitled, "Inquiry and Knowledge: Asking the Impertinent Questions." Shug held that we learn everything from stories, including all matters scientific. Science and fiction are both stories. Science is a story that someone's trying to prove; fiction is a story that defines a truth. Science is God's story; fiction is ours. Science is reductive; fiction expansive. Science seeks answers; fiction, questions.

Shug then shared his optimism with the group, said he thought that eventually we will come to understand what we need to understand, but our language is not yet capable of conceiving the image or of constructing the correct interrogative, which must be other than, but including, *Why?* And, *How?* Only language will enable us to know. God is in the syntax. And that is why we study Euclidian geometry in a quantum universe and read Homer 2,700 years later: understanding is not about progress; it's about process. What we may finally come to understand is that we won't, can't, understand and that incomprehension is essential to our existence. Mystery is our maker.

When you're ready, we'll move on to Chapter 13.)

Dinner on the Grounds

We're all of us Time Travelers, Bo.
We each got the one-way ticket.

—DELANO 6SMITH

Adlai stepped out of the Black & Lovely, saw that the Rambler had not yet arrived to fetch him, and sat on a milk carton beside Delano. He put the sack of groceries at his feet, looked straight ahead across the bridge beyond the lake in the direction of Monroe, trying to place Ariane back in his world. If he could just see where she was, what she was doing, then he would be comforted, and maybe she would feel him watching her—not in a creepy way, but in a wistful, ardent, and virtuous way. What he saw was Ariane and Grisham, arm-in-arm, laughing at something they're staring at in a store window.

Delano said, "How you coming, Adlai?"

"Nicely, thanks." Adlai looked over his shoulder at Delano's win-

119

dow painting, studied the flying woman whose skin was whiter than her ivory gown, but who had no face.

Delano offered Adlai a sip of his beer. Adlai declined.

"You in love, Birdsong. I see it 'round your head."

"You believe in auras, Delano?"

"I believe what I see. And I see plenty."

Earlene drove the Rambler up to the front of the store and waved.

Adlai said, "Got to go."

Delano waved to the car, raised his beer can in salute.

"We're fixing to pay our respects to my brother Rylan."

"Sweet boy."

Once you cross the Bridge of Sighs, Rue Royale becomes Temperance Street. To get to the cemetery, you take Temperance past Fortitude and over the railroad tracks. Take a right on Justice, which carries you over Fontana Bayou and becomes Hope. About a quarter mile beyond Prudence you'll see a bias road to your left. Take it. This is Golgotha Lane and it leads you to Dispersed of Judah.

We call this part of town Mount of Olives on account of the old Indian burial mound. An archaeological team up from LSU determined that this exact spot has been a necropolis for fifteen hundred years or more. How the team came to investigate the site at all was that after a particularly wet winter upstate, the bayou flooded, several mummified bodies surfaced not twenty yards from the bank. Turns out that the lack of oxygen in the boggy soil, the alkanizing plant life, and the presence of certain minerals which inhibit bacterial and fungal growth have conspired to keep the bodies of the interred from corruption, which means that the legend carved on the cemetery gate—*The Worms Shall Feed Sweetly on Them*—is more wish than fact. The archaeologists reburied our incorruptibles, except for the one who resides now over to the Shiver-de-Freeze Museum of Social and Natural History. (We named him Slim Marshbury, and he shares a closet with Boyd Hammond's caul and with Elna Schimmelpenningh's calcified baby, a child she carried fifteen years in her abdominal cavity, and which was the cause of the inexplicable chronic pain in her right side.

Earlene scrubbed Rylan's headstone with bleach and a stiff brush. The pungent smell brought back summer days at the Monroe municipal swimming pool at Forsythe Park, and just like that Earlene heard the laughter of splashing children and felt the burn of chlorinated water in her nostrils. She saw herself in her peach two-piece bathing suit—must have been seven or eight—wearing her earplugs, in water up to her eyes, holding her breath, watching the big girls cannonball off the diving board. And something about that recollection triggered another: she and Billy Wayne are arguing. Or she is anyway, because he won't talk. They're sitting in the parlor of the first house on Concordia. He won't look at her. His face is set like concrete.

Earlene worked a toothbrush into the curved *o* in *Beloved.* How were those two memories, twenty years apart, connected? She understood the smell of bleach now and the pool then. But the other? She smelled her hands. There must be some common thread. A word? A song? Earlene closed her eyes. What she felt was shame. She knew that emotions do not deceive. Had no reason to. You can deny them, but what sense would that make? You may not understand them, but they are unignorable.

But what did she experience at the pool? The shame of being too small or too young? The shame of not being happy when she should be—hadn't Papaw taken her here on the bus so she could have fun with the other children? And then she knew. Earlene remembered that the girl in the water felt ashamed at not being good enough to be liked. How does that happen to a seven-year-old?

And with Billy Wayne? Did the shame arise from failing at the argument? at the marriage? How can you love someone and be unable to reach or save them? Now she felt angry. What is it with men and arguments that they panic and go silent? Are all men like that or is she for some reason perversely attracted to those who are? Varden's an emotional black hole. Royal Landry was pitifully inarticulate.

. . .

There's folks who think Dispersed of Judah is a bit trashy for a graveyard. Those who do bury their kin over to the new Shady Glen Memorial Gardens. We like to think of our charnel yard as expressive, peculiar, and charming in a shambled kind of way. It's not tidy and is not particularly somber. (We almost said *grave*.) There are some vaults made from cinder block and tile, others from concrete. We have a monument to the Confederate dead and another to those who died of yellow fever. Aleta Clark's onyx headstone is shaped like a telephone and is inscribed, *Jesus Called and I Answered*. Sophronia Wilson's headstone features a clock face whose hands indicate the minute of her death (11:53). The epitaph reads, *Time to Go*. Bobby Griffith's grave is marked by a granite Camaro and these words: *Highway to Heaven*. Bobby died out on 165 in Sterlington when his Z-28 wrapped itself around a utility pole and somehow Bobby himself came to rest folded over a telephone wire like a pair of slacks, twenty feet off the ground. Willy and Lucy Allen are buried together under a marble four-poster bed, Roosevelt Lincoln under Mount Rushmore, Alice Beale under a pair of shoes. Alice was six months old when she died. Her epitaph is, *I'll Take My First Steps in Heaven*.

Family and friends of the Dearly Departed tend to stay awhile when they visit, which is why there are so many wicker and chrome chairs scattered about. Folks like to catch up, reminisce, carry gifts along for the dead. Boudou, who had made it his job to water all the flowers in the cemetery, had already examined the following items left on graves: a stuffed and mounted smallmouth bass; a wrought-iron birdcage; a Volkswagen bumper; a collection of bleached seashells and brain coral; an oak pulpit; Scrabble tiles; an X ray of a lung, featuring an unmistakable and appalling shadow; a yellow billiard ball; assorted fishing lures; three bottles of Ouachita Amber Ale; an enamel bowl of plastic fruit; a color photograph of a tandem disk harrow; nursing bottles; a wooden crib; cloth diapers; a thin and worn bicycle tire; ceramic rosary beads; a deck of Aquarian tarot cards; a sno-globe, and a fez.

What happens is that every Graveyard Day (the fourth Friday in August, a municipal holiday) before the clutter gets too ostentatious, before the grounds begin to look like Branson Tilley's front yard, folks come out and gather up the old gifts (some of which end up in the museum, some in the dump, some at Peyton Pepper's House of Junque). They'll weed the plots, plant flowers, spruce up the place, and they'll present their deceased with new gifts. It's like Christmas for the dead.

Adlai imagined that Ariane was watching him from some secluded prospect as he set the picnic table for dinner. Adlai would *compose* his table. And Ariane would note his grace, his prudence, his careful eye for detail. Of course, there is only so much you can do with paper plates and napkins. Adlai folded six napkins into coffin-shaped sleeves and slipped the clear plastic utensils into them. He borrowed a lard can of fresh lilies from the nearby tomb of one Crompton "The Cunning" Knowles, 1902–1977, to use as a centerpiece. He thought about who should sit where, and who could reach what, and he arranged the seasonings and condiments accordingly. He checked his watch. Alvin Lee ought to be arriving shortly with food. Adlai considered his table. He thought of the sadness of meals. Too soon the food is eaten, and then the cleanup, the trash, the getting on with life.

What Adlai couldn't know was that while he was imagining Ariane watching him, she was in Monroe with Grisham and Duane, sitting in the Mohawk Tavern, listening to those two laugh about the man who took Viagra with his coffee and stayed up all night, listening to them, but thinking about Adlai, how unlike Grisham he was, how peculiar, and how comfortable to be with. Grisham finished telling Duane about the elderly newlyweds who honeymooned in Viagra Falls. Grisham put his hand on Ariane's knee beneath the table. He startled her. She smiled and crossed her legs. She counted thirty-six bottles on the top shelf. Grisham thought about what's-her-name, the girl in Lafayette. Miranda. What an odd duck, he thought. That refrigerator.

What Grisham couldn't know was that while he was remembering Miranda, she was just then towing her Airstream out of the trailer park, saying so long to Lafayette and chicken-sexing. She turned north on 182 so she could drive one last time by the chicken plant. From there she'd head north to Alec and pick up some highway to Arkansas. She had saved five hundred dollars. Her stomach shook like nervous pudding, and she wasn't sure why. Was this what her life was always going to be like? Always moving, always alone, always uncertain. All her childhood she had wanted to be free. Couldn't wait to be old enough to beat it out of Orange. And here she was at twenty-three, rootless, independent, on the loose, unfettered, unclaimed, untaken. Was this freedom, this disconnectedness? Why had she ever thought that freedom meant escape and simplicity? She began to hum the song she heard the other night at the House of Blue Lights. "Leaving You/Wanting To." Or was it ". . . Wanting, Too"? Or ". . . Wanting Two"? A cowboy sang it, but you could tell a woman wrote it. Miranda sang what she remembered of the lyrics, the lines that drew her attention away from Varden Roebuck's dimpled cheeks:

> You're married to the single life
> And coupled to the road,
> And I'm in bed with loneliness
> And I'm borrowed and I'm blue
> But I'd rather be alone
> Than be alone with you.*

Miranda stopped at a red light in front of Molly Bloom's Florist Shop and saw Wyman Gordon at his post, taking notes. She waved to him. He saluted, snapped his heels together. She realized she wouldn't ever see old Wyman again. Wyman works for Plutonians, who'll be arriving directly to conquer the earth, just as soon as they have a spare moment, Pluto being the busiest planet, the duty-free planet, the shopper's paradise, the banking center of the outer planets and nearby galaxies. Wyman's job is to write down anything odd, strange, out of the ordinary. His bosses will want to know.

Once, he told Miranda that one day while they were gigging frogs, he asked the Plutonians did they believe in God? Had they accepted Jesus Christ as their personal Lord and Savior? They said, Who? He said, God. A Supreme Being. They looked perplexed. A Creator, he said. Blank stares. He said, Someone who can be in many places at the same time. They smiled (which means they brightened and warmed the air around them). They said, We all can do that. The light turned green. Miranda yelled, Hey, Wyman! See you in the funny papers! And she drove off. Wyman took his pen from his pocket.

Earlene sat down at the table. She felt calm and wasn't sure why. She realized she'd slept through the night, a deep and dreamless sleep. It was the absence of Varden, wasn't it? She had relieved herself of him, of the turmoil and unpleasantness that their relationship had become. And at that moment she understood she had already decided somehow that she would not be going back to him or on to anyone else, and she wondered was it the embrace of family that had enabled and emboldened her. Her life suddenly seemed simple and splendid. If she wanted trouble and complication, she'd write about it. There are men and there is love. She loves Boudou, loves this family.

Adlai said, "I love Ariane."

"Then stop."

Adlai stared off down Golgotha at the cloud of rising dust, at what must be Alvin Lee arriving with the picnic hamper.

"I don't think I could ever find anyone as great as Ariane. She's it for me."

Boudou ran to the table, sat, caught his breath, settled himself. He wrangled out of Earlene's hug and told her and Adlai that there's a Fontana buried down by the stone wall. Like me. Only the first name is Ponder. 1912–1946.

"One of your daddy's uncles," Earlene said.

Alvin Lee parked his car and waved. Boudou and Adlai helped

him haul the food to the table. Earlene asked Alvin Lee which Fontana Ponder was.

"The boneheaded boy who worked the road crew. Remember?"

"The one who electrocuted himself stealing copper wire?"

"That was Muse. Ponder was here building the old Monroe Road. He and his buddies was at a party at some roadhouse, and they were drinking the high octane and trying to blow up a goat. Had a blasting cap kind of deal tied into its mouth and were poking at it with a pickaxe."

Boudou said, "Why would anyone do that?"

Earlene said, "They were dull-witted boys. Didn't have a complete thought among them."

Alvin Lee said, "The kind of lightweights that fish with electrical cable. Anyway, they can't seem to get the goat to explode, so Ponder takes the cap from out the goat's mouth, wipes it clean on his overalls, says he knows how to blast it. He puts it in his mouth and bites down. The blast blows off his lips, his tongue, shatters his teeth, rips a hole in his cheek, and clefts his palate."

Alvin Lee stood at the head of Rylan's grave and recited the Lord's Prayer. The family bowed their heads. Amen. Alvin Lee said, "My old friend Rylan had a saving knowledge of the Lord Jesus Christ. He never got too high to fall on his knees, never too low to raise up his eyes unto the Lord and behold His fourteen-carat majesty."

Benning said, "I miss you, boy. We got all your favorites for the meal—iced tea, buttermilk biscuits, country ham, and hoppin' john, pound cake, and banana pudding." Benning raised her eyes to heaven and closed them.

Royce said, "It's the Smiling Mighty Jesus took Rylan, right?"

Benning said, "Yes, dear, the spinal meningitis."

Royce said, "And there was nothing we could do?"

Benning said, "We did everything we could." She patted Royce's hand.

Alvin Lee said, "Amen."

. . .

Benning poured herself another glass of sweet tea and asked Boudou to mind the flies off the pudding. She took a photograph out of her purse, studied it, passed it on to Earlene. Earlene smiled. In the picture, Rylan, who's about eleven, has his head caught between the bars of a wrought-iron fence. And he's laughing about it. Benning said, "That's Dewey Bowditch's fence. We had to call the fire department to release that monkey." Earlene passed the picture to Alvin Lee, who showed it to Adlai.

Alvin Lee said something about Rylan's first seizure, how he locked himself in the closet that day.

Benning said, "Rylan claimed the light was too bright in his room."

Royce said, "My teeth hurt."

Alvin Lee said, "I remember how he started drowsing all the time. Then how he didn't wake up. By that time he was deaf, the doctors said. Poison blood drove through his body."

Royce took out his dentures. Earlene asked Boudou to rinse out a coffee cup over by the Bayles vault. See the spigot there. "We'll put Royce's teeth in it. Fill it up halfway. Go ahead."

Benning said, "My cousin Thalassa—she married one of the Meades—well, she just snapped, got gripped by the devil, some said. Tossed her little baby boy to the hogs. Nothing but bones and scalp in the morning."

"Every family has tragedy in it," Alvin Lee said.

Benning said, "Adlai's uncle Beryl fell out a fourth-floor window of the Grand Hotel in Monroe and landed on a parking meter."

Boudou returned with the cup and set it before Royce. Royce dipped his uppers into the cup. Boudou took his spyglasses and roamed the cemetery. While the family talked about wedding food and wedding gifts and wedding etiquette and about nursery necessities and baby clothes and the drive time to St. Francis Hospital, Adlai imagined Grisham standing up at the rehearsal supper to say he was sorry and embarrassed to let this drag on, but he had to tell everyone before it was too late that he and Duane were deeply in love or that he was the carrier of a rare genetic time bomb and would not take the chance of having children and so he was leaving immediately for a monastery in North Dakota, don't try to stop me, it's the right thing to do.

Boudou leaned back against the cement bass boat that was Boozy Harper's tombstone. He turned his glasses on the group at the table. He looked at each of them. He saw the label turned up at the back of Alvin Lee's jersey. An oak leaf had trapped itself in the cobweb of Benning's hair. Royce rocked himself in his seat. Adlai, he was smiling brightly, but beneath the table his foot was tapping as quick as a lizard.

(And in Monroe at about this moment, on the couch in Boudou's house, Varden Roebuck came to the conclusion that he would not, could not live without Earlene. This was not so much a decision as an impulse. He was tugging his boot onto his left foot. Just because two people don't get along doesn't mean they shouldn't be together. He stamped his foot, picked up the right boot. And wasn't he the King of North Louisiana Singing Cowboys? And aren't gals of all ages and all persuasions just dying to bed him down? Varden stood. He shook his legs till the jeans fell just so over the boots.

All right then, how does he explain to Earlene about what she called the fire sale in his romance department? Sweetly, that's how. Honey, he'll say, sex is overrated. It's a small part of a successful relationship. Sex is great when you're young. And sure it's terrific when you're with someone new—as we both found out a while ago. But it is ultimately degrading to the woman, and you know that, Earlene. In your heart you do. And I do not wish to degrade you, darling. You are precious to me, my treasure, my china doll, my sugar angel. Varden thought, Am I fucked up?)

Every Picture Tells a Story

*Even to this day Arkansas is ruled by
the Lord of Vermin and Louisiana by
the Prince of the Southern Cross.*

—DURWOOD TULLIVER

Because Boudou asked her about curses, Benning fetched her *Best of Durwood Tulliver* cassette tape and snapped it into the player. She pressed start, shook the machine, gave it a slap. She told Boudou how to play "A Picture Is Worth a Thousand Words," which was Rylan's favorite game. She told him to find a photo he liked in the album and give it a title. When we each have a photo we tell the story about it, and the best story wins a dish of Double Chocolate Deluge ice cream and no one's momma has to know.

Durwood said, "The curse of the bastard follows the bloodline. Yes, it does. Stay with me, now," Boudou saw a photo of the side of commercial building with *Tom Moore Cigars* painted on it. Where the paint was fading, you could see *Rooms* and *Coca-Cola* and Something *Brothers Saloon*. He put that one aside. Maybe.

Durwood said, "A person begotten out of wedlock shall not enter into the assembly of the Lord, even unto the tenth generation. Hallelujah! The demons of lust will follow all the children of the line!"

Boudou said, "That's not nice."

Benning said, "*Nice* is not Brother Durwood's concern."

"I meant God. Blaming a person, a baby, for what someone else did. Anyway, my momma says there isn't any such a thing as a curse."

"It's a metaphor." Benning studied a picture of Morin's Funeral Home and pictured the wake going on inside. Alice Cole is on her knees in the reception parlor saying good-bye to Betty Gundelfinger, Betty who worked beside her for seventeen years in the stitching room at Monroe Leather. Alice is praying over the body and weeping, not for Betty now, but for Betty then, the blue-eyed girl she shared her lunch with at the plant, whose dream it was to marry Bobby Joe Gaddis, help him with his plumbing business, have a pile of kids, and buy a place right on the bayou. Then Bobby Joe went and died in Vietnam.

Durwood said, "Now suppose all the women in your family die of the cancer, generation after generation. You got you a curse, don't you?"

"You see there, Boudou. Genes. *Curse* is the old word for genes." She turned the page, found a photo of an old gas pump, a padlocked door.

Durwood said, "What was the original sin that started the generations of cancer? Was your granddaddy practicing wart removal or water-witching? Forgive him if he did. Did your grandmother wear pierced earrings? Did she fool with the Ouija board? Did your daddy wear a peace symbol—ain't nothing but a busted cross? Did he listen to rock and roll music? Did he hang a horseshoe over the door? Collect four-leaf clovers, rabbits' feet, wishbones? Did he have a puppet?"

Boudou said he'd go first. He found a picture of a derelict house

that seemed to have a face with one eye shut, the other opened but damaged. His story was called "Mr. Wilde."

Benning switched off the tape. "Let's hear it."

Mr. Archibald Wilde died because his heart stopped just like that. His heart stopped and his wife—his second wife, Barbara Jean—ignored him when he gripped the sides of the kitchen table—and here Boudou acted the role—looked across at her and managed to say he thought he was having a heart attack, just before his arms relaxed and his face smashed into the bowl of tapioca pudding. Boudou slapped the table. *Barbara Jean didn't call the ambulance, didn't carry Archibald to the hospital. After he died, the whole family pretended that Barbara Jean was so sweet and everything. They tapped her on the back, hugged her, said, "There, there, Barbara Jean, you mustn't blame yourself." They dabbed her eyes with Kleenex. Gave her some Beeman's gum to chew. Aunt Rita signed over her share of the inheritance to Barbara Jean, and the family persuaded Archibald's other sisters, Rose, Lily, and Violet, to do the same. Barbara Jean was amazed at her good fortune as was her boyfriend Timmy. Barbara Jean tried to sell the little white house, but everyone thought it smelled of rancid pork and mold, and so she just abandoned it and moved into town. Timmy was thinking, No more drive-ins, no more Fat Willie's Fish Camp. Timmy was thinking multiplex, Red Lobster. The end.*

Benning said, "You just made that up right now?" She told him how wonderful that was. She knew a woman just as mean-spirited as his Barbara Jean. She told Boudou he was better at "Picture" than Rylan was, and he was something.

"My turn." Benning said her story would be called "The Marches" because it was about August and Jan March and their daughters April, May, June, and Julie. She showed Boudou her picture of what had been a house with a huge tree growing right up out of it. Only the outer wall was left and a shuttered window where someone had improbably left baskets of fresh flowers.

Mr. March took his three oldest daughters into town to Mr. Rodney Pomeroy's Photographic Studio on a Saturday afternoon. Julie was feeling a bit punkish, so she stayed at home with her momma and they played "A Picture Is Worth a Thousand Words."

Boudou laughed at that

April had borrowed her aunt Emma's cashmere tea gown, her mother's star-and-crescent brooch, her lace hanky, her friend Grace Fournier's Ceylon brilliant studs. The hat she bought from Montgomery Ward's. Mr. March thought it looked like an accident, like an ostrich had blown into a rose on a velvet lily pad. April would give her photo to her beau Leander

Harris, who was going off to Tulane in the fall. May was bored with the whole adventure. Mr. Pomeroy asked her to smile five times, and Mr. March tapped his foot like mad. Finally she cracked a smile that did not include her eyes. June thought the whole business was a fraud. This is not her. They can make her wear rouge and lipstick and curl her hair, but they cannot make her who she is not. She stared right through Mr. Pomeroy's camera, right through Mr. Pomeroy and on to all of her kin through all of the years who will ever look on her image, and she told them that this moment was a lie.

Back at home, Julie was in the middle of her story of the house with the gas pump when the tornado struck and lifted the roof off the house. When the wind stopped, Julie's mother was gone. I should have held on tighter, she thought. And so was all the furniture. Julie had a swollen leg, a bruised back, three broken ribs. She went looking for her momma. She found a dead horse where the Heflin place used to be. She saw an Oldsmobile wrapped like tinfoil around a leafless tree. She found her parents' chifforobe by the bluff, but her mother wasn't in it. She found a painting of Jesus whose eyes followed her. She found her cat Beezer. She found her momma on the couch in the creek. Her momma opened her eyes, smiled, said, You would not believe the dream I just had.

Benning served the ice cream. Boudou asked how old was Julie. Your age. Benning put Durwood back on.

"Go home now and cleanse your houses, brothers and sisters. Remove the marks of Satan. Throw out all pentacles and shamrocks, tulips and unicorns, distelfinks and lucky stars. Say, I break any curse placed on me by my ancestors. I break theses curses in Jesus' name back to ten generations and even back to Adam and Eve. Say to Satan, I am closing any door I may have opened to you through contact with astrology, chiropractic, hypnosis, the lottery. Be gone, Beastmaster!"

Boudou said, "Julie brings the flowers for the window, right?'

The Social Ocean

We see the happiness of young lovers,
and we're moved because we've seen the
unhappiness that awaits them.

—SHUG JOHNSON

The Kingfish had a soft spot in his populist heart for Shiver-de-Freeze because as a young man he had sold his very first bottle of Hadacol to Miss Shaundollyn Evans who lived on Mercy in a flat over Rayburn's Hardware and who was herself prone to seasons of disabling lassitude. Miss Shaundollyn the Envigorated told her friends all about the straw-hatted young gentleman with the charming voice and the pep and about his miraculous potion, and before Huey left town, he was well on his way to becoming the #1 Hadacol salesman in the Deep South and then the governor and then the U.S. senator and then the president for certain if the unthinkable had not've happened. And the folks in Shiver-de-Freeze were themselves relieved of headaches and were decongested.

So when Huey got elected governor, he wanted to do something special for the people of Shiver-de-Freeze. Folks in town, however, had had enough of the kleptocrats in Baton Rouge who siphoned their monies off so's New Orleans could have another bridge. Townsfolk told Huey thanks but no highway, thanks but no railroad depot, thanks but no textbooks, thanks, we're fine. Huey said, Then I'm fixing to build you a fountain, a civic monument. Shiver-de-Freeze, he said, Rome in the Delta! How about that! Folks said, We've got us a river, a lake, a swamp, and a bayou, and you want to build us a fountain? We're damp already. Huey said, Listen at me. Don't make me look bad in front of the Frenchmen down here. We're all of us rednecks. We got to hold together.

And so the Long Fountain was built on vacant land between Prudence and Piety. The fountain was a simple affair with a circular base about thirty foot in diameter. Carved into the base was, *Every Man a King*. Inside was a circle of four paunchy bronze fish with jets of water spitting out their mouths.

At first folks tolerated the piece, then grew to like it, then they cleared the land around it of plum thickets, Spanish dagger, and trash, planted grass, installed benches and tables. The fountain became the centerpiece of the park we call the Social Ocean, and every night our citizens gather to sit and listen to the soothing gurgle, hiss, and splash of the fountain, to watch each other, to gossip, joke, wait for the colony of thirty thousand fishing bats to spiral out of the trees in Tohu Bohu and descend, some of them, to the river and the bayou to hunt dace and darters, others off to southward to the Ouachita and the Red.

By tradition the nights at the Social Ocean are free of entertainment, commercial enterprise, public spectacle, and other distractions. This is a time for reflection and contemplation, for conversation and communion, for fooling with the kids, for games of euchre and cranbo, and for relaxation. Of course, every so often one of the intolerant and self-absorbed will hold forth on a bullhorn, subject his neighbors in the park to a strident recitation of all his bright ideas. This person is inevitably a fundamentalist Christian preacher, often from another parish, and on some kind of divine mission. What is it, people wonder, with these arrogant and rackety little bigots insulting us with their self-righteous disregard for tranquillity and thought?

On the evening of the family's cemetery picnic, Earlene and Adlai tried to ignore the man standing in the fountain, knee-deep in green water, ranting and occasionally speaking in tongues. Boudou held his ears, closed his eyes, blocked his nose. The man clutched a Bible and shouted about how you got your place in life just like a postage stamp has a place on an envelope, how you do the best you can. If you're a twenty-cent stamp you deliver a postcard. Radley Smallpiece sat in his wheelchair, a pistol in the holster slung over the hand grip, a mirror in his hand. God's unnerved postmaster saw the depravity in Radley's eyes and sloshed a few steps to his left. Radley rolled himself a few feet closer. The preacher said, The Lord is my whirlwind, my mighty searchlight, my plague of locusts, my brazen serpent, my smitten rock, my refuge, my father. Radley held his mirror so that the light of the setting sun shone into the preacher's eyes. When the disconcerted preacher stumbled over the phrase *Ain't God All Right* (he said, *God Ain't All Right*), a gentle, if somewhat mocking applause went up from the exasperated townsfolk. Radley asked the preacher to talk on the Fifth Commandment if he would. The preacher asked God to smite the crippled infidel. Radley said, God already tooken my legs and I ain't quit. At that the preacher stepped out of the fountain and squished away.

Earlene sipped her iced tea and watched Boudou walk toward the river. She smiled, shook her head. She told Adlai, "He worries me sometimes. He gets up in the morning and he's happy and singing and he hops in the shower, and he daydreams about school, and the daydream is so vivid that he doesn't get out of the shower to catch the school bus. He's already in class as far as he's concerned."

Grisham and Ariane, Duane and Ouida approached from Mercy. Earlene waved, but the group didn't see her. They took seats at a picnic table. Adlai saw Delano, alone, drinking from a can in a paper sack. Delano saw him and waved. Adlai saw Mélia and Father Pat strolling along the riverbank. Father Pat smoked a ropy-looking cigar and fanned himself with a—what is that?—with a restaurant menu. Adlai saw Boudou talking to somebody or somebodies.

. . .

"I saw you in the boat," Boudou said. "I heard you sing, didn't I? What's your name?"

"Tous-les-deux," the left-handed one said. She laid down her jump rope, took a loop of red, green, and blue string from her pocket.

"That's what Mother calls us," the right-handed one said. "She read it in a book."

"What's your real name?"

The left-handed girl said, "I'm Kate."

The right-handed girl said, "I'm Alice."

The sisters shared the one body. Two arms, two legs, two hands. He watched the girls play cat's cradle.

Kate said, "We're identical twins, but we're distinguishable sisters."

Alice said, "We're like two pies on the table or two eyes in your head."

Boudou said, "Do you remember the same things?"

Kate said, "Yes, only differently."

Alice said, "Kate thinks you're cute."

"I do not."

Boudou said, "How do you walk?"

Alice said, "Without thinking."

Kate said, "Do you have a girlfriend?"

Boudou said, "I'm only eleven."

Kate said, "Perfect."

Adlai asked Delano did he bring the love charm. Delano told him not to take this business lightly. What he was giving the boy was a grigri, a vial containing the powdered heart of a hummingbird, the she-bird, you understand. I know you're bad to have that girl. What you got to do is you sprinkle the heart dust on her hair and shoulders. She's yours then. Never get rid of her. I don't care you don't believe in it. It'll work on its own whether you do or don't do. It's the only way you'll beat your cousin's time.

Adlai thanked him, slipped the vial into his pocket. Delano said, Me, once I loved a plus-sized gal from up in Crosset. Clarice Benoit. Plump as a dumpling. Um-hmm. Rather they shake than rattle. We had our fun till Clarice started in with, 6smith, honey, here's a job of work for you in the newspaper right here. I told her I didn't drive no forklift. Or she'd say, My cousin Bernard, he'll fix you up over to the lumberyard. I said, Momma, I got a job. I think about things, and I paints what I see. She told me I was born tired and raised lazy. I said, What's lazy is your sorry cousin trading in his brain for a paycheck. Clarice told me if I don't have a money-paying job then I can't dip my spoon into her sugar bowl. So when I got back to Shiver-de-Freeze, Purvis says, What took you so long?

Grisham kissed Ariane on the forehead, put his arm around her shoulder. He watched Adlai talking to the black guy. He knew Adlai would be joining them shortly, could see him walking over here before he even did. In a few days Grisham would be a married man, a settled and sober man. This was a good thing. He knew that. Sometimes Grisham felt like nothing was important in his life, or nothing was more important than anything else. Was like he didn't care enough. Marry Ariane or don't. He'd survive. When he held Ariane like this, when he could smell her hair, feel her press gently against him, when the world stopped like this, then Grisham believed he loved her. Sometimes when he heard an old song on the radio, Grisham would break out in goose bumps and feel his face flush. He would feel exalted and benevolent and fortunate. That's how he knew he liked the song, in fact, realized that the lyrics had resonated in his heart. And he expected that love would feel something like that, that it would call attention to itself the way it does in books and movies.

Ariane was so glad that Grisham had finally quit his philandering ways, that they no longer had to play the game where she pretends not to know he's fooling around until the woman throws it in her face and then she has to be indignant until Grisham mollifies her with a gold bracelet or something and lies about how he'll never do it again, blah, blah, blah. It's a guy thing, but it got boring. She wasn't sure why she put up with it so long, but she was glad she did now that he had said, yes, he'd marry her, yes, he was hers exclusively. With some men you had to be patient, let them get it out of their system. Ariane sat up, arched her back, massaged her neck, asked Grisham where did Duane and Ouida run off to.

"Went to eat, I think."

"Here comes Adlai. He should comb his hair once in a while."

Grisham told Adlai, Sit down, take a load off. Adlai looked straight ahead, then at his red sneakers. Grisham didn't think he could sit here another second. He said if they didn't mind he was going to duck into the Crown for a quick Tequila Mockingbird. Maybe see if Duane and Ouida were there. He kissed Ariane on the forehead, said he'd be back in ten.

Adlai said, "You look great."

"Well, thank you, that's sweet."

"Close your eyes a sec."

"Whatever for?"

"Surprise."

Ariane closed her eyes and Adlai sprinkled the powder onto her hair.

"What did you just do?"

"Open." Adlai handed Ariane a sack.

She opened it and took out a pair of shell-encrusted salt and pepper shakers, souvenirs of Biloxi Beach. "Oh, I get it. Something old. For the wedding. Thank you, Aldai." She kissed him on the cheek.

"Got it over to Peyton Pepper's collectibles store."

Ariane asked Adlai if he ever thought he'd get married. He told her that depended on her. She laughed and said, "Don't you be flirting with me, Adlai Birdsong. Really," she said, "you must think

about your future. How will you live? What do you want to be when
you grow up?"

"I don't need much."

"You need to pay your bills."

He had a house. Renting out some acres paid the water, gas,
electric, property. He knew ambition's what Ariane meant. A defin-
ing aspiration. Well, he could open a restaurant. Right in the house.
Serve one meal a day. No menu. You eat what he cooks. Get himself
one of those handsome checked chef uniforms. Plant a garden for
the herbs and vegetables. He saw himself in the kitchen, Mozart on
the stereo. He's stirring grits into the water. He sees Tyler Pate park
his car out front. Tyler's got himself a date. Looks like Mavis Willig
from here. He's cooking barbecued shrimp tonight because this morning he remembered for no reason at all the old Shrimp Man and his
wagon on the streets of Flandreau. And the Shrimp Man's song:

Lady, gets you dishpan,
Heah come da Swimp-man.
Swimpee! Swimpee! Raw raw swimp!
I gots da hebby pan of chaupique
And da mudbug and redfish all two!
And da mudbug walk
And da redfish talk
And da chaupique eat wid a knife and fork!
Heah come da Swimp-man!

Barbecued shrimp, chaupique caviar, and grits soufflé. Huckleberry
cheesecake for dessert.

"What happens when your daddy gets so bad he has to live in a
nursing home? They'll take your house, your land—"

"They can do that?"

"I worry about you."

Adlai smiled. He knew he was behaving oddly, even foolishly;
after all who traffics in love potions these days? He apologized for
flirting but said he couldn't help himself.

"I'm marrying your cousin in four days. And anyway you don't even know me."

"Do you love Grisham?"

"Of course I do. I don't want to discuss this." Ariane stood. "What are you trying to do to me?" And she turned and she walked toward the Crown of Thorns.

After Alvin Lee and Lorraine excused themselves and retired upstairs, Royce and Benning had the parlor to themselves. Royce sat in the Queen Anne chair, his slippered feet on the ottoman. Benning put a record on the hi-fi—Louis Duclot and the Ladelta Cooperative Association Orchestra. She listened to the opening notes of "*Filles a la Cassette*," and lowered the volume. She sat on the davenport, kicked off her shoes, flexed her toes and her ankles. Her lower back hurt. How many years since she'd lived a day without some physical pain or other? Royce poured cognac into her snifter, set the bottle on the occasional table between them. He said, Well, here's to us! And they toasted. They fell silent, listened to the "Napoleonville Waltz."

Benning knew she had been blessed. With a fine husband, darling sons. A loving family. With a sharp mind into old age. And unlike Royce, she'd been gifted with a full-dress memory. The older she got, the sharper were the details of her youth. A mixed blessing. Everything she had locked away and tried to forget now reappeared.

Like the time she stole a kerchief from the Kress store when she was seven. She's never been able to dismiss the episode as innocent bravado or childhood defiance. Benning felt that her future had been determined at that moment. It allowed for little deceptions to become a way of life. Another time, she was fifteen or sixteen, she sat in a phone booth at Patenaude's Drug Store gabbing to her friend Delia Hubbard while a woman stood nearby the booth waiting for her to finish. Benning giggled and told Delia how this incredibly fat woman was tapping her foot, tsking, rolling her bulgy eyes, squeezing the nickel in her thick little fist, checking her wristwatch. Benning kept talking about the woman in a tawdry and demeaning way, wondering to Delia if the woman would even fit into the phone booth. Only thing is the woman heard every word Benning had uttered and repeated them to Benning when she opened the folding glass door.

Benning looked at the old brass floor lamp across the room, at the blue crepe and pink satin scalloped shade. She said, "Royce, do you remember dancing with that lamp?"

"I did not."

"You cut the fool that night. You did the bamboula, you called it, to 'Hernando's Hideaway.' You had us all in stitches. Your brother's first wife Reba nearly wet her knickers."

"My brother's dead."

"So's Reba. That girl had a tongue loose at both ends, didn't she?"

"My brother Phin was a wild one. Ride bareheaded through a shit storm."

Benning's idea was that they should get dressed up in their evening clothes, see if they fit after all these years—when was their last formal affair? She helped Royce into his black tux, his starched shirt.

Benning wore a white sleeveless evening dress. The V-neck was trimmed in black. She wore black heels and elbow-length kid gloves, pear and pink. The gown looked another shade of white than how she remembered it, more fog than frost. Could be the light in the bedroom. Benning entered the parlor with a sweeping turn the way she remembered Loretta Young doing it on the TV. Royce applauded, told her she looked like the queen of Denmark, and kissed her hand. They stood in the middle of the room, listened to "Tensas Sunset." When the needle skipped, Benning took the opportunity to switch the radio on and tune to the classical station from Ruston.

They sat on the davenport. Royce felt something against his chest. He reached into the breast pocket of his jacket and pulled out a folded invitation to a New Year's Eve celebration. He put on his reading glasses. "Welcome in 1966 with the Ouachita Parish Light Opera at the River Oaks Country Club."

Benning smiled. "Nineteen sixty-six. My goodness. I think we did the twist. We went with Hollins and Barbara Vanderhague."

Royce shook his head.

"Hollins was a dean at the college."

Royce brought the snifter to his nose. "I can't smell the cognac."

"We've never been to Europe."

"I'd like to see you in a summer dress riding in a gondola."

Royce took Benning's hands in his, said, "I've been considering what makes life not worth living."

"Royce—"

"Not having a mind you can rely on. At first you say, Do I really need to know how to turn on the radio? Do I have to remember so-and-so's phone number? I can look it up. But then you don't know where to look it up or why you are or who this person is anyway. The world gets smaller, and you know at some point it'll squeeze you till you can't breathe.

"Who am I without a past? A baby. I was a baby once and that was enough. I don't want anyone changing my diapers, feeding me strained carrots, explaining to me what I'm looking at.

"Every day is sad because I look at a sunset or at a heron and see how beautiful it is and think this may be the last time I see the bird take flight against an orange sky. I get out of the boat with Boudou and think we may never get in the boat again. This is my last wedding.

"It doesn't seem like my world anymore. You're all that's left of the world I knew. I never thought I'd feel this way. I wanted to live forever."

Benning wiped her eye with a tissue. "Royce Birdsong, what am I going to do with you?" She realized it had been ages since the two of them had engaged in conversation like this.

Royce kissed her hands. "Shall we dance?"

The scent of Royce's jacket carried her back to that New Year's Eve thirty-something years ago. This was the perfume of Royce's younger body, still joined to the fabric. She remembered that night and how, when they arrived home, they walked out into the fields and gazed up at the clear sky, the millions of stars, the constellations. And Royce named them. Leo, Cancer, Orion, and a dozen others she can't recall now. He said the star in the middle of Orion was really four stars. He was always a surprise. Royce would know something cold that you never even knew he thought about. Like you could mention a particular degree of dog, like a Catahoula Leopard Dog, and well, Royce would tell you a history of the dog, how they were bred by Indians from the dogs the Spanish left behind and red wolves. They looked at the sky that night, and at the clay beneath their feet. Then they went into the house and made breakfast.

Upstairs Alvin Lee sat in a cane chair and watched Lorraine sleep. She snored a little. He heard the music from the parlor. He was going to be a father. How would he support a child and two wives with no gainful employment? He remembered his daddy Skeet and how Skeet slapped him silly when he caught Alvin Lee sucking on a stick of chalk that he'd stolen from school. Alvin Lee loved the taste of chalk. It was like free candy. Then he remembered how he imagined he could run incredibly fast when he was dripping wet and barefooted. So he'd skinny-dip in the bayou and go running like mad along the dirt road, so fast the fishermen couldn't see him. His daddy beat him more than once for that, too, said was he possessed with the devil or something.

Little Alvin Lee had another secret. He could fly. But he could fly only in an emergency—to save someone's life. It was a comforting power. He could have, for example, flown to the Branding Iron to save his daddy if he got attacked by rednecks the way Cousin Crosley did. Crosley got his mouth placed on a curbstone and the back of his head kicked at till all his teeth were shattered. What a funny kid he'd been. Used to sleep in his clothes so he could jump out of bed and get the day started. He wondered about his own child, what he or she would be like. He pictured the two of them walking down the road to Purvis's store.

Ariane rubbed her bare foot along Grisham's shin, stirred her drink with a cocktail straw, remembered to smile while Grisham told his story about deer hunting with his uncles in East Texas when he was ten. She wondered why it was she felt so peculiar around Adlai. She looked at the armless, bare-chested woman carved into the mahogany back bar. Looked like one of those maiden figureheads who rode the prows of sailing ships in the old days. You couldn't tell if she was emerging from the wood or was trapped there. Ariane fiddled with her ring. Grisham said something about being washed in the blood of the buck. Ariane thought, Well, I'm new to Adlai. With him I can be who I want to be. With Grisham—she touched his knee with her hand—I have to be who he thinks I am. With Adlai I get to re-create myself, be better than I am. With him it's invention; with Grisham it's performance.

Up All Night

Fidelity is an idiosyncracy, not a virtue.

—GRISHAM LOUDERMILK

Normally, it's death keeps Adlai awake at night. But tonight it was love *and* death. Whenever Adlai considered not being, he'd feel certain that somewhere deep in the soup of his cells something catastrophic was brewing, that he was, in fact, already decomposing, inside to out. This sort of nocturnal disturbance had been going on since he was a child. It wasn't that he was afraid of sleep, it was that his brain, pretending that it was not terrified, accelerated into overdrive and pumped all kinds of fuel to Adlai's nerve endings.

Adlai kicked off his sheet, got out of bed, put on his T-shirt and pajama bottoms. He slipped out of his room, eased the door shut behind him. He looked for a wand of light below Ariane's door, saw none. He listened to the creaks and cracks of the old house. He heard the whistle of a screech owl. He thought he'd take a short walk and hope that maybe Ariane was peeking out her window and would see him. He followed the road to the end, noticed a light on in the house and a man in the window, arguing, it looked like, with someone. He thought he recognized the man from those commercials on the TV. Says who? Says me, Royal Landry, the king of cars. You all need to come on down to Royal Landry's Kar Kingdom! Have we got deal for you!

What Royal was talking about was this essay Shug had found in the *Quarterly Review of Southern Literature*: "Faulkner's Unfortunate Legacy: the Grotesque in Contemporary Southern Fiction." The author, Professor J. Daniel Pointforth, decried what he perceived as the retreat of Southern narrative from social realism. Southern fiction has become, he wrote, a sanctuary for deviants, monsters, freaks, the miserable, the evil, and the downtrodden, the wretched, and the enfeebled.

Royal wanted to know what's so grotesque about infirmity, about girls with wooden legs or farmers with snaggled teeth, or alcoholics or dirt roads or unbottled water or unreliable automobiles (not that he would sell one) or raggedy wardrobes.

Shug reminded Royal about his blood pressure, said, Don't blow your shoes over this. Margaret went for the Tylenol. Ted Muto opened a bottle of whiskey, set it on the coffee table. Shug said, Relax, Royal, nobody pays any mind to academics. They're just writing for each other. It's like a pissing contest.

Ted said what he heard was that ninety percent of the readers in the country live in New York City. Shug said, Horseshit. Maybe ninety percent of the people who buy bestsellers live in New York. People we know read all the time, just that we don't all want to read about cocaine-snorting stockbrokers. And we don't need to wait for a talk show host to tell us what to read this month. Ain't one Armani suit in Shiver-de-Freeze, or one Rolex wristwatch, or one Lexus. Does this mean we ain't normal? We got folks trying to decide should they put Granny in the nursing home, got women living with husbands who beat them, got children who miss their daddies, folks learning their cough is more than a cold.

Shug poured whiskey into his jelly glass. What the hell is grotesque about poverty? Isn't it greed what's grotesque?

Margaret picked up the *Times Book Review*, cleared her throat. She read the capsule descriptions on the "Best Seller" list to get an idea of what New Yorkers were reading:

A terrorist uses a genetically engineered virus to attack New York.

A woman on the trail of her brother who has vanished along with stolen jewelry.

A young woman, posing as a widow, is hired to be a nanny in Regency England.

"And so on," Margaret said. "Terrorists, wealth, murder, lawyers. The fluff of social realism."

Royal said, "Do you suppose Pointforth has mistaken amusement for thought?"

Shug said. "Academics are twisted, petty, and forlorn people." And to illustrate his point, Shug told them about the business at Arizona State, how this instructor taught Shakespeare, Aeschylus, Ibsen, and Chekhov in his theater class. But the department head told him his syllabus was offensive, sexist, Eurocentric, and asked him to reinterpret the texts. And he had to teach a play *Betty the Yeti: an Eco-Fable*.

"You're making this up," Margaret said.

"Wish I were. Play's about a logger who has sex with a female yeti and is transformed into an environmentalist."

Ted tried to picture the copulation. You'd want to hold your breath, probably. Did they do it onstage? Did the logger take off his boots? Cicero wondered what on earth was going on in the world. And he reminded himself to reread Revelations.

By that time Adlai had returned to Paradise. He lit the hurricane lamp, set it on the kitchen table, turned the flame low. He thought how it could have been 1870 in the kitchen, the flickering light, the perfume of kerosene, the ocean of night swelling outside the window. Maybe it was a night like this when Thurlow Loudermilk sat right here courting Ella Mae Pinnix, the girl who would become his wife, who would birth Laymon, who would sire Witt, who begat Benning, who gave birth to Adlai. And Thurlow was here because his daddy before him and all the daddies back through the Tidewater and back to Ireland and to Scotland and before that—what?—the caves of southern Europe, the Fertile Crescent, the Rift Valley—because all these men had settled down with women whom they loved. What if a single one of those matings had gone wrong? What if Benning had not stayed up late that night reading *Intruder in the Dust*? And what if Royce had not decided to come home early from the Volunteer Fire Department meeting? Or what if another of the fifteen million sperm, or whatever the number is, had penetrated the egg? Suddenly Adlai realized how he was completely improbable, but absolutely inevitable. And all those ancestors were depending on him, on Adlai Birdsong, to keep them alive.

Adlai looked up at the ceiling. He knew that Ariane's bed was just there over his head. He tried to look through the ceiling, through the plaster, the studs, the floorboards, through the box spring, the feather mattress, to her. He saw her asleep on her right side, left arm and shoulder out from the covers, a bit of drool on her chin, a strand of hair at her cheek, bangs slightly damp. Her sleep is soundless. Her eyes move. She's dreaming. And then he's in her dream, and in the dream, he watches her fall and fall into an abyss, but he's paralyzed and can't save her.

Adlai jumped when the lamp flickered. Where had the draft come from? Had he fallen asleep? He thought maybe he should cook something, bake some bread maybe. But he'd wake the house. Or he could read. No, he couldn't—his mind would be all the time drifting to Ariane.

Adlai decided he'd write a letter which he would slip under her door.

Dearest Ariane, Like gravity, you are everywhere and always attractive. My heart and my light bend to you. I circle you. You are my sun. You warm the cold dark matter of my heart.

Adlai read what he'd written. What had seemed so romantic a moment ago sounded ludicrous now. He crumpled the note. It was one a.m. He'd make breakfast for her later, take it to her room, knock quietly. Leave the tray at the door with a flower and a simple note. *Good morning.* He stood, heard a creak from the stairs. Someone was coming. Could his thoughts have summoned her? He froze. Listened to the steps approach.

Ariane said, "Adlai, do you know why I cant sleep?"

"No, I don't."

"I think you do."

"Strange house?"

"I think it's you doing it."

"How?"

Ariane walked to Adlai, stared up into his eyes, cocked her head. He felt her breath on his skin. He flushed.

She said, "What are you doing to me?" She kissed him. She said, "I'm spoken for, Adlai," and she said it so her lips grazed his as she pronounced the syllables.

"Hi, you two. What's keeping you all up?" Lorraine said.

Ariane stepped back and turned from Adlai. Adlai gathered his senses. He said, "Can I make you a coffee, Lorraine? Some warm milk? We were just—"

Ariane said, "I was just going on up to bed." She excused herself, thanked Adlai for getting the lash out of her eye.

Adlai watched her leave. Lorraine said milk would be nice. Adlai poured her milk while he drank coffee.

Lorraine said, "Jesus set me free because I was not afraid to wear my makeup and my wigs and my clothes. What I believe is you got to keep the male ego intact. It's a fragile thing. Sometimes a wife has to take a little walk with God, where the Lord can speak with her, show her the way. I talked with Jesus, and now I love being under submission to my husband. Praise God." Lorraine began to cry.

"Maybe you just love Alvin Lee so deeply you'll do anything for him. Maybe it's not a theological idea at all."

"God told Eve, 'Thy husband shall rule over thee.' The husband is head of the wife."

They heard the kitchen door open. Adlai's hand jumped, and he spilled his coffee. He turned. Duane and Ouida walked in, each holding a pair of shoes.

"We went for a walk," Ouida whispered. "Lost track of time."

Adlai said, "Sit, join us. We've got coffee."

Ouida asked Adlai did he see the Siberian twins.

"The girls? Yes, I did."

Ouida said, "Duane and I found out tonight we had a lot in common."

Duane said, "We both like dogs and silk, the color red and Southeastern Conference football."

Just then Boudou walked in from outside. He had a flashlight and a prong he'd made from a tree branch. Said he'd been frog-gigging. No luck. He opened a box of Sugar Pops and ate a handful dry.

Adlai touched his lips with his fingers. He thought maybe his life was just beginning. He thought if only everyone would get themselves to bed he could find out.

Adlai rapped 1-2-3 on Ariane's door with his knuckle. He whispered her name and listened. He put his ear to the door. He tapped again with a finger. He looked at the glass doorknob and willed it to open. "Ariane." He sent her a telepathic message to open up, let him in. He hoped that she hadn't frightened herself into reconsideration with her kiss. All right then, he'd wait in his room for the sound of her.

He eased the door shut behind him.

Ariane said, "I don't know why I'm here."

Adlai held the wall to steady himself. He saw that she was in his bed, under his covers. He said, "Because you want to be?"

"But why do I want to be?"

Adlai walked to the bed and sat on its edge, one foot on the floor. "I can't believe you're here." He smiled.

"What have you done to me?"

"I told you how I feel about you is all."

"I don't throw myself at men."

"That's not what you're doing."

Ariane took Adlai's hand. "I'm supposed to be getting married."

"But maybe you weren't meant to."

Ariane pulled back the covers, and Adlai saw that she was naked, and there fell from his eyes, as it were, scales, and he drew next to her, and she said, Hold me, and his left hand was under her, and his right hand did embrace her, and she said, Make love to me, Adlai. And after they had made love, Ariane wept, and Adlai held her, thanked her, asked her if she was all right. Her shoulders trembled, her body shook. Adlai lifted a lock of hair from her damp cheek and curled it behind her ear. He nuzzled into her, inhaled the balm of her, held her until she stilled. He hoped she had done this for love, but if the seed had been confusion, apprehension, still, he knew, it would blossom to love.

Adlai realized how much his life had just changed, and how much more it *would* change. Naturally, the family would be upset. But he would mollify them. He dared to think they all might still have a wedding to celebrate come Saturday. He would speak with Grisham in the morning, apologize, explain how this was all for the better, wasn't it?—to find out now rather than years into a marriage that Ariane loved another. He could not wait for morning to arrive. He thought he might never sleep again, but he must have dozed off because he suddenly realized that Ariane was gone from his bed, though her scent remained.

Crisscross

*It's a simple love story as I see it.
You know, boy meets girl, boy wants girl, boy
pursues girl despite obstacles. And so on.*

—AUTHOR

(That's what he says, but you get the feeling he wants to kill someone. If it's a love story, why's he loading all these weapons—the curse, the pistol, the lake, the swamp, the infidelity? We're not sure he can be trusted.)

A. See How Great a Flame Aspires.   Adlai said good-morning to Ariane, said, "Breakfast is ready. Please," he told her, "sit. Your timing is perfect." Ariane stood with her hand on the back of the chair. Adlai set Ariane's plate on the place mat. "Creamed stuffed eggs, oyster fritters, juice, and coffee." He pulled out the chair for Ariane. Adlai got his own plate and sat across from her.

"This is so good. It must have taken you hours."

Adlai shrugged. "You could wake up every morning to a gourmet breakfast."

"Adlai, I hope you understand that nothing has changed."

When Ariane didn't smile, Adlai reckoned she had a drier sense of humor than he had figured her for. The world had changed. He sprinkled his fritters with pepper sauce.

Ariane said, "I don't know what I was thinking last night."

Adlai wiped his mouth with his napkin, swallowed. "I think you do, too, know."

Ariane pointed at Adlai with her fork. "You have no idea what's in my heart, Adlai Birdsong. Please don't presume that you do."

"We made love last night."

"And that's our little secret."

"But it was wonderful. More than wonderful. It was paradise."

"Don't make it out to be more than it was."

"Isn't the guy supposed to say that?"

"I'm marrying Grisham on Saturday."

"How can you do that?"

"I love him."

Adlai put his face in his hands, shook his head. He opened his hands and peeked at Ariane. "You betrayed him."

"An indiscretion I'm not proud of. Maybe I just needed to be bad, just this once."

"Bad?"

"Wild, then. I wasn't thinking clearly."

"You knew what you were doing."

Ariane folded her napkin in half, in quarters, in eighths. She creased the napkin with the meat of her hand, and then unfolded it. "All right, suppose I was charmed by you—"

"Don't blame me."

"I knew if I were ever going to cheat on Grisham, it would have to be with someone kind, safe, someone I could trust, someone like you."

"Dammit, Ariane, we made love."

"Not so loud, please and thank you." Ariane looked over her shoulder, listened.

Adlai said, "You can't marry Grisham now."

"I must. It's more important now than ever. I've sinned against him."

Adlai couldn't believe what he was hearing. "I won't go away, you know."

"That's your affair."

"When we made love, I knew you were the one."

"There'll be others. You need to distinguish between love and sex."

Adlai stood, walked to the stove, turned and leaned back against it. "Ariane, people do this all the time. They rush to marriage. They're anxious to grow up, move on. So they plan the wedding, the honeymoon, the future. The date is set, the guests invited. And then they realize what a terrible mistake they're making. But they are too ashamed or too embarrassed, too afraid of upsetting the family and friends to do anything about it. They don't even tell each other. They determine that their folly must not go unpunished, so they proceed with the mortification of matrimony. Ariane, what will it be—a day of embarrassment or a lifetime of misery?"

Ariane watched Adlai, saw the way his hands and his eyebrows punctuated his speech. He was intriguing to be sure, sweet, she'd give him that. She'd never met a guy so honest, so guileless. Or was that just his novel way of being shrewd? And he was attractive enough. Grisham was handsome in a straightforward movie-star kind of way. He had a face you could stare at. Easy on the eyes. Adlai's face was always reminding you of someone else that you couldn't quite place. His eyes were too large, and sometimes they were brown and sometimes they were green. His cheekbones were too high, his nose too freckled. He was, in some ways, more interesting-looking than Grisham, but is *interesting* what you want in a man?

Adlai said, "Are you listening to me?"

"A woman should have a husband and a lover."

"That's ridiculous and immoral."

"An unapproachable lover. That way their love is pure, unde-filed. They always must ache for each other. Then they have something to live for. Then nothing can damage them."

"Ariane, this isn't you talking. I refuse to listen. We'll talk later when you're out of this annoying mood." Adlai cleared away the remains of Ariane's breakfast. "I won't be provoked or infuriated by your outrageous comments. I know what you're doing." He took a paper sack from the top of the fridge and put it on the table in front of Ariane and told her he'd bought her a few things over to Pepper Peyton's House of Junque. "I saw that you liked the shakers yesterday." Ariane took out a French poodle pincushion, a cracked ceramic teapot shaped and painted like a strawberry, a spin-art beer bottle pencil holder, and a dozen or so tintype photographs from the turn of the century.

"I don't favor old things. You see, Adlai, that's my point. You don't know me. I grew up in a house cluttered with tacky, old, useless odds and ends, and I don't want any of it in my new house."

"I'll take them back."

She put the items back in the sack. "I appreciate the thought, Adlai, I do."

"I hope you have some time today. I've got something I want to show you. We'll take a walk."

"I'll check with Grisham." Ariane looked at the clock. "I need to wake him up anyway."

B. The Shiver-de-Freeze Museum of Social and Natural History. It was Macky Ptak's day off from Pug's Curl Up and Dye. And his day to volunteer at the museum. He took Royce and Boudou's money and ushered them into the museum proper. "You've got the place to yourself this morning. You all enjoy."

Royce thanked him. Macky didn't leave. He was obviously bothered by something. Royce asked him what that was.

"Pronunciation."

"What do you mean?"

"It's gotten so slack. I have to listen to people all day saying *nucular*. How hard is it to say *nuclear*? They say *foilage*, not *foliage*. *Foilage* like it's some kind of sandwich wrap."

Boudou had never heard anyone who talked as fast as Macky. And all his words seemed to come from the front of his mouth.

Macky folded his arms. "And they say *jagwire* for *jaguar.* That one I just can't figure. These are the same people who pronounce the *t* on *often* or say *haich* for *h*." Macky brought his fist to his mouth and took a calming breath. "I'm sorry to carry on like this. It's just that if I hear someone say *supposeably* when they mean *supposedly*, I think I'll scream. As it is I can't sleep some nights. They sit in the chair and tell me they want more *heighth* on their hair, and if I make a face they accuse me of being *mischievious* or *laxadaisical*. So I tell them I'm just *disorientated*, and they don't even get it." And then he left Royce and Boudou alone.

Boudou wasn't sure why anyone would need a machine that measures the sweetness or bitterness of blood, but now he knew that such a contraption existed and that it had been invented right here in Shiver-de-Freeze by Terry Schimmelpenningh, father of Elna. Elna's calcified baby was on display, as was the tanned skin of a Yankee soldier, a fossilized peach, and little Boyd Hammond's caul that we mentioned, and so was the providential minie ball responsible for the birth of Henry Fontana.*

Boudou liked the story of Parthana Tanzy, which was presented as a narrated slide show. Parthana, a woman with a prodigious blond beehive hairdo—a model of which graced a Styrofoam head in a glass case—found herself slowly going deaf, but did nothing about it really for the longest time—except to pray over it, to worry, to pay attention to the Engrams when they signed each other, to talk to her cousin Estelle Kartheizer about it. When she could no longer hear Pastor Phipps's mellifluous voice at Sunday service, Parthana spoke with the Lord one more time, and the Lord suggested—in that soundless but rousing voice of His—that she visit Dr. Norris Bunch, an allergist and addictionologist. Well, Dr. Bunch solved the problem in no time. Parthana's ears, it turned out, were clogged solid with Queen Helene Super Hold hairspray. Dr. Norris poured warm milk into Parthana's ears. She needed three gallons over a two-week period.

Royce and Boudou examined a diorama of an Indian village along Bayou Fontana, saw displays of local flora and fauna (stuffed fishing bats, pressed bellicose orchids, pinned checkered drugstore beetles, and so on). They looked at exhibits on soap-making and on mattress-making at the turn of the century (cotton and moss, cornhusks and human hair). In the reconstructed apothecary shop asafetida bags were on display next to Old Judge and Gypsy cigarettes. There were vintage advertising posters for Zograin, *The Asthma Conqueror and Catarrh Cure*, for Addison Diaphragms, *the Secure Vaginal Tent*, for Shepherd's Best Condoms, *Your Cobweb Against Danger*.

In the manuscript room among the letters, maps, deeds, and wills were 126 leather-bound volumes of the world's longest diary, kept continuously by Mims Lugenbuill from his fifteenth birthday in 1921 (*Daddy says I should write down what happens so when I'm old I'll never have to strain my memory nerve for the truth*) until the moment of his death on December 3, 1982 (*Am struggling with the idea of getting up and calling the doc*—), in the course of which, by his own count, Mims went through 7,181 bottles of peacock blue ink, 828 blotters, and 260 pens.

Boudou called Royce's attention to a compact made between Our Lady of Immediate Succor Industrial School and Model Farm for Girls and the Fontana clan, signed by Mangham Fontana (his mark) and by Sister Mariette of the Holy Cross, and having something to do with wives.* Boudou said, "My great-great-great grandfather wrote that. Look at the nice *X*, so symmetrical and everything." He couldn't get over the fact that someone he knew (in his cells, not in his life) could have written his mark on paper over a century ago and that he, Boudou, would be here in the future to witness it.

Earlene had told Boudou about the Fontana Room, of course, said she didn't care to visit it herself—she had all the memories she needed right in her head. Boudou could give her a report when he got back. The room was crammed with artifacts. On one wall were blown-up photos of Positive Wassermann in his Recline-o-Chair out in the Bottom, and of Jupiter and Saturn at their own hanging. (You wonder what they had to smile about.) Boudou and Royce flipped through a scrapbook of newspaper stories about various Fontana disasters. "Seems like no one died of natural causes in my family," Boudou said. "Sure had lots of bad luck."

Royce said, "You could say they did, or you could say they were fortunate to live eventful lives."

Tennis's straitjacket was there in a glass case. And so was the charred leather helmet that Ott was wearing when he flew his Huff Daland Puffer into the Union Oil Mill storage tank. There were a pair of armadillo handbags that Napoleon had made before he lost his fingers, and the ecru evening dress that Mendel wore the night he won the 1925 Miss Monroe Beauty Pageant and Bathing Girl Review. A few of the sequins were missing, and it was a tad moth-eaten, but still dazzling. In a corner of the room, hanging on the wall was Billy Wayne's altar boy cassock and surplice. Boudou touched the hem.

Royce said, "Looks like it would fit you."

Boudou smelled the cassock for evidence of his daddy and he heard echoing footsteps like someone in new shoes walking down and empty corridor.

Boudou took his daddy's LP&L hat down from the hook. Just a blue ball cap with the company's logo on the front: a sun with rays of lightning bolts shining down on a cypress swamp. Boudou put the hat on. His head itched. His nose dripped.

Royce said, "You could be him."

"I don't want to be."

In the gift shop, Boudou suggested a cross pendant made from polished mussel shell for Ariane and a tie woven from Spanish moss for Grisham. Royce thought maybe a single gift for both would be better. They considered the catfish-shaped napkin rings, the plastic model of the UFO that supposedly landed at Black Bayou Lake in 1979, scaring the grits out of Trace and Mark Ryalls, and decided on a set of serving trays decorated with a Delano 6smith map of Shiver-de-Freeze. Macky wrote up the bill, gift-wrapped and boxed the trays.

Macky said, "You know what this one sweetheart told me yesterday? I asked her how her knees got all skinned. She told me she and her amorous husband were warming up with some *floorplay*. I don't even want to think about that."

C. Flight. Earlene let her eyes adjust to the darkness. The waiter whose name she once knew—was it *Gary? Cary?*—brought her a napkin and a flute of something dryish, white, and Californian.

The only light at this end of the room flickered from the TV. She was waiting on Varden. Better to meet him here at a bar in Monroe, on mutual turf, than back at Paradise. He'd said on the phone that he wanted to return her house key now that he was *persona non garter*—that's what he said, *garter*, like the snake. She told him to leave it under the rock by the back door. No can do, he said. First place a thief would look. Mail it, she said. Do you know how many crooks with AK-47s and headaches work at the post office? he said.

It was here at the Mohawk—maybe in this very booth, she couldn't quite remember—where she and Billy Wayne once sat eating crawfish etoufée and discussing his sperm count. Earlene sipped her sparkling wine, began a list in her memo pad. *THINGS THAT FLY: monarch butterflies, dreams, rumors, pilots, pollen, sounds to our ears, light to our eyes, prayer to our gods, planets in the firmament, birds in the air, their songs, the wind, the clouds, the dead, a tossed stone, a shouldered door, bullet trains, bullets, kites, balloons, happiness, opportunities.*

When he arrived, Varden ordered a bourbon and cola. "You look good, Earlene, real good," he said.

"Where's the key?" she said.

He leaned to his left, took his wallet out of his rear pocket, unfolded it, spread the bill compartment, and retrieved the key. He handed it to Earlene. She thanked him and slid to the end of her bench. Varden said, "Just listen to me for one minute, Earlene. Just one minute." Earlene relaxed in her seat, looked at her watch.

He said, "I can't live without you." He reached across the table to Earlene's hand. "You just can't toss away three years like it was nothing. I swear to God, Earlene, if you leave me I'll kill myself. I can't live without you."

"If you were capable of suicide, Varden, you wouldn't need to commit it."

Varden cried. Earlene looked up at the TV. All the laundry on the clothesline was singing about the soap. Varden sniffled.

She said, "I was so lonely all the time when I was with you. You were gone even when you were around. I don't feel that ache anymore, knowing it's over. We tried to make it work—at least I did— and we failed."

"I'll try harder this time, Earlene. I promise."

"I'm not angry with you, Varden. I'm not resentful or upset or anything. I'm relieved. I'm happier right now than I've been in years. And maybe I'm a little sad."

"You'll miss me."

"Not as much as I missed you when we were together."

"What about Boudou? I loved that boy."

"Listen to yourself—it's all about you. You were good to him when you were there, but you weren't there enough—so how much did you care? That boy can't have people walking out on him, people who see him at their convenience."

"I was going to teach him to play guitar."

"Well, you lost your chance."

"You're not being fair."

"I cared more about you than I cared about myself. I let you humiliate me with your silence, your chill, your girlfriends."

"I admit I fucked up, Earlene. But I can change."

"Varden, you don't get unlimited chances in life. That's something adults understand."

"You can't go," he said.

"I'm already gone."

D. Float.   Grisham rowed the boat away from Paradise. He couldn't see where he was aimed, only where he'd been. Ariane watched him, listened to the squeal of oarlocks, the slap of water against the stem. She shaded her eyes from the hazy sun, looked beyond Grisham to Tohu Bohu. She said, "In three days we'll be married."

"Doesn't seem real, does it?"

She said, "How will things change, do you think? Between us, I mean."

"We won't have to wonder where we are."

"Are you excited?"

"I've been too busy to get excited. That's why I rowed us out here." Grisham lifted the oars from the water, let the boat drift in the breeze. Grisham smiled. "We've invested five years in each other, and now that investment begins to pay dividends."

Ariane dipped the finger in the black water of the lake. She watched a Jesus bug skate on the skin of the water, darting in rapid, direct, and unpredictable spurts, inscribing a pentagon, she thought, on the face of the water.

Grisham put his head back, closed his eyes, watched specks of life drift across his eyelids. How had he gotten here—to the verge of marriage? When had he proposed to her? He couldn't recall. She hadn't asked him. That he would remember. Their first date? Mardi Gras in Mamou. He was a pirate. Ariane was an angel, had to take her wings off to get into the car. He had been dating—what was her name? the dance major, red hair, Linda, yes, Linda . . . Merceaux. Linda went to New York and became a Rockette. Last he saw of her was on TV. Linda was up there on Santa's float in the Thanksgiving Day parade, waving at the crowd.

Ariane had never learned to swim, in fact was terrified of water, and should never have come out to the middle of the lake without a life jacket at least. She knew if she slipped over the side of this boat that weeds would ensnare her ankles, drag her under, and catfish with heads as big as turnips would begin to scrape at her skin, nibble her eyes. She simply wasn't buoyant, she told her daddy when he tried to teach her to swim. Just relax, the water will do the work. But it never did. She sank like a sack of cats. She was terrified of heights, bothered by caves, by cockroaches, by anything behind her.

Grisham said, "When I interned with Meek, Mason, and Dean, a man who wanted a divorce after fifteen years of marriage told me, 'I like my wife. I respect her. Sherri is a good mother to our children. I do not want her hurt in the divorce.' Then he looked at me, leaned over my desk. He said, 'And that's your job, son. See that she don't.'"

"We should go back," Ariane said. Did Grisham mean to hurt her with this divorce talk? Was this some left-hand way of speaking?

Grisham dipped the oars in the water, turned the boat, looked over his shoulder, and began to row. If he kept the stern in line with the dead cypress yonder, he would hit the dock at Paradise. "Had this other client who was raised a strict Catholic. Married thirty years to the one wife. They had eight children. Buster Huddleston, you know, from the Feed Store Huddlestons."

"Isn't this a little on the unethical side, talking about your clients this way?"

He winked. "Buster's wife, the way he tells it, began to heft up, to lose her sheen. I got to tell you, Buster himself is no Robert Redford. Built like a furled umbrella. His wife, he said, had become an old cushioned sofa. He went and found himself a pretty young thing. According to Buster's thinking, in order to do something as reprehensible as cheating on his faithful wife and jeopardizing his children's happiness and welfare and all that, well then, he would have to be in love with the young woman."

"That's perverse."

"He sets the girl up in a shotgun house near the college, buys her a coffee grinder, a big-screen TV, a waterbed, a Toyota Camry, a Pomeranian. The wife pretty much decides she'll put up with Buster because she's got all those kids to mind. And they're all going to need money for college. Being freed up from sex would give her more time to read. And then what happens is Fiona the trophy tells Buster that she's pregnant, showed him the test results. Twice. So Buster told his wife that he was leaving her. She did not contest the divorce. The children were provided for. Adios, Huddleston, she said."

"I hope the story has a happy ending, Grisham. Like old Buster gets hit by an ambulance on his way to Confession or something."

"One week after Buster moved into Fiona's apartment, she lost the baby."

"Let me guess. He found himself trapped in a dingy, suffocating, and quiet apartment with a woman he suspected of duplicity, realized what a holy fool he had become, and he called his wife and his wife's lawyer, and he tried to stop the divorce, tried to inveigle his way back into his wife's heart and good graces."

"He married Fiona."

E. Grace Is No Stationary Thing.   Miranda sat on the steps of her Airstream eating a kiss-me-not sandwich and water lily pie. The trailer was parked off Temperance on the flat and grassy bank of Bayou Fontana. She could look across the bayou to Prudence and to the Social Ocean beyond. She sipped her iced tea, opened the Monroe newspaper, and saw on page three a photograph of a Holstein with the likeness of a heralding angel blazed on her flank. Pilgrims from all over Mississippi were coming to Sunflower County to drink the blessed milk and to be healed. What Miranda noticed, but the paper did not mention, was that there was also a white map of Brazil on the animal's forehead. What might that mean?

She looked up and saw a man across the bayou carrying a bundlesome sack of groceries. When he shifted the sack to his other arm, the sack ripped open and the groceries dropped to the sidewalk. He picked up the produce, piece by piece, and smashed it all on the ground. A muskmelon, a grapefruit, a resilient green pepper. He stomped on the carrots, tore the sack to shreds, and walked away in tears. Miranda thought how so often it's the inconsequential that defeats and disheartens. It's not that your lover has left you, it's that the toast has burned or the car won't start or you can't find your glasses again. She took a bite of her sandwich, watched a priest and the woman he was with step around the wreck of canned goods and broken fruit. The priest was cleaning his fingernails with a key.

Father Pat was thinking how his life might have been different had he grown up in a town like Shiver-de-Freeze, a place so much a part of the spongy land it grew from. He might have become a trapper, a crawfish farmer, maybe a mechanic. He might have married, sired children. And now he never would. Celibacy is the renunciation of marriage made for the more perfect observance of chastity. When he'd taken that vow, he'd looked upon virginity as a higher call. A priest is a man who sacrifices himself for the sake of his flock. He has no children in order that all of the parishioners might be his children. But what had once been regarded as a noble and admirable profession was now considered a curious one. What sort of man, after all, renounces his human nature, sets himself apart from his neighbors, and claims moral authority? Where once upon a time a priest had been teacher, shepherd, advisor, he was now ranter, tax collector, pest. Father Pat saw Mélia's shadow across his path. He stepped on its back.

Mélia wondered what she'd do now that Ariane was leaving her. At what would she aim her day? Had it all come down to this, then—this horror of being free from all things? Mélia didn't know what to do with her arms, her hands. The arms hung like sausages. She folded them. She saw Duane and Ouida walking toward them, and she waved like crazy.

Duane and Ouida turned down Mercy. Duane seemed unable to stop talking about his childhood. He told Ouida that his daddy O'Neill was an alcoholic even though he drank only a dozen or so well-spaced highballs a day and never missed work and never became a monster or turned maudlin or anything.

"Duane, are you telling me all this about your daddy and all so that I'll like you?"

"Well—"

"Because I do, you know."

Duane wasn't paying attention, and he walked into Radley Smallpiece's wheelchair. He apologized to Radley, who said, No harm done, and to the blind man who was pushing Radley along, and who said nothing. Duane thought just because he's blind doesn't mean he has to be rude. Radley said, "To the Social Ocean, Homer. Follow the wheels." It ain't like he's deaf, Duane thought.

What was attracting Radley's attention was some kind of commotion going on over to the gazebo. Turned out to be the Great Books people rehearsing for a play, or trying to at least. Actors, Radley thought. Dissemblers, liars, pretenders, fakes.

Shug Johnson already had a headache. What's so difficult about putting on a little play, an entre'acte, for the wedding?

Ted Muto said, "So what is Pyramus? A lover or a tyrant?"

Shug said, "A lover that kills himself for love."

Margaret Grimes said, "Is that really an appropriate theme for a wedding? Dead lovers?"

"All your great loves come to sorrowful endings," Chiquita Deal said. "Romeo and Juliet; Samson and Delilah; Elvis and Priscilla; Bonnie and Clyde."

Tommie Nash said, "Let's do *Evangeline*. This is Louisiana. It's perfect."

Shug said, "Evangeline and Gabriel as played by the mechanicals of the Delta."

Margaret protested. "That's a story of separation. It's too depressing."

"Not our version," Ted said. "It's about how you'll find your love if you persist."

"Find your love and die," Margaret said.

Bobby Sistrunk took a step downstage (as it were), raised his arms, and declaimed: "This is the forest primeval. The murmuring pines and the hemlocks—"

Ted said he wasn't playing no tree.

Sandy Van Veckhoven said, "Why, Ted, you do know how to murmur, don't you? You just put your lips together—"

Lorraine fanned her face with her hand. Her back ached and the bench wasn't helping. She told Benning she'd only ever been to the Passion Play in Eureka Springs, and while it was heartrending and awe-inspiring, of course, she had been disconcerted the whole performance by Jesus' bad teeth.

Benning kept her eye on Shug, who was turning mauve. She told Lorraine how she and Royce saw John Barrymore play Hamlet one time in New Orleans. And it like to take her breath away. And Benning thought how she and Royce would not be visiting New Orleans ever again.

And Lorraine understood just what Benning was thinking, and she took Benning's hand and held it. She tried to imagine her own world without Alvin Lee in it. She saw a dark room and there's a draft blowing in from somewhere and it's rattling the pages of an opened book. She squeezed Benning's hand, looked up at the gazebo.

One of These Mirrors Is

LyING *to* Me

Jesus lied just the single time. Lied about
"Blessed are the meek." Lied to be kind, but
lied all the same. Jesus knew wasn't nothing
the meek would inherit but the wind.

—DURWOOD TULLIVER

Adlai drove Ariane to Newlight to where the secret was. He didn't want to frighten her, so he didn't tell her that he usually wore window screens wrapped around his legs when he walked out here. He took a walking stick along and told her to stay behind him when they weren't on a trail. He did not say *water moccasin*. They trudged along the south bank of the Tensas River for a quarter mile and then hiked into the woods a few hundred yards and stopped at a clearing. Adlai looked up, listened. Nothing yet. He saw a pile of fresh-stripped bark at the base of a honey locust. They sat and waited, shared a bottle of water.

It had never occurred to Ariane to learn the names of natural things. What could it matter? She knew that they had passed six submerged logs along the riverbank, had stepped around seven mounds of scat, had seen four turkey vultures wheeling overhead. But Adlai could tell a water oak from a basket oak, a tupelo from a cypress. He had pointed out lantana, passionflowers, pitcher plants, and snakemouth orchids that she hadn't even noticed until he named them. This was looking with a purpose. Adlai told her there were two ways of looking, hard and soft. When you look hard at something, everything else disappears. When you look soft at nothing, anything that moves attracts your attention. So first you look soft, and then you look hard.

They heard what sounded like the high and sour note of a clarinet. And then a nasal *kent!* Then *pait!* Adlai pointed to an enormous black and white bird that dipped and swooped from one tree to another without seeming to flap its wings.

"What's so special about a woodpecker, Adlai?"

"That's a female ivory-billed woodpecker."

"That's your secret?"

"Ivory bills are extinct. At least that's what everyone thinks. As far as I know this colony is the only one in the world, and you are only the third person who knows. You, me, and Kebo."

"Why not tell folks?"

"Then the Tensas would be crawling with ornithologists and worse. The birds wouldn't last a day. They'd end up in a zoo somewhere. Or worse."

Ariane was flattered that Adlai had trusted her with his secret. But, really, who could she tell that would care? No one she knew would have ever heard of an ivory-billed woodpecker.

Adlai opened his knapsack and took out the sandwiches he'd made for lunch, handed one to Ariane. "Pimiento." He opened a plastic sack of dills. He told Ariane how one day in Shreveport a man, a perfect stranger, walked right up to him and out of nowhere said, "We're here for character development, not for the fulfillment of desires." The man wore a white shirt and had his red suspenders x'ed across his chest. Then he said, "We're all impressed with your strength of character and your sense of self-worth." Anything can happen in Shreveport.

But Ariane wasn't listening, at least not after the phrase "fulfillment of desires." She was trying to sort out the distressing but undeniable attraction she felt for Adlai. Was she flattered by his attentions? Apprehensive about the wedding? Was she having second thoughts? She knew she would never have met Adlai except for these unique familial circumstances. He just would not travel in her circle of more conventional friends. He was unlike anyone she knew. Of course, it's easy to be fascinating if you're new. And maybe he only behaved this way with her and was Mr. Bland with the rest of the world.

And why had she agreed to come all the way out here to the middle of this unpleasant nowhere—and that's all it was—with Adlai. Why had she placed herself once again in the near occasion of sin after she had just this morning extricated her wanton self from her imprudent and ill-advised romantic entanglement with him? She said, "I don't get what you see in nature."

He said, "Beauty."

Ariane looked around her. "It's just ordinary trees, dirt, water, muck, and bugs."

"My daddy says when you see something beautiful, it's because you looked at it beautifully."

"That doesn't make sense."

"And if you see something unattractive, you were looking in an ugly fashion."

That got Ariane thinking about the ways she sees herself, how she looks so exotic in the storefront window at Landry's Bakery and how that's different from how severe she looks in the revolving door of the Citizen's Bank. And at home the bathroom mirror makes her look bloated, tired, old, but the full-length mirror on the closet door makes her look slender and vigorous. She's the same. Walked from one room to the next. How's that possible? And which is the self that people see? The bathroom Ariane or the closet-door Ariane? She does know that when she's all dressed up, she looks her best. She's sure she'll make a radiant bride, not so sure she'll make a lovely wife.

"Adlai, you can kiss me if you'd like to."

"I wouldn't do that unless you wanted me to."

"Well, let's just say I do."

You could take that response in a couple of ways, Adlai thought. "I do."

"You haven't." Ariane moved her face closer to Adlai's. "What are you waiting for?"

And Adlai kissed Ariane on the lips, and one kiss led to another, and so on. And Adlai thought how pleasure this intense and pure was an impossible and undeserved gift, and Ariane thought how would she explain these scrapes on her back and her knees, the dirt all in her hair. And when they had finished, Adlai opened his eyes and saw, not fifteen feet from where they lay, a water moccasin, thick as a motorcycle tire, sunning himself on a fallen cypress.

Boudou and Royce sat at the kitchen table with their rubber spatulas and their stoneware bowls of what was left of the caramel icing that Benning had made for her chocolate Waldorf cake. Royce was trying to explain how it wasn't so bad as maybe it sounded, how he was more articulate with himself, when he didn't need to speak. Did that make any sense? When he let his thoughts just happen, they were as clear as Karo syrup. But when he tried to share them, something misfired between his brain and his mouth. Even now he wasn't sure if he had said all this to Boudou or just thought it. Boudou smiled, ran his fingers along the shoulder of the bowl, licked his fingers. He told Royce he had icing on his chin. Royce swiped it away.

Boudou heard his momma and Benning talking in the parlor about kin, about how Cousin Nell was a high-tempered gal and Uncle Walker was weak in the intellectuals and Aunt Juanita was economical with the truth. Benning told Earlene how Cousin Eula's first husband Norwood Hastie, the electrician, had a stroke while he was walking laps inside a shopping mall over to Greenville. What kind of sense does that make? What kind of person would care to exercise around all those stores? Maybe the kind of person who dies watching TV, Earlene said. Boudou loved being in the house with his family. He'd like to close all the doors to Paradise and not let anyone get away.

Royce couldn't make out what they were saying in the parlor. He heard voices understood the tone to be befuddlement and resignation, but he couldn't make out the words. Can't talk, can't hear. He looked across the room to where the calendar hung—couldn't see. He was getting tired of not being a part of the world. He felt disconnected, redundant, knew that he was losing what was important, but didn't understand quite what that was.

Boudou thought how all this pleasantness would end in a few days, and the happiness he felt today he would not feel again. He felt like he was losing what he had been denied till now.

Royce said, "What's going on, Boudou?"

"Do you think we could just live here?"

"We do."

"I mean forever. That way we can talk every day."

"And I'll have someone to eat icing with."

"What do you think?"

"Sounds good to me."

On the drive home, Adlai suddenly noticed that they were in Archibald, and he didn't remember how he'd gotten there. He waved at a couple of men loitering outside the Shuffle Inn. He turned on the radio and heard Jim White sing about ten miles to go on a nine-mile road. Ariane turned off the radio. She said, "What we're doing ain't right."

Adlai said, "How could love be wrong?"

"I'm not in love with you."

"You have a funny way of showing it."

"You don't know what love is."

Adlai didn't believe anyone really knew what love was because love wasn't something you *knew*, it was something you felt, you believed in, and he believed that what he felt for Ariane—the adoration, the obsession, the tenderness, the gratitude, the longing, all of it—was love. He looked at her out the corner of his eye, and he understood that he was helpless and free.

And everything that happened to Adlai for the rest of the day seemed to him like it was happening to someone else. His real life was a secret, and this was all pretend. Ariane went off with Grisham somewhere still insisting that nothing had changed, but Adlai felt that nothing in his life would ever be the same again. He cleaned, he baked, he thought about Ariane's body thrust against his, and when he did his eyes closed, and his groin ached, and he moaned right out loud. Couldn't help himself. And that made him smile, and the smile made Earlene ask him did he have some money in the bank or something. Even Boudou noticed how he was acting peculiar. Boudou said, You're in some other world, aren't you? Not another world, Adlai thought, but another life, a better one. Love doesn't change the world. Adlai could see that. But it changes the lover.

Adlai went to bed but couldn't sleep. And he couldn't read. Every sentence reminded him of Ariane. And he was reading Fabre's book of insects. *The moment the fly came within reach, the watchful devilkin turned her head, bent her corselet slantwise, harpooned the fly, and gripped it between her two saws.* He put the book down, cut the light. He lay awake waiting for her return. He'd go to her, explain how the sooner they canceled the wedding, the easier it would be for everyone, and the sooner they could all get on with their lives. He pictured himself speaking reasonably with Grisham, saw Grisham pale, collapse into a chair, saw himself offering his devastated cousin solace and pledging his undying friendship. Adlai heard the car doors slam. He got up and peeked out the window. He heard Grisham's voice, Ariane's squeal, heard them climb the stairs. He listened at his door, heard Ariane tell Grisham to stay with her, not to leave her alone tonight. He heard her door open, click shut. He thought, Now what? What if I don't get to see her alone again? What if she's tied up with rehearsals, fittings, manicures, and whatnot? What if she's willing to sacrifice herself for the sake of decorum and decency?

The Key to Wedlock

Seaux.

—OFFICIAL STATE EXCUSE,
LOUISIANA

Adlai chopped onions, bell peppers, and celery. He put the radio on for company, low so he wouldn't wake anyone. He got the butter and the defrosted crawfish tails out of the fridge. He'd never heard of such a thing—a call-in talk show at five in the morning. A gentleman caller from Luna told the host about the Great Red Dragon of Revelation. Adlai melted butter in the skillet. Then the caller said he was an end-of-times preacher, and he needed to let everyone know about the Satanic machinations of what he called an Illuminati proprietary group. Funny thing was the host seemed to know what the preacher, Gideon Kline, was talking about. The host asked Gideon could he hold for the news.

Adlai swept the chopped vegetables into the buttered skillet, stirred for a minute, and dumped in the seasonings. The host read a story about how in New Orleans some funeral director cut the hands off a corpse and filled its chest cavity full of pinned voodoo dolls. Now how is that news? Adlai wondered. He switched off the radio. "Too early in the morning for this, my friends."

"Good morning," Grisham said.

Adlai dropped his spoon.

"You always talk to yourself?"

"I do, but I don't listen." Adlai poured a bowl of chopped, peeled tomatoes into the skillet, added garlic, stirred, let it sit.

Grisham said, "I couldn't sleep." He sat at the table.

Adlai wiped his hands on the towel tucked into his pants. He put two cups on the table and poured coffee. "Cream and sugar?"

"Black."

"I expect you're just all wound up over the wedding and all."

"People walk in and out of your life every day. Some you'll see again, some you won't. You never expect a stranger is going to be important in your life, but then it happens."

"How did you meet Ariane?"

Grisham told Adlai how the girl he'd dated three or four times— nothing serious—invited him to a wedding reception. One of her cousins was getting married. The girlfriend's name was Darby Nichols. Grisham didn't know a soul at the reception.

Adlai said, "You want some red-eye gravy over doughnuts?"

"I'll pass for now, thanks."

"So Ariane was a friend of Darby's?"

"She was our waitress. First time I laid eyes on Ariane she was placing a goblet of fruit cocktail in front of Darby's aunt Belinda."

Adlai got up to add more tomatoes, onions, peppers, and butter to the stew. He scraped the crust at the bottom of the skillet. He tasted, spooned in more seasoning. Meanwhile, Grisham explained his theory of weddings, how they provoke hormonal changes in the single women present. They suddenly want to cuddle, talk about the future. Grisham wasn't sure what exactly caused this—the sight of a white gown, maybe, or an acquiescent groom, or maybe it's the idea that if you plan anything with enough energy, attention, and tenacity, it will turn out splendidly. He hardly knew Darby, and out of nowhere she started naming the children they might have together (two boys, two girls—Cindy Lee [We'll call her Dee Dee] and Paula Louise [Polly], Matthew Mark and Luke John), decorating the family room of a house on Metarie that Grisham knew would never exist.

"So you saw Ariane, and then what?"

"While all the single ladies were lined up to catch the bouquet, I slipped into the kitchen, found Ariane tossing slop into trash buckets, and got her phone number."

Grisham poured himself another coffee. Adlai stirred the crawfish tails into the stew, added seafood stock. He said, "I've always been good at that—at getting phone numbers, addresses, dates. I don't know why. If I want someone I go after her."

"That's a good way to be."

"Nothing stops me."

Adlai thought if he disliked Grisham, then his pursuit of Ariane would not be so problematic. Anniece Pate once told him that his tolerance of people's sins and peculiarities, their stupidity and vulgarity was a serious character flaw.

Grisham thanked Adlai for the coffee, took his cup, said he was going to take a shower. Adlai went back to his stew, turned on the radio. The host was telling the listeners wasn't it funny how a computer company was named after the forbidden fruit of Eden. And what about the Walt Disney company? You look at that corporate logo, Walt Disney's signature, and you'll find three 6s concealed there in the *W* and in the *Y* and in the dot over the *i*. So it shouldn't surprise us that they run a Homosexual Day, should it? What about that dog Pluto, god of the Underworld? And the duck who won't wear pants?

Earlene stood at the stove. She sipped crawfish broth from a wooden spoon, let the liquid cool on her tongue, clicked her lips to taste. What's missing? Paprika? She thought how a person's death really happens at different times. She didn't know why she was thinking of this—maybe she'd been dreaming about it. When her papaw had his second stroke and lapsed into his final coma, well, he was dead to her right then. His body lived for another year, but the man did not, and she had finished grieving for him by the time he—*expired* was the word that came to her—expired like a drugstore coupon. She dusted the stew with paprika and stirred.

Or let's say your husband died on a hunting trip but his body was never found. Your life would come to a stop, wouldn't it? It could be ten years later, and you'd still be waiting for your thirty-year-old husband to come walking up that sidewalk to the front porch, to take you in his thick arms and hug you to pieces. Someone knocked.

Earlene saw a man at the French doors. He smiled and waved. He held up a black leather bag. Earlene smiled back. She opened the doors. He introduced himself: Parnell Broadway. They shook hands. Earlene, she said. He said, I'm the doctor. I'm here to see Royce Birdsong. Earlene said, Of course. Come on in, come in. She said, I'll get Royce. She pulled a chair away from the table. Sit, she said.

Earlene found Royce locked in the bathroom. He didn't understand how to unlatch the hook from the eye. Parnell sat on a mohair chair in the parlor, picked up the old stereograph on the chairside table, and browsed through the 3-D views of the world at the turn of the last century—at Mammoth Hot Springs, at the ruins of Ross Castle in Ireland, at the Garden of the Tuileries, where Parisians in 1905 were caught in midstride on a cool, sunny afternoon. In another view a milkmaid sits on a wooden fence, a bucket at her feet, cattle over her shoulder. A gentleman in a gray suit and gray fedora leans his elbow on the fence and asks her, "Where is your father, my pretty maid?" At least that's what the caption says. Parnell wondered if the baby in the carriage being wheeled through the Tuileries might still be alive. Earlene got the lock undone with a knife. She led Royce downstairs.

When Ariane walked into the kitchen, she tasted the stew. Needed salt. Adlai said hello and went back to writing. Ariane sat, watched him, wondered why he was ignoring her. She asked Adlai what he was doing. He said, Writing fortunes for the wedding cookies I'm going to bake. He read some to Ariane: *All the Women at the Office Have a Crush on You*; *You Really Were Your Mother's Favorite*; *Your First Husband Thinks About You All the Time*; *Nobody's Ever Had That Thought You Are Just Now Thinking*. Ariane said she had one: *The Man Who Insulted You at Work Has Been Fired*. After last night's rebuff, after this morning's chat with Grisham, Adlai's plan had been to ignore Ariane, and by ignoring begin to unfetter himself from the bonds of hope and get on with his life, such as it was. But here she sat like the morning star drawing his vision to her, and Adlai understood that seeing is also not seeing, and as he beheld Ariane he lost sight of the future and himself. "Have you told Grisham what's been going on?"

"Why on earth would I?"

"We need to talk about our future."

"I'm fond of you, Adlai. If we had met under other circumstances . . . But then we never would have."

Adlai took Ariane's hand, stroked her cheek. "I love you."

"Please, don't." Ariane stepped away from Adlai. "You're an affliction I need to get over. Being near you won't help me do that."

In the parlor, Earlene looked at Parnell who must have felt her gaze because he looked up to meet it. They heard Adlai out on the veranda with his violin. Royce said, Adlai's not getting any better with that fiddle, is he? Benning said, But he plays with such enthusiasm. Earlene said, Sounds like he's trying to play "Jesus Sails Home to Zion." Parnell explained to Benning how she should administer Royce's herbal supplements—wolfberry, black ginger seed, fleece flower root—said he'd be by with some lecithin caps later on. Royce thought, Pills you wear on your head? Can't be. Earlene walked Parnell to the door. Such a handsome man. She was surprised that she wasn't attracted to him. Too bad.

(And it's too bad, by the way, about Varden Roebuck. The previous evening he got kneewalking drunk over to Simmie's Diddy-wah-Diddy in Monroe. He was there listening to Tremaine Davis and His Pleasure Kings. Varden met a married lady there and took her to the newly renovated Palms Motel. He woke up alone at three a.m. His car was not in the lot, his wallet not in his pocket. All of which meant what? He wasn't sure. He took another swallow of bourbon and headed off in the direction of the Diddy-wah-Diddy. He became lost, disoriented, cold. Shortly, he became out-of-bourbon. He looked at the sky, knew you were supposed to be able to tell directions from looking at the Big Dipper or something. But what good is direction if you don't know where you are? He couldn't walk anymore anyway. Better to rest now, get his bearings come light. It was so damn cold. Varden sat on the tarmac. He ain't about to sleep in that field. The tarmac was warm. He stretched out and closed his eyes. He heard a skittering in the grass. Once he's asleep it can crawl all over him, whatever it is. He'll be asleep and he won't care. He heard a rumble like the road was snoring. The noise grew louder, and in a few seconds, Varden understood that the rising pitch signaled an oncoming semi. Hauling ass, too, sounds like. He wondered what it might say on the side of the trailer, but he knows he'll never know because he is too tired to open his eyes. [It said, *Let's Go Krogering!*] He wondered why he was not getting up, wondered is this suicide he was pursuing, and if it was, how would anyone ever know?

What the driver thought was he'd hit a fox or a coyote. He'd hose down the wheel well when he got to Winnsboro. Louisiana, by the way, leads the nation in lying-in-road deaths. Varden's body would not be identified for a week yet.)*

The End of Passion

Happy love has no history.
—DENIS DE ROUGEMONT

Adlai cleared away Royce's plate, swept the crumbs into his hand, asked Boudou would he like another one-eyed egg. Have it ready in a jiffy. Boudou said he wouldn't care to, thanks anyway, Adlai; had me an elegant sufficiency. Royce and Boudou excused themselves. They were heading into town to take in the Bible Expo over to the fairgrounds in Sodom & Gomorrah. Royce said that Benning and Lorraine, if she was up to it, would be meeting them there—Durwood Tulliver's got him a booth. Adlai shook out the tablecloth, washed the dishes, and dried them. He picked up the new issue of *The Vindicator* and went out to sit on the veranda.

On the society page, Adlai saw a picture of the Great Books Club in the middle of a discussion, it looked like, of *The Magic Mountain*—that was the book lying on the coffee table. And just as Adlai studied the photo, someone said hello from the road, and wasn't it Cicero

Wittlief, second from the right in the photo, and Adlai's first thought was, There are no coincidences—but then he thought, of course there are—life is full of accidents. Adlai waved to Cicero, said, Hey! He watched Cicero walk toward the bridge and noticed he was pigeon-toed and buck-kneed. Adlai imagined Cicero's whole life just from watching him walk: Lives in a modular home with wood-grain paneling and shag carpets. On top of the TV he's laid a towel and on top of the towel an aquarium. In the aquarium are guppies and a ceramic sponge diver. Over the living room window is a print of DaVinci's *Last Supper* laminated onto a slice of a cypress log. Adlai saw Cicero sitting in the La-Z-Boy, snacking on vanilla wafers, reading Thomas Mann. He's rehearsing a point he would like to make at the Great Books discussion, something about Clavdia's emotional promiscuity, but he keeps thinking about who he would cast in the movie: Billy Bob Thornton as Leo Naphta; Anthony Hopkins as Settembrini. Cicero feels bad that he never speaks much at the meetings—not as much as he should, not as much as he thinks he should. Cicero is convinced he's not as smart as the others, and he wishes he were. He should have gone to college like his aunt Frankie told him to.

Ariane said, "You don't even know I'm here." About scared Adlai to death.

"You sneaking up on me?"

"I was sitting here when you came out."

"Are you sure?" Adlai watched a tanager light on the Rose of Sharon. He listened to the bird's *chip-burr*. Not much of a singer for a voluptuous bird. "I thought you'd be with Grisham."

On the second-floor gallery, Boudou saw the flash of the tanager in the cypress and heard Adlai and Ariane, and he sensed not danger exactly, more like a gathering storm, sensed a threat in the stillness between their sentences, in the crispness of their pronunciation. He peeked through a gap in the deck and he saw the side of Adlai's green rocker and Adlai's foot flat to the floor.

"What's going to happen when I marry Grisham?" Ariane looked over her shoulder at the kitchen window.

"I'll have to make do with the charm of distance. When something goes wrong, you'll know how to reach me."

"Adlai, we can be friends, I hope."

"Are you flirting with me again?"

"Do you want me to go away?"

Boudou had noticed this about adults: they want an awful lot, but they don't always want what they have. Something dreadful must happen between eleven and twenty. Like you reach a certain height or something and your body releases the chemical of discontent.

Ariane watched the scarlet bird lift off the bush and fly toward the lake. "Grisham's never really said he loves me. Except when we're—you know—and then he can't stop saying it."

"When I look at you it's like I'm standing on the edge of a cliff or the ledge of a building and I'm dizzy, afraid to move."

"Some people are freer with their emotions."

"What are we talking about?"

Alvin Lee stepped out onto the veranda, said hello. "Duane just asked me for Ouida's hand in marriage." He sat down.

Ariane said, "Why, that's wonderful. Isn't it?"

Adlai said, "What did you say to him?"

"I said, It's up to Ouida. When I said that, she smiled and then she cried and I felt a wonderful relief."

Ariane excused herself to congratulate the couple.

Adlai said, "Now you're back to a normal marriage."

"I've learned my lesson."

"Have you told Lorraine?"

"She's sleeping."

"She'll be happy."

Alvin Lee said, "What were you all talking about—if it's any of my business?"

"My future."

"Tell you what I think, Adlai. You'd make you a fine preacher if we could just get you to believe in Jesus Christ and all. You got you an A-number-one mind, a magnanimous soul, and a bountiful heart—but you ain't saved yet. I'm on a pray for you, Ad. That doesn't offend you, does it?"

"It tickles me. But I think you're wrong about me and preaching. Preachers—no offense—believe in universals."

"You saying you don't believe in no kind of God?"

"I believe in our need to have a God."

"I'll be praying double-time, I can see that."

Reverential Awe

No tobacco use of any kind.
Men with long hair, mustache or beard.
Dresses above the knee. Sleeveless shirt.
Jewelry or make up. Women cutting hair.

—SIGN ON THE DOOR,
Holiness Church of God in Jesus' Name

Boudou had not expected this at a Bible Expo. He hadn't thought the first thing he'd see would be this big old aquarium full of—he counted them—five spade-headed pit vipers. His daddy had died when he fell into a nest of water moccasins—suicide by serpent, one reporter wrote—and maybe that should have made Boudou apprehensive, but he was, instead, fascinated. Of all the beasts, he wondered, why had snakes been chosen for revulsion? Because of their silence, seclusion, subtlety? A message made with that black plastic tape and pressed white letters was stuck to the aquarium glass. It said, *They shall lick the dust like a serpent.*

"Those are copperheads, son," the man behind the table said, "the ones on top. You can tell a copperhead by the hourglass body patches." He pointed them out with a pencil. "See right there. There's a rattler on the bottom of the pile. You want to touch one, do you?" he asked Boudou. Royce interrupted, said he was in charge of the boy, and he didn't think fooling with poisonous snakes was such a bright idea.

The gentleman smiled, shook their hands, and introduced himself. The Reverend James Henry Flowers, a herpetologist at Tennessee Mountain College of Christ and an ordained minister at the Holiness Church of God in Jesus' Name in Rocky Fork. "Pleased to make your acquaintance, gentlemen. We're not fanatics or nothing," he assured them, "not like the church across the valley in Damascus. We don't handle fire none, but we are serious," he said. "You'll meet lots of people here today who profess to belong to Jesus, but they ain't serious."

"And you're the judge of them?" Royce said.

"Sometimes Jesus wants to prove to the world that what we do on our Wednesday evenings and Sunday mornings in Rocky Fork is very dangerous, that we don't hypnotize the snakes, don't milk their venom, don't render them sluggish with ice, don't feed them into a stupor. And so he allows a snake to bite." He stepped back a little and bent to look into the aquarium. "That fellow on top of the heap there, that's Belial, and he killed my double cousin, Delphina Flowers. Bit her on the wrist. Before she died in the kitchen of her trailer, her hand, her shoulder, and head swelled up three times normal size. She never complained the whole time while the saints were praying over her."

Royce nodded, held out his hand. "It's been a pleasure to make your acquaintance, Reverend." They shook. "We got a lot to see. Enjoy your stay in Shiver-de-Freeze."

Royce and Boudou stopped at the Bethel Bookshop booth. Royce picked up an autographed copy of *Wrestling with Satan: the Intelligent Use of Nuclear Weapons.* The author, Neville Hettich, had lovely Palmer Method handwriting. Royce asked the lady at the counter if this was a joke.

She said, "We don't think Communism is funny."

Royce put the book down. "No offense, ma'am." This was the first religious bookstore he'd ever seen that had a Military section. He read the jacket to *The Coming Nuclear Crusade.* He said to the lady, "Aren't you worried what with Jesus coming back and all that he'll get radiation poisoning or something?"

Royce and Boudou walked around a bit, keeping their eyes opened for Lorraine and Benning. They stopped at the Ryre's Study Bible booth but not the Witness Panty Hose booth. Boudou fiddled with the telephone at the Heavenly Touch Personal Answering Machine display: *Spiritually Inspired Phone Messages for your AT&T, GE, or Sony Machine.* At the end of the Dispensational Millennialist aisle they came to the Loaves and Fishes Food Court and found themselves an empty table. Royce bought corn dogs and RC colas.

A man with a T-shirt advertising *Awake and Sing Records* on the back and with *Jesus Is My Rock and My Name Is on the Roll* written across the front sat down at the adjoining table. His friend folded a copy of *The Sword of the Lord* and said hello. They hadn't seen each other in a while and were catching up. The T-shirted one told the other, "My little Ronnie, Jr.—here's a picture—he was made a certi-fied genius by the Lord. I mean to tell you."

"Praise Jesus," the other man said.

"He's eight years old, but he can read at the twelve-year-old level."

"You're a lucky man, Ron."

"Read the New Testament, all of it, at Vacation Bible School. Boy might could be a preacher someday."

Royce and Boudou kept quiet and learned that the other man had not enjoyed the parental good fortune that Ron had. He had brought his daughter Nadine up strict, God-fearing, but she reversed on him. One day she's in the First Baptist Chorus, organiz-ing car washes, going to Teen Bible Study. Went off to Liberty Uni-versity and reversed. The man snapped his fingers. "Just like that."

Boudou found Durwood Tulliver's booth listed on the map of the Expo. He and Royce headed for it. Boudou asked Royce why some people thought Jesus was God and others did not, why some folks thought Allah was. And couldn't God clear up this confusion in a skinny minute if He wanted to? Why doesn't He want to?

Royce looked to see what booth they were standing by—the Homemakers Evangelical Missionary booth. Number 146. "What number is Durwood Tulliver's booth again?"

"Next aisle," Boudou said. He saw that Royce's pajama bottom was sticking out his pant leg.

While they stood in front of the Proverb Study for the Widowed booth, watching a security guard try to defuse an altercation between two ministers, Royce and Boudou met Dr. John Ryland, Associate Professor of Natural Science in Connection with Revelation at Bob Jones University. Boudou thought how sweet it was to give a university two names just like a person. Dr. Ryland didn't mind telling them about the coming pestilence and famine, about the United Nations' Food Distribution Centers—a euphemism if ever there was one. A fourth of the world's population will die shortly, he said. One and a half billion people.

Boudou said, "There they are," meaning Benning and Lorraine. He waved.

Benning hugged Royce, introduced him and Boudou to Brother Durwood. Durwood said, "I was just letting the ladies know how there's no gossip allowed in the Signs Following church. No talebearing, no lying, no backbiting, no bad language."

Boudou thought how Brother Tulliver didn't look anything like he did on the radio. He was not a man of girth at all, didn't have a ruddy complexion or a shock of greased black hair. Here he was just as thin as a mink in his white suit. The flowerdy band on his straw hat matched his necktie. His skin was rashed and papery, and his eyes so pale and blue that they looked like ice. Boudou saw Tous-les-deux down the aisle talking to a man in a blue flannel suit. Boudou excused himself. Boudou stood beside Tous-les-deux, said hello. Alice smiled at him.

Kate looked at the man, said, "I don't have two heads."

"Neither do you have two souls," said the man, "and so you are one person, you see?"

Kate looked at Alice, said, "Are you thinking what I'm thinking?"

Alice nodded. "Let's go. Come on, Boudou." They went back to the food court and sat. Boudou could see the girls were upset and told them don't listen to what the man said because no one knows where the soul's at for starters. Or what a person is, for that matter. "When you say *I*, who are you talking about?"

"We can't be apart," they said.

"Except when we're asleep. Sort of," Alice said. "Once I dreamed I was separate." She took her sister's hand. "It was a horror."

Kate said, "Maybe the man was right. Maybe we are just one person with two—what?—personalities?"

Alice said, "We have the same circulatory system."

Kate said, "Watch this." She told Alice to close her eyes and turn away. She told Boudou to take something out of his pocket and show it to her. He did. She said, "Alice, what am I looking at?"

Alice said, "A green cowboy on a yellow horse." And she was right.

Alice said, "Why do you have a little cowboy in your pocket, Boudou?"

"I found it."

Kate said, "We could talk to each other before we could speak."

"When I have a headache," Alice said, "Kate takes the medicine."

Boudou said, "You have a dad?"

Alice said, "He's somewheres."

Boudou said, "You don't know?"

Kate said, "We scared him away."

Boudou said, "Ever wonder where he's at?"

Alice said, "No."

Boudou said, "Wonder does he think about you?"

Kate said, "We don't want him to."

Alice said, "He might get to feeling guilty and come home."

Kate said, "Spoil everything."

Meanwhile Brother Durwood was explaining how he was going to bust the devil wide open on tomorrow's *Holy Minute* program.

You be sure to listen, now. He said, "Jesus told me last night that I'd meet a man today failing in his mental faculties. He said to me, 'Durwood, lay your hands on that man and he will be healed.'" Durwood stared at Royce's head, walked slowly around him. "You're that man," Durwood said. "Praise Jesus! The Holy Ghost gives me the X-ray vision. I look into your skull and I see the brain glowing red in some places like the glowing embers of a fire in the hearth. But it's stone-blue in other places." Durwood placed his hands on Royce's head, bowed his own head, and asked the Lord to heal this man. Royce felt a pleasurable warmth blanket his body, and he remembered how when they were first married, Benning would wash his hair at the kitchen sink and how he would want her never to stop, how it was the calmest, the tenderest feeling he could imagine.

Behind the Visible World

*It's when you don't know what you're
doing that you do the right thing.*

—BOUDOU FONTANA

Boudou sat beside Earlene on a bench at the Social Ocean. She asked him who was that man he was talking to. Doyle Cantu. Told me the dark is all around us. She said, You think you ought to just talk to every Tom, Dick, and Harry you meet? He did. Earlene said, You worry me, Boudou. I think you . . .

Boudou listened to her, but not to the meaning of her words. He noticed how he perceived the sound of words inside his head, but how everything else—the smell, the texture, the shape, the temperature of the words and of the voice were just outside his body. He wondered if that could be why other people claim they don't apprehend all the senses in words—they only pay attention to what's inside their head. Earlene's voice was a warm wave of smooth green and blue amoebas.

Boudou told his momma Royce had bought him a banana ring with hot fudge at the Expo. He told me not to tell you. Boudou noticed the doctor who had come to see Royce this morning, sitting with a family who were assaulting him with sign language. The signers seemed agitated—you could see it on their faces, in their rapid and erratic—so it seemed to Boudou—arm movements. Every part of their faces was used to express a sort of tone of voice—forehead, eyebrows, nose, lips and teeth, even the chin. When someone got real wound up, his speech took up more space, and people backed away. The doctor jotted notes, nodded his head once in a while. Here was language, Boudou realized, without color, without words even—a language of gestures.

Earlene told Boudou that Varden wouldn't be coming back and how she was sorry that this had to happen, how she knew that Boudou liked having a man in the house and all. Boudou said, "Where did you get that idea?" He said he had an Oedipal complex.

"What do you know about Oedipal complexes?"

"I read."

"So you're jealous of my boyfriends?"

"I require a lot of attention. And besides, I have a dad."

"No one will ever love you like your momma. Remember that." Earlene hugged Boudou, kissed his cheek.

Boudou saw that the doctor was walking toward them. Earlene waved. She introduced Boudou to Parnell. Parnell shook Boudou's hand, suggested lunch, his treat, at TLC, right over yonder. Earlene said, Tender Loving Care? Boudou said, Tastes Like Chicken? Parnell said, Best restaurant in town.

On their way across the Social Ocean, Parnell pointed out his plants—beds of gentian, peppermint, rosemary, milk vetch, skullcap—nature's Prozac, he said. Earlene wanted to know what was this plant with the bristle-toothed leaves and the purple flowers. Parnell told her, Eyebright, usually only grows in Canada. Good for allergies. In the alley beside the restaurant, Parnell pointed out a large, yellow thistle with hairy, leafy bracts. Blessed thistle. He said how they used this plant in the Middle Ages to cure bubonic plague.

Boudou figured Parnell knew the difference between neutrinos and molecules and quarks and atoms. He should ask Parnell how come if neutrinos have zero mass, and neutrinos are the building blocks of life, and zero plus zero is zero, then how come anything at all is here and visible? When he asked his teacher, Mr. Piersall, that question, Mr. Piersall said there were some things in the world that we are not supposed to know.

In the restaurant, Parnell made sure that Boudou slid into the booth beside his mother. Parnell ordered the baked armadillo and Earlene the Cajun squirrel ravioli.* Boudou asked the waitress could they make him a grilled cheese, orange Kraft American, white bread. They sure could. And a chocolate milk, thank you.

Parnell said he grew up in Hot Springs, Arkansas. His momma pressed towels in a bathhouse laundry. His daddy tended bar at the Ohio Club. Parnell went to college up in Fayetteville, to med school in Little Rock. He interned at Baptist Hospital in El Dorado, worked at a public health clinic in Crossett until he came here. Happened to drive through Shiver-de-Freeze one spring day when he was out admiring the redbuds in bloom. Moved here first chance he got—six years ago.

Across the dining room, Royal Landry heard a voice he recognized and looked up from his script. He could only see the back of her head, but that was all he needed. He knew Boudou the Memorious was in town, should have figured he'd run into Earlene soon enough. When Earlene and Billy Wayne Fontana separated—what was it, twenty-five years ago? (Could it be?)—Royal and Earlene dated, he guessed you'd call it. Kept company. God, he loved her then. Loved her so much he finally told his wife everything. His revelation drove Sandy into the arms of a man twenty years older than she was. Lamar Crow. Nice enough fellow, a widower, sang tenor in the First Baptist choir, sold appliances at the Sears and Roebuck. Royal wasn't even angry about it, wasn't devastated like he should have been. And then Earlene left him. What he deserved, really. He and Sandy stayed together despite her ongoing relationship with Lamar. About a dozen years ago now, Lamar died suddenly (hair dryer/bathtub). Royal and Sandy put betrayal aside then and resumed a kind of reasonably happy married life until she dropped dead at the Pecanland Mall of a massive stroke. She was dead before her head hit the marble fountain and split open. Royal no longer looked for love or intimacy in his life. He thought, maybe he should just study his lines. He's Snug the Joiner playing Gabriel Lajeunesse in Shug's "A Cajun Midsummer Night's Dream." But no sense trying to study with Earlene in the room. Royal paid his bill, stood, walked toward the door. Earlene caught a glimpse of him and turned.

Earlene did not like being reminded of that squalid time in her life—the time with Royal, who was a kind man, of course, considerate of her, but who was her ally in a great betrayal. How could she have behaved so treacherously?

Bone of My Bones

Jesus dying as we speak.
Jesus ain't never stopped dying.

—DURWOOD TULLIVER

On the walk to Pug's Curl Up and Dye, Ariane asked Grisham, "Can you imagine living without me?"

Grisham knew the answer she wanted—the fatuous, rhetorical answer. He tried being honest. "I wouldn't want to live without you, but could I imagine it? Yes."

"Then why are you marrying me?"

"Are you looking for an excuse to call this off?"

Ariane felt brittle, like if she misstepped, caught her foot on a clump of grass, say, her ankle would shatter, like if Grisham were to squeeze her hand, the hollow bones would snap. Sometimes you asked questions for reassurances, not for answers. "Am I always on your mind?"

"Do I think of you every day? Yes. Do I obsess about you? No. We're past that stage, Ariane."

Ariane felt like lead. "I need to sit."

Grisham walked her to a bench alongside the bayou. She shut her eyes. He wished she'd stop playing these games. He put his arm around her shoulder.

Ariane stared at the bayou. She could understand where some-one might suddenly leap into the water and sink. And not even struggle for the surface. Despair shuts down all your systems—of survival and will and pleasure. She said, "You look at other women?"

"I look. I'm alive. I admire beauty. I admire you, don't I? And don't tell me you don't look at other guys."

Ariane wiped her eyes with the cuff of her jersey. "Used to be we couldn't take our hands off each other. We used to boil."

"And now we simmer, which means we'll cook for a whole lot longer." Grisham smiled. Ariane leaned into his shoulder. He hoped she was done with her insecurities for now.

She sat up, looked at Grisham. "What do you see us doing in five years?"

"We'll just be getting our second house. Out by the golf course. I'll be a full partner by then. Might be I'll run for Police Jury."

"And where am I?"

"You're pregnant with our first."

"You've got your whole life planned out, don't you?"

"*Our* life."

"Would you ever divorce me?"

"I don't think so."

"You don't know what marriage is if you can say that."

"Marriage is an act of faith. You don't have to understand it to believe in it. You have to believe in it to understand it."

Adlai stood in Pug's window and watched the bride and groom approach the shop from down Faith. Benning asked Macky to tune the radio in to Durwood Tulliver's afternoon program. He did, and then she told him she'd like her hair done the way she's had it done for the past fifty years—up in a chignon.

Durwood said that the Lord had asked him to speak this morning on marriage and adultery. Amen. Yes, He did. Durwood said he had a confession to make, said he spent some of the happiest moments of his life in the arms of another man's wife. Macky lifted his eyebrows and his comb. Benning closed her eyes and prayed that this was a lie. Durwood said, "Did you hear me, brothers and sisters? I have spent some of the happiest moments of my life in the arms of another man's wife. And I don't give a dime who knows it. That woman was my mother. Praise God!"

Macky said, "Durwood, you lowlife, playing us like that."

Adlai took a chair by the manicure station. Durwood was saying how some men think of adultery as a little bit of paradise on the side. Say they aren't feeling love at home, so they'll look for some on the streets. Adlai heard the door shut, saw Ariane standing there without Grisham. Macky hummed the "Wedding March." Durwood told husbands they need to drink from the cooling waters of the river of wedlock and to avoid the sweet stolen waters of adultery. Ariane kissed Benning and Lorraine on their cheeks and followed Pug to the sinks. Pug secured the silk cape around Ariane's neck, laid her head back into the shampoo basin, warmed the water, and washed her hair. Ariane relaxed under the insistence of Pug's scalp massage and gave herself over to the pleasure of the shampoo. She felt herself drifting away, floating above her cares, fastened to the world by Pug's fingertips. If only this could last forever, the tingle down the neck and shoulders, the rapture of lemon and coconut. She'd have to get a sink like this for the new house, one with a lip to lean back into. She'd insist on it. Grisham could wash her hair every night. She heard Durwood say that God's got His eyes on you. She felt the pulse of the hand spray. Pug said, "Upsey daisy," and helped Ariane sit up.

Durwood said, "If you're hungry, eat the gospel. If you're thirsty, drink the Word."

Pug wrapped a towel around Ariane's head and led her to the styling chair. Adlai said, "Ariane, can I speak with you later?"

"I'm getting fitted for the gown. Then there's rehearsal."

Benning said, "You leave Ariane alone. She's got a lot on her mind."

Macky said, "Adlai, if you want to kiss the bride, you're going to have to wait till after the wedding with the rest of us."

Durwood said, "I don't mind the deep water; Jesus is my scuba tank. Don't mind the fast track; Jesus is my crash helmet. Don't mind the free fall; Jesus is my parachute. I want you to know."

Lorraine said, "Amen."

Adlai looked at Ariane in the mirror. Saw her see him. He smiled. She looked away, not like she meant to, but like she had to. When she glanced back at him, Adlai knew they would talk, knew that he still had hope.

Grisham walked up Mercy to Fontana Bayou and saw two shirt-less boys fishing with cane poles. He sat on the bank and watched. Lots of nibbles, but no catches. One minute you're eleven, and you're lying on your bed reading *Kon Tiki*, listening to Rockin' Dopsie on the stereo, and the next minute you're twenty-five and getting married and fixing to start a family and a career in jurisprudence, and there's no time now in your week to lie around and imagine the lives of people you'll never meet anyway, and nothing you could have done or thought or fantasized at eleven could possibly have prepared you for this moment.

Grisham realized he was getting maudlin, sentimental, was feeling vulnerable and childish, yet he did not dislike the feeling more than he felt embarrassed by it. In fact, he wanted to prolong the condition, indulge in this nostalgia as long as it lasted—this was as close as he ever came to appreciating his own internal life. He wondered could he talk to Ariane about all this or would she flip at what she might think of as his misgivings, cold feet, call them what you will? He stood, dusted off the seat of his slacks, and that's when he saw it shimmering in the sun—the Airstream trailer parked by the Social Ocean. Surely it couldn't be hers.

Grisham investigated. Texas tags. He walked up front to the

hitch. He looked around, grabbed hold of a propane tank, and boosted himself up to the window. Zebra-striped couch looked familiar, but maybe that's standard in this model.

"Why don't you just knock?"

Grisham jumped, slipped off his perch. He turned to see Tous-les-deux standing there. "You about scared the devil out of me." And he explained, "I figured it's unhitched, so whoever lives here wasn't at home."

Kate said, "She isn't."

Grisham said, "I thought it might be an old friend of mine. Do you know the woman?"

Alice said, "She makes the best brown sugar sandwiches."

"Is her name Miranda?"

Kate looked at Alice. "Yes."

"Are you sure?"

Kate said, "I bet you're the kind of guy who thinks everyone is lying to him."

At the Black & Lovely Miranda introduced herself to Purvis and to Delano, said she'd seen them both around. She asked Purvis did he carry canned gravy.

Purvis shook his head. "Don't get much call for it. Folks as make their own. I'm guessing you don't do much cooking."

"No, but you stop by and I'll make you and Delano a Velveeta and crabmeat log that you won't believe. And cottage cheese apple-sauce."

Miranda waited for Purvis to box her groceries, total the purchase. She watched Delano outside painting the window. Right now Delano had these thick yellow blotches where the eyes would be. Miranda walked outside, said, "Who is she?"

Delano said, "She's a queen."

"Going to leave the eyes like that?"

"Waiting for the eyes to stare back, so I can paint them in." Delano stepped back, cocked his head, squinted.

Exemption from Oblivion

I think we agree, the past is over.
—GOVERNOR GEORGE W. BUSH

After supper (barbecued brisket, sweet potatoes, cornbread, Waldorf salad—Gravenstein apples) and after folks had carried their saucers of ginger snaps (a mistake, Adlai realized too late: unduly loud) and their tumblers of lemonade to their seats, and after Boudou had set up the music stand to be used as a lectern, and after Benning had introduced her distinguished guest, had welcomed him back to Paradise after an absence of, my goodness, ten years! (Has it really been that long, Underwood?), and after the heartfelt applause had ended, Underwood Abdelnour, a slight, darkly complected man with black hair and white sideburns, with black eyes—irises and pupils indistinguishable (so black you think he sees what we cannot, so black that Underwood's ex–significant other, Macky Ptak [long story; another time], swore that Underwood's eyes absorbed so much light that he could see in the dark, and for that reason Macky made him wear an eye mask to bed because Macky didn't want to be spied on while he was at his most vulnerable—gave him the heebie-jeebies)—looking splendid in his tan flannel suit and suede Birken-stocks, coughed by way of preface, announced the title of this evening's discourse on memory, "The Cabinet of Imagination," bowed slightly from the waist, and smiled.

Boudou's cowboy hat was too large for his head. His ears flat-tened out under the brim. He cinched the lanyard to his chin, tilted his head back to see. What he saw was Adlai watching Ariane, Ariane brushing crumbs off her knee, Grisham yawning, checking the time on his watch.

Underwood began his address with a quotation from E. M. Forster: "Unless we remember, we cannot understand," and from Nietzsche: "Many a man fails to become a thinker because his mem-ory is too good." That caught Boudou's attention. He'd already assumed that memory *was* thinking, and wouldn't this be a terrible fate—to be trapped inside a brain too busy recollecting to discern. He heard Royce's nostrils whistle, wondered should he poke him awake.

Underwood's thesis was that there is no such thing as memory, only the process of remembering, which involves effort and respon-sibility. He talked about Simonides and Matteo Ricci and about a man with a shattered brain; about procedural memory, skill memory, episodic memory, semantic memory, long- and short-term memory. He discussed forgetting and how memories fade naturally or they get distorted as new experiences crowd them, or new knowledge interferes with old, or they get repressed. He said, "Memory is our way of knowing who we are."

Royce awoke just then, said, "Behind the sofa or underthe-neath."

Benning touched his arm. "You were dreaming, dear. We're here in Paradise."

Earlene brought Royce a glass of water. Benning said, "Please, Underwood, go on."

He said, "Where was I?"

And no one quite knew except Boudou, who said, "Knowing who we are."

Underwood said, "Right. Thank you, son." And he repeated his last sentence, and that seemed to propel him on to the next: "Memory is our autobiography, and our earliest memory is where we have decided that our life began. Begins."

Adlai said he wasn't certain he could buy that notion. After all, you got from birth to that earliest memory, and that journey must have taken place. His own first memory was the cloying smell of honeysuckle wafting through his bedroom window, he assumed, although he couldn't remember the window or the bedroom, just the smell. He was a baby.

Benning said she remembered showing her granddaddy Claude a little clay frog she had shaped and him saying, "Well, butter my butt and call me biscuit." Earlene remembered waking in a dark room, seeing light leaking under the door, hearing voices, trying to climb out of the crib. Alvin Lee remembered watching his daddy take off his overalls after coming in from the field. Why that? Why not Momma, whom he adored, who was in that house with him all day. All night? He felt a twinge of shame.

Lorraine said, "I broke my foot or my ankle somehow, and I was sitting on the porch showing off the cast to Cousin Harlan. Only Momma says I never did break any part of my body." She smoothed her hands over her belly. "So is the beginning of my life a lie?"

Father Pat recalled kneeling on the divan, praying the rosary. He was three. He was reciting along with a priest on the radio. Ariane remembered an enormously fat man eating twelve chicken wings, and he had a pearl of mucus under one nostril. After sucking the last bone, he picked his teeth with a plastic straw. Boudou remembered that tennis shoe we told you about. Duane said he couldn't recall anything before the first day of school, when he wore a plaid shirt, new brown shoes, and carried a pencil case. The pencil case he remembered best. It was red plastic with a clear yellow plastic six-inch ruler, pencil sharpener attached. It slid to open. He liked to open it and watch the green pencil turn blue.

Grisham told how he was being carried out of a burning house by a fireman and he remembered the sting of smoke and the smell of rubber. Ouida said her first memory was of Vanna White on *Wheel of Fortune* on the TV. Mélia asked Ariane didn't she remember her stuffed bunny Pootzy or the wonderful Holly Hobbie wallpaper in her bedroom or the way she was lullabyed to sleep by her momma or anything decent or sweet? Ariane said, no, no she didn't. Mélia said, "So why do we knock ourselves out for you children?"

Underwood asked the assembled to consider what it would be like to have no memory. You would be fixed in a single moment, wouldn't you? How can you comprehend the here and now without the there and then? Like when you wake up suddenly from a heavy sleep and you don't know where you are or what day it is or maybe who you are—it's memory that rescues you.

Adlai thought, Why have significant moments dropped away? Like reading his first word or understanding his first joke or naming his first tree. And why do trivial moments and objects remain? He remembered holding candy in his mouth until the powder dissolved, and the licorice, in the shape of a doll, was shiny black. He doesn't remember kindergarten, but remembers walking there. He heard Underwood say that stories are memories in order. The future, he said, is invented by memory and story.

Adlai would have asked Underwood to explain except that Royce stood just then, walked to the plant stand, lifted the larkspur from the vase, reached his hand inside, and plucked out a soggy peppermint lozenge. He would have popped it in his mouth, but Benning stopped him and return him to his seat. By this time Underwood was saying how memories are the most durable feature that we acquire in our lifetimes. Memories can last a hundred years or more. They are the scar tissue of our minds.

Earlene remembered Billy Wayne and her going to see a movie with Peter O'Toole and how it made her feel so optimistic about their marriage, their love. She remembered humming the song as she held Billy Wayne's hand and they walked across the Cinema 3 parking lot.

Suddenly Grisham, who had seemed, at least to Underwood, to be disinterested or preoccupied at least, said how he himself was afflicted with these déjà vu experiences, and what was that about, do you think? And he wondered was this some kind of loop in the time field, and why was it always happening to him? Underwood suggested that Grisham was not remembering at all and called the phenomenon *fausse reconaissance*. He said this feeling of Grisham's was not an affirmation of the past but a negation of the present. Grisham said, "I knew you'd say that."

Underwood said, "This is delightful, all this interest, energy, enthusiasm. Not all my evenings are so spirited, not all my listeners so engaged. My recent lecture over to Dolphus Higdon's seemed to put people to sleep."

Earlene wondered was this the Dolphus Higdon who'd saved her life. How many Dolphus Higdon's could there be? Underwood told Earlene Dolphus lived on Prosperity, over in Sodom & Gomorrah. She'd go see him tomorrow. She didn't expect he would remember her. She was just a girl he'd driven home from Memphis to Monroe one Saturday night in July. A girl he didn't know. But he was her angel.

Instruments of the Passion

If you don't sleep, you can't dream.

—EARLENE FONTANA

If you don't wake, you can't live.

—BOUDOU FONTANA

Ariane's Dream: Ariane has never been to this bar & grille or lodge or whatever it is. And she doesn't much care for this scribbled sign in the window: *You may be a loser, but beer is still your friend.* This is where Grisham said to meet him—at Zig Roebuck's House of Games. Even though the sign over the entry says, *Asker Inn (Lady's Invited)*, Ariane knows this is the place.

And then she's sitting with Grisham in a dark corner and there's a ceramic pig in a chef's hat and an apron standing on their table, and he's staring at her. Grisham has a clipboard full of papers that he flips over leaf by leaf and asks Ariane to sign by the *x*'s. "Sign here.

And here. Here. Here. And here. Initial. Initial. Sign. Here. Initial. Last one. Sign." The pig looks at Grisham and winks and then stares straight ahead like he's completely innocent.

Ariane awoke. She thought she heard footsteps in the hall. She was grateful to be interrupted.

Adlai's Dream: Adlai slips out of bed, thinks for a second about where he is and who he is. He rubs a grain of sand from his eye. He gets dressed, steps across the hall to his parents' room, and slides the note under their door, the note that explains everything—his love, his joy, this impulsive decision to elope, of all things, that reassures them he'll be back in Flandreau at the end of next week. He'll be back with Ariane, of course. In the meantime, he'll call from Mississippi somewhere. You don't need a blood test to get married in Mississippi. He's pretty sure about that. Adlai hears the wheeze of his daddy's breathing, the click and hum of the ceiling fan. Could use some WD-40. He slides the note under—wait a minute. Didn't he do that already? He could have sworn . . .

He slides the note under his parents' door, the note that explains it all—his heartache, his guilt, this reckless decision to elope, that assures them he'll—they'll—be home in Flandreau at the end of next week at the latest. Adlai hears the rattle of oak leaves outside the open window in the hallway. Funny, he never noticed the window before and can't figure how an outside wall got to the middle of the house. He hears a thud coming from Ariane's room. He taps out a *shave-and-a-haircut* on her door—their signal. She opens the door and she's crying. She kisses Adlai's cheek, hands him her overnight bag. He says, Wow, what have you got in here? She wipes her eyes, sniffles. She tells him she's packed a Dutch oven and don't even ask. Adlai knows that Ariane thinks this running away is cowardly, but it *is* the only thing that can save her from a most ordinary and therefore a most terrible life.

They hold hands and slink down the stairs, steal through the kitchen and out to the drive. Oyster shells crackle under their feet.

They get in the Rambler. How to start the car without waking the house? Hmm. Ariane giggles. Adlai is puzzled. She tells him she was thinking about Elvis Presley asleep in van Gogh's room at Arles.

Which jolted Adlai out of the car and back into bed. Adlai looked at the alarm clock. Two-thirty. He kicked off the sheets, slipped out of bed. So why can't he do now what he just imagined doing? Why doesn't he march into Ariane's room right now and carry her off like Paris did Helen? No, it's not that simple. He'll write her a letter.

Excuse us, but this telling is turning out to be more complicated than we might have wished. At the start, our plan was to hurry the players onto the stage and let them perform, a somewhat disingenuous notion, of course. Complications arise from the conflicting needs of narrator and author. *We* tell the story, but *he* writes it. Our needs are literary and dramatic; his needs are emotional and, frankly, embarrassing. Our author—and we don't mean to be coy here—seems driven by a lamentable and peculiar need to be loved by his characters, and he purchases their affections with the only currency he has—words. He figures (and we're speculating here, our omniscience being limited to those who live in *Shiver-de-Freeze*) that if he spends enough time with his made-up people, he'll have to like them, and they him, his theory of endearment being that knowledge leads to understanding, understanding to caring.

And then there's his wish to live a thousand lives, the one little life he has being routine like it is, being sedentary, adventureless. All he does is sit in that room and imagine other worlds. Then he writes down what he sees. When he does leave the house it's only to search for material. He's a thief of deportment, and ruthless at it. Steal your gesture without a second thought. Now, why would anyone choose to live like this? Because telling a story is a way of being told a story, and ever since he heard about the fisherman who caught a golden fish and was granted three wishes, he's loved listening to stories. What he'd like to do is write an enormous book that you couldn't put down—in any sense. You'd forgo dinner, sleep, sex, and money to keep on reading.

What we'd like to do is tell a story that a million people would hear. We told him, "We want an audience."

He said, "You're not the Pope."

"You know what we mean. Sales."

He said, "All you have is one reader—she who holds this book."

This was his high-and-mighty self speaking, but for once he was right.

Every character has a story, and our author's impulse (some would say *regrettable* impulse) is to let each character have her say, her go at sympathy and redemption. And our job in part (ours and Jill's [Jill his beleaguered and sensible editor]) is to rein in this profligate and self-serving tendency. When he wanted to tell Macky Ptak's story earlier—how Macky did what all his friends and kin had done and married, had a child, took a job as a junior high English teacher in Chalmette, and how he acknowledged some ten years into the marriage that he was indeed homosexual, but did not tell his wife Ruthanne, not at first, and how he remained faithful to her, faithful and confused, frightened, and sad, how he finally fessed up, said he loved her and his son dearly, said he would stay married if that was what she wanted, and how Ruthanne, horrified by the disclosure and betrayed by the only man she had ever loved, ever could love, took little Zack and went home to her momma in Hammond, and how after two years of phone calls and letters and visits from Macky, she came on back to him and they all moved to Shiver-de-Freeze and took rent houses next door to each other and were best of friends, and how little Zack was thrilled to have his daddy back in his life even if his momma's boyfriend Underwood was a pretty neat guy, too—we suggested that perhaps Macky's struggles were too peripheral to our story to warrant the space and the time.

"But it's thematically related," he said.

We said, "Macky is tickled. He got to do his spiel on mispronouncements, to style Ariane's hair for the wedding, and he's invited to the reception. And maybe he'll bring a date, and maybe we'll eavesdrop on their conversation."

He said, "But that's what a novel is—a machine you build to show how everything is connected."

We won that aesthetic argument. Sort of.* And we know what you're thinking. You're thinking, *Not coy?* You've noticed that he indulges us immoderately, as he's doing now. But here's the thing: You may be giving him more credit than he deserves. He doesn't do the thinking. We are his thoughts thinking for him. Here's Adlai's letter to Ariane and Ariane's response.

Dearest Ariane,

I feel that I'm choking. I feel the buzz of electricity charging through my body. My bones hum your name, my parched heart murmurs its love. I could cry at the breaking of a pencil. I could live without sleep. There's a fire inside me that I can't put out. You set it there. I am a fool without shame. I should not write to you, but what can I do? I write because I cannot speak. I write to have my say. I write to break the intolerable silence. I write so you will think well of me. I write because it keeps me attached to the paper, to the table the paper is on, to the floor, the earth. Otherwise I fear I would float away. I live in the last moment we were together. Give me a glance, a smile, a sign, and I will give you everything, anything.

I'm sitting here below you, in the kitchen with your photo in front of me, hoping that you'll walk in, allow me to behold your face, inhale your perfume. I sit with the cup you drank from. It's sacred to me. See what a disturbed person you've made me. I want to tell you everything. Is that love? I'm so happy and so unhappy, happy to drift in your wake, unhappy that I can't have you. I'm elated and I'm desperate.

Remember that you are thought of every minute by him who would kiss your eyes, your hands, your feet,

Adlai Birdsong

Adlai sat rocking on the veranda, watching the restless, sallow moon toss and wriggle on the lake's black sheet. He listened to the mournful howl of Loup Garoup. He smelled the incense of honeysuckle and wisteria. Adlai loved the water and the night because they made him think of things he loved. He understood that solitude connects you to the world.

Ariane stepped out onto the veranda and took a chair beside Adlai. She wrapped her robe over her knees. She looked at him, then up into the magnolia. "I read your letter." She heard a voice from the Great Books house say, "He's a heart specialist," and she realized how darkness amplifies sound. She whispered. "I do care about you, Adlai. I always will. But you need to stop doing this. What I feel for Grisham is more complicated than mere passion."

"So why have you been spending yourself with me?"

"Because I'm confused. Afraid maybe. Because I wanted to feel what it was like to be the unfaithful one—so I could understand what Grisham feels. Because I'm attracted to you. All of the above. I don't know. Because I wanted to punish myself."

"For what?"

"For being happy."

"I love you."

"Adlai, it's too late for us. Grisham and I have history."

"We could run off right now. Get in the Rambler and drive away. Find a Justice of the Peace to marry us."

"This isn't a romance novel."

"We drive till we see the shingle by the front door: *Justice of the Peace*. We knock. A light goes on upstairs. An old woman answers the door. She's tying the cord on her flannel robe. We tell her we want to get married. She remarks how unusual this is, but she can see how in love we are. She tells us to wait in the foyer while she fetches the judge."

"You see, even you can't take it seriously."

"And in the morning we come back here, and there's nothing anyone can do about it."

"Marriage is not supposed to be spontaneous. It has to be deliberate, premeditated."

"Only in the first degree."

Boudou had his eye in the crack between slats, but he could only see the top of Adlai's head. He heard Ariane tell Adlai that maybe he wanted to be in love to feel lovable. She told him he was, so he could stop trying to prove it. That's when Boudou heard Grisham's door open, heard Grisham yawn, and heard footsteps on the stairs.

Ariane touched Adlai's cheek, and Adlai felt the fire of her hand and then a sharp sting on his head like he'd been tapped with a hammer. He grabbed his head and stood. "Damn!"

Grisham said, "What are you two doing up so late?"

"Grisham," Ariane said, "you scared me."

Grisham sat. Adlai looked at his fingers—no blood.

Grisham said, "I'm glad you two have hit it off." He smiled. "Adlai, you'll have to come visit us in Lafayette."

"I will."

They were quiet. They heard a creak in the wood from above. Adlai said the house must be settling, not knowing what he was talking about. They heard a voice from the Great Books house say, "The man died at his wife's grave."

Grisham said, "We should go upstairs and get some rest, Mrs. Loudermilk."

Adlai said good-night. He thought about what Ariane had said, how he was lovable. So why hadn't he ever been loved?*

Later that morning, Boudou set his chocolate milk on the table, wiped his mouth with the back of his hand, wiped his hand on his pants. He explained to Adlai about the scrapes on his arm, how he reached into a catfish hole and a big old blue clamped down on him up to the elbow and spun itself crazy until finally he was able to tickle her belly and pull the arm free. She was bigger than he'd reckoned on. Adlai told him he should salve that arm with balm of Gilead. We'll see if Purvis has some. He said, You sleep well last night, Boudou? Like a rock, Boudou said.

Adlai stirred vanilla into his scrambled eggs. Benning asked him did he and Alvin Lee clean out and furnish the boathouse for the bride and groom. They had. She reminded him to carry down all the old pots and pans from the attic for the shivaree. She said, Shush now, let's listen to Brother Durwood.

Durwood said how a boy is an easy prey for Satan, how all those scintillating nerve cells and boiling-over hormones and sexual juices were churning up inside his pernicious little body. Durwood said, "Brothers and Sisters, I, too, was a depraved child, and I went so far as to one day I expressed my carnal, my bestial, my whoremongering desires to Ashley Valentine. And I was punished by the Lord for my abomination. I lost my ability to speak. Jesus took it away from me, yes, He did. I barked like a dog for a year, and I was infested with vermin and ran naked as a boar in the swamp."

Durwood caught his breath. He sniffled. Sometimes you want to cry a little bit, he said. Sometimes you need to die a little bit. Yes, you do. Praise God! I was dead, but now I live. I live because I repented of my atrocity and accepted Jesus Christ into my ulcerous heart. Because Jesus came unto me who was more disgusting than the viper. He sat there with me on the front porch of Uncle Danny's camelback house and He looked at me, and His eyes were like unto a flame of fire. I looked at Him and saw my corruption reflected in the mirror of His face, and He gave me back my voice, and I said, Get thee behind me, Satan. I said, Thank you, thank you, Blessed Lord. Yes, I did. I told the Lord I would fight against Satan, against the filthiness of fornication, with the sword of my mouth.

"So when you are worshiping that woman you have, ain't nothing but Baal. When you are worshiping that woman you have, remember that her house is on the road to hell. When you are worshiping that woman you have, you may live, but you are dead."

Benning pointed out how weren't they all talking about memories last evening, and here's Durwood talking about a childhood memory, and don't even tell me that's a coincidence. She said, It's like when I have a dream and then something that day happens like in the dream.

Adlai spooned eggs into his mother's plate, into Royce's plate. "What's keeping Royce, do you think?" he said. Boudou said he'd fetch him and scooted off.

"Like I dreamed a while ago," Benning said, "that we had these adorable three kittens—lively, fresh, frisky, cute as the dickens. One of them had tissue paper stuck to the butt. And that very morning I see in the Flandreau *Avalanche-Gazette* about an animal shelter wanting to place kittens. Or Johnny Cash will be singing 'Ring of Fire' in my dream, and the next day he's arrested for drug possession or whatever. I don't pretend to understand it."

Adlai asked Benning what she dreamed about last night. She said she could only remember a part of it. "Lorraine had her baby, and it's already talking a blue streak, wanted to know was it a boy or a girl. I said for some of us you're a boy, for others a girl. You're the best kind of baby."

Adlai said, "Well, maybe we'll have a birth today."

Boudou led Royce to the table, helped him on with his bib. Royce smiled hello to everyone. Boudou said what happens in his dreams is all the different things that went on in the day get connected up in one long story. Royce poured juice into his glass. Poured right over the rim and kept pouring till Boudou said, Whoa! and grabbed the pitcher. Royce said, What did I do? Benning sopped up the spill with her napkin. She said, You're fine, darling. You just eat.

Earlene said good-morning and she'd love to sit and chat, but she was going to try to find Dolphus Higdon, an old acquaintance. Catch him before he sets off to work. Meet you all at the Social Ocean around noon. How's that? Deal, Boudou said. Earlene said, We'll have lunch. Adlai said, We'll have a picnic.

People Who Might Be

Dead or ALiVE

Love makes sense because
indifference is so dangerous.

—DOLPHUS HIGDON

The house on Prosperity was a porchless little pink box lacking in any decorative detail. The paint company would have called this shade of pink Nosegay or Bride's Blush, but it had long ago faded to Bleached Shell. This was the *idea* of a house, really, more than an in-fact house, something an unremarkable preschool child might draw—front-gabled, a central door flanked by single windows—a house with a congenial and guileless, if not memorable, face. The warped screen door didn't shut all the way. A tear in the screen had been bandaged with a rectangle of duct tape. Earlene took a breath and knocked. She heard the scrape of a chair, the creak of footfalls on a plank floor. She recognized him right off. She said, "Dolphus Higdon."

He opened the screen door. "Can I help you?"

Earlene stuck out her hand. "Earlene deBastrop." They shook hands.

Dolphus clipped the pen he was holding onto the bib pocket of his overalls. "I know you, don't I?"

Earlene reminded Dolphus how when she was fifteen and stranded in Memphis, penniless and ill, he had driven her home all the way to West Monroe in the middle of the night.

Dolphus thought it couldn't be, could it? The girl on the sidewalk outside the bus station. But who else would know about it? He said, "Come in, come in, please. My God! Earlene. I can't believe this. You remembered me after all these years."

Dolphus led Earlene to the table and offered her a chair. "Excuse the mess. I'll make us coffee. Sit."

On top of the fridge was one of those carnival prize chalkware statues—a spray-painted dog in a red sport coat with silver glitter where his tie would be. The image carried Earlene back to the Parish Fair when she was ten or so. She was eating a funnel cake, standing in line to ride The Whip, and she was staring at a tattoo on the ticket-taker's arm—a skull and crossbones and the words *The Less Deceived*. She looked at Dolphus. He was staring at her. He blushed, turned back to his coffeemaking. She said, "You don't know how many times I told myself to drive on up to Memphis to look you up."

Dolphus put the pot on the stove. "I've never before had the door open and the past walk in." He opened a cabinet and took down cups and saucers.

In the middle of the table was a glass bowl of old wooden treble-hooked fishing lures. "You don't still drive that old Falcon, do you?"

No, he didn't. Wrecked it. He'd just been driving along, not paying attention to the road evidently, and the next thing he realized was he was smashing through the plate-glass window of Hens' Nest Hobbies and Crafts. The body on the windshield turned out to be a mannequin, thank goodness.

Dolphus set the sugar and cream on the table.

Earlene told Dolphus about Billy Wayne, their marriage, and how he left her and then came back long enough to get her pregnant before he died.

No, Dolphus said he didn't have children, didn't have a wife anymore, either. Did have a girlfriend of sorts and a steady job for the first time in a long while. Wrote for *The Vindicator*. Feature stories. That's what he was doing when Earlene knocked at the door—transcribing an interview he'd just done with Radley Smallpiece.*

Dolphus poured the coffee and set out a plate of Chessmen cookies. He sat.

Earlene stirred cream into her coffee. She said, "Until today, you were on my list of people who might be alive or dead."

"Was I in good company?"

"Well, there was Bobby Carrigan from elementary school. He had freckles all over, and he could make me laugh without even talking. And then his daddy married a lady from Mobile, and they moved away. And then there was Caroline Davis, a girl I was pals with at the paper mill where I worked after school. I'm going to get sad if I keep talking about this."

Dolphus smiled, shook his head. "I think it's such a hoot that you've thought about me every now and then."

"Did you ever think about me?"

Dolphus nodded. "After I dropped you off that night, I felt exhilarated. I'd done something good for someone else. I stopped the car by an oxbow lake in Lula, I think it was. I didn't want to go home, back to my desolate bedroom and my sulky sister and my cynical mother, and back to washing cars at Bill Maggio's Downtown Auto and Detail Shop. I told myself I was worth more than that—more than wasting away in Memphis."

She told him how she was in town for a family wedding, how she lived in Monroe these days and he should come visit.

Dolphus poured them each another cup of coffee—it's not too strong, is it?—and gave Earlene a tour of the house, which was just this one square room and a bathroom built onto the back of the house. He showed her the desk with the interview-in-progress on it, showed her his books in their cases. Physics, theology, food, and fiction. Here's the undistinguished stove and fridge, the fold-out sofa bed, the paint-by-numbers portraits of a collie and a German shepherd, the collections of linen postcards (*View of Klinger Lake from Oakwood Tavern, Klinger Lake, Mich.*; *Boats at Anchor, Lake Chargoggagoggmanchaugagoggchaubunagungamaugg, Webster, Mass.*), View-Master slide reels (*Cypress Gardens; Sun Valley*), ballpoint pens (*Return Dan Foley to the State House; Zesto Shoppe Drive-In, 422 S. Sanborn Blvd., Mitchell*), cocktail stirrers (*Sammy White's Hollywood Lounge; Purple Porpoise*), gasoline station road maps (*Esso, Sinclair, Atlantic*), menus (*Sam's BBQ, Ronnie's Fried Clams*), marbles (swirls, flames, bloodies, diaper folds, cats' eyes, agates), matchbooks (*DeNiro's Supper Club, Sullivan's "Where Steak Is King"*), and stones. Dolphus pointed with his foot to an old varnished wooden beer case in the corner. "Photographs," he said.

Dolphus had hundreds of old snapshots in the crate, many of them in cardboard frames, some of them hand-tinted. Formal, mostly, from studios in towns like Warren, Pennsylvania; Broken Arrow, Oklahoma; and Cle Elum, Washington. Weddings, graduations, First Communions, installations for various fraternal organizations. Distressed-looking men stood stiffly in tweed suits, starched collars, hands resting on pedestal tables. Women posed in front of painted backdrops (gardens, Roman ruins) wearing elaborate hats of puffed velvet, showy flowers, and ostrich plumes and chintz and lace dresses with cinched waists and shoulder ruffles. Babies in long, white christening gowns sat propped up on mohair daybeds.

Earlene said, "Do you know any of these people?"

He picked a photo out of the pile, a color picture of a blond woman with teased hair and loud makeup. Pretty enough, but maybe trying too hard. "This's my ex-wife, Noreen." Dolphus took the photo from Earlene and examined it, like he may have been looking for something he missed the last time. He said, "I should have listened to her first husband, Zip Beaty. He found me in a bar when I first took up with her. He brought me a drink for taking her off his hands, told me she had a heart like an artichoke—a leaf for everyone." Dolphus fished in the pile of photos and pulled out a photograph. He showed it to Earlene. "That's Noreen when we met."

"What did Noreen do for work?"

"She was a bank teller at the Planters & Merchants Bank until the ATM machines put her out of work. She got depressed and wanted to leave Tennessee, and so I quit my job painting houses and we moved to Boise, Idaho. One of Noreen's girlfriends was a dancer at a club there and said Boise was a land of opportunity. I got a job mucking stalls at Les Bois Racetrack and Noreen started dancing at Solid Gold in Garden City. She'd be coming in at four a.m. And I'd be leaving for work. She changed her name to Capri Bardot and got her hair bleached. She got a whole new crew of friends that I didn't fit in with. When I found her sleeping with a jockey from the track, I left, came on back to Memphis."

"She still there?"

"I was gone about a month when she started calling me morning, noon, and night. Said she was sorry, lonesome. Said she wanted me back in the worst way. She loved me, needed me, and all that. She said, Come back and we'll work it all out. Promise. I'll quit dancing if that's what you want."

Dolphus took the photo from Earlene, added it to the others, dropped them into the crate, closed the lid. They took their coffees back to the table and sat. Dolphus looked out the window. "I drove to Boise, but I found out she didn't want me back at all. She just wanted to see would I come back. She had a good laugh about that with her dancing friends. I said goodbye. She said the car was registered in her name, and if I left with it, she'd have me arrested. I said, I bought it. She said, I own it. I took the bus back to Memphis."

Earlene told Dolphus about her songwriting and about Boudou. Dolphus said his sometime girlfriend Susie Robichaud and he had been on and off for two years. "Husband's a drug addict, left her and their two boys, but she hasn't made any move to divorce him. I keep a little distance, you know. Don't know why I do it. Reassurance, I guess."

"Dolphus, this has been so wonderful seeing you again. I can't tell you."

"Let's stay in touch this time."

"And since I'm just down the road in Monroe, we're neighbors."

"Your number in the book?"

"It is. Fontana, not deBastrop."

"No wonder I couldn't find you."

Earlene sat on the grass by Fontana Bayou and added what Dolphus had said about indifference to her list of *THINGS OVER-HEARD IN SHIVER-DE-FREEZE*:

Radley Smallpiece: *I wouldn't trust that reptile behind a dime, and I mean to anoint his scaly ass.*

Purvis Cheniere: *Life is doing, not selling.*

Boy fishing with cane pole on Bayou Fontana: *Refrain means you stop yourself. A refrain in music is the part you'd better not sing.*

Homer St. Onge: *Radley keeps telling me I'll see again. I like hearing that.*

Delano 6smith: *You're going to have to lick more than asphalt.*

Durwood Tulliver: *Send me a letter. I'll lay hands on it and pray.*

Lady in Macky Ptak's chair: *I just think the most delightful thing is to take a piece of land and make it more beautiful than it ever was.*

Royce: *I'm putting my teeth on the back of the toilet.*

Father Pat: *Religion used to be full of suffering and awe, but it's become accommodating and benign. Life isn't painless. Why pretend it is? Why anesthetize the pain? Pain is a warning that something is wrong. Without pain, we are not whole, and we are in danger.*

Earlene saw Royal Landry across the Ocean. She thought how love can sometimes lead to being strangers. They really had had fun together, but they weren't particularly good for each other. Too much drinking, too much trying to be wilder than the other. Still she smiled to remember how they would drive all night to Gulfport on a whim, eat oysters all day, stay at the Jeff Davis Motel, swim naked in the Gulf—like they were in some French movie. And then she sang the lines that came to her head: *Cornbread for your husband, Biscuits for your man, Biscuits in the oven, Cornbread on the pan. Royal's in the kitchen, Marzael's in there, too, Little Early Pearly don't know what to do.*

Picnic

*A few weeks after George died, I could no longer
see him clearly. He was an afterimage, like the red
café curtains that turn green and float in the
purple darkness when you close your eyes.
The only image I have now of George's face
is my own parabolic mug looking back
at myself from George's pupil.*

—BILLY WAYNE FONTANA

Alvin Lee lifted the three card tables out of his trunk and carried them to the grass beneath an oak. He unfolded the legs and set the tables alongside each other. He leveled the wobbles as best he could by sliding old issues of *Annals of the American Pulpit* beneath the table legs. He counted on his fingers: Lorraine, Earlene, Benning, Royce, Boudou, Adlai. Six. Seven with himself. Father Pat and Mélia. Nine. On his way back to the car for folding chairs, he saw Earlene walking down Mercy toward him. He leaned the chairs against the car, noticed a man and woman on a bench, his arm over her shoulder. Alvin Lee knew the woman, but not who she was. He knew if he stared at her then her identity would reveal itself. He almost had it. He wondered if she belonged to his youth or to the nursing home years. To the ministry, perhaps. Yes, that's it! Bastrop. Or Mer Rouge. She wore a black, sleeveless dress, stood on her tiptoes when she spoke to . . . to whom? Then he had it. She's Rance Usrey's wife. His lawyer's wife is holding another man's hand on her lap, is resting her head on his shoulder, is closing her eyes. A car door slammed and someone called out, "Heavenly!" Emma Usrey, who was just then hoping that she and Douglas Bleeker don't go home at all; they drive to Biloxi, stay at the Beau Rivage, looked up and saw Alvin Lee. He looked away, called to Boudou to give him a hand with these chairs. Emma thought, I've seen that man before. He's crazy in the head.

Miranda watched the boy and his father, she guessed he was, carry the folding chairs to the tables. She took a bite of her mayonnaise toast, a spoonful of hurry curry. The older man and his wife took their seats in the shade. The father helped the very pregnant woman into her chair. He handed her a tumbler of ice water. She held the tumbler to her forehead. The woman who had walked down Mercy hugged the boy and kissed the top of his head. Miranda could hear their voices, but not what they were saying. They laughed a lot, touched each other. The cute one serving food seemed a little distracted. When you leave home as Miranda had, you don't get opportunities like this to share your life and your food with people you care about. Of course, Miranda's own mother did not care to eat outside like some nomad and would never have prepared food on a greasy and crusty grill—my goodness! the filth—nor would she have cooked chicken with the skin on it—you could choke to death on all those little hairs. Miranda's parents considered eating a duty, not a pleasure, and were wary of meals as the near occasions of sin.

Miranda thought of her childhood as silence and space. She had felt cared for, certainly, but never cherished like she saw that her friends were, not indulged, not spoiled. Her parents seemed to tolerate the day and to welcome the escape of sleep. They were anonymous, nice—meaning courteous, polite, respectable. Miranda could not recall even a single moment of abandonment—the good kind: exuberance and inhibition—in her childhood. Strong emotions were suspect in her family. Amusement replaced joy; disgruntlement, anger; fussiness, ambition. And in her heart, the love she once felt for her parents had been replaced by a fondness. She didn't miss them. On her occasional visits home, Miranda felt like an intruder, felt that her presence was a bother, not because her parents, Clyde and Melody, altered their routine to accommodate her, but because they did not.

Miranda looked at the clock above the door to Lazarus Funeral Home. Twelve-thirty. So then it would be one, Central Time, back in Orange, and Claude would be finishing lunch at his desk at Al's Trophy World, would be rinsing his thermos bottle, folding his paper lunch sack in three and putting it in his jacket pocket where he wouldn't forget it. Melody would be sitting down in the comfy chair by the living room window with the first of the two romance novels she would read today.

Miranda remembered her mother telling her about the eight female archetypes of the romance novel. "The nurturer, the librarian, the crusader—"

"The harlot," Miranda said.

"That's a man's idea."

Miranda heard the bleat of a horn and turned to see Purvis driving an old pickup truck. He waved to the family she was spying on.

Alvin Lee spit out a watermelon seed, stopped his waving, said he wondered where Purvis and Delano were off to and who's minding the store. Royce watched the truck turn onto Piety, saw Purvis at the wheel, his dead son Rylan beside him, saw himself riding shotgun with the window down, the wind whipping the hair into his eyes. They're rattling down some dirt road in the wilderness area, and it's dark as a dungeon, and the air reeks of methane. Royce looks into the headlights and sees a wood hog skitter off into a bluejack thicket. Purvis passes him the bottle of Fighting Cock, and he drinks, swallows, smacks his lips. He sees heat lightning silhouette the Fairbanks Lookout Tower.

Adlai said, "The cooler, Boudou. Get the lemons out of it."

And Royce realized he'd just been daydreaming about driving with Purvis. Would he and Purvis have taken a drive like that in those days? "Rylan, do you remember driving out by the lookout tower one night? Me, you, and Purvis, the three of us in the . . . the . . ."

"I can only remember what you tell me."

Royce said, "Sorry, Boudou. I called you Rylan, didn't I?"

"I enjoy being Rylan once in a while."

Benning said, "Only two days to the wedding. Are we all in order, do you think?"

Earlene said they were. Father Pat said he'd hear confessions Saturday early for those who needed it. Mélia said she could hardly believe her baby girl was about to walk down the aisle. Why, she recalled her own wedding like it was only yesterday. Married her high school sweetheart, Remy Thevenot, in Mamou.

Later, after the others had driven back to Paradise, and after Earlene and Adlai had cleaned and packed the Rambler, they sat in the front seat, and Adlai told Earlene that he had told Ariane that he loved her and that she was not happy about it.

Earlene told Adlai he ought not to get involved with someone otherwise engaged. Can only lead to heartache. When he said how could he do it, she said, "Wet your finger. Turn the page."

Adlai watched the woman outside her Airstream juggle a cantaloupe, an egg, and a martini glass. And then he saw Boudou and Royce sitting there applauding her. And then the three of them were waving at him like he was arriving on a boat from Europe. Adlai waved back.

Royce said, "My boy, Adlai."

Miranda said, "He's as handsome as his daddy."

Is That the Same Moon?

Time's not real, but eternity is.

—KEBO HALEY

Duane followed Grisham into the men's room at the Crown of Thorns and told him he ought not to keep talking like he's doing about old girlfriends in that lascivious way. Or any way, for that matter. "It's upsetting Ariane. Can't you see that? It ain't funny neither. What's gotten ahold of you?"

"Jesus Henry Christ, Duane! I'm only reminiscing. What's the big hairy deal?" Grisham read Duane a headline from the newspaper page tacked to the wall above the urinal. *"Photon travels faster than the speed of light.* Won't be long before we're traveling back in time."

"How can you travel back in time without getting younger? Being born would be the same as dying in that direction."

"Maybe you've come to us from the future, Duane. Maybe you've been sent here on a mission."

Duane zipped up, washed and dried his hands. Grisham joined

him at the sink. Duane told him, "You're getting married. I'm your best man. My mission is to look out for you." He took hold of Grisham's shoulders and looked him in the eyes. "Straighten up now, you hear? I'll see you in a minute."

Grisham realized he'd been acting like a horse's ass, like a bore, a lout, a cad, and in front of his best friend, his cousin, and this woman who's at the same time his other cousin's second wife and his pal's girlfriend. Why was he making a show of his cruelty and his ignorance? He didn't want to behave obnoxiously, but seemed incapable of controlling himself. His mind said, Stop!, but some rage inside said, Go! He splashed cold water on his face, wiped his face with a paper towel. He looked into the mirror at his puffy, murky eyes. When had he become his daddy? Some days you look good without even trying. Other days you look repulsive. And that can't help your self-esteem, won't elevate a downcast attitude. Must be the lighting in here. Lights are the secret to looks. But why is he even thinking of appearances? And why had he said what he did about doing the wild thing with Birute O'Sullivan in the choir loft at North American Martyrs during High Mass? And it wasn't even true. He was tense and irritable and wasn't sure why or when this crankiness had started. He shook his arms and hands, shrugged his shoulders, rolled his head, loosened up. He took a deep breath, exhaled slowly. Yes, he could still salvage the evening. Go out there and apologize. Be decent and all his churlishness would be forgiven and forgotten. Be sweet. Give Ariane a peck on the cheek. In a couple of hours they'd be making love, and then he'd sleep like a baby, wake up the old competent Grisham.

On his way to their table, Grisham stopped at the bar to buy another round: one sparkling water, two Mockingbirds, no salt, a Bourbon Sprawl, and a Manhattan Project, easy on the pepper sauce. He admired the bottles over the bar, shoulder to shoulder on three shelves, labels forward, spouts back. He was cheered by their neatness and order and by the bartender's crisply starched white shirt and his snappy bow tie. Grisham played waiter, carried the drinks to the table and served. He told Adlai, "Easy on the Evian, pardner." They all laughed. He sat, folded his hands in prayer, said he was sorry, smiled broadly, and, as a prelude to his kiss, offered a toast to the bride.

Ariane said, "Don't you think you've had enough, honey?"

Grisham, his glass still raised, looked at Ariane. He said, "Dearest Ariane, I'm out now with friends, and we're having a wonderful time. Wish you were here."

Duane said, "Come on, now, you two, kiss and make up."

Ariane said, "I just don't want you getting sick is all."

Adlai looked at the pair of them not looking at each other. He thought, Here's Grisham, who doesn't exactly want to be with anyone other than Ariane for the rest of his life, but who doesn't always want to be with her. And here's Ariane, who thinks she can change Grisham, brighten him, descend into his hell and return with his soul. Adlai felt sad for the both of them.

Duane asked if Jolene the bridesmaid had arrived in town yet. Ariane told him she'd arrive in Monroe on the morning bus from Opelousas. She put her hand on Grisham's knee, which Grisham knew to be a gesture of reconciliation, and knew as well he should graciously reciprocate. Instead, he crossed his legs. He said, "Adlai, you've been quiet tonight."

Duane stood, announced that he and Ouida were going for a walk if anyone would like to join them. No one did. They said their good-nights and left. When they had gone, Grisham said, "Enjoy the fresh air."

Ariane said, "Grisham, we should be going."

"I'll let you know when I'm ready to go."

The bartender used a remote to click through the TV channels. Riotous laughter. Frothy music. Sober discussion. Stadium cheers. More laughter.

Ariane said, "Adlai, would you walk me home?"

Grisham said, "I'll be fine right here. You two scoot along. Remember: the safest way home is the straightest way home."

Adlai and Ariane left the Crown of Thorns, but they did not return to Paradise. Ariane said she needed to collect herself, asked could they just sit awhile on a bench in the Social Ocean. She apologized for Grisham. He gets like this when he drinks too much.

"He'll be okay."

"Why is he being so hurtful?"

"Grisham's my cousin. He's a good man, but that doesn't mean he'd make a good husband. If he can't control his drinking, what else can't he control?"

"He almost never drinks."

"And yet he chose to drink tonight."

"Don't get on your high horse, Adlai. It's a long way to fall. From the time I read my first love story, I've been dreaming of this, of getting married and living happily ever after. When I closed the book, I went out into the world searching for my love. And I found him." Ariane wiped her eyes with a tissue, sniffled. Ariane told Adlai to go on without her. She wanted to wait for Grisham. "I'll fetch him if he doesn't come out soon."

Grisham knew that he should bolt out that door and run after Ariane. His goddam future was a stake here. The bartender laughed at something Benny Hill said. A couple of tables away, a serious-looking young man wrote furiously in a notebook. He's been in here every time Grisham has. Doesn't even drink. Grisham wanted to know what the guy was writing. He stood. The man flipped his notebook to a blank page. Grisham waved good-night to the bartender.

Ariane watched Grisham come out of the Crown of Thorns and look around. She thought, Let him walk back and find out I'm not there waiting for him. She watched him cross the Social Ocean and walk up to the Airstream. What the hell? He knocked on the door. The door opened.

A Spy in the House of Love

*A lover is a man who, embarking on
a conquest, does not know what to do.*

—UNDERWOOD ABDELNOUR

Grisham stood on Miranda's doorstep, said, "Imagine my surprise at finding you here in Shiver-de-Freeze."

"Have I been following you?" Miranda stood at the door, a can of fruit cocktail in one hand, a spoon in the other.

"You're just lucky, I guess."

"What brings you here"

"A wedding."

"You're letting in the bugs."

Grisham stepped up and into the trailer, closed the door behind him, kissed Miranda on the cheek, said, "Patchouli."

Miranda put the can in the fridge, the spoon in the sink. She sat at the table.

Grisham said he sure could use a beer.

"Help yourself."

He took a can of Pearl out of the fridge and sat across from Miranda. He noticed an old sign on the wall over the table. *Tourists Meals Rooms.* How had he missed it the last time? What else had he missed? He said, "If women really want to attract men, their perfume should be vanilla or sautéed garlic or fresh bread. You'd have to beat us off with a fry pan."

"Which is why we don't."

"What brings you here?"

"On my way to somewhere else."

"Where's that?"

Miranda shook her head. "Somewhere beautiful." She turned the radio on, fiddled with the antenna to clear the reception, tuned to a jazz station. Grisham couldn't stand how damned cute she was. He could leave now or he could stay. He dribbled beer on his chin, wiped it with his hand. "I've been thinking about you."

"What have you been thinking?"

"Maybe not thinking. Picturing. Just seeing you."

"You've got a secret, don't you?"

"Every person has a secret life that no one else can know about. It's what you don't know about a person that attracts you to her."

Miranda put her finger to her lips, lowered the radio. "Shh." She went to the window, looked out. She shrugged. "Thought I heard something." She sat and turned the music up.

"Shall we dance?"

"Why have you come to see me?"

"I was hoping we could make love. The other night was so amazing."

"You must think you're very charming."

"Just being honest."

"Are you only honest when you're drinking?"

"I'm more honest then, yes. Honesty is disarming to women, isn't it? You all don't expect much from us."

"I don't suppose you can stay the night."

"Can't." Grisham reached across, took Miranda's hand.

"Where do you have to go?"

"Paradise."

"A metaphor?"

"Name of a house."

Grisham kissed Miranda's palm, held it to his cheek.

Dolphus laid a blanket on the step in front of his house, and he and Earlene sat. He sipped his coffee, handed it to Earlene. She said she probably should feel embarrassed showing up like this in the middle of the night, but she didn't. "I'm glad you looked out. I saw your light on."

"I was reading the dictionary."

"A good word, I hope."

"*Quipu*. It means variously colored strings tied to a lead rope and knotted in a code that kept accounts. The Incas thought of it."

Earlene smiled. Dolphus said he was memorizing the *Q*'s.

Earlene said, "I thought you might be with your girlfriend."

"Not likely. Like I said, she's married."

"Do you love her?"

"Sometimes I'm not sure I even like her."

Earlene put the coffee mug between her feet, listened to what must have been a possum scuttling through the brush. "I don't think you should be messing with a married woman."

"I know that."

Earlene laughed. "So will you be my date for the wedding?"

Adlai stood in the hall with his ear to Ariane's door. He heard her sobbing, tapped the door with the tip of his finger. The crying stopped. He tapped again. He put his mouth to the doorframe. He whispered, "Are you okay?"

"I'm a wreck."

"Do you want to talk?"

"I want to scream."

Adlai considered opening the door. He touched the glass knob, but let go. Ariane told him, Wait a sec. And then, Come in. She knotted the belt on her chenille robe. There were yellow beach shoes and sunglasses embroidered on the back. She wiped her eyes with a folded tissue. "I look at how sweet you are to me, Adlai Birdsong, and I think of Grisham's indifference."

Adlai sat beside Ariane at the edge of the bed. She smelled of lemons and cinnamon.

Ariane said, "I don't deserve it." Ariane touched Adlai's cheek, looked into his eyes. "Maybe I should love you instead." She managed a smile.

Adlai saw the robe fall away from Ariane's thigh, saw her tuck it back between her legs. He wondered just how much he would risk to have her. He took her in his arms. She seemed to be on fire. For a moment, Ariane allowed herself to be held, comforted. She wept onto Adlai's shoulder. And then she sat up, took a deep and composing breath, dried her eyes.

Adlai said, "You could chose to love me. I wouldn't hurt you."

Ariane stood, walked to the window. Adlai watched the breeze lift the hair from her damp cheek. She looked lovelier than ever.

Adlai said, "He's making you miserable. Is that what you want? A life of squalor?"

He tried to read her face. She turned from the window, crossed the room, opened the bedroom door, peeked into the hall, closed the door, and leaned back against it.

Adlai said, "Did you hear someone?"

"Making sure the lights were out."

Ariane stepped toward Adlai, untied the belt of her robe, dropped the robe to the floor.

"You're naked."

Ariane crawled onto the bed, lay on her back, held out her arms to Adlai.

"The door—"

"I locked it."

"I'll switch off the lamp."

"Leave it."

Adlai leaned his face over hers, kissed her, lay down beside him. She told him it would go a lot smoother if he took off his clothes. He sat up and slipped his T-shirt over his head. He heard the ticking of the clock on the night table, heard a squirrel scratching along inside the wall. He took off his jeans and briefs.

Ariane said she had made love 139 times.

"You keep count?"

"I count everything. There are forty-seven stairs to the third floor, thirty-four windows in the house, seven streetlights on the way to the Social Ocean. What are you waiting for?"

This was not the invitation to romance that he had envisioned. He slid his hand to Ariane's belly. She jumped, said it tickled. He kissed her arm, drew his leg up along her thigh. Ariane stared at the ceiling. He massaged her breast. She inspected her fingernails. Adlai stopped what he was doing, laid his head on the pillow, and waited for her to do something. She turned her face to his. "I'm sorry. I can't."

"We've done this before." Adlai kissed her nose.

"But this time I was using you to get back at Grisham."

"I don't mind being used." Adlai smiled, wiped a tear from her eye.

"I saw him with another woman."

"But we—"

"I didn't say it made sense. But it did make me incensed."

Adlai sat up on his elbow. "What happens next?"

"Take me away from here."

"You mean it? Now?"

"If you still want to."

"We could go to Flandreau, to my house."

"People will hate you for doing this."

"At first maybe."

"I would."

"I can't help what people think. I can't help myself."

"I was hoping he'd burst in and catch us at it."

"Grisham?"

"I arranged all of this. Got you in here with the sobbing. Left the light on, the door unlocked. Pathetic, isn't it?"

"You'd do that to me?"

"I would have done anything for him." Ariane cried. She wiped her face on the sheets, took a deep breath. "I even left a note for him on the woman's door. Told him it was over." She shook her head. "He didn't care enough to come back."

Adlai swung his legs off the bed and stood. "We should go if we're going."

"Do you still want to?"

"We could stay and face the music."

"I'm afraid of what I'd do if I stayed. Something crazy maybe, like get married."

"I'll meet you downstairs. Be quiet. Don't wake the house."

Adlai told Ariane to wait a sec. He wanted to leave a note for Benning. Tell her they were okay and he'd call tomorrow, explain everything.

"Don't tell her we're going to Flandreau."

When the Rambler pulled away, Boudou left the gallery and went down to the kitchen. He sat at the table and read the note. He didn't know what was going on exactly, but he did know that when adults say they are okay, they pretty much are not. But they seem to believe in the magic of the spoken word—saying will make it so. He put the note in his pocket. No sense getting Benning all upset. It's like when they say they are in love and then they act so self-absorbed. Well, he knew this. They hadn't gone missing because he knew where they were.

As they drove past the Mount Zion rest area, Adlai told Ariane that this was the very spot, right at that table there, where he had first seen her photo and fallen in love. "I was on my way to your wedding. Can you believe that? I didn't know you, didn't know myself." He looked at her and smiled. "And here we are driving away from the old life and into the new. Sure, we'll have a lot of explaining to do, but the only people that really matter are kin, and blood is thicker than irony, and when we explain how it was with Grisham, how you felt abandoned and all—" Adlai saw that Ariane's eyes were shut, and he stopped, let her sleep.

Ariane thought he'd never stop talking. She focused on the ache at the front of her brain and tried to imagine it dissolving, washing away. She didn't understand what was happening to her. Yesterday, she and Grisham had been attached, and today they were not. Grisham and Ariane were greater than the sum of each other. That's what she thought. She thought of them as the bee that needs the rose that needs the bee that needs the rose. Without each other they would die. And now she's supposed to go on living.

Grisham came blasting into the house and ran upstairs. Boudou heard a door open, another door, heard Grisham come down the stairs two at a time, it sounded like. He came into the kitchen. Boudou looked up from his bowl.

Grisham said, "Don't you ever sleep?"

"Did you lose something?"

"Have you seen Ariane?"

"Earlier."

Grisham sat at the table. "What are you eating?"

"Butterscotch pudding. You want some?"

"No, thanks."

"She went away."

"Ariane?"

"With Adlai."

"Where?"

"Do you love her?"

"And she loves me."

"I think she loves Adlai."

"Boudou, you can't love two people."

"Why not?"

Grisham shook his head. "You're too young to understand."

"Sounds pretty selfish to me. Maybe that's the problem with it."

"I've been a damn fool."

"If you want her so much, you'll have to fetch her back."

"How will I do that?"

"I know where they went."

"What are we waiting for?"

"You won't do anything mean, will you?"

"Adlai's our cousin. If Ariane wants to stay with Adlai—and she doesn't—then she can stay with him. I'll be their best man."

"I can just picture myself sleeping through the night—takes me about two minutes—and I get all the rest I need."

"You're too weird for me, Boudou." Grisham laughed, stood, raised his eyebrows, nodded toward the door. He put his arm on Boudou's shoulder. "Let's go."

"When everyone else wakes up, I want it to be like nothing ever happened tonight. I love keeping secrets."

Love in General, Ariane
in Particular

*The only thing better than
being in love is falling in love.*

—PURVIS CHENIERE

Adlai sat on the mohair couch beside Ariane. He handed her a box of tissues, put his hands on his knees, smiled, lifted his eyebrows, tapped his foot. Ariane blew her nose, dabbed her eyes, asked about all those newspapers piled three feet high around the walls of the room, and who was that severe-looking woman in the photograph on the mantelpiece. Adlai told her the papers were copies of the *Lincoln Parish Citizen-Call* from 1934 to 1997 when it closed down due to Ashton Beggs's failing health and his boys' disinterest in the publishing business. "Whole history of the Louisiana century sitting right here: the first Sugar Bowl, the death of the Kingfish, the Lake Pontchartrain Causeway, Hurricane Audrey, Desegregation,

Bonnie and Clyde killed. That happened just up the road a piece."
Adlai went to a pile of papers by the floor lamp, flipped through a
dozen or so, and pulled out an issue. He read, "The twenty-four-
year-old desperado and his quick shooting accomplice whizzed their
merry way along a deserted back road near Gibsland and sped right
into a carefully-laid death trap. When lookouts recognized the
eight-cylinder sedan approaching, officers in the ambuscade trained
their weapons on the criminals and riddled the outlaws and their car
with a deadly hail of bullets. They died with guns in their hands."
Adlai put the paper back in its place. "You don't hardly read words
like *ambuscade* in the newspaper anymore." He asked Ariane would
she like a Mr Pibb or something. He sat on the couch, told her how
Royce had all the papers filed by week and year beginning over by
the credenza. "The woman in the photo is my great-aunt Fanny
Orbison.

"Was she mean?"

"I heard she didn't tolerate any funny business."

"She has nothing but spite for the photographer."

"Ran a boardinghouse in Ruston. Catered to commercial
travelers."

Ariane sneezed. "Guess I'm allergic to history."

"We could sit outside. Why don't we do that." Do that as
opposed to what else, he didn't know. Suddenly Adlai became aware
of the disturbance in their magnetic field, a perplexing awkwardness
between them.

On their way to the brick patio outside the kitchen, Ariane
remarked that the house in general could do with some tidying up.
"Like do you need to have all those photo albums cluttering the love
seat?"

"We like to be able to get at our things."

"Get at them in the attic."

"You can open an album at random at any time and see someone
you maybe haven't thought of for years. I kind of like that."

Adlai opened two folding chairs and they sat. It was so dark you
could see a million stars.

Ariane said, "I haven't done anything wrong."

"I didn't say you had."

"I may have cheated a bit, but I've been more cheated on."

"I was thinking how if I had grown up in Lafayette instead of here, then you and I would have been getting married now without all of the complications."

"You can't run your life saying 'What if?' You deal with what is." Ariane saw a flash of light in the sky and looked at Adlai.

"Sheet lightning."

Now the light shone on the poplar trees along the bayou and seemed to brighten and shimmer and then spread across the cotton field and then it moved toward them, shone fiercely in their eyes, and then went out, leaving them blind.

Boudou said, "Hey, Adlai. Hey, Ariane."

Grisham said, "Ariane."

Ariane said, "I have nothing to say to you, Grisham Loudermilk." She looked at where his face ought to be but saw the green and black afterimage of a headlight.

Grisham said, "When I got your note, I came to my senses. I was frantic. I ran all the way back to Paradise, but you were gone. I'm so sorry. I've been a reprehensible fool. I know I have. I'm begging you for one more chance."

"Years of your hollow promises are ringing in my ears."

"Please, Ariane. Forgive me. I love you. I need you."

"How did you find us?"

"Boudou."

Boudou looked at Adlai and smiled.

Grisham turned to Adlai. "He also told me about your crush on Ariane." Grisham patted Adlai's shoulder. "I don't blame you one bit."

Adlai said, "I'd hardly call what—"

Ariane said, "Adlai, hush!"

Grisham got down on one knee. "I want to marry you, Ariane."

Ariane said, "Grisham and I would like our privacy. If you boys could make yourselves scarce for a while."

Adlai said, "This is crazy, Ariane, we—"

Ariane said, "Now, please."

Boudou tugged at Adlai's arm.

Boudou and Adlai walked to the bayou, followed it to the property line, then turned and headed back. They could hear the occasional plunk of a bullfrog diving into the water and the steady electric buzz of the tree frogs. And they could hear Grisham and Ariane's voices, but not their words. Boudou said it was like listening to opera. You know the singers are all worked up, but you're not sure why.

Adlai said, "How did you know?"

"That you were here?"

"About me and Ariane."

"Just from paying attention. I could see you were going under."

"So you betrayed me?"

"I saved you from drowning."

"How so?"

"What I think is that Ariane likes you on account of you're dangerous, but she feels safe with Grisham. She wants security."

"I think you're wrong."

"Well, I'm only eleven."

They heard the honking of Grisham's car, saw the headlights go on, and saw Ariane standing there illuminated, and then Grisham and Ariane, holding hands, waving at them, summoning them.

Boudou said, "Looks like we'll have a wedding after all."

We Crave for Hunger

You put strange memories in my head.

—BOUDOU FONTANA

Delano and Purvis didn't like the way Adlai was moping around the Black & Lovely, so they carried him along to the cookout at Miranda's. Delano said he was interested in what repeats, what comes around, what's natural. He said he paints a scene to find out what it would be like to be there, to learn what was on folks' minds, what they felt, and so on. "Me, I look for angles of trouble," he said. "That's the music in the painting." He and Miranda and Adlai were sitting at a card table outside the Airstream in the partial shade of a bead tree. Purvis stood over by the grill poking at the coals, sprinkling in the mesquite chips.

Though he wasn't used to drinking, Adlai said he'd enjoy a beer. Miranda pulled a bottle of Caddo Lager out of the cooler. He sipped. Delano said he should take a good pull. He did. He said,

"Taste's fine." Delano said, "You like that I've got some high-test for you." Adlai wiped the beer off his chin, smiled at Miranda.

Delano poured three fingers of Fighting Cock into his tumbler. "I'm looking for the moment that's gone in the blink of an eye."

Purvis brushed unsalted butter on the fillets, dusted them with fresh, ground cayenne and Tellicherry pepper. He went inside the trailer to check on the sweet potatoes.

Delano looked at Adlai. "Adlai's all broke up about a gal. He deloves her."

Miranda said, "What happened?"

Delano said, "She's getting married to Adlai's cousin tomorrow."

Adlai told them the story of his abiding love and about the events of last evening, how he had been brought to the brink of sublime love and then dropped off the edge.

Delano said that's one tough gal. "Course, you got no one to blame but your own self. You the one been chasing the gal."

Purvis offered a theory. He said some couples go to desperate measures. "Their relationship can't stand the dullness of nothing happening. You understand? It's trouble what holds them together, and when they ain't got it, they begin to drift apart. You were the trouble they needed, Adlai."

Adlai said, "I even used Delano's love potion, and it didn't work."

Delano said, "Must be you misapplied it, Adlai."

Miranda said, "You got any left, Delano?" She smiled at him, raised her eyebrows.

"I don't think she loves Grisham, either," Adlai said.

"Grisham?" Miranda looked at Adlai, and for a second thought this whole conversation, this whole lunch must be a joke on her.

"Loudermilk."

"Goddam," Miranda said.

After they had eaten the grilled channel cat (fine-grained and fragrant) and the sweet potato croquettes (honeyed and delectable), and after Delano had said that if you eat the heart out of a black cat, no bullet can kill you, and after Miranda had said she wanted to love someone novel, unsolvable, and multifarious, and after Purvis had ground the beans and brewed the yergacheffe coffee (clean, bright, flowery) in a French press, one cup at a time, and after Delano had said that part of love is fear, then Adlai, who had no idea what Delano meant, leaned back in his chair, smiled, watched a flock of goldfinches rise off a box elder, and though how odd this was, how close he felt toward these strangers, how he seldom got to talk to people who think love is worth talking about, how usually the folks he encountered talked about prices and scores, fashions and scandals, and Adlai wished this afternoon would never end, and then Delano poured double shots of bourbon all around and stood, and raised his glass and said, "First human act was naming; second was disobedience. I'd say Adam got us off on the right foot," and they all toasted man in his (and her) battle against those who would be gods, and that got Miranda off on a rave about how one time people looked at paintings and read stories as sources of nourishment and understanding, but today art is entertainment, and we end up with movies about superheroes and the literature of body counts and body parts, and it's depressing, disheartening, and dishonest. Purvis looked at his watch and said, We need to think about getting back, and Adlai considered the fuzz and hum in his brain and found them pleasant and tranquil and thought he'd just close his eyes a second, and when he opened them again, the sun was hidden behind the trailer, Purvis and Delano were gone, the table was cleared, the fire had died, Miranda was sitting in her chair smiling at him, and he could see Alvin Lee walking toward them from across the Social Ocean. Miranda said, Welcome back. They heard a gunshot.

When Boudou arrived at Paradise, Royce was not dozing on the chair on the veranda. And he was not at the kitchen table, though evidence suggested he had been—his medications were lined up in a circle: Ativan, Thorazine, Phillips' milk of magnesia. Dimetapp, aspirin, estrogen, Senokot syrup, Sinequan, Provera, Thera-M vitamins, Pepto-Bismol, Hydergine, Cognex, Haldol, Metamucil, Stelazine, Compazine, choline with lecithin, neuropeptides, gingko biloba. None opened.

Boudou heard water coursing through pipes in the wall; heard the snap of a shade against a window frame, the rattle of blinds; heard a creak from the ceiling. He called out, "Royce!" and his voice was an icy blue cone. He walked into the dining room and then the living room. He sniffed the air. He skulked up the stairs, pausing at each step to listen. On the second floor, all the bedrooms were opened, and all the airy rooms were empty, expectant. On the third-floor landing, he heard what he hoped was the drone of someone snoring in Alvin Lee's room. He knocked. Knocked again, harder this time. In a second he heard the screak and squeal of bed springs and then three shoeless footsteps. Alvin Lee opened the door, said, "Boudou. Hey. What's up?" He stretched his face and mussed his hair.

"Royce disappeared."

"In front of your eyes?"

"No, he left. I mean I guess he did."

"Let me get my pants on."

Lorraine sat up in bed. "Hello, Boudou."

Alvin Lee told her what was going on, said he'd start looking for Royce. He helped Lorraine out of bed. She needed to stand just a second before she could walk. He told Boudou to stay with Lorraine in case she went into labor. "You ever delivered a baby, Boudou?"

Boudou shook his head.

"It's a joke. You call Dr. Broadway and ask could he come sit with Lorraine till we get back with Royce."

In the kitchen at last, Lorraine told Alvin Lee they needed to switch rooms with someone on the second floor, didn't think she could even make it back up. She said she wished she new where everyone was. "I'll call TLC, see are they having lunch."

Alvin Lee stepped through plum thickets and onto a carpet of blue flag. He called to Royce, listened. He thought he could hear a distant voice. Could be a radio maybe. He stood still, heard his own ears ringing, and thought he heard, "She gasped, drew her swollen and bloody tongue from his nipple to the hollow of his collarbone. She sucked at his throbbing jugular." But maybe he heard wrong. "She sank to her knees in the cold mud, her fingernails digging into the solid flesh at his flanks." Sounded like the voice was coming from the book club house over yonder. "Lorna's hand found its way beneath Otis's kilt and freed his fevered, rubescent manhood, and he groaned like some giant, wounded beast. She laughed and sque—"

"Hello," Alvin Lee said, startling the three on the deck.

Ted Muto looked up from his book. "Hello."

Sandy Van Veckhoven shaded her eyes to see the visitor in the yard. Her sister Cindy brought a sweaty tumbler of iced tea to her cheek.

"Reading to the ladies from the *Hearts in the Highlands*," Ted said. "Ever read Tiffany Craven?"

Alvin Lee shook his head, introduced himself. "I'm your neighbor from next door."

Ted said, "We know you. We're all of us going to the wedding. Some of us are out back rehearsing a play for the deal."

Ted said no, neither he nor the twins had noticed an old guy wandering in the vicinity. They'd see to it he got home if they did. "You might want to check with the others though."

Alvin Lee thanked them, went in through the screen door to the parlor. Last he heard from Ted was something about Laura's "inferno of desire." He came upon an older couple in the kitchen, said hi, introduced himself, told them what was going on, how he wasn't worried yet—Royce hadn't been gone long, but he was so forgetful.

Margaret said she'd put her shoes on and they could all go looking. Shug told Alvin Lee that Margaret was making truffled turkey to carry to the wedding reception.

The three of them went out back and checked with Royal and the others. They hadn't seen a soul except for Tous-les-deux out in the boat an hour ago. Would keep their eyes peeled for Royce. Alvin Lee told folks that Royce was wearing gray flannel trousers, a checkedy shirt, and cordovan house slippers. "At least he was the last time I saw him."

When they walked by the front of the house, Ted was reading a passage dripping with adverbs and bodily fluids. Margaret mumbled something about Craven's turgid prose. As far as Alvin Lee knew, he had never heard the word *turgid* in his life before yesterday when he heard Adlai mention his turgid bladder. And now here was that word again.

"Speaking of overblown," Margaret said, "I just hate *Evangeline* to death. It's not a love story, that's what I'm saying. It's a story of bad luck and regret."

When they crossed the bridge, Alvin Lee asked Shug and Margaret to walk to the museum and then circle back to the bayou. He'd check the Black & Lovely, follow the river, cut back to the Social Ocean.

Royce couldn't quite remember where he was going, but he trusted it would all come back to him. He stopped, closed his eyes to think, and saw himself with a pen, but not writing, and then in a car, but not driving; with a fork, but not eating; in bed, but not sleeping; on fire, but not burning. He walked to the bayou, and its smell helped him remember the past (he and Rylan in a johnboat on Bayou D'Arbonne, fishing with cane poles among the cypress knees, and it's real hot and some kind of green bird lands on Rylan's shoulder—could that be right?) and the present. He remembered that he was off to see Radley Smallpiece. Royce rested on a bench. He wanted to get back to fishing with Rylan and sort out the truth of that bird, but he sensed danger. If he returned to the past, he may lose the present. It was like the price of admission. And in the present he had something important to do. What was it? Oh, yes. Radley.

Earlier this morning when he looked in the mirror, Royce saw a man he didn't know, a man with slack and lumpish skin like distressed leather. And then at breakfast he forgot what he had said as soon as he finished saying it. He could not be certain that he had even spoken. After breakfast and coffee, he felt less muddled even though the coffee was tasteless and the grits could have been dust for all he knew. At the museum, he and Boudou saw something unsettling, but now he couldn't remember what.

He thought that the best thing about old age is memory, carrying your life and your friends and kin—alive and dead—along with you. And the worst thing about old age is memory. How do you live with how you were and how you have become? He looked at his left palm where he had written the address. Now if he could just remember how to get to Charity from here. Cross the tracks into Sodom & Gomorrah. Royce stood, put the river to his back, followed the bayou east. Royce understood what awaited him: the drooling, the falling down, the being fed, the soiling himself, the forgetting what is, the noise, the not knowing who or what.

The house and porch were up on cinder blocks. The shingled roof had been extended over the porch, where it sagged like a damp blanket. The house paint had long ago flaked away, and the clapboards had bleached to silver. The exterior chimney was blackened with soot. The front door's screen was torn and puckered. Windowpanes had been here and there replaced by cardboard and duct tape. Salvaged furniture littered the dirt yard. Radley Smallpiece and Homer St. Onge sat drinking beers beneath a fruitless, leafless, and clearly ailing peach tree.

Royce stopped a dozen yards from the men, stood beside a baby stroller and the plastic grill from a played-out window fan. He said, "You found me."

Radley said, "I think it's you found me."

"No matter. Here I am. Now kill me."

"Come again?"

"I'm the man you're looking for. I'm the Chameleon."

Homer said, "He done kilt the Chameleon already."

Royce said, "You saying I don't know my ownself? You got the wrong man, my friend."

Radley said, "All right then. Tell us what you did. Tell us how did you kill Seal Boy?"

Homer said, "And why you killed him."

Royce said, "I shot him because he irritated me."

Radley said, "You shot him where?"

"In his house."

"On his body, I mean."

Royce said, "Shot him everywheres."

"Why?"

Royce shook his head. "I don't remember why very well." He said, "My life is like a photo album." Royce took a seat on the bench beside Homer. "It's like here I am trimming the wisteria bush. Here I am standing by a 1938 auto, my foot up on the running board. Here I am pulling a trigger. I'm not sure how they're connected." Royce put his hands on his knees, rubbed the fabric of his slacks. He balled his hands to fists. "I don't think we always do what we do for a reason."

"You're wrong, Mr. Whoever-you-are. We always have a reason."

"Well, my reason here is this. I came here so you could do your job of work."

Radley said, "Was it revenge? Did Seal Boy deal with your sister as with a harlot? Did he smite thee? Accuse thee falsely?"

Royce said, "Death is not the worst thing that can happen to a person."

Homer asked Royce would he enjoy a beer. Royce took the bottle from Homer, held it. Homer said, "Twist off." He took the bottle back and opened it. "There you go."

Radley drew his pistol from the holster draped over the handgrip of his chair. "I've kilt some. But you reach of a certain age, and you lose your resolve, I guess." He laid the pistol in his lap, stroked it. He took a swig of his beer, wiped his mouth with the back of his hand.

Homer said, "Friend, you going to tell us your honest name?"

"Royce Birdsong."

"All right then. Paradise. Adlai's daddy. Am I right?"

Royce said he was. Royce apologized, said he hadn't taken his medication.

Radley said, "Me neither."

"Why not?"

"When I'm medicated I realize I'm otherwise crazy. When I'm

crazy all the time, crazy's normal. I've only ever wanted to be normal." Radley said he needed to see a man about a horse. He set his
pistol on the bench and wheeled himself around back to get into the
house. Royce said, "What's it like being blind?"

Homer said, "I don't know what you mean by *seeing* exactly. To
me it's like taking noise and giving it a form that is in the air, a form
with weight and substance and all, and it makes no sense. Nearest I
can tell, seeing's like silent hearing, and that ain't possible."

"You ever dream?"

Homer said he did. "Last night I dreamed I heard a scratching
like maybe a possum was trying to open a kitchen cabinet—and the
scratching got louder, and I could feel cold from it, and then the
scratching became the touch of a wool blanket covering my face, and
I couldn't breathe, and what I could smell was the stuffy, acid, rank
odor of fear, and I woke up."

"And everything is dark?"

"Everything is how it always is. You know, I can tell when the
sun comes up. If I'm not sleeping with lots of blankets on. I can feel
morning on my skin."

"I've never heard the beat of that."

Homer asked Royce for the pistol, handed Royce his empty beer
bottle. "You're going to toss that bottle in the air, and I'm going to
hear the hum of wind through the mouth, and I'm going to blast
that bottle with one shot.

Royce stared at Homer. Was he serious?

"Are you with me?"

Royce didn't say a word. He just underhanded the bottle in an
arc that would land it in the old bathtub, and Homer fired, and the
bottle looked to Royce like the explosion of some coppery star.

Alvin Lee said, "Did you hear that?"

Miranda said it sounded like a gunshot or a backfire. Adlai said it
came from past the tracks.

Alvin Lee told Adlai about Royce gone missing.

Adlai said, "Shit, you don't think—"

Miranda said, "Let's go."

Royce looked across the yard at the brown Naugahyde La-Z-Boy recliner by the dilapidated porch, and he couldn't imagine what it was. Just bulk and color at first. Apparition without significance. And then the chair seemed to have a mouth low down in its curious head and a tall, comical-looking hat. He picked up the pistol Homer had laid on the bench. He realized he had never shot a pistol in his life. Not any kind of firearm. That seemed pathetic and irresponsible now. He put the gun barrel in his mouth. Tasted like Vaseline and vitamins. How hard can it be? His heart raced a mile a minute and he wondered was it frightened and trying to save itself or was it releasing the adrenaline that would help him squeeze the trigger? He kind of wished he could see the result of what he was about to do, but that would mean he hadn't done it.

Homer said, "You okay?"

Royce took the gun out of his mouth to answer. "Fine." He put the gun in his mouth and squeezed the trigger, heard the click.

"Mine was the last of the bullets, Royce."

"Shit."

"Why you want to kill yourself?"

"I'm a burden to Adlai and Benning. Oh, they'd be sad. They'd feel guilty. But they'd also be relieved."

"You ain't no burden."

"I don't even know who I am anymore."

"You be dead, we wouldn't be having this chat. You wouldn't be getting to know me. And I'm worth knowing."

Radley wheeled out of the house. "My whole life I got into trouble by not thinking. So I've commenced to think. I ain't Norman Einstein, but I'm getting there."

Homer cocked his head. "Someone's coming." He cupped his ear. "Three of them."

Radley said, "Royce, I believe your kin have come to fetch you."

When Adlai saw Royce, he yelled, "Daddy, are you all right?" and he ran ahead of the others. When he got to Royce, he knelt in front of him. "You okay then?"

Radley said, "That's your boy, Royce. Spit and image."

Alvin Lee arrived, nodded to Radley, said, "Hey!" to Homer. He said, "Royce, come on home now."

Talking in Bed

Well, then, just be better than you are, Boudou. Be
happy and be beautiful. And don't forget to be sad.

—EARLENE FONTANA

Duane and Ouida. Duane wanted to know did Ouida need to
wear the toilet paper turban. Yes, she did if she wanted to keep her
hairdo intact until the wedding. The pair of them were naked and
kneeling in prayer by the side of her canopied bed. Ouida closed her
eyes and moved her lips. Duane couldn't help it; he peeked at
Ouida's wonderfully voluptuous bottom. They hopped into bed, and
Duane asked Ouida did she feel bad about what they were doing
with each other, you know, fornicating and all, since she was such a
devout Christian woman. She certainly did not. How could something so natural be a sin? She said, "He knew that our time here
would be one of constant sorrow and strife, and so He gave us our
sexual conveniences to comfort and console us. He said, This is as
close to heaven as you're going to get for now, children."

"That's why He's our God," Duane said.

"He is truly good."

F*ather Pat and Mélia.* They have had this conversation before.

Father Pat sat at the edge of Mélia's bed in his cassock and slippers, his back to her, and tried to explain. He said, "The most highly developed of the flowers in our garden can only be obtained at the sacrifice of its fertility." But to whom was he trying to explain this? He thought he still believed that virginity was the higher calling. It was certainly the more burdensome.

Mélia lay under her sheet in a silk nightgown. She said, "Suppose, then, you're a flower, say you're a pasture rose, and I'm the worker bee who has just lighted in your silky petal—"

"Mélia, don't."

"I've come to fill my pollen basket, and there you are waving your pistol at me."

"Holy Mother the Church has her reasons, Mélia. Now, what if we were married, and I heard sins that day in confession, and I was troubled by them? Would I want to tell you what I had learned?"

"I would hope so."

Maybe if he *could* talk to someone about the atrocities that assaulted him in the confessional he could find some release from the horrors that held him awake at night.

Mélia said, "I won't always be around to tempt you."

Father Pat was not a machine. He often thought about the unspeakable pleasures of sex, and he was obsessively and uncomfortably curious about the riddle of copulation and about the intimacy of carnal engagement. And he did, too, care so much for Mélia, too much, and if he were ever to violate his vow of chastity, it would only, could only, be with her. And if he did succumb to his urgent and relentless lust, if he did fall from grace, then he would have to leave the priesthood, forsake the man he had been for thirty years. He would leave in shame and would marry Mélia to save his vile soul. And could he survive his regret if he did? He did not, he knew, have the ordained power to forgive his own sins.

Mélia said, "You'll miss me when I'm gone."

Father Pat heard the buzz of a fly, looked up at the lamp on the dresser. He watched the fly butt its shadow on the plaited paper shade.

Mélia said, "Resisting me will not make you a saint, Patrick McDermott. Loving me will not condemn you to hell."

Now the fly was hurling itself against its own reflection in the dresser mirror. And Father Pat could see the fly and himself and behind himself Mélia watching him. He saw her lift herself, squirm a bit, cross her arms, lift her nightgown over her head, and drop it to the floor. He saw in the flesh what he had never seen before.

R*oyce and Benning.* Benning said, "I woke you up because you just stopped breathing. Are you all right, sugar?"

Royce looked at his wife, touched her arm. "Yes."

She helped Royce settle back into sleep. She fluffed his pillow, kissed his forehead, tucked the sheet up under his arms, and lay on her back, staring up at the ceiling. As her eyes adjusted, she was able to make out a crack in the plaster that outlined the profile of a jowly man in a bowler hat.

Benning realized, not for the first time, of course, that she was losing her husband, and she felt leaden, chilled, immovable. And not just her husband, but her consummate friend and constant companion. In fifty-three years of marriage they had never spent the night apart, not even those nights the boys were born, not the desolate night that Rylan died. Royce had been Benning's anchor, her compass, her lighthouse, and now she felt she could drown in sorrow. Other loves may have been more spectacular than theirs, who's to say, but no other love, Benning was certain, could have been more steadfast or more devoted. Their love was a durable fire. And when it was finally doused, wretchedness would fill the rooms in her head like smoke. She would collapse in the cold ash.

Even worse would be if Royce were to leave her before he died. Benning did not think she could survive the knife of his not knowing, not recognizing her. She glanced at the serene mask of his sleeping face, took his hand in hers, and squeezed. He stirred, mumbled, and snorted, but did not wake.

Here at the end of their marvelous affair, Benning remembered seeing Royce for the first time. Remembered it clearly, the most indelible second of her life. She was at Cousin Lily Sudduth's house in Monroe for oysters and croquet. She stood in the living room admiring Cousin Lily's walnut hutch when she heard a stirring behind her and turned and saw him in his seersucker suit, collarless white shirt. He was carrying a mallet over his shoulder, a mallet with green stripes. What she remembered most was his thick brown hair, his sleepy blue eyes, his easy smile. He introduced himself, and she was sure he said *Roy Bartson*, so that later when Cousin Lily was complimenting that Birdsong fellow in conversation, Benning had no idea whom she was talking about. Right here in bed, fifty-seven years away from that afternoon in Monroe, Benning watched as Royce Birdsong took aim, swung his mallet, and sent Brewster Robertson's croquet ball into the goldfish pond. A brilliant stroke.

Royce opened his eyes. He squeezed Benning's hand. "Do you want to?"

Benning smiled. She said, "Yes, I do," and she turned to her husband and took his face in her hands.

Ariane and Grisham lay in bed, their foreheads touching so that when one spoke, the other felt the words shudder through her skull, so close that one's breath warmed the other's skin. Grisham told Ariane that all of his unwarranted doubts about her, about them, all of his petty resentments, all of his truculence and nettle, all of it had washed away in the moment he thought he had lost her. "I had never felt fear until then. It choked me. I hated myself for what I'd done to you, hated that I was even capable of such cruelty. I looked at what my life would be without you and all I saw was darkness."

Ariane said, "I needed to protect myself, let you know what you were losing, what I was capable of in my wretchedness. I couldn't live without you, Grisham."

Ariane turned away from Grisham, stared at the wall, and thought about Adlai. She saw his face, and saw him smile, and saw the dimple on his right cheek. How sweet he was to fall for her. How terrible she had behaved toward him. She owed him a debt. She felt Grisham turn, and she rolled over and spooned into his back.

Grisham thought about the first little girl he had ever liked. Sharon Someone. He probably never knew her second name. They were both five or six, living in the same subdivision. She was taller than he was. Sharon won all his baseball cards in a game of flip. Wiped him out. And then she offered to give them back, but he couldn't accept and went home to cry. And then Sharon's daddy took a job in the Texas oil patch, and she was gone.

Grisham remembered them all. Suzie, who didn't make a face when he asked her to dance; Lisette, whose green hair ribbon he still kept in a cigar box in his closet; Maris, who's married to a heroin addict; Randa, the astrologer (Scorpio); Frances, the dental hygienist; Lindy, the urban planning major; Mercedes, who ate only raw foods, studied art history, and went off to work for Greenpeace. If there was anything common among these women—and Ariane—he couldn't see it. What was it he was attracted to? And then he saw himself in Miranda's bed watching Miranda. Her short, gingery hair is disheveled. When she smiles you think she's talking to you.

Ariane said, "What are you thinking about?"

"Why people get married," Grisham said. He turned on his back.

They were quiet a moment, and then Grisham said, "Worst I ever heard of was this guy from Iota, I think it was—this is before my time. Bobby Walsh told me the story. The guy gets drafted into the Army in Vietnam, and his wife—I think they got married after he got the draft notice—his wife told him he had to go in and fight for his country or she'd divorce him. She wouldn't be married to a coward. So he enlisted. While he was over there getting shot at, she left him for a draft dodger."

Grisham slid his arm beneath Ariane's head. He squeezed her shoulder, said good-night. He thought about his parents, dead now these six years. Drowned in Bayou Lafourche in the middle of one hot July night. Grisham liked to think his momma was asleep in the passenger seat and that his daddy dozed off, and neither felt a thing as they eased off the road and slowly sank in the fifteen feet of water like babies being lowered into a crib.

A*lvin Lee and Lorraine.* Lorraine held the damp washcloth to her forehead, cleared her throat, and read her list of final boys' names: *Ezra, Josiah, Amos, Llywellyn, Obadiah, Micah, Dusty.* Alvin Lee considered. Nothing sang to him. He read his finalists: *Brick, Cal, Elvis, Zeke, D'Artagnan, Shane, Reece, Hopalong.* Lorraine rolled her eyes. She said she was sure they were having a girl anyway, and she read those names: *Grace, Ruth, Tanner, Cherish, Tourmaline, Kylie, Tangerine, Zipporah.* Alvin Lee read his: *Daley, Sparkle, Rayanne, Kit, Silk, Skylar, Dixie.*

Lorraine said, "*Sparkle?*"

"No *Sparkle*, no *Tangerine.*"

"*Rayanne* sounds like synthetic fabric."

"We could take the first name from one list, the middle name from the other."

"*Llywellyn D'Artagnan?*"

Lorraine kissed Alvin Lee on the nose, touched his lips with her finger. She adjusted her unwieldy body as best she could. "The baby's kicking." Lorraine took Alvin Lee's hand and placed it on her belly.

Alvin Lee felt the baby turn, saw the swell where its foot pressed against the edge of its world. Alvin Lee kissed the spot. Lorraine shut her eyes, Alvin Lee cut the light. When he thought of the baby's future, he thought of his own, the one he needed to launch just as soon as the wedding was over. He didn't ever want to work in a nursing home again. His old friend Harley Davidson would hire him to work at his plastics plant in Lincoln Parish. But what kind of life was it, making those little table deals that keep the pizza box from squashing the pizza? Maybe he could congregate another flock of needy Christians, start up another church. He had the calling, the talent. But he no longer had the will. The whole idea of church was disagreeable to him now. Maybe religion was becoming a substitute for a spiritual life. Alvin Lee sat up. He should write this down. Religion . . . no, faith . . . no, your relationship to God ought to be personal, secluded, and ought to aspire to ecstasy. It ought to lift you out of yourself. At least that. Get your mind off real estate; set your feet on higher ground.

Alvin Lee was wide awake now. He was on to something, he just knew it. He'd think some more, think harder, think longer, follow the trail of thoughts wherever it led him. He found a pencil and a box of envelopes in the nightstand drawer. He sat by the window and took notes in the moonlight. He noticed for the first time in his life that the leaves on a magnolia are not always green. Like right now they were gray. And the flowers were creamy. Sometimes you look, but you don't see, or you see, but you don't get the picture.

He said, "Llwellyn D'Artagnan Loudermilk." He said, "Tangerine Sparkle Loudermilk," and said it like a prayer.

M*iranda* sat on her bed, staring out the window at the clear night sky. She used her melted vanilla ice cream like ketchup, as a dip for her french fries. She put her bowl on the floor beside the bed and stretched out. So quiet here, not like back at the trailer park. Dogs barking all night. People wailing and screaming at all hours. Children dying mysteriously. Pythons getting free. Fires and molestations. She didn't want to think about all that. But there was one more thought and it was Grisham that son of a bitch, hardly saying goodbye the other night, turning her into a cliché, the other woman. And then she thought how Adlai didn't know of her connection to Grisham. Maybe she'd tell him someday. Now, why did she say that—she and Adlai and a mutual future? Miranda longed to live in solitude with someone she loved. If she were with that someone now, she thought, he would know the constellations and the stories of how they came to be named, and he would tell her. *Once upon a time*, he would say . . .

Adlai. He opened his eyes, thought about Royce, and Royce's health, and getting Royce ready for the festivities, and then he began to make a list of everything he had to do to get the house ready for guests, and by the time he got to *weed the flower bed*, he was wide awake, and considered getting up and getting at it, but he didn't want to wake the house. Here in the bosom of his family he felt lonely.

Earlene and Boudou. Boudou knocked, opened the door, and peeked in. He said he couldn't sleep. Earlene put down her book and told him to hop in under the covers. He said he was sad because this afternoon when Adlai and Miranda brought Royce into the house, he ran to him and hugged him. Royce stood there, didn't say dot. "I took his hand. He pulled it away."

Boudou told Earlene he felt fatherless all over again, which was stupid because Royce was *a* father, not *his* father. It felt like what Radley Smallpiece called phantom pain. His legs aren't there, but he can feel them. Sometimes they itch, sometimes they throb, sometimes they cramp, and sometimes it's like someone's got this billhook buried halfway through your knee. "My daddy's missing, and it hurts like an ulcer in your mouth, only it's in your heart or your brain or whatever it is that hopes."

Earlene hugged her boy. "Royce's pain is he's losing himself. When he looks at you and he can't quite remember your name, it makes him sad. Because he would do anything before he hurt your feelings."

"You think he wants to die?"

"Nobody wants to die."

"But maybe life isn't the best deal for everyone. What if you hurt so much you can't even think? What if you can't eat or sleep or be touched or anything?"

"That's a hard question, Boudou."

"Like if I was in pain, and I couldn't do anything about it, if I couldn't even move to kill myself, that would make me want to die, even if I wouldn't choose to."

"Well, sugar, I won't let anything like that happen to you."

R*adley and Homer.* Radley wrapped his stumps in warm towels, laid a heating pad over them. He exercised the limbs that were not there. He said, "I just don't think it's safe for a blind man to smoke in bed."

Homer flicked his ashes toward the ashtray on his belly. "Ain't burned the house down till yet."

Radley shook his head. He tightened the muscles in the stump, then released them slowly. "Homer, what do you think when I say *face?*"

"Where the voice comes from."

"I look at a man's face, I can tell you all about him. What he's feeling, what he's thinking. Character is written at the face—in the lines, in the light of the eyes, the set of the brow." Radley took off the pad, the towels, put shrinker socks on his stumps. Homer extinguished his cigarette in the ashtray, put the ashtray on the floor beside the bed.

T*ous-les-deux.* Kate wondered what it must be like to sleep on your side or on your belly. It had been her idea that one of them should fall asleep early and the other sleep late, so that both would have an hour of private time. That way one could think without disturbing the other. Some nights Kate tried to imagine herself apart from Alice, but she would feel too guilty to hold the image in her mind.

She brushed Alice's hair off her own chin. Alice moaned. The wedding. Kate saw herself at the reception in the yard at Paradise. She's talking to Boudou, and she tells Boudou how she wants to be a doctor when she grows up, a surgeon. And all of a sudden, as she's talking, she feels a profound emptiness at her left—not empty like space, but empty like there's not even space, and the emptiness is pushing her into its void. She whispered, "Alice?" She thought how her whole life was a compromise—every step she took in any direction was a mutual decision. Kate knew there would be no romance without Alice's cooperation, but Alice refused to even talk about boys anymore. Kate wished she could get out of bed, walk to the lake, wait for Boudou to meet her there. She kissed her sister on the cheek, wrapped her arm across Alice's chest.

Now You Will Feel No Rain

Rapture is the best medicine.
—DURWOOD TULLIVER

A. Happy Is the Bride the Sun Shines On. Adlai turned off the radio when Durwood Tulliver started in on *Can two walk together, unless they are agreed?* He made spoonbread, shirred eggs, and sausages. Grisham and Duane ate and ran. They'd been relegated to the boathouse by Jolene Thevenot, Maid of Honor, who evidently was a nuptial traditionalist and a believer in the taboo against the groom's seeing the bride before the ceremony. Jolene had chosen to stay in town at the Dreamland Motel, and walked over this morning at seven. Alvin Lee told Father Pat how he understood sin, was intimate with depravity, and people could sense that about him, and so they trusted him. Alvin Lee said he was one time bit by a rattlesnake named Azazel at a worship service, bit in the neck, and his feet commenced to go out from under him; he lost control of his body, would jerk every once in a while and in every which way. He couldn't tolerate the sound vibrations from a whispered voice or the blinding light of a candle.

Father Pat bowed his head, thanked the good Lord—and Adlai—for the delicious food at our table and for the resplendent day. Alvin Lee *amen*ed. Boudou helped Royce on with his bib. Adlai served the food and sat. Father Pat said what a lovely day for a wedding. Our Lord is truly shining down on us today. He had expected to feel guilty and ashamed for what he had done last night with Mélia. What he felt instead was exhilaration, what he felt was fellowship with every single man and woman privy to the glorious open secret of sex, what he felt was regret that he hadn't done this long ago. What he and Mélia did was no sin. Abstinence, unnatural and perverse abstinence, that was the sin. Soul and body are one. He would perform the marriage ceremony today. Tomorrow, he and Mélia would return to Lafayette. On Monday, he'd hand in his resignation to the bishop. He'd have to serve the Lord in some other way. But what on earth would he do to earn a living? He'd think of something. He had opened his heart and let the world in. That's how he felt.

Adlai said, "You look like you swallowed the canary, Father."

Father Pat blushed. Adlai felt a pang of jealousy. He guessed Father Pat's secret. How old would he be finally when this cramp in his heart would relax with bliss? Not so old as Father Pat, he hoped. He did not have the consolation of God to keep him occupied. He thought of Ariane this afternoon, about to recite her vows, and Father Pat asks does anyone object to this union, speak now or forever hold your peace, and to everyone's shock a woman stands and tells Grisham—and the world—that she is having his child. And Adlai imagined consoling Ariane. And then he thought, This is pitiful.

Alvin Lee said, "Adlai, are you listening to me?"

"Sorry."

"I said, what about the music?"

"We've got a band called Red Wheelbarrow, and Dolphus's bringing a stereo, a CD/tape thing."

Jolene peeked her head into the kitchen. She said did anyone have a silver dollar or some special coin—a Kennedy half maybe. For Ariane's shoe. They didn't, but Boudou remembered the Confederate coin in Royce's memory sack. Royce told him, you fetch it then. He told Jolene, You tell Ariane it's hers to keep. Guaranteed to bring her money and children. Father Pat cleaned his teeth with the blade of a Swiss Army knife.

B. Music Hath a Far More Pleasing Sound.   Red Wheelbarrow began Mozart's adagio from Sonata in E-flat. Grisham and Duane joined Father Pat up front. They all shook hands. Boudou gave the rings to Duane. He noticed his mom and Dolphus smiling, whispering. Earlene motioned for Boudou to stand up straight. Adlai stood behind the rows of chairs and fussed with the flower arrangements on the serving tables. Grisham wondered what would have happened had he not gone after Ariane, had not thrown himself at her feet. Where would he be this morning? Where would all the others be? He remembered his panic at reading the note, his overwrought behavior. He was not ordinarily given to melodrama . Ariane wanted him so badly that she had forgiven him his indiscretion. Or had she? Overlooked it, at least. Yes, she still did have that bullet to fire, he supposed. He saw an angel bird lift off a cypress limb and glide out over the lake. He'd be halfway to Gatlinburg with Miranda is what. No sense letting luxury lodgings go wanting. Leave a note saying he'd explain everything when he got back. Why am I thinking like this? Pull yourself together, Grisham. Focus.

The music stopped. Ariane appeared in the doorway flanked by Jolene and Mélia. She wore an ivory A-line, floor-length gown with a sleeveless bodice and a chiffon drape across the back. Jolene and Mélia wore green and blue versions of the gown, but without the drapes. Ouida stood beside them with brush and hair spray. She scrutinized the three of them, feathered Ariane's bangs, adjusted the beaded crown of her veil. She pouffed up Jolene's hair a bit, spritzed it, checked the tension of the wave with her hand. She told Mr. Lenny Stranieri he could take his photos now.

Red Wheelbarrow played the wedding march from *Lohengrin*,

and the three women made their way across the lawn. Miranda saw Adlai duck into the house. Ariane squinted in the sun. She hoped the light didn't make her sneeze into her veil.

Grisham watched Ariane approach and saw Miranda sitting in the back row, and noticed, too, that she had seen him notice her. His eyes darted from her glance. What in pluperfect hell was she doing here giving him the bad eye? Come here to bless him out at his own wedding? Or worse? This wasn't right. Ariane joined Grisham. He took her hand, smiled, squeezed. They turned to face Father Pat.

Boudou returned to his seat. Benning patted his shoulder. She remembered her own wedding day, how it poured rain all day and all night, how she never got to take the photos by the magnolia in the yard. Memory ought to be kinder than this, ought to account for a sense of long time passing. She looked at Royce. Royce looked up into the trees, trees like he'd never seen before, leaves not just green, but blue and white and gold and waving in the breeze. Benning thought how time's a thief and a deceiver.

Father Pat asked the bride and groom to join hands and face each other. He said, "Dear Father, Bless these hands You see before You this day. May they always be held by one another. Give them the strength to hold on during the storms and stress and the dark of disillusionment. Keep them tender and gentle as they nurture each other in their love.

"Help these hands to continue building a relationship founded in Your grace, rich in caring, and devoted to reaching for Your perfection.

"May Ariane and Grisham see their four hands as healer, protector, shelter, and guide.

"We ask this in the name of Our Lord and Savior, Jesus Christ, who lives and reigns with you now and forever. Amen."

Adlai leaned back against the kitchen sink and looked out the French doors to the yard. No one, he realized, was about to object to this marriage. Father Pat was not even going to give anyone the opportunity to do so. The guests seemed rapt in the ceremony, except for Miranda, who was looking at him. She gave a little wave. He waved back. He heard Grisham say, "All that I am and all that I have, I offer to you, Ariane, in love and in happiness, I, Grisham Loudermilk, take you, Ariane Thevenot, to be my wife from this day forward. I will love and comfort you, hold you close, prize you above all others, and remain faithful to you all the days of our lives."

And Ariane may have said something similar, but Adlai didn't hear it. For some reason he thought of Anniece Pate, about the first time he saw her. He was standing at the corner of Choudrant and Grambling by the First Baptist Church, when she walked by him in a yellow slicker. It wasn't raining. She was alone; she was carrying library books; she was whistling.

Father Pat finished the ceremony with a blessing and with the Apache Wedding Prayer: "Now you will feel no rain, for each of you will be shelter to the other. Now you will feel no cold, for each of you will be warmth to the other. Now you are two bodies, but there is only one life before you. Go now to your dwelling place to enter into the days of your togetherness, and may your days be good and long upon the earth."

Red Wheelbarrow struck up the allegro from the Brandenburg Concerto No. 4 in G, and the guests broke into applause. Ouida told Mélia she was just memorized by the service, so beautiful, so moving. Purvis asked Delano was he okay. Delano maybe looked like he'd swallowed some nasty medicine, but really, he'd just had a glimpse into a tragic future.

In the kitchen, Miranda approached Adlai. She smiled. "I'm here to help with the food. What do I do?"

C. What Will Survive of Us Is Love.   Adlai told Miranda the food here was just for this little reception. The shivaree's tonight. Most folks will probably go home for a nap, rest up, then come back about day down, and we'll start eating and drinking and whatnot, and then by dark-thirty, the revels really begin. Grisham and Ariane will be in the boathouse, and we'll keep them up until they join us. Miranda said she'd stay this afternoon and help set up. Clean up, decorate, whatever. That's sweet, Adlai said. Thank you.

. . .

When Red Wheelbarrow took a break, Boudou loaded his CDs into the player: Rancid, Bad Religion, Cramps, Green Day, Ween. He pressed *Shuffle* and waited for people to dance. Earlene asked could he turn it down a tad. Jolene blocked her ears. A song about a time bomb? At a wedding? Mélia walked to the table to ask Boudou could he play something more matrimonial, more sedate if he could, but a strange thing happened. The Engrams, all six of them, Kit and Razzie, and the four children, Cody, Jane, Belle, and little Bill, got up from their seats and began to dance like dervishes. As we mentioned, every single Engram for one hundred years has been stone deaf, a condition brought on, some of our fundamentalists believe, by Cassidy Engram's refusal to stop listening to the devil's music. Boudou and Purvis clapped their hands to the beat, which the Engrams in their flamboyant, gangly, brow-furrowed way were somehow dancing to, and each one of them was smiling up a storm, using their bodies to sing, to raise a joyful silence unto the Lord. Macky Ptak did the bump with Pug Wolfe, and she did not spill a single drop of bourbon. Jolene wandered over to the only single man she'd noticed, a bit old for her, but cute, and introduced herself. He said his name was Parnell Broadway. He told her he came from Hot Springs, Arkansas. Arkansas? Yes. Well, do you know a Walter Romano? He'd be about thirty, I'd say. Dated my sister Queenie. Dark hair, but maybe he's bald by now. Could be. Some folks as call him Snitz. Snitz Romano. Parnell said he didn't know any Snitz, said he was living here in Shiver these days.

Ariane, needing to use the bathroom, walked into the house. She saw Adlai washing dishes, his back to her, Miranda drying. How cozy. She shouldn't have, but she felt jealous. She somehow felt that Adlai belonged to her, or at least his attentions did. She didn't want his love, but she did want his notice and regard. She kept walking—only slowly, quietly, tiptoeingly—and she heard Adlai tell Miranda that he didn't like small talk. Ariane thought, Well, there's an arrogance she'd never detected. And where was he at the reception line earlier? Didn't kiss the bride, congratulate the groom. Where were his manners?

With Red Wheelbarrow playing again, Boudou got a chance to dance with Tous-les-deux. Earlene watched him. His first dance without her as a partner, and he was doing quite well.

Kate said, "So, Boudou, when are you leaving?"

"Maybe Monday."

"And will you ever come back to Shiver-de-Freeze?"

Boudou shrugged, watched his feet, tried to glide into a turn, but Kate and Alice just stopped. He said, "I'll ask my mom."

Alice said, "You could ride your bike. Monroe's not that far."

Tous-les-deux let go of Boudou's hands, stepped back from him. Kate said, "I told you he didn't like us."

Kate cried. Alice hugged her, then she cried. And then they turned and ran past the other dancers and out of the yard. Boudou said, "What did I do?" Only no one heard him.

Red Wheelbarrow announced the final song and asked the bride and groom to begin the dance. The song was Ariane's request—"Sentimental Journey"—her daddy's favorite song. Ouida leaned her head on Duane's chest and cried. Mélia asked Father Pat if he was going to change his mind. He said of course not. She said, Let's dance. Father Pat hesitated. He said, I don't want to scandalize folks. I should tell them, tell everyone I'm leaving the priesthood for you. Mélia said, Yes, but this isn't the time. Even Benning and Royce got up to dance, though Royce seemed perplexed. The band played on. Ted Muto told the twins how there are these cleaner fish that live in groups of one male and a half dozen lady fish, and if the male dies, the most dominant female changes into a male in a matter of days. Sandy asked him what he was driving at.

Miranda and Adlai sat at the kitchen table. Adlai refilled their cups of coffee, pushed the sugar bowl toward Miranda. "I don't go to work. I run the house. Cook, garden. Plants all over the house. I pay the bills, collect the rents, like that."

Adlai took a strawberry from the bowl of fruit, ate it, wiped his fingers on a napkin.

Miranda said, "I believe in traveling, moving. I love meeting new people, talking to them, getting the feel of a new place."

"And you travel alone?"

"Better alone than not at all."

Adlai and Miranda listened to the shouts and shuffles of people going.

"I'll walk you to your trailer."

"I'm staying. We got work to do."

Epithalamium

I love you once, I love you twice,
I love you next to beans and rice.

—TRADITIONAL LOUISIANA LOVE SONG

Alvin Lee stood by the barbecue pit cooking up the last of the three-and-down ribs over a hickory fire and feeling panicked for the first time in his waking life. Of course, he's been panicked plenty in his dreams, like he's supposed to be preaching at the First Church of the Last Chance in Luna, but he can't find the church; or his teeth fall out or his privates lose their purchase on his body, the putty or wax or whatever it is that holds them in place softens, and the whole unit oozes out of position, slips, droops, then thumps to the floor; or he's in hell, and it's even worse than you or Dante had imagined—the fire they all talk about, that's inside, and hell is the grave they put you in, dark, dank, vermin-infested, foul-smelling, and all you want to do is turn over, but you can't—all that earth is crushing down on your face and chest and suffocating you, and you can't even brush the worms from your eyes.

Lorraine sat nearby drinking iced tea, talking to Duane and Ouida. Duane's got his whole life sussed out, Alvin Lee thought. He's what—twenty-five?—and he already knows that in two years he'll move up from real estate sales to managing his daddy's realty office, and eventually he'll own Daddy's business, and he'll use it as a springboard to his dream job, the one-word oxymoron—Developer. He'll have the grand home in Lafayette, of course, a holiday cabin on Lake Pontchartrain, and a townhouse in the French Quarter. And all this prosperity talk has swept Ouida off her tiny feet. Duane's going to set her up with her own beauty shop. Three chairs, manicure station, the works. He said, You could call it Age of Aquarius, but Ouida said she wanted to serve ladies and straight men, too. And here I am, Alvin Lee thought, just to the soft side of forty, and I still have no idea what I'm going to be when I grow up. It's pathetic. He turned the ribs over, basted them with sauce, put the paintbrush in the bowl, took another swig of bourbon. He caught Lorraine's eye, threw her a kiss. She touched her belly and smiled.

Alvin Lee couldn't think of a thing he was any damned good at except preaching. Maybe he'd be good at sales—that's all preaching comes down to. But to be any decent kind of salesman, he'd have to believe in his product, and Alvin Lee couldn't think of one. If a product is any good, it sells itself. If it's not any good, then a salesman's a falsifier. Might need to head for the big city. Bound to be more opportunity in Monroe. He remembered a matchbook he'd seen at the Black & Lovely, advertising for job training in tractor-trailer driving, locksmith, computer repair, vending machines, refrigeration, things like that. Of course, it's sad, isn't it, looking for your career on a matchcover. Must have an aptitude for something. Of course, it could be an aptitude for something that makes no economic sense, like an aptitude for finding four-leaf clovers or for recognizing birdcalls or for looking at paintings.

If someone were to ask him right now to pick the one job he'd have for the rest of his life—the perfect job—Alvin Lee would say disc jockey. Late night disc jockey, but only if he got to play the music he liked: Five Blind Boys of Alabama, Dixie Hummingbirds, the Soul Stirrers, Bo-Weevil Jackson, Jaybird Coleman, Blind Willie Johnson.

Kate and Alice marched right up to Boudou while he was eating a particularly sharp-edged peach compote and sat beside him and said he had to promise to visit them once a month, at least, and they'd already talked with Earlene about it, and she said that she thought she and Boudou would be spending more time at Paradise than they have in the past, so there's no excuse. And we'll come to see you in Monroe and we'll all go to the movies. How about that?

Jolene joined Earlene and Dolphus, asked them if they'd tried this wonderful buttermilk-sky pie. They hadn't. She fed Dolphus a spoonful. Earlene passed. Jolene asked where Parnell was. Earlene said he's on a house call. Should be back soon. Dolphus and I were talking about tamales and how good they are in the Delta. Jolene said, Have you ever stuffed tamales with crawfish tails? Earlene noticed the Great Books people setting up a stage by the boathouse. Shivaree's about to start, she said. Jolene said she could stay 'cause Parnell was driving her to Lafayette in the morning.

Grisham and Ariane stood on the stage—a few pallets covered with a plywood floor—and thanked their guests, said they were retiring now to their honeymoon cottage, stepped off the stage, and walked into the boathouse. They closed the door. People cheered. Adlai switched on the white bridal lights that he and Alvin Lee had garlanded the boathouse with.

Royce didn't know what on earth all this commotion was about, but he didn't want to ask. He was tired of asking. He was sick to death with all this confusion in his life and in his brain. Benning squeezed his hand, leaned her head onto his shoulder. Royce figured the source of his turmoil was probably something simple, something reparable. So Royce tried not to think about the man onstage or Adlai with his violin or all these laughing people.

Shug Johnson stood alone onstage and cleared his throat. Adlai and Boudou passed out candles to everyone. Shug unrolled a scroll and read. With apologies to Catullus he said:

And now, Rosy-crowned Hymen,
Join us to witness this marriage
Of Evangeline Bellefontaine
To Gabriel Lajeunesse,
And ask the blessing of your
Azure-robed mother, the Queen
Of Beauty and Generation,
Join us, Urania's son, in our
Celebration, in our joy,
As we raise our voices in song . . .

At which point Earlene and Adlai took the stage. Adlai played his violin, Earlene sang, "In Our Boathouse."* And the performance began:

EVANGELINE, AS PERFORMED BY THE MECHANICALS OF SHIVER-DE-FREEZE

Enter Shug, carrying scripts, Royal Landry, Chiquita Deal, Cicero Wittlief, and Boudou.

    Shug: Is all our company here?

    Cicero: What play do we perform, good Shug?

    Shug: Marry, our play is that most romantic comedy of the marriage of Evangeline and Gabriel.

    Chiquita: (incredulous) But, kind sir, verily, such tale is a most tragic one. The lovers, pray, do not reunite until the dying Gabriel's last breath.

    Shug: This Longfellow had it wrong. What miserable manner of story would that make? Tell me. Star-crossed lovers who never meet, who—

Shug hesitates, covers Boudou's ears.

    Shug: —who never consummate their love, exploit their passion? Whose lives are ruined by a chance passing in the night? Consider that our revised interlude is meant to please our bride and groom on their wedding night, not depress them.

Shug steps upstage to the boathouse window. He listens. He mimes lifting the curtain, peers inside, is clearly embarrassed.

Shug: And they are clearly not yet depressed.

Royal: What part am I for?

Shug: Royal, the salesman, you are set down for Gabriel Lajeunesse.

Shug hands Royal a script. Royal leafs through the pages.

Royal: What is Gabriel? Lover? Or Loser?

Shug: Lover most gallant and noble, with countenance thoughtful and careworn.

Royal: Noble lover. I shall need a sword, then, of good measure. A pistol, at least.

Royal hitches his pants, steps downstage, and delivers:

> *In the sweet hereof,*
> *My light o' love,*
> *Dear lady-dove,*
> *I've searched all over.*
> *I've sailed by ship,*
> *And trudged a clip,*
> *A mighty long trip*
> *From Scotia Nova.*

Shug: Enough, my Royal flush! *The sweet hereof?* Chiquita Deal, the waitress.

Chiquita: Here, Shug the Johnson.

He hands her the script as Royal admires his lover-to-be, his comely costar.

Royal: Proceed.

Shug: Cicero, the certified public accountant, for you the part of Loup Garoup. Boudou, you play the Island.

Shug hands them scripts.

Boudou: I lie in water?

Shug: More precisely, a screen of palmettos on the island. Now go and learn your parts. We will meet back here anon. Take pains. Be perfect.

All except Shug exit stage.

Shug: And you, too, gentle audience, have your role to play. When you see fair Evangeline searching for her beloved Gabriel and cursing the darkness, then light your candles and hold them aloft. And when you spy Loup Garoup come from behind the palmetto screen, bang your pots and pans as loudly as you can to alert Evangeline and frighten the werewolf.

And while Shug the Chorus summarized the story thus far, the British-enforced exile from the homeland, which separated families and lovers, the arduous journeys to Louisiana, etc., etc., and while Macky Ptak dressed Boudou as a tree, and while Adlai and Miranda distributed cookware drums and utensils to beat them with, and bells and whistles, and horns and matches, Ariane and Grisham sat inside the honeymoon boathouse celebrating their wedding with Veuve Cliquot Ponsardin Brut, the taste of which neither of them really liked.

Ariane said, "This is depressing."

"What is?"

She handed Grisham the Polaroid photo of herself that Lenny Stranieri had taken this morning. "Do I really look like that?"

Grisham told Ariane how the usual way we see ourselves is by reflection—in a mirror or a store window, the rearview mirror, like that, in which our unsymmetrical faces are reversed. Your left is really your right—but it's the only idea you have of yourself, and that "ideal" self is upset by a photographic image, which is a true image, which is what everyone else sees.

"And that's supposed to make me happy?"

"Sounds like they're having a good time out there."

"You look forward to this day your whole life. If you're a girl you do. And then it comes, and you know it can never come again. It's over in a flash."

Boudou took his place onstage. He stood stiffly at center stage facing the audience. Palmetto fronds were tied to his shoulders and

Spanish moss hung from his outstretched arms. Earlene motioned for him to stand up straight like a proud young tree. Macky lifted an office chair on wheels onto the stage. The crowd hushed.

Shug enters.

> Shug: We beseech thee, Venus Urania
> Goddess of love, queen of laughter,
> Mistress of graces and pleasure,
> Venus, sprung from the froth of the sea,
> Guide your virgin Evangeline
> To her beloved Gabriel.
> Fire her heart, girdle her loins
> With Beauty, Charm, and Elegance.
> Excite her love and her passion.
> Come on your swan-driven chariot,
> Bless this couple as you have blessed
> Pyramis and Thisbee,
> Romeo and Juliet,
> Odysseus and Penelope.

Shug bows, stands on stage uncomfortably. He turns to the cast, offstage, and whispers:

> Shug: Actors, your cue. Odysseus and Penelope!

Cicero leaps onstage, crouches behind Boudou the tree. Chiquita takes a seat on the chair and begins to row herself across stage with a broom/paddle.

> Shug: Every stroke of the paddle brought bereft Evangeline nearer and nearer to her love. And an angel of God there was that guided her to this one island among the thousands.
> Chiquita: I'll stop here. I feel that my love is nearby. I feel a chill I cannot warm.

She steps off the boat and onto shore. Shug removes the boat.

> Chiquita: Gabriel! Gabriel! Oh, curse the darkness!
> Shug: *(to audience)* Light your torches! Hold them aloft! Let them blaze!
> Chiquita: *(looking up)* Ah, Moon, sweet Moon, I thank thee for thy sunny beams. Gabriel, is that you?

Cicero growls.

    Chiquita: Oh, Gabriel, come closer that I might behold thy
        splendid semblance.
Cicero creeps closer to Boudou.
    Chiquita: Why, Gabriel, what big eyes you have!
Cicero growls.
    Chiquita: What big ears you have!
Cicero growls.
    Chiquita: What big teeth you have!
Cicero growls and leaps out at Chiquita.
    Chiquita: Loup Garoup! Help!
Cicero chases Chiquita around and around the tree as Shug leads the audi-ence in noise-making. Cicero stops, stands, holds his ears against the din. Chiquita keeps running around the tree, passing him once, twice. On her third pass, Cicero, the Loup Garoup, grabs her. She screams just as Royal, in coonskin cap, bounds onto the stage wielding a spatula, his axe.
    Royal: Unpaw that beauty, you beast!
Cicero drops Chiquita, who collapses to the floor. Royal chases him from the stage. Royal then kneels beside the fallen Chiquita, lifts her head.
    Royal: What dreadful dole is here!
               Evangeline!
               My Valentine!
               Alas, thy death I fear.
Overcome with grief, he drops her head. He stands, addresses the audience. As he speaks, Boudou shakes Chiquita awake and makes her aware of her beloved's presence.
    Royal: Oh, wherefore, Nature, didst thou wolves frame?
               Since Loup Garoup hath here deflowered my dame.
               So near, yet thou canst not behold me.
               So near, yet my voice canst not reach her.
He sobs.
    Chiquita: Gabriel, rejoice! Thy love is not lost.
She indicates a stain on her blouse.
    Chiquita: Here's not blood, but barbecue sauce!
Royal rushes to Chiquita. They embrace. Kiss. Boudou the tree closes his eyes.
    Royal: Come, honey, do!

        We can elope!

Chiquita: Such my fruited hope!

        Adieu! Adieu! Adieu!

They exit arm in arm. Shug walks downstage center.

Shug: And so our tale is ended

        But not our revelry.

He turns to Boudou.

Shug: Take a bough, Good Tree,

        No pun intended.

Boudou bows. They exit.

Later, Grisham joined the revelers, but Ariane did not. She was dead for sleep, Grisham explained. Adlai knew that he would not have left Ariane to sit or lie in bed alone, not on her wedding night, not on any night. Grisham sat with Earlene and Dolphus. Boudou and Tous-les-deux had the guests up and dancing. They played Boozoo Chavis, Camray Fontenot, Clifton Chenier, and Beausoleil. Macky danced with Underwood. They discussed their common ex, Ruthanne—she thinks she's got the curse of turning straight men gay, and who could blame her?—about their own bygone romance, and neither could now recall why they'd broken up. Underwood tried to explain the difference between Cajun music and zydeco. He started with Amedee Ardoin, the king of diatonic blues, but Macky was not listening. Macky said, "Belvedere martinis? My place?" Underwood said, "Let me find my shoes."

Miranda danced with Kebo Haley, who had arrived in time for the Evangeline sketch. She danced with Adlai, who apologized for his clumsiness, his stiffness, his lack of rhythm. Miranda told him she could have him waltzing like Fred Astaire in a week. She danced with Delano, who asked her what color she would call Benning's gloves. She danced with Purvis, who barely moved his body to the beat and whose every move was understated and eloquent. And Grisham watched Miranda dance, was thankful Ariane had never seen her face.

Dolphus ate the sweet potato pie Earlene had saved him and a bit of the rice salad. Earlene waved good-night to Lorraine and Alvin Lee, who were heading to bed. She told Boudou it was maybe time to turn down the music and start thinking about bedtime himself.

Delano told Miranda he was going back to the Black & Lovely to finish his painting. She said, You paint every day, do you? He said, I tried to quit. I couldn't. She said, What do you think a painting should be? He said, Evidence.

When Adlai came back from helping Benning with Royce, most everyone was gone. Kebo was cleaning up. Grisham was asleep, his head on a table. Adlai shook him awake. Grisham looked confused. He said, "Where is she?"

"In the boathouse, where you ought to be."

"Miranda."

"She left with Delano."

When Grisham went off to bed, Adlai sat with Kebo, told him he was holding up fine, considering. He told Kebo to take Grisham's room in Paradise, said, "You go on to bed, I'll clean up here."

"I'm not tired. Had an easy day. Fixed the exhaust system in Tyler's Gremlin, closed up early. Funny thing," he said. "I stopped at the Pecanland Mall in Monroe to get a wedding gift. Went into Bath & Body Works, and this young lady lectured me just out of nowhere on the varieties of massage products. I bought one of each. She intimidated me, and she was only like eighteen. At the desk I was paying and she tells me to rub this lotion in my hands. Alpine Summit. She said, "I like to rub it in my hands during the day. Smells like men.""

"You bought some."

"Yes, indeed." He held up his hands for Adlai to sniff.

In Dreams

In dreams I am well and in a pleasant place.

—PURVIS CHENIERE

Father Pat strolls through a cavernous church, his hands buried in his pockets. He's wearing cleats on his wingtips. He looks up, sees daylight shaft through the clerestory windows. Smells the lingering incense of a recent Requiem Mass. Funeral incense has that pine-and-honey fragrance, like a paschal candle. He's thinking about Cain and why his chaff of wheat was rejected by God. For no good reason, as far as he could tell. Not that God has to explain Himself, but not to do so seems unduly stubborn. After all, He did provoke a good deal of nastiness with His disregard. Father Pat stops near the sacristy by a stained-glass depiction of St. Catherine, Virgin and Martyr, tied to a spiked wheel, milk flowing from her wounds. He is seized with apprehension. He knows enough to look outside. He opens the door, sees a column of flying saucers hovering over the city, and it's like they were waiting for his appearance to begin their siege. The UFOs attack, exploding buildings, incinerating trees. Father Pat slams the door, takes Mélia's hand, and they run past the high altar and the choir screen to the Lady Chapel, where he feels they'll be safe. The saucers release smaller saucers—the size of dinner plates. Father Pat knows this but doesn't know how he knows. It's like he's here with Mélia, but he also has eyes in the sky. And then he realizes he and Mélia aren't in the sanctuary of the church at all, but in an empty office on the tenth floor of a downtown building. The UFOs—they're even smaller now, the size of drink coasters and silver dollars—soar through the open window and strike at him and Mélia, and when the saucers hit the body, they open vicious paper cuts. Father Pat heroically manages to close and lock the window, and for a second he and Mélia are safe. But the UFOs are so thin that they squeeze between the sill and the window frame, and in seconds a horde of them blizzard the room. Father Pat swats at them, beats them off with a broom, but they are legion, are relentless, are razor-sharp. Mélia has ceased her screaming, is unconscious and awash in wine-dark blood. Father Pat drops to the floor, spent. He takes a fallen UFO in his hand. It feels like linen. He examines it, sees to his horror the monogram *IHS* stamped onto its fuselage, and knows that he and Mélia have been slaughtered by a host of Communion wafers, by the unleavened bodies of Christ.

Duane sees Ouida holding a scroll. They are on their honeymoon, on a bus in the jungle. Ouida's hair has curled in the humidity. Duane sees Ariane sitting toward the front and Grisham, wearing a Smoky Bear hat, driving the bus. Everyone on the bus knows that there is a reticulated python loose under the seats. Duane asks Ouida what the scroll's all about. She says it's her Emasculation Proclamation.

Royce has a holographic camera set up to work with the headboard in the bed. The way it operates is you have this clear, quilted

plastic draped over the headboard, and when you touch it, it acti-
vates the camera mounted on the wall opposite, and your three-
dimensional image is frozen in that position on the bed itself and in
the air above it. The space is the printing medium. It's quite a
remarkable invention. Benning says, It's like photo-sculpture. Royce
says, Smile, and reaches for the headboard.

Adlai's on the front porch of a log house out West, and he's
drinking the local beverage made from mulled wine and bouillon
cubes. He thinks it's called mullion, but it's not. Miranda, who's sitting next to him on the glider, says they call it *grape-beefoline*. There's
also *lemon-beefoline*, and *tutti-fruitti-beefoline*. Adlai looks up to the
sky and sees right through the atmosphere, sees a blue eye with a
white pupil in a black sky, and he understands this is a white-hot star
flashing in a sapphire pool of gas, and it's all encased in a brown
cloud. Miranda says, It's all poetry out there, isn't it?

Alvin Lee lives in an abandoned egg-crate factory across the
highway from a ten-thousand-head feed lot. The lowing is driving
him berserk. Lorraine is sick from the stench. Alvin Lee has an
annoying hernia under his rib cage. It's popped out to the size of a
softball. When he pushes it in, it pops out in a new location. So he
opens his body to fix the problem. The keys to his '69 Chevy drop
out. He does a little jig, and he rattles and clatters. Out fall sunglasses and coins, pens, paper clips, rings. Lorraine says, Your vac-
uum sack must have torn.

Homer's in a room watching cartoons with Buddhist monks.
That's when he realizes he has eyes. He's not blind and never has
been. The monk beside him says that the best way to see is not to
see.

. . .

Miranda's in a white room with a pile of babies on the hardwood floor. She picks one up, adjusts its mouth into a smile, opens one of its blue eyes, and fastens it to a wall, like artwork. The audience applauds. She picks up a pudgier one, musses his hair, puts him on the wall. The audience cheers, whoops, barks. Pretty soon the four walls are plastered with naked babies. She calls the installation, *Flight of the Bumble Bees.* And you can actually hear them buzzing, see their little honeyed legs twitch.

Grisham is driving in bad weather. It's either pouring sheets of rain, or the wind is tossing his car around, or it's snowing. The woman with him is a motivational speaker and she's wearing a tempered gold cross on a thick gold chain. She tells him the cross was retrieved from a Spanish galleon in the Gulf. They are going to see Grisham's friend Sidney Taylor whom he hasn't seen in ten years, but they are always heading in the wrong direction. The woman, Miss Apprehension she calls herself, tells him he has to let the car know who's in control.

Shug's dreams are downloaded on a computer, and he watches them in a monitor. He gets the menu. He scrolls past *Brother's Hat in River* and clicks on *Arrivals/Departures.* Everyone he has ever known is staying at this hotel for the weekend. He's in the lobby waiting for them to come down. It's night. It's Europe. He looks under the cushion of his chair and finds all the checks he's ever written. He forgot to mail them.

Earlene is with Billy Wayne at a restaurant, and Billy Wayne says, I hope you appreciated everything I've done for you. She says she does and goes to kiss him, but he stiffens, says, They don't like affection. Earlene notices that all the other diners are priests. Billy Wayne collapses and is tended to by the paramedics who've just materialized. He may have had a stroke. His left arm is strapped to his neck with a leather belt, and he keeps babbling about getting on disability. A monsignor tells Earlene that the latest findings indicate that all strokes originate in Antarctica and are communicable through sexual intercourse. Billy Wayne's alert and happy. He waves goodbye from the gurney. Earlene sits back down and asks Dr. Parnell Broadway for his prognosis. Parnell paints his face with different shades of red to indicate the degrees of pain that Billy Wayne is feeling. The priest at the next table is eating his toast with a knife and fork. He opens his beer can with his teeth. There's a live, but skinned, rabbit on the priest's plate. The priest tucks a napkin into his collar, stabs the rabbit with his fork. The rabbit screams like a woman in labor. The priest slices the rabbit in half from head to tail. The blood is everywhere.

Lorraine is walking in a city. The city is massive, but silent and empty. She sees the Statue of Liberty on the sidewalk. The statue is pea-green, and Liberty, like herself, is pregnant. Lorraine reads the inscription on the plaque at the base of the statue:

> *Give me a chair, I'm tired*
> *Just need to catch my breath.*
> *You know what its like*
> *To be on your feet all day?*

She turns a corner and Willie Nelson's standing in the bed of a red pickup, singing "Pancho and Lefty." It's just Willie and Mickey Raphael on harmonica. They go to Denny's for a Grand Slam breakfast. It's Willie's birthday, so he eats free. Mickey says, What's the baby's name? Lorraine doesn't know. Willie says, Every woman dreams the baby's name just before she delivers. She says, Don't tell me it's named *Denny*. Mickey shakes his head. *Willie?* Nope. Lorraine says, Tell me. So Willie leans over and says, It's a girl and her name's *Brooklyn Charisma*.

Ariane's in jail with a boatload of Chinese stowaways and no one will listen to her when she tells them she's not Chinese, she's Cajun. She doesn't even like duck sauce or those black cloth slippers. The warden wants to order takeout. Ariane looks at the menu. She tells the warden it's *Maine* lobster, not *Main* lobster; it's *dumplings*, not *dumpings*; *lunch*, not *launch*; it's *curry flavor*, not *curry favor*. He says, And you tell us you're not Chinese. She orders #39, tender squid in garlic and pepper sauce, topped with peanuts. The fortune cookies are cruel jokes, she thinks.

Boudou had set his alarm clock to wake him in an hour so he would finally remember a dream. He's in a large house and walks from room to room. In every room he looks into a mirror, and each time he sees someone else in the reflection. He likes some mirrors better than others. The alarm goes off and startles the dream right out of him.

The author's sitting with Kebo Haley over to Kebo's garage. The Interstate Battery clock says it's 7:17. Kebo's wearing his blue jump suit and a red ball cap with grease stains on the bill. Author's got his feet up on a pile of Chilton manuals, says he's frustrated with the book, doesn't know what's wrong with it or how to fix it. Just going to move on, write a memoir like everyone else is doing. He and Kebo are drinking cognac out of coffee mugs. He tells Kebo, I can pretend as well as the next guy to remember conversations I had when I was three. Kebo tells him a story's like a car. When you have trouble with it, you look inside. The author wants to know whatever happened between Kebo and Mrs. Haley. Kebo shakes his head. I won't say because anything people tell you, you just shove it in a book. They laugh about the author's being a thief by trade. Kebo says, I got one you can have: Two old boys over to Trailerville— Buster Carnegie and Scooter Rothschild—used to play this game where if one of them bought a new ball cap, the other one could shoot the button off the top. One night Scooter missed, caught Buster full on the forehead. Talks a little slower than he used to. Kebo and the author aren't in the garage anymore. They're 507 miles from Needles. That's what the sign says. The highway's empty, the dust blowing. Kebo says, You can't quit, Bo. You owe us.

Kate's falling. She can only see where she's falling from, not where she's falling to. Where she's falling from is darkness. She knows she's in the funnel of a whirlpool. And now she's outside her body watching herself and her sister as they accelerate into the void. Alice puts out her arm, her leg, opens her mouth, and this slows the fall. She's gliding now and sees at last a place to alight. She and Kate tumble into soft grass. Alice says, That wasn't so bad, was it? Kate says, So this is the country of our fears.

Benning sits in a sleek, black gondola eating nuns' breasts, soft meringue kisses, the peaks lightly browned—like swallowing clouds. Royce holds her in his arms, and they drift down the Grand Canal. Benning is so happy that they've made it to Venice. She likes the way the pastel palazzos reflect off the water more than she likes the palazzos themselves, likes the way they shimmer on the surface, the way they dissolve into discrete pearls of color on the undulating water and then come back together. Night falls, and the canal becomes a starry sky. Royce reminisces about his younger days in Venice, about knowing Pound—a fraud, and Mann—a saint. He says, And every Saturday we took the vaporetto to Murano—you loved the glass. Benning feels herself becoming less substantial, gauzy. At the merest ruffle of a breeze, her body flutters like a gossamer blouse. She is lifted by the wind, out of Royce's embrace, over the buildings. She floats over Venice and over Shiver-de-Freeze. She knows what's happening, and knows that she needs to say goodbye to Royce and to Adlai, but they're sleeping below in Paradise. It's not important. She is unconcerned. She's dying, and she's delighted that death is a lightening. And life is but a dream. (Sh-boom! Sh-boom!) Things happened in life, and you felt them, but it was all in your mind, the colors, the fear and anxiety. People surrounded you and houses did, and towns, but what you saw was not so important as what you felt. Life was one thing after another, a brief insanity, a series of inexplicable transitions that seemed at the time sensible, but at second sight ridiculous, a succession of unconnected incidents, accidental relationships. You die, as Benning realizes she has, and it's like waking from a dream—the first thing you forget is the plot. That way you never mistake confabulation for memory. Life's a dream. Death's something else again. It's . . .

Might I But Moor
Tonight in THeE

Rouse them up! the disbehaving, the
unaneled and unhousled, those whose bright
hearts have dinged, and reposit their souls
in the broad-open daylight of the Lord!

—THE LOUISIANA BOOK OF THE DEAD

. . . unimaginable and inexpressible. It's not being there. It's not being anywhere. It's repose without sleep, essence without being, space without form. It's the end of gravity, the sloughing off of desire, the collapse of the trillion-starred galaxy that was the self. It's the not-being-born.

Royce awoke, his throat dry, his eyes itchy, the room not a blur. He'd slept with his glasses on. He looked at the maple rocker in the corner, the paisley shawl draped over its back, the onyx lamp beside it, at the three-wing vanity there beyond his feet. In the vanity's mirrors, he saw himself from three slightly different angles. His life was like that now, like a puzzle that someone takes apart while he's sleeping and scrambles all the pieces. And every morning he snaps the pieces back together until he can see enough of a room or a landscape to know what the whole picture will be. It's like if you were to see a photograph of a young lady wearing a straw sailor hat. You see the red silk trim around the crown—well, there's the problem—*around* is not a word you can use with a photograph. You see the trim and know that it circles the hat and is, maybe, bowed in back. You can't see it—all you can see is a flat hat, shaped like the *Monitor* or the *Merrimac*, whichever it was that looked like a cheese box.

Royce needed water, but his teeth were in the glass on the night table. He scooped out his upper plate and sipped the water. He put the dripping teeth into the table drawer. Benning lay beside him in just the same position she'd taken in his dream of the hologram. And then he wasn't certain if he wasn't still dreaming. He touched her wrist with his finger. Thank God—we're both here. Benning smiled in her sleep. In her slump. In her slumber. Royce shook Benning's arm. "Sweetie!" He pulled the blanket up to her shoulders. Royce closed his eyes. Better to dream again, where everything is effortless.

When Lorraine went into labor—yes, she was certain this was it—Alvin Lee scooted down the hall to Earlene's room and knocked. He stuck his head in the door and told Earlene what was going on. Earlene dressed and went to Lorraine. Alvin Lee said shouldn't he boil some water. Earlene said, Get Lorriane's necessities packed and loaded in the car. Within a few minutes, Earlene, Lorraine, and Alvin Lee were pulling out the driveway. Ouida woke up in the midst of the commotion, and Adlai filled her in. She woke Duane, told him to get dressed pronto. Lorraine was labor-intensive and they needed to get to the hospital in Monroe as quick as a blink.

Adlai carried breakfast out to the boathouse. He saw Ariane in the rowboat in the lake, drifting. He set the tray by the door, knocked, walked back to the house. He waved to Dunae and Ouida as they got in their car. When Duane drove past the Black & Lovely, he saw that Delano had finished his painting on the window.

Delano, Purvis, Miranda, Radley, and Homer were all standing there admiring it. Well, maybe Homer wasn't.

Adlai switched the radio on. He sat at the table with Father Pat. They listened to a story on the news about a woman in Virginia who murdered her newborn son by putting him in a microwave oven. She cooked the boy for one hour. Father Pat said, "May the Lord have mercy on her soul."

Adlai said, "*His*. Baby was a boy."

"I meant the mother."

Adlai asked Father Pat would he feel the same way if it was a daddy or some boyfriend that murdered the child, and Father Pat said he could only hope that he would. Adlai said he found it curious how when a man abuses a child our outrage is undiluted, but if a woman does, we're suddenly concerned with motivation, with extenuating circumstances, and we assume some undo stress or mental incapacity or whatever drove her to it. It's like we don't want to believe women can be evil.

Father Pat said it's easy to forgive the righteous their occasional malfeasances, but it takes courage and humility to forgive the wicked. And we will not enter heaven until we do. Adlai said was evil always a deed or could it be an idea alone. Father Pat said that evil was the absence of God in the world and in our hearts. Durwood Tulliver began his program by asking, "Don't you feel lonely sometimes?" He said, "Give me your hand, friend."

Adlai glanced at the clock. "Benning never misses Brother Durwood."

Father Pat said, "She had a long day yesterday."

Durwood Tulliver said, "We thank Thee this morning, Lord. Thank Thee, thank Thee, thank Thee. We come before Thee, heavenly Father, to ask You to stand by us."

Adlai heard footfalls on the staircase and expected to see his mother walk into the kitchen, but, instead, Royce did. Slipperless and in his pajamas. Adlai said, "Daddy, where's your teeth at?"

Royce felt for his teeth with his tongue.

Adlai said, "Can't eat breakfast without you have your teeth in. We've talked about this."

"I know they're wet."

Adlai hoped they weren't wet from the toilet again. He said, "Where's Benning?"

"In the drawer."

"Benning's in the drawer?"

"She is not."

"The teeth, you mean?"

"She's sound asleep."

Durwood said, "Didn't He say it!"

"Well, I'm going to fetch your teeth, your robe and slippers. Sit here with Father Pat."

Adlai tiptoed across the room, eased the night table drawer open. Sure enough. He picked up the teeth with a Kleenex, put the teeth in the robe pocket. He looked at Benning, whose arm was extended above her head and touched the headboard. She looked like she was fixing to fly away. He checked under the bed for the slippers. He checked the closet, the dresser. He found them under the pillow along with a watch and a slice of wedding cake. Benning hadn't stirred during the muffled commotion. Adlai straightened the picture in the wall by the rocking chair. The same framed print that Benning had at home in the guest bedroom, a painting Adlai had never much cared for. A solitary blond figure, forlorn and ragged, is stranded on a rock—in the middle of the sea, he had always thought, but that's not clear from the picture. The person is barefoot, blind-folded, and chained by the head to what, as a child, Adlai had thought was some kind of vise, but which turns out to be a lyre. He would call the painting *Despair*, but the artist called it *Hope*.

Adlai looked at his mother again. He got closer, kicked at the mattress with his knee. And again, harder this time. He whispered his mother's name. He backed away from the bed. Adlai sat in the rocking chair, stung with this wretched knowledge. Numbness spread through his body. It became an effort to breathe. He knew if he just sat there that Benning would continue to live for the others. He said he loved her. He said goodbye.

Adlai asked Boudou to help Royce into his slippers, robe, and teeth. He motioned for Father Pat to join him out on the veranda.

He told him. Father Pat made the sign of the cross. He asked Adlai
if he was all right. Adlai nodded. Father Pat said he'd perform
Extreme Unction. "We don't know if the soul's left the body."
Father Pat hurried to his room for his vestments and oils. Adlai went
to the kitchen, consulted the calendar for Dion Lazarus's phone
number, went to the living room and made the call. He left a message on the machine. Adlai asked Boudou if he'd go wake up Kebo
in Grisham's room. When Boudou had left the room, Adlai said,
"Daddy, I got something to tell you."

In Benning's room Mélia helped Father Pat. She held back the
covers while he anointed Benning's feet and the hand down at her
side. Father Pat leaned over the bed and whispered into Benning's
ear, "O Lord, Jesus Christ, receive my spirit; Holy Mary, pray for
me; Mary, Mother of Grace, Mother of Mercy, do thou protect me
from the enemy and receive me at the hour of my death."

Boudou stood at the bedroom door. He could see that Benning
was more than asleep, that the bustle by the bed signified conse-
quence. Her face had changed shape, the orbit of her eye was more
pronounced than it had been, her cheekbone more obvious, her skin
purple where it touched the sheet. And he knew she was dead. He
had seen death before. When he was two he sat in the driveway
pushing trucks through the oyster shell. He looked up to see his
momma racing out the house, not toward him, as he had hoped, but
toward the bread man's truck. When he saw his momma hugging
another woman, he walked over, left his payloader with a full bucket,
and saw a little girl in a red jacket, his age about, red leggings—it
was winter—red cloth cap, visored and tied beneath her chin, saw
her lying there in the road behind the truck, next to her red and
white tricycle, lying in a pool of lustrous and plentiful blood—not
that he knew it was blood then, not that he knew what that meant.
He watched the woman wail, saw the bread man collapse on the
lawn, saw his momma go to the bread man. When Momma spotted
him, she told Boudou to go back and play. A week or so later he
asked her, "Where's that little girl who was hit by that truck?" Earlene said, "She's dead." She hugged Boudou. "She won't be coming
back."

Boudou remembered Benning from yesterday at the wedding, remembered her with such clarity and detail that she was there; he could feel her gloved hand on his shoulder, hear the whisper of her dress when she moved, smell the fragrance of her voice. Benning would always be with him, but she wouldn't ever change, wouldn't ever surprise him with something new. Boudou backed away from the room, wiped his eyes, sniffled. Why did she have to die when they were just becoming friends?

He ran to the gallery and down the outside staircase, across the yard to the road. It was like he was crying for every sorry awful thing that had ever happened in his life, for the chameleon he kept in a popcorn box that died and stiffened in the night, for the boy in the schoolyard who punched him in the stomach and took his Walkman, for the hours he waited in the dark after the movie for Varden to pick him up, for the sound of his momma crying behind her locked bedroom door, for the toys he had broken, the bike that got stolen, for the time he lied about his momma's missing watch, for the lost watch, for being too late to ever know his daddy. Boudou didn't know where he was running to, but he knew he was running from the misery in Paradise.

Adlai said, "So you understand then? She's gone from us."

Royce nodded.

"And you're okay?"

Royce took a bite of toast. The phone rang. Adlai answered. Earlene said, "It's a girl. Six pounds, twelve ounces. Lorraine popped her out like a watermelon seed. Cutest little bald-headed girl you ever saw. Ten fingers, ten toes, a little raucous and disappointed at being here, I think. Duane and Ouida took a roll of pictures, went out to get them developed."

Adlai told Earlene.

"Oh, Jesus, Adlai. Oh, God. I'm so sorry. You okay?"

"I'm okay."

"I'll be there directly. You hold tight. Boudou doing all right?"

"I haven't told him. He went up to wake Kebo."

On the drive back to Shiver-de-Freeze Earlene thought about Benning, how she used to have a gold filling in her front tooth—not a filling, a crown; anyway her front tooth when she was younger was edged in gold, and Earlene had wanted one just like it. Earlene cried; her chin trembled. She bit her lip. When Earlene was little and staying at Paradise for the summer, Benning would cook breakfast for her and Rylan, make them smiley faces out of bacon and eggs, and call them to the table yelling, Smiley Rylie and Early Pearly, come and get it.

Earlene found Adlai and Kebo in the kitchen scrubbing down cabinets and counters, putting things away. Royce sat at the table stirring his coffee. Earlene told Royce she was sorry. She told Adlai to sit. He said there was a lot of sprucing and cleaning to do. Need to get the house spic and span. He said Parnell was stopping by before the drive to Opelousas and would certify the death, get what had been Benning ready for Dion Lazarus.

"Where's Boudou at?"

Royce said, "Adlai, tell your mother she's missing breakfast."

Adlai looked at Earlene. Royce stirred his coffee and stirred his coffee. Earlene touched his stirring arm and his shoulder.

Adlai said, "I told you, Daddy, she's gone."

"She wouldn't go without saying goodbye."

Adlai put his fist on his hip. (Perhaps he should have asked himself why he did.) "Daddy, she's dead."

Royce said, "What kind of shit is that to say about your mother?" Royce pounded the table. "I let it go the first time." He shook his trembling finger at Adlai. "Who do you think you are? You're trash, mister. Your mother is worth of two of you!"

Adlai said, "Please, Daddy, calm yourself."

Royce threw the coffee cup at Adlai, hit the sink. "Don't you ever say your mother is dead, hear me?"

Adlai blinked slowly, a slightly exaggerated, if involuntary, closing of the eyes, as if to broadcast his proper exasperation, and as soon as he did, he knew the gesture was an insult to his father, to the memory of his mother, knew it was provocative and uncalled for. What kind of person was he becoming, anyway? And he winced, just slightly, just so you'd barely notice, just so you'd think he tried not to, but he might as well have been rending his clothes, pounding his breast, saying, See how I suffer! You see what I must go through! It wasn't pity he was after. He had plenty of that for himself. He wanted to be thought of as the noble and forbearing, the magnanimous Adlai. Earlene surely knew this. Kebo knew it. And worst of all, Royce knew it. Adlai felt unmasked by his blink and wince, revealed to be the ungrateful, self-serving pomposity that he surely was. Before Adali could apologize, Royce slammed his own face into the table, shattering the saucer. Earlene sat him up. Royce's glasses hung from one ear. He bled from his nose. Kebo dampened a washcloth. Earlene said she'd take care of Royce, told Adlai to find Boudou and keep him out of the kitchen awhile.

At the Black & Lovely, Radley told Delano it looked like the picture was done to a finish. After they watched Dion Lazarus drive his hearse over the Bridge of Sighs, Miranda asked Delano how he knew to paint Benning up there on the window. He said painting's not about knowing. It's about feeling.

Earlene found Boudou at the museum, sitting on the floor beneath his daddy's cassock. She sat down beside him. "We were worried about you. Looked all over."

"How did you find me?"

"Royce told me where you'd be. How did you get in?"

"Macky leaves a key under the mat."

Earlene took a tissue out of her pocket and handed it to Boudou. He wiped his eyes, blew his nose. "Are you okay, Bou?"

"Benning's dead."

"We all die, sugar, that's why we need to love each other so hard."

"It isn't fair."

"Everyone's death is tragic, not just the Fontanas'. It's not the Fontanas who are cursed. It's all of us."

Boudou held his daddy's LP&L cap in his hands, ran his fingers over the stitching.

"Why don't you forgive him?"

"Daddy?"

"For dying." She hugged Boudou. He cried. She reminded him how she didn't have a momma or a daddy. I had Papaw and Memaw is all. Don't know who my momma was." Earlene rocked Boudou in her arms, tried not to think about how her daddy dropped her off with his parents, said he was going out for milk, and never came back.

They heard the door open, saw a shaft of light brighten the ceiling, heard footsteps. Macky said, "Hey, you two."

Earlene said hi. Boudou sat back up.

Macky said, "Nice hat."

"It fits." Boudou put it on.

"Tell you what. I'm going to trade you that hat for a photograph of you that I can put up here in the exhibit."

"You'd do that?"

"Under the photo, I write, 'End of curse.' "

Benning had the feeling death might not last all that long, that like everything else, it was a process. Oblivion follows. She thought if she could talk to her kin, she'd tell them this—death is the sadness at the center of our lives, but it's also the source of the beauty.

A Formal Feeling Comes

*I suppose the goddam tragedy here is not so much
that I will not get up and save my sorry ass, but
that I don't have the will to want to rise.*

—VARDEN ROEBUCK,
last articulated thought*

At the funeral home Alvin Lee sat with Adlai and with Royce. He noticed Royce was having trouble staying awake. He looked a mess without the teeth and with the bandage over his nose. When Earlene arrived with Boudou, Alvin Lee said a prayer over his aunt, took his leave, and drove to the hospital in Monroe to be with Lorraine and Esther Benning. He sat by the bed and watched the baby nurse and sleep. He peeked under her pink cap at her fuzzy blond hair and pointy head. Wasn't bald at all. He watched her spread her fingers and wince. He wished she would open her teeny eyes. He touched her cheek with his knuckle. Alvin Lee cared about the baby more than he cared about anything, cared more for her than he'd ever realized he could care for a person. When the nurse took the

303

baby back to the nursery, Alvin Lee stood at the window and tried to imagine what the swaddled Esther Benning might be dreaming about—about the warmth and reassuring pressure of skin, he figured, about the loamy smell of Momma, the recent surprise of air.

There was no doubt in Alvin Lee's mind that he would give up his own life to save this baby's, no doubt that he was not nearly as significant a person as she was. And he thought this must have been how Jesus felt about us. And if He did, then His death was no tragedy at all, no sacrifice even. Was pure joy, immaculate love. Maybe that's the secret of the Crucifixion. And a man's love would be greater even than God's. After all, Jesus knew He would rise from death.

Ouida and Duane stopped by. Ouida said they bought a box of exposable diapers for the house. Ouida brushed, combed, and styled Lorraine's hair. She filed Lorraine's nails and painted them pink. Duane had a confession. When he first heard the baby's name, he thought Alvin Lee said Easter Bunny. Anyway, he went out and bought a furry little bunny puppet for the baby. Duane put the puppet on his hand and had it talk to Esther Benning through the nursery window. Ouida and Duane took Alvin Lee to the Mohawk for crawfish while Lorraine napped. Alvin Lee said the child's got herself quite a grip for a one-day-old. She'll just latch on to your finger so's you could pick her right up.

Duane was sure he had never seen a happier person than Alvin Lee in his life. Not that the happiness was undiluted, but the sadness Alvin Lee felt at his aunt's death seemed to make his delight in the child all the more precious. Duane squeezed Ouida's hand, and she knew what he was thinking, and she smiled. Ouida wanted a passel of children one day. She wanted them crawling all over her, up her legs, around her neck, down her back. She wanted to inhale the berry and grass and milk of them, to kiss their round little bellies, to suck their toes till they laughed themselves silly.

Later that afternoon, Ariane came by with Grisham, their honeymoon in Gatlinburg (mercifully) postponed. They bought a spray of red roses for Lorraine and little yellow booties for the baby. Ariane walked to the nursery and stared at the row of cribbed babies and noted how you couldn't tell one from the other really. She wondered why some people thought they were cute. They were rashed, round, blank. She and Grisham would have children in due time. Two children—but not until she and Grisham had taken the time to enjoy each other, build up some equity, fashion a suitable nest. A boy and a girl would be perfect. Kyle and Celine.

Alvin Lee told them Lorraine and the baby would be leaving St. Francis first thing in the morning, in time for the graveside service. Grisham said they'd be stopping by the funeral home to sit awhile and then they'd get something to eat before going back to Paradise. Lorraine said she was famished. Alvin Lee said he'd scoot downstairs to the cafeteria for something. What would she like? She'd like him to run across the street to Brer Rabbit's and buy her a bucket of spicy chicken, a tub of fried okra, and some molasses biscuits. And a diet RC. Grisham and Ariane kissed Lorraine goodbye and left with Alvin Lee, who said did they want to stop by the nursery on their way out. They did, but the blinds were down. Nap time.

Lorraine closed her eyes. She could still smell Esther Benning on the bedclothes, on her gown, on her arm. And when she inhaled the fragrance she could feel the pulse of the baby's sucking on her nipple.

Royce looked behind him. He shifted in his chair. His back had stiffened. He breathed through his mouth. His feet hurt. The sun through the window made his eyes water. Why can't Adlai draw the shade? Royce could imagine not one good reason to keep sitting here, but he didn't know what else to do. He looked at his watch. He might as well try reading spilled milk. So what else did he need to know? *On what river are New Orleans and Baton Rouge?* He raised his hand. Adlai grabbed Royce's arm and tried to lower it. Royce said, The Mississippi. *On what river is Shreveport?* He's in school. Geography. Last class of the day. Can't wait till the bell rings. He said, The Red. *An earthen bank along a river is called?* Levee, Royce said. Adlai said, Daddy, are you all right? Royce put his fingers over his lips, shushed Adlai. He said, A break in the levee is called a crevasse. He's in Mr. Kirby's classroom, and he's bored to tears, and he's imagining himself an old man sitting in a close room with his body seized up and his mind banjaxed. *New Orleans has had rapid growth in manufactures. It takes high rank in the refining of sugar.* Royce heard someone talking in class and looked around. The new kid in class causing all the ruckus is named Boudou.

Boudou waved to Royce and took a seat beside his mother. Adlai kissed Earlene, shook hands with Boudou, told them both he thought he should get Royce back to Paradise. I think it's all too much for him. Royce said he'd go back when Benning was ready. Earlene helped Royce to his feet, gave him a hug. She said, Honey, Benning's waiting on you back to the house. Boudou kept his confusion to himself, said he'd stay, keep his momma company. Adlai said he'd see could Mélia keep an eye on Royce. He'd be back in a couple of hours if she could.

Earlene sat and regarded Benning's body, which seemed both more and less than it had been. As matter without vitality, it seemed to have achieved some profound density. But this body was empty of exuberance, and so it was meager and inconsequential, like so much lint under a bed. Earlene made a new list—*WHAT DEATH IS: Silent. Abiding. Corruption, annihilation, dissolution. Blind. Privation. Sleep without sleep. Formidable. Banishment. Vacancy. The name of despair. Not a verb. Shame. Nothing. The "I know not what." The void. Ignorance. Deaf. Loss. Absence. Foul. End without end; end without beginning. Nowhereness. Not. The Undoing. The food of worms. Timeless. Indifference. Indecent. Without consolation. Forgetting. Where you fall to in dreams. Paradise lost. Stillness. A barren womb. Formlessness. Where everything leaves off. Not brimstone; not choirs of angels; not ice at the eye. The surprise of where God cannot be found. Senseless. Proud. Waiting. Unimaginable, unimagined, imaginationless. An element of blank. A thief. A catastrophic collapse. The only immortal. What something was. Not here, not after, not hereafter. Matter out of reach. An empty bed. Lethe. The expiration of hope. The fountainhead of gods. The candle consumed by its flames. The fire that saith not, It is enough. Tick, tick, tick.*

Earlene knew that what is interred is not the person, not the nut, but the shell. The cadaver, the corpse, the remains. But what of that which flies? Like in Delano's painting. The essence of a person is beyond the laws of physics. And holding on to that departed essence is our job, is what culture is, what hope is, what defiance is, what love is. What do we owe the dead? Everything.

When Duane and Ouida and Ariane and Grisham came by, Earlene decided she'd relieve Mélia and Father Pat back at the house. Ouida admired the nifty job Pug and Macky had done on Benning, said she just loved the flagrance of the gladiolus. Ariane sat beside Grisham on the sofa and wept on his shoulder, occasionally drying her eyes with Kleenex. She wasn't crying so much for Benning, whom she didn't really know, but for every little death we suffer every day, every sneer and every leer, every unkind and unnecessary remark, everything shoddy and mean and impoverished; she wept for thrift stores and off brands, plastic plants and tooth decay, for polyester blouses, for duct tape on door screens, tinfoil on TV antennas, radio talk shows, Lee Press-on Nails, Swedish meatballs, canned chop suey, velvet paintings and Crock-Pots, spool tables and Cremora, shag carpets and aluminum siding, flocked wallpaper, plaid furniture, wood-grain paneling, filthy language, Muzak, cinder-block bookcases, board games, unicorns, rainbows, astrologers, dragons, aerosol cheese, L'Eggs, and all the bamboo curtains draped between us and lives worth living. All of it insulting, demeaning, and unspeakably sad.

Grisham let Ariane cry, knowing he was not the cause of it, but wondered if his own self-control made him appear insensitive. He knew he missed his aunt, knew in a few days he'd allow himself a dark and private place for tears, just like he did when his parents died, but for here and now he was thinking about the future, about which suit to wear to work on the first day, what gadgets to buy for the new office, what totems to bring in for the desk, about how to arrange the electronics in the entertainment room at home. Grisham wasn't trying to be disrespectful, wasn't consciously avoiding the dire truth that stilled the room; it wasn't his fault, was it, that his mind sheltered him with distraction?

Duane could hardly keep himself from smiling, which he knew

would be impolite and indecorous. He was intoxicated with love for Ouida, drunk with the waters of the river of hope. Love was all the grace and providence he would ever need. He felt indestructible, indomitable, immortal, exalted by a blessing of Ouida's devotion. Life, he thought, could not get better than this. And that sudden understanding sobered him.

At closing, Adlai said he wanted to be alone awhile. He told the others he wasn't hungry—but now that he'd thought of it, he was— and they went off to TLC for supper. Dion told him to stay as long as he needed. He said he'd button the front door so all Adlai would have to do is shut it, and it would lock behind him. Adlai stood before the casket and examined the body that was now like the surface of nothing, this waxy mound of stiffening flesh, this intimation of what had been, of what might have been. He wished Benning could have died at home in her own bed among her familiars.

Adlai thought it might be best if he closed his eyes, turned away, and never looked at his mother again. He thought he should reach down and touch her face, thought, perhaps, he should leave something of his in the casket to be buried with Benning. A photo from his wallet maybe, or a lock of his hair. He had to remind himself that this wasn't Benning, that sentimentality was false emotion, false and easy, disappointing and disrespectful, crass and ignoble. When he did look back at the casket, Adlai saw a cockroach, one of those with the dark stripes behind its eyes like at home, saw it crawl out from behind the satin pillow, stop, test the air with its long, swept-back antennae, and then slip beneath the corpse's shoulder.

In a Time of Sore
Bereavement

Why is it dark?

—RYLAN BIRDSONG, last words

From the Flandreau *Avalanche-Gazette*:

The pillar and strength of a happy home has toppled. Time, Death's twin, has carried off one of our most treasured citizens. Her radiant countenance made the sun shine in a shaded place. None ever entered her home without a most cordial and sincere welcome, nor left it without luxuriating in the flattering warmth of her genuine hospitality and good grace.

Yes, a good woman has passed to her reward, a loving mother, passionate wife, the soul of sweet earnestness and careful culture. A fine woman has been summoned by the Sovereign of the Universe and has departed from her devoted husband and son, whose anguish is unfathomable, whose grief unconsolable, whose hearts bleed with sorrow and ache with desolation.

But hers is the glorious promise of a magnificent future.

When news reached Flandreau on Monday afternoon last that Mrs. Benning Taylor (Loudermilk) Birdsong, beloved wife of Royce Harper Birdsong, was dead, a gloom of sadness fell over the entire town. Mrs. Birdsong enjoyed the highest respect and esteem of all who had the pleasure of knowing her. Our shock is barbed with pain and with profound melancholy. Vain is the attempt to measure the loss of a wife and a mother to a husband and a son.

Mrs. Birdsong was born in Ouachita Parish in 1931, the daughter of Witt and Tennessee (Pettiquois) Loudermilk. She was the last surviving sibling, Batchelor, Nola, Nixie, Cadmus "Skeet," Berry Jayne, Harmony, and Pyne having predeceased her. In 1950, she married Royce Birdsong and moved with him to Avondale Plantation. Her first born, Rylan Russell, passed away under tragic circumstances at 15. Mrs. Birdsong is survived by her husband and son Adlai Estes, the child whose birth had surprised and pleased her late in life. She also leaves several nieces and nephews.

Mrs. Birdsong's loving heart gave out during the night. Gave out, but never failed. She died as she lived, in the bosom of her family at the Loudermilk home in Shiver-de-Freeze whence Providence had directed her. Mrs. Birdsong, on the day of her death, had been in attendance at the wedding of her nephew Grisham Loudermilk and the former Ariane Thevenot.

To the devastated husband and son, to the shaken bride and groom, to the other members of Benning Birdsong's family, to the host of friends and neighbors who will grieve for her as if she were kin, this writer and the *Avalanche-Gazette* extend our heartfelt sympathy and condolences and ask them to remember that their loss is her gain, and in their suffering, she for whom they suffer, has found rest, repose, and the sweet rewards of her noble and honest life.

After the sitting-in at Lazarus Funeral Home, a graveside service was held at Dispersed of Judah Cemetery presided over by the Reverend Alvin Lee Loudermilk.

God bless her memory. God bless the loved ones in their great loss and sad hour.

We loved her, yes, we loved her. But angels loved her more, and they have sweetly called her to that distant shore.

—by Mavis Willig

Heart, Without the Swoon

He assended into Heaven.

—SIGN ON HIGHWAY 165,
NEAR THE FLOYD PLACE

A dlai said good-night. He told his mother—she wasn't here in the casket, he knew that, but she could be somewhere and watching (he thought not, but then he could be dead wrong about this whole shooting match)—told her he'd see her in the morning. He dimmed the lights, closed the door, heard the lock snick behind him as the bolt entered the chamber, a quiet sound, crisp, prudent, certain. He sat on the porch steps. He had nowhere he wanted to go. He thought of big-shouldered crows he'd seen hopping on the tarmac out on 165, dancing with the husk of a dead possum.

"I've brought you something to eat." Miranda sat beside Adlai. "I'm sorry about your mother." She held a covered dish in her lap. "Three-can casserole and pickle pie." She smiled and passed the dish to Adlai. "Dills." She took a fork out of her pocket and handed it to him. "Ritz-cracker crust."

Adlai thanked her, balanced the dish on his knees, peeked under the plastic cover, inhaled, raised his eyebrows. "Smells wonderful." He smiled. "This is so sweet." They heard, "Help! Help!" and looked up to see Dion's peacock, Thomas Love, on the funeral home roof.

Adlai took a bite of the casserole and chewed. Miranda asked Adlai would he rather be alone. He wouldn't, he said. He said he'd been wondering what would be wrong with living forever.

Miranda thought not a thing if you could stay healthy. "If you didn't age. If your pals and kin stayed around, too."

Adlai said, "If you kept your Paradise Body, the resurrection body, the one you'll carry to Armageddon."

Miranda asked Adlai how was the casserole. He took a forkful and held it to her mouth. She tasted it, dripped a little on her chin, and wiped it. "Not bad."

Adlai said, "What do you think death is?"

"Something we can't experience."

Adlai set the dish behind him. "It's the end of the self, I think."

"But what's the self? Surely not the body." She looked at Adlai and lost her train of thought in his hazel eyes.

Miranda's eyes darkened in those few seconds, Adlai thought. Adlai smiled, made some idiotic face. Miranda dropped her eyelids and stared away, across the Social Ocean to the lights of TLC and the Crown of Thorns. Adlai wondered what just happened.

Miranda leaned forward, parked her elbow on her knee and cradled her face in her hand. She saw that her shadow from the porch light touched Adlai's shadow.

The self, they decided was a flux, like a river, always changing. And then they were back to death.

This time when Adlai moved, his knee bumped hers. Miranda wanted to say something that would require the punctuation of a touch, something apparently less accidental. She put her hand on Adlai's forearm—he became so still, you might have thought he'd been shot. She said, "Why worry about a future nonexistence when you don't worry about the aeons of nonexistence in the past? Just like the present and the past, the future ends."

Adlai couldn't believe how startling this touch was, how every hair, every nerve was alert, edgy, like they knew something he didn't. He leaned toward Miranda. He said, "The past doesn't end."

She said, "It will."

Adlai and Miranda continued to talk about death, and it seemed to Adlai that if they just kept on talking, he and Miranda could figure out all of life's mysteries tonight. And if you had been standing, say, across the Social Ocean and were watching these two in conversation—as Ariane and Grisham, having finished supper at TLC, were doing—you would notice how they shifted and shrugged and swiveled and bent and angled and turned as if they were dancing with each other. One's move seemed to mirror the other. One leans in, the other leans in; one crosses his legs, the other crosses her legs; one scratches her nose, the other scratches his nose. They rotate, you would notice, toward each other. You would hear them laugh—a little too heartily, you might think. You might walk closely enough to hear the music of their voices, but not what they are saying, and you might notice how they seem to keep each other's time, seem to be in harmony.

Mirror Without Glass

WHAT DEATH IS (PART II):   a cool night with a clear moon;
angels with mourning figures; a thirst you feel within; the
unexpected hand at your shoulder; what you always suspected; a
scream from the attic; sleep without dreams; the motive for birth;
zero at the heart; the bride stripped bare; the land of lotus-eaters;
the aspiring flame; the curve of forgetting; near though distant;
mirror without glass; persuasion; the mind goes blind; the price paid;
the unsticking; subtraction; insensible and still; a dumb show;
nothing to touch; the slumber of nonbeing; the curse of quiet; the
stupor of darkness; no they, no I, no you; extinction without end.
Amen.

—EARLENE FONTANA

A. The Black & Lovely Gro.   Delano set his grave marker* to
dry by the window fan and cleaned up his brushes, paints, rags, and
whatnot. The grave marker was temporary till Dion completed the
granite headstone. Purvis laid his poached catfish on a bed of white
rice and cucumbers. He stirred a tablespoon of McDermott's Fire on
the Bayou pepper sauce into a bowl of egg yolks and added that to

his Allemande sauce. He covered the fish with Saran Wrap, poured the sauce into a Mason jar, and carried the platter of fish and the jar of sauce to where Macky and Pug sat. Purvis untied his apron, hung it on the coat tree, and went to the back room to work, shave, dress for the service.

Macky and Pug had volunteered to stay behind at Paradise, get the house and food ready for the gathering after the burial. They sat here drinking coffee, waiting till they saw the Loudermilk clan pass over the bridge and head for town. Pug reached across the table and picked a bit of lint off the lapel of Macky's blue suit jacket. She dropped the fuzz into the ashtray and burned it with her cigarette.

Delano began humming a tune, and the humming became mumbled words and then audible words, and then Macky and Pug began to sing along. They sang "There's a Fountain." *Filled with blood.* Sang of sinners plunged beneath the flood and a dying thief, a dying Lamb, and about salvation. *Redeeming love has been my theme and shall be till I die.*

Purvis returned in his brown suit and shined shoes. Had a white handkerchief in his breast pocket. They sang "Rock of Ages, Cleft for Me." *Let me hide myself in Thee.* And as they sang, the cars from Paradise approached, made the hump of the bridge, kicked up dust, drove on. Macky looked at Pug. "I reckon we ought to go."

Pug lit another cigarette. "How come singing makes you feel better?"

Delano said, "Not singing, but singing together."

B. Dispersed of Judah. Father Pat said a prayer over the grave recommending Benning's soul to heaven. He made the Sign of the Cross. Boudou leaned into Earlene's side. She put her arm around his shoulders. Alvin Lee thanked Father Pat and stepped toward the coffin and looked at his baby there asleep in Lorraine's arms and smiled. He read from Ecclesiastes: "For in him that is joined to all the living there is hope: for a living dog is better than a dead lion. For the living know that they shall die: but the dead know not any thing, neither have they any more reward: for the memory of them is forgotten. Also their love, and their hatred, and their envy is now perished: neither have they any more a portion for ever in any thing that is done under the sun." Alvin Lee bowed his head, wondered why he had chosen to read this passage of meager hope, of desolate possibility. He looked at the others gathered around the grave.

Royce asked Adlai where Benning had gone to. Adlai shook his head. Royce said, "She's just being a lazybones today."

C. Paradise.   The dining room table was crowded with food. Besides Purvis's catfish, there were buttermilk and beaten biscuits, spoonbread and cornbread, red beans and rice, boiled shrimp, fried chicken, crab puffs, black-eyed peas, collards, green beans, fried tomatoes, sweet potato pie, and banana pudding with vanilla wafer crust and whipped cream. In the kitchen was the coffee on the stove, iced tea and lemonade in the fridge, beer and soft drinks in the cooler. Liquor was on the buffet in the parlor. Folks helped themselves, sat where they would, and ate, talked. Hospitality smooths the edges of grief, and it wasn't long before people loosened neckties, unbuttoned collars, kicked off shoes, sipped drinks.

The Van Veckhovens huddled in a corner of the parlor with Tous-les-deux and talked about the telepathic communication between twins. Sandy said how one time she was out at County Market buying a case of Slim Fast when a lustful feeling came over her of a sudden. Come to find out, at that very moment, Cindy was at home romancing her then boyfriend, Leander Fontaine. Of course, she said, that won't ever happen to you two exactly like that. Kate said, What's intercoursing like? Cindy looked at Sandy, at Kate and Alice, said, Well, let me tell you about my first time.

Boudou and Royce sat on the glider out on the lawn. Boudou dropped peanuts into his Pop Rouge, took a sip, held the cold glass to his forehead. He told Boudou about this cake he'd seen one time at a wedding, not sure where or when. "It was three-tiered, maybe four-foot tall. Had icing like latticework and these live roses on each layer and like climbing up the sides, like this was a trellis or something. Was marvelous to look at. The first layer was charlotte royal cake, the second layer was almond, the third Grand Marnier. The icing was butter cream and marzipan. Magnificent structure. And delicious. I can see it right now on a white linen tablecloth. There's people muddling around. A band is playing." Alvin Lee came out with Esther Benning and asked Boudou would he like to hold her. He sure would. Boudou cradled her head by his face. She sucked on his nose.

D. The Writing Table.   As long as dear readers like yourself open this book, then we get to tell this story. But the author—there he is at his writing table—can tell it only once. And right now he knows two things—that he has to stop, and that he doesn't want to. He has, after all, lived with these people for years. He goes to bed with them, wakes up with them. We know the story's over, yet he sits there with his orthopedic back pillow, his coffee, his legal pad, and his fountain pen, and takes notes about what's become of Rance Usrey, poet, actor, barrister, cuckold.* He's furnishing Kebo Haley's shotgun house; he's down in Opelousas with Jolene, who's having drinks with friends at Guidry's. Remember Donnie Carr? Well, our author thinks Donnie's got a novel in him. Donnie doesn't know it yet, but he and Anniece are splitting up (mutual, overdue), and he's quitting the store. He's going to run for mayor of Flandreau and sell Mexican pottery out of the vacant lot beside the Malcom X Car Wash. And what about Shug and Margaret? Will they ever admit they love each other and finally get together? And while our author's been distracted by minor characters (no characters are minor, we can hear him say), Adlai and Miranda have walked back to her trailer, have talked about how tomorrow she'll follow Adlai back to Avondale. They've speculated about what Miranda's presence in the house might do to Royce—well, he can't get any more confused, can he? And then they made love, and they snuggled and dozed, but our author will not let them sleep, fearing, perhaps, they'll dream of him and then awake from their dreams. For him, the book exists in the writing, and after that it's merchandise. So he's got Adlai fretting about Royce, about nursing homes, about grief all over again, about being the last Birdsong, about the sixty-four items on his list of things to do when he gets home: (1) pay the light bill; (2) fill the hummingbird feeders; (3) call lawyer; (4) call Payne Herbert at Lincoln Parish Bank; (5) call the pharmacy; (6) have Kebo over to upper . . .

Miranda's eyes are opened. She's staring at her pink robe draped over the bathroom door. From the bed, in this dim light, it looks like a silhouette of Sister Benedict John from first grade. Bought the robe in a thrift store in Lake Charles. She can't believe how happy and tranquil she feels right now, and how lucky to be happy. What if she hadn't stopped in for a drink that afternoon, and hadn't taken Grisham home, hadn't gotten so blue when, like all the others, he left, so she decided that's it, I'm out of here and she left the motor court and the job and drove north. Why north? And what if she had stayed on 165 and had lunch in Bastrop like she'd planned? And imagine her surprise at seeing Grisham Loudermilk himself in this tiny little town.*

Miranda says, "Adlai?"

"What?"

She wraps her arm over Adlai's chest, kisses his shoulder. "Tell me a story, a long, long, long story that you never finish."

"Can you have a story that never ends?"

"Yes, if you tell it right."

Epilogue

You do not need to live for the future,
for the future lives for you.

—RADLEY SMALLPIECE (1938–2003)

Human reason is not sophisticated enough, not adroit enough, supple enough, discerning enough to penetrate the profound mysteries of existence, but perhaps our imaginations are. That's what Alvin Lee's come to think. If we ever figure out what God is, it'll be because we discovered the unmasking metaphor for *Him* (wrong metaphor), whether that metaphor be a breathtaking mathematical theorem, an exalted musical phrase, or an elegant figure of speech. So then, Alvin Lee figures, religion ought to be a creative act, not an act of veneration. Or maybe worship and creation are one and the same. These are the sorts of issues he's dealing with at the renamed Church of the Many in Search of the One. Alvin Lee's temporary pulpit became permanent when it was disclosed that the Reverend Engarazz Walker had absconded with the meager church coffers and fled to Talkeetna, Alaska, at least that's where his letter was posted.

Between the church and his night job at Taylor's Tavern, Alvin Lee and family are getting by. And with Esther Benning in school, Lorraine's been able to take art classes at UNO and pick up some part-time waitressing. They all three are looking forward to next month's reunion at Paradise. Boudou's grown a foot in a year, Earlene says. It'll be so much fun. Of course, it'll be sad, too.

When Grisham got killed by the Illinois Central freight train (cops know he'd been drinking, suspect he was racing the train to the crossing—tie goes to the train), Ariane settled his, it turns out, muddled financial affairs,* sold the house and furnishings, took the kids, Celine and Julie, and moved in with no-longer-Father Pat and Mélia—Mr. and Mrs. McDermott. For several years now Pat's been the host of a classical music program on KLAS-FM. He and Mélia are heartsick at the loss of Grisham, to be sure, but they're also delighted to have a family in the house. They're not just doing for themselves anymore—that's how they feel.

Ariane is doing as well as you'd expect, but she's not ready to socialize as yet, and she's certainly not ready to return to Shiver-de-Freeze, the site of her nuptials. Which is fine. Pat and Mélia will take the kids, no problem. Ariane's got a new attitude, a new way of thinking about herself. She feels competent, ingenious, powerful. She didn't collapse when Grisham died; she fortified. Still, she's lonely at night, so she sleeps with the kids in her queen-sized bed. She may need to get used to that. Jolene Broadway told her, *Men don't make passes at girls with two lasses.* Jolene meant it as a joke, but that night Ariane poured herself a glass of wine and sat up in the dark house and cried for hours.

Earlene and Dolphus got married in Start at Buddy Embanato's house, Buddy being the justice of the peace. Adlai and Miranda were witnesses. Boudou and Tous-les-deux were there and so were Purvis and Delano. After the ceremony they all went into Monroe and took photos of one another in Forsythe Park and then had a celebratory crawfish boil at Bryant's Crawfish Cabin. That was the day that the gunman opened fire with an AK-47 at the NRA National Convention in New Orleans, killing Charlton Heston and all those others.*

Adlai and Miranda spend as much time these days on the Airstream as at Avondale. They make some money from renting out the farmland, but sometimes Adlai worries that they don't have enough. Miranda's idea is, why do we need money if we already have what money will buy? After the reunion this summer, they're driving out to New Mexico, out to the desert. One more year of vagabonding (Miranda wants to see the Northern Plains), and then they start having children. Lots of them.

The last thing Royce said was, "I'll think of you after I'm dead if I can."

Boudou's passion is memory. He volunteers now with UL–M's David Jeffrey Institute of Vanishing Languages, where his job is to learn endangered languages from the last of their native speakers. They tell Boudou about their loneliness and distress, and about the comfort they feel in knowing that their culture and history will survive them, if only for a little while. Boudou's become a repository of singular and untranslatable ideas. What Boudou doesn't know yet is that he will begin to dream in these languages, and to remember the dreams, but will be unable to tell anyone about them because the events he dreamed can only be spoken of in Chamicuro or Cocama-Cocomilla. In the same way that *I am dying* is only a thought in English, and is, indeed, senseless in Qmilgau, where self and death are incomprehensible in a single sentence, so Boudou will come to understand that when he dies, his inherited ideas and the potential therein for new ideas will die with him, like the marvelous notion of a Land Without Evil and Death—a dense and timeless jungle where people live fearlessly and forever, deep, deep in the shade of a canopy of happiness.

Appendix

Page 56:

February 3, 1863, Vicksburg, Mississippi, C.S.A.

Dearest Sukey,

No struggle is ever unsuccessful, no matter how faint. Is it? My deepest affections to you, Suke, and my warmest salutations to your honorable father and goodly mother. (If your father, by the way, continues to suffer from toothaches, have him try this receipt that has proven efficacious here in camp: equal quantities of alum and salt, pulverized, mixed, and applied to the tooth with a wet wad of cotton.) I write knowing that I will be unable to post this letter until our dreadful siege is ended, until the Federals realize our inviolable position and take their leave, by God, or until we are all too weak, too decimated, too broken-hearted to resist.

As I write this evening, missiles launched from beyond the Yankee saps whistle above our tents. We stop, tense, await percussion, we tremble, and if there are no screams, we relax and carry on. There! A strike not fifty yards away, I would guess.

Though the shelling is often fierce, much of our time is passed in boredom. The men play two-base townball in the cemetery. I read old issues of Southern Illustrated News. *Pemberton has said there will be no carnival this year, news not warmly received by the ranks, some of which had busied themselves with the construction of masks already. You will recall, perhaps, that breezier time when I wrote you from Dallas Station, one year ago, during carnival. Didn't we have a time then? The old man himself was Dionysus and Colonel Pincus (rest his soul!) was Persephone, Queen of Carnival, and our regiment pronounced itself Krewe of Cerberus, Hellhounds of War. That's when I met that queer little trapper and his albino sons, remember? They brought us gator and bear meat. Stood there slack-jawed, the trapper did, seeing the army in dresses, feathers, and paint. Jeff Davis know about this? he asked me. I told him he should stay for the fandango, but he said his kind didn't antic with boys. That's just the way we are, Colonel, he says. No offense. I asked his name. I said, Peregrine, where you all from? Where's your home? We ain't home people, he said. We's abroad.*

Now that I am chief medical officer, my usual greeting to the men is, You're looking like your bowels are regular. Regularity being an uncommon though devoutly desired condition, rarer still now that our diet includes mule, canine, and weevil-infested pea flour. Excuse my lamentable irritability, darling Sukey.

It is now three quarters of an hour or so beyond the last sentence. I spoke with a young boy just now, a boy of fifteen years, a private from New Roads, who died in my arms of a defluxion of the breast. I am going to die, ain't I, sir? he asked me. Yes, son, I told him. You are going to die. He closed his eyes. I asked the nurse who this boy was. I said to him, the boy I mean, I said, God bless you, Charlie O'Toole. He smiled and nodded.

I fear another outbreak of malaria as the weather warms toward spring. And we are nearly out of turpentine and castor oil. Nearly out of anvil dust as well and will soon be unable to treat iron deficiency. I use the saw on the wounded. At the elbow, the knee. I am surprised at how rickety are the bones of our men, how easily sliced, like goat cheese.

*Until we are together again, Suke, dearest, sweet Suke, pray
for us, for our country, for our freedom.*

Yours in love,
Starkey

Page 64:

Excerpt taken from the transcript of Tape #1 of Tavis Sadberry's
recorded memoir, as edited and abridged by Professor Fleming
Oliver, Ph.D., of UL–M, and presented by him at the 15th Annual
Louisiana Cultural History Conference at the Bonnet Carré Holi-
day Inn in Kenner, Louisiana. The tape is archived at the Shiver-de-
Freeze Museum of Social and Natural History.

Course the Fontana I knowed best was Fluellen. This is
when I was working for Mrs. C. J. Breedlove, selling her
congolene door-to-door right here in Shiver-de-Freeze and
over to Monroe. I rode the blinds on the Illinois Central
from Delhi to get to Monroe. I had a family and all. Lived at
1094 Hope—just south of Prudence where they's a voodoo
shop nowadays. Whole family, two wifes, six children, they
children, all of them, gone years ago, and here I am the
same.

Fluellen's job was making bottle trees. Course he didn't
get paid for it. He was like on a mission to rid the town of
evil shades which he claimed he could feel all around him.
Fluellen was a banjo-belly, so fat he was in his own way. I'd
go cart-riding with Fluellen, say, along the bayou, and when
he'd feel a chill we'd stop. He'd strip the foliage off the clos-
est cedar, wash his Co-cola bottles in the dye he made from
wild indigo, slip the bottles over the up-pointing branches.
When the wind blew, you heard the captured haints moan-
ing inside them bottles.

Fluellen said though they weren't spirits and this wasn't
nothing to do with God or nothing. These evil characters
ain't from hell. They's from out there, he says. From the

stars, he meant. Evil ain't no spiritual affair to Fluellen, you understand. It is real. I knowed it was real already. Not many other folks as did, however. Well, this one afternoon, me and Fluellen is fishing in the slough off the river by the Ledbetter place, and we was surprised by a eclipse. We ain't read the newspaper, so we don't know. Fluellen says how some fool from space is put a bottle over the sun, and he says, "Blind your eyes, Tavis. The sun is black sackcloth." He says, "The moon is red as blood. We ain't gwine catch no fish today."

Page 70:

Dr. Calvin Speed of the Lamkin-Baker Institute for the Study of Memory was generous enough to share with us the notes of his May 6 session with Boudou in which Boudou tells the story of a Social Security number.

5/6 11 A.M. This morning Boudou drove his pulse from 75 beats to 160 beats a minute by imagining himself running up the stairs of the Ouachita National Bank building. He raised his body temperature to 101 degrees by recalling a fever he had when he was three. I had to ask him to stop before it went much higher and he became delirious. He reminded me that my sixteenth wedding anniversary was next week. I thanked him and made a note in my Daily Planner. He told me that Sears was having a sale on electronics. He said my wife had mentioned home theater systems to him in the waiting room. He asked me if I wanted to see him bleed. I did not. He said if he thought about the time he got his ear pierced, thought about it clearly, his lobe would bleed. I asked him if he was ready for a little test. He said, "You should have seen it, Doctor, your voice just went from sable to soot."

I showed Boudou an index card with his father's Social Security number, which, to my knowledge, he had never seen. I had typed the number in Courier 12 point. Boudou has remarked in the past that font styles, italics, and boldface will slightly alter the numerical imagery. For example, his number *1* is a man who lives alone, wears overalls and a straw Stetson. In Goudy, the man might wear a purple shirt. He'll be shoeless in Times New Roman. Shoeless and squinting into the sun in Times New Roman italics. Like that. Boudou looked at the number and said:

This is a sad one. By the time their handsome son died in the bed in the hospital room that had become his home, Mr. and Mrs. Warren were not living with each other, were not speaking to each other, were not visiting their son together. Mr. Warren stands by the bed and the dead son and realizes that as you are dying, all the hard work that went into making your body a person, all that work begins to show.

Page 73:

From *No Cure Was Found for Their Life: a History of the Fontanas of Northeast Louisiana,* by Johnny Ash. Monroe, Louisiana: University of Louisiana–Monroe Press, 1997.

Chapter 3: Eugenics

Boudou Fontana is now the last representative of a durable but bedeviled clan that lived out most of its days in a marshy clearing here in Monroe called Chauvin Bottom. To help you understand a bit about Boudou's pedigree we'll back up a bit to 1922, when we almost lost the Fontanas because of a misguided (although at the time it was considered progressive) policy of our amusing state government. Mind you this is the very state government that had a few years earlier decided to—what the hell—burn the rafts of water hyacinths clogging our waterways, burn them with flamethrowers "hot enough to melt blocks of steel." The result, unhappily, was that the hyacinths thrived on the fiery pruning and will be with us, it seems, in perpetuity.

(It might be said here, in defense of the government, that short-sightedness has often been applauded, admired, and respected here in Louisiana. Consider, for example, that in Bayou Goula, parishioners built the Madonna Church, which is so tiny that only the priest, not even the altar boy, can fit inside. In fact, it wasn't long before the pastor, Father Thihiol Prudomme, gourmet and confessor, could not fit inside. Or, listen to the words of one of our prominent state legislators, Nedra Espenschade, who in a recent debate concerning the ten-mile-wide dead zone off our Gulf coast, where no animal life can now exist, and why aren't we doing something about it, said, "What our esteemed colleagues across the aisle do not seem to understand is that extinction is not always a terrible thing. Did not the dinosaurs become our remarkable and profitable oil fields?" And this is just the manner of addled thinking that nearly eliminated our Fontanas.)

The goal of the Louisiana Institute of Eugenics (LIE) was to cleanse society of its undesirables. Humanely, of course. LIE concerned itself with the racial and inheritable qualities of the population and held that in time, if not dealt with, the objectionable, the noxious physical, mental, and moral traits of the few and the corrupt could and would pass on to the general population, understood to be the many, the white, the Christian, the principled. The Institute trained workers from the social-control professions (clergymen, teachers, welfare clerks, and so on) to identify the mentally incompetent, the morally repugnant, to study their families, and to make recommendations as to the handling of those families found to be afflicted with "bad gene plasm."

The fieldworkers were taught that feeble-mindedness generally manifested itself in physical stigmata, which rendered said dimwits more easily recognizable, what with their crossed-eyes, deafness, swollen joints, or what have you. And, naturally, the morally deranged—who could sometimes look like you or us—could be identified through police records. The eugenic solutions recommended for deviants and deficients might range from preventative breeding to institutionalization. Genetic and social worth, you understand, were thought to coincide. The idea—a venerable and cherished one to be sure—was to blame the victim. Blame and punish, to be precise. The national and state eugenics institutes, our own Louisiana Committee on Provision for the Feebleminded, and the Regional Conference on Charities and Corrections were all underwritten by the philanthropies of the Rockefellers, the Harrimans, the Carnegies, and other such noteworthy social and moral desirables.

It didn't take long for fieldworker Elnora Hibbard to locate the Fontanas. Who she stumbled upon first was Paris Fontana, who, if truth be told, was not the brightest star in the Fontana galaxy. Elnora sat fanning herself on the gallery of the Hotel Monroe and watched Paris walk down Grand Street swinging a chicken on a rope over his head. Elnora called to Paris who only just laughed (*cackled* is what Elnora would scribble in her report) until Elnora offered to buy him a lemon phosphate. The chicken was dead, and had been, it smelled like, for some time. Paris was pleased to escort Elnora out to the Bottom where she could interview the rest of the tribe and could scrutinize their domestic arrangements.

Elnora Hibbard wrote her first monograph on the Fontanas, entitled "A Study in the Social Degradation of Hereditary Defectives." In the paper, which the Fontanas and Monroyans did not know about at the time, Elnora called the Fontanas a "cocogenic [bad-gened] family" and accused them of, among other things, "insanity, criminality, indolence, vagabondage, loquacity, licentiousness, insolence, and promiscuity." She called their residence "the aptly named Bottom, a hotbed where human maggots spawn in their own excrement." Other papers and other studies by other fieldworkers followed. One paper took a historical slant and traced the Fontanas to a place called Valle Fontana in Italy, a place known for its kettlemenders and itinerant vendors, who were so generally disliked and mistrusted in the region that they were barred from many alpine villages.

All the fieldworkers seemed appalled by the same couple of things: the alleged promiscuity of the Fontanas and their apparent indifference to material possessions. No one with intelligence and civility would choose to live like this—in wood and tin shacks, in lean-tos, in canvas tents in the swamp, without so much as an oven, a credenza, a chest of drawers. Therefore, they reasoned that every man, woman, child out there was mentally incompetent, and the plan was to ship the imbeciles to the Parish Home for the Feeble-minded, the "high-grade morons" to the Parish Poorhouse—where at least they'd get grits and blankets—the underage to the State School for Spastic Children, and anyone who wouldn't leave the Bottom to jail.

At about this time, some of our citizens got wind of the plan, and a couple of them sat down in the hotel lobby with Elnora and her supervisor, Harvey Kunkel, Professor of Eugenics and Sociobiology at the Institute. Sweet iced tea was served. Norval Blake explained to the pair that sure there were a few instances of polyandry amongst the Fontanas, but that was due to the lack of females. The clan hadn't fully recovered from the Spanish flu or the War.

And just because they didn't bother with proper marriage licenses didn't mean they weren't married. This amused Elnora and the Yankee professor. Elnora sipped her tea. The children are bastards, Elnora said. This made Norval twinge. That a woman would use that word.

Professor Kunkel piped in. "Elnora—Miss Hibbard—advises me that there are men and women in Chauvin Bottom who can neither count their children nor name them."

"Is that a crime?" Norval said. "Being slow?"

"Your dim-witted are your criminal element, Mr. Blake," Elnora explained.

The professor explained his theory of social sanitation

slowly, so Norval and Wyatt Dyer, who was with him, could understand it. When he thought they did, he smiled.

Wyatt squinted. Norval sucked his teeth.

"Elnora," the professor said.

Elnora smiled at the professor, nodded. She opened her carpetbag and handed a tin box to the professor. He held it up. "Do you know what this is, gentlemen?"

Wyatt thought this might be a trick question. Norval said, "Seems to me you're acting a might slow now. That's a tin box."

The professor explained that inside the tin box were file cards with names, addresses, ages, etc., of all the mental defectives in Ouachita, Madison, and Morehouse parishes. We'll soon have a complete listing for the state, and we'll make the roster available to schools, sheriffs, clerks, and whoever else needs one.

Wyatt wondered was his own name on that list. Wondered what it would look like all stretched out on a page. Norval slapped his knees. The gentlemen stood and excused themselves. Norval said, "What you say, Professor, it's all bug-dust." They nodded, put on their hats. "You won't be hauling any Fontanas out of the Bottom."

"Oh, but we will." The professor smiled.

Oh, but they didn't. No one, not the sheriff, not the mayor, not any public official would lift a finger to help. The *Daily Star* ran an editorial against what it termed a conspiracy to kidnap. Elnora Hibbard and Professor Kunkel were invited to leave town by a citizens' committee. When the pair explained how the good townspeople of Alexandria had been grateful to be relieved of their hereditarily enfeebled, the professor was told, "We don't care how they did it down south. That crap don't flush in Monroe," or words to that effect.

"All right then," the professor said. He stood tall, adjusted his suit jacket, puffed himself up like a grouse. "It doesn't matter in the long run. Defective lines," he said, "tend naturally toward extinction."

Page 91:

Thoughts on plots. In 1894, Gustav Freitag suggested that the plot of a story takes the shape of a pyramid. Like this:

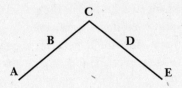

A is the introduction, *B* the rising action, *C* the climax, *D* the falling action, and *E* the catastrophe, the end. Such fearful and improbable symmetry.

At midcentury last, John Barth and others suggested a new geometry for plot:

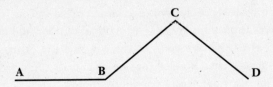

Here, the line *AB* represents exposition and point *B* the introduction of conflict. Line *BC* represents the rising action; point *C* the climax. Line *CD*, which may or may not exist, represents the denouement.

More recently, Janet Burroway offered the inverted checkmark:

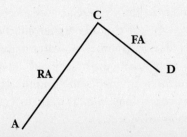

Closer to Freitag, perhaps, than to Barth, but without the nineteenth century insistence on harmony.

(Our three models, you will note, share the masculine notion of the single, isolated climax—the Big Bang, so to speak—our Aristotlean legacy. We can only speculate about what might have become of Western literature [not to mention Aristotle's household] if on that brisk Attic evening long ago, as Aristotle dutifully [his point of view] mounted his loving wife, if his mind had not drifted— as it so often did—to thoughts of Sophocles and the problem of the dramatic paradigm, if instead he had attended wholly to the business at hand, then he might have heard sweet Pythias whisper in his ear that rising action can generate multiple climaxes, darling, sometimes coming so quickly as to seem continuous, yes, uncontrollable, oh, yes, and resulting in a thunderous shuddering, a seizure of insight and transcendence. I've got your catharsis right here, honey. Had her sensible husband helped her ascend that rapturous ladder, Pythias might have gripped Aristotle's ample flanks with her viselike thighs, and with her fingernails might have inscribed on his hairy back the blueprint of her ecstacy, the shape of her euphoria:

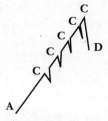

And in her postbrisance serenity, a blissful Pythias might have snuggled her randy philosopher, told him about serial consummation, how the emptied vessel needs refilling, how every fall has its rise, how every story is, at least, a trilogy, my dearest. And she might then have fondled her flaccid spouse, teased him to action. However, before any of this could happen, Aristotle, having achieved his own hasty purgation, spent now and weary, drifted off to sleep and to dreams of peripeties, leaving his wife, the unmoved mover, alert, distressed, her desires unresolved.)

Our own plot thus far could be diagrammed like so:

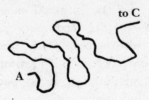

We're on our way. Our own seismic-looking side trips are digressions, not distractions. The latter are to be avoided at all costs, in art and in life.

Page 101:

Underwood Abdelnour is the last of the parish's fabled Lecture Men. At one time lecturing door-to-door in the community was a competitive business, and two or three gentlemen might be pitching their wares on a person's doorstep of a Saturday night. Lecture was a popular entertainment in the days before television and movies and singles' nights at Piggly Wiggly. People today would rather sit around playing Trivial Pursuit than engage in serious social discourse. Underwood's daddy Chandler was a Lecture Man (specializing in Bible history) and his daddy before him (Reconstruction). Chandler once spoke to a crowd of three dozen men, women, and children in Augusta Thompson's home on the subject of *Weatherwise Gardening*. There were people in the kitchen, on the staircase, poking in through windows. Of course, that was during the Great Awakening in Shiver-de-Freeze, back between the wars when the rest of the country was dealing with the Depression.

Underwood uses his lecture profits to pay for correspondence college (Ayn Rand Extension University). When he finally gets his distance-learned Ph.D., Underwood plans to quit his day job (sales associate at Baxendale's Casual Male, *For the Big and Tall Man of Style*), open a philosophy office near the Social Ocean, do a little consulting on occasion (government, service industries, the usual). The days when a learned man makes house calls to share his expertise and rhetorical skills with assembled guests in a patron's parlor may be nearly over.

Underwood is no longer a spring chicken, and the traipsing from house to house is becoming a grind. Many of his regular clients have died, and their children have perhaps heard all their favorite addresses several times. Once he gets his foot in the door, he knows he's okay. It's just the getting in the door that's becoming more difficult and more humiliating. "You'd think I was peddling headache powders," Underwood told the Monroe *News-Star*. "Some folks are afraid of enlightenment. It's a physical thing with some of them. They tremble when they see me. One time I could count on four lectures a week in Sodom & Gomorrah. Now I'm lucky if I get four a year." The more educated folks are also getting picky. They want to see the paper, the degree. "They'll as much as say to me, 'Who are you to hold forth on a subject which you have not specialized in studying?' I hand them my business card: *Underwood Abdelnour, Polymath.* That's who I am. They'll listen to Oprah Winfree blather about anything, like she's the Queen of Discernment, Our Lady of Understanding, but they won't listen to me. When did a camera become an advanced degree?"

We print, with Underwood's approval, his business brochure for your examination.

Underwood Abdelnour / The Lecture Man

Available for: Salons, Socials, Birthday Parties, Anniversaries, Church Suppers, Box Lunches, Barbecues, Baptisms, Conferences, Rent Parties, Quilting Bees, Union Meetings, Brunches, Teas, At-Homes, Drop-Ins, Shivarees, Rotary Luncheons, Commencements, Ribbon Cuttings, Radio Call-Ins, Funerals, Wakes, Graduations, Annual Meetings, Family Reunions, Cocktail Parties, Convocations, Conventions, Banquets, Cotillions, Coffee Klatches, Company Picnics, Field Days, Press Clubs, Bon Voyages, *Wherever Two Or More Of You Are Gathered . . .*

The Five-Dollar Lecture (Approximately 45 Minutes): *The Surrender of Vicksburg; The Happiness Instinct; The Successful Tomato Garden; Poverty Point*

Culture; How to Roast a Wild Boar; A Brief History of the Fontanas; From Here to Maternity: the Politics of Conception; You and Your Cocker Spaniel; Write That Sonnet!; Collecting Ephemera; Weatherwise Farming; Mr. Sears and Mr. Roebuck; The Bo Diddly Beat; Self? Help!; Training Your Maine Coon; Introduction to Mycology; Collecting Fiestaware; The Bourbons and the Know-Nothings; The Personal Correspondence of Jesse James; A Deconstructionist Examination of the Interoffice Memos of Wallace Stevens, Insurance Executive.

The Ten-Dollar Lecture (Approximately 50 Minutes to an Hour): *The Moving Image of God; Love Is an Appetite; A Natural History of the Louisiana River Basin; Know Your Waterbirds (with slides); Fuzzy Similarity Clusters; Hume's Dogmatic Slumber; Folk Artists of Northeast Louisiana; On the Road to Mermenteau: an Adventurer's Tour Through Louisiana (with color slides and postcards); If Immanuel Kant, Then Genghis Khan: Order and Chaos in the Life of the Mind; Beauty Cannot Be Bad; The Climax of Emptiness; Breathing as Metaphor; The Myth of Coherence.*

The Fifteen-Dollar Lecture (Approximately One Hour with Q & A): *The Oort Cloud; Embracing Paradox; The Ipseity of God; The Nag Hammadi Library; The Note of a Note Is a Note of the Thing Itself; The Tradition of the Picaro in Louisiana Politics; Blue Genes; Weakly Interactive Massive Particles; The Imagined Attic; The Wind Is Free; Troy Brodie: One Man Sawmill; Asian Pen Pals; 1-800-Redfish; An Evening with Huey Long; Salvador Dali: Visionary Fascist.*

Underwood will also offer spontaneous opinions on the subject of your choice!
For a scheduled lecture call Baxendale's Sportswear Department
and leave a message.

Page 106:

Seal Boy was born with a genetic condition called ectrosyndactyly in which his fingers and toes had essentially fused at the ends of his foreshortened limbs, leaving him with flippers rather than the usual arms, hands, legs, and feet. He worked in the Pelican State Carnival sideshow, married, sired three kids, two with his unfortunate condition and one without. He murders the normal daughter's boyfriend—straps on his prosthetic hands and blasts young Elliot

Nault in the groin with an elephant gun—and gets a merciful fifteen years probation because of his deformity, maybe, or because of his emphysema or his cirrhosis.

Then Seal Boy's wife of nineteen years, Roberta, divorces him and marries the world's tiniest man, Bob Muldoon, known as Banty Bob, and they have a boy they optimistically name Hoss, who grows up to be the Human Blockhead—drives nails up his nostrils with a hammer. Meanwhile normal daughter shoots herself in the head during her father's act, and people applaud, thinking it's part of the show. It takes her weeks to die.

Roberta grows tired of Banty Bob's constant philandering and leaves him. She remarries Seal Boy, and they honeymoon in Grand Isle. Seal Boy by now is drinking heavily and slapping Roberta around. She and her son conspire to rid themselves of Seal Boy and avail themselves of his handsome bank account. They hire the boy next door to do the job. The boy next door is the Chameleon, so called because of his bulbous eyes, leathery skin, and the ability to blend with his surroundings. Chameleon knocks on Seal Boy's door and comes into the trailer and stands behind Seal Boy's recliner. Seal Boy is watching wrestling, smoking reefer, sipping whiskey. Chameleon drills two bullets into Seal Boy's brain. At the trial, people who knew the couple, like the Limbless Lady, Rubber Man, Radium Boy, the Human Porcupine, and Leopard Lady, all testified for the prosecution. How hard, they reasoned, would it have been to walk away from the Seal Boy when he got nasty?

Page 110:

Margaret Grimes had been disheartened so often at restaurants by the scandalous preparation of what she called porched eggs that she took to carrying recipe cards with her, which instructed the cooks in the proper method of porching. Her own preferred porching medium was water, but milk would do or wine (if you've got certain pretensions) or chicken broth—most any liquid, in fact. But you cannot boil the egg hard. We pass along Margaret's advice:

Boil three inches of salted water in a skillet. Add a drop of apple cider vinegar. Break your egg on a saucer (two eggs two saucers). Slide the eggs into the water, turn off the heat and cover. Cook for three minutes. Not three minutes and ten seconds. Three minutes. Remove with slotted spoon. Trim the edges. Thank you.

Page 116:

Jean-Paul Sartre walks into a café in the 2nd Arrondisement and settles into a quiet corner in the back. Simone is not in the café. He's here to prepare a philosophy exam for his students. He's not feeling all that well—a touch of nausea. The waitress is busy with the phenomenologists across the room. That could take a while—they all have to touch the beans, inhale the aroma. The exam then will be one question:

Why did the chicken cross the road?
 A. to live deliberately
 B. to die
 C. to be true to itself
 D. it had no choice
 E. all of the above
In answering, please consider Zeno's paradox, Heisenberg's Uncertainty Principle, Chicken-Nature, the possibility of not-crossing. For Extra Credit: Is there a road?

Finally the waitress arrives. Sartre asks her for a coffee without cream.

She says, "Monsieur Sartre, I'm so sorry. We are out of cream today."

"All right, then, I'll have it without milk."

Page 124:

LEAVING YOU/WANTING TO
Earlene Fontana (Cousins Music, Inc.)

You're married to the single life
And coupled to the road,
And I'm in bed with loneliness

And I'm borrowed and I'm blue
But I'd rather be alone
Than be alone with you.

You're married to a single wife
Your supper's getting cold.
I was your one and onliness
Too much sorrow now, it's true,
The sadness that I've known
I've known because of you.

Leaving you and wanting to
Loving to and wanting you
Haunting you and grieving too
Loving you and leaving you.

Page 159:

The Fontanas laid claim to being the only family in northeast Louisiana to have borne a child without the mess and turbulence of the sexual act. This would be the birth of Mangham and Bosco's half-brother Henry in the spring of 1864. Peregrine, you see, had gone smitten with a Miss Twyla Whatley, a seventeen-or-so-year-old schoolteacher in Madison Parish. Peregrine, whose woman, Velma Littlejohn, the twins' momma, was just then ailish with the slows, found himself setting his traps closer and closer to Miss Twyla's lodgings south of Young's Point. For a while he was content to stay his distance from the handsome schoolteacher and to await the proper opportunity to make his affections known. That opportunity knocked when Miss Twyla advertised by word of mouth for an escort with a farm wagon to haul her and five students to Vicksburg to watch the battle being fought there. Peregrine volunteered.

Miss Twyla, wearing a sapphirine dress and a wide-brimmed hat, sat up front with Peregrine while the children, three redheaded brothers, another boy, shoeless and drippy-nosed, and an eleven-year-old girl, sat in back. The girl sang to the others and later read them from *Nights in Biloxi*, which Miss Twyla told Peregrine was written by an officer who served with General Braxton Bragg and was cousin to President Davis himself. Miss Twyla, for her part, read silently from a leather-bound book. Her lips moved, Peregrine noticed. She told him the book was Mrs. Stowe's *Sunny Memories of Sunny Lands*. Yes, she said, the same Mrs. Stowe.

Peregrine took the cart path along the torn-up tracks of the Vicksburg, Shreveport and Texas Railroad to Grant's canal at Tuscumbia Bend. He followed the canal southeast to a corduroyed road that led along the river to the Brown Plantation. From there, the adventurers were ferried across the river to the mouth of Big Bayou. Once the children heard the distant reports of musketry, they were too excited to sit, all except the eleven-year-old girl, who kept right on reading out loud to no one but herself. The others got on down from the farm wagon and ran alongside it through the raddled field all the way to the Warrenton Road, a quarter of a mile or so below the Marine Hospital.

Peregrine parked the wagon on the bluff south of town. He tied the skittish chestnut mare to a sourwood bush. This was a marvelous prospect indeed. The class could watch the skirmish on the river below or could turn and study the thousands of foot soldiers battling on the plain to their right. Peregrine pointed out a Federal gunboat sitting off DeSoto Peninsula and firing on the city's river batteries. He showed the children the Confederate earthworks and then to the east the Yankee lines. The hills around Vicksburg were covered with spectators and the yellow clay hills themselves were honeycombed with caves.

In no time at all, counting the casualties became an arithmetic lesson. The class counted to near two hundred before they grew bored. The youngest boy asked Miss Twyla why it was you could see the smoke of the rifles before you could hear the discharge. She explained as to how the sound slowed as it climbed the bluff while their vision, on the contrary, was all the time going down the hill—Isaac Walton's Law of Gravity, she said.

A young gentleman toting a cloth shoulder bag, smoking a cheroot, and wearing a flat-crowned, narrow-brimmed hat, walked toward them through the sedge and thickets by the river and across the open field. He introduced himself as Jim Richardson, correspondent for the Augusta *Constitutionalist*. Jim Richardson told Peregrine and Miss Twyla that Pemberton had been routed just two days ago at Big Black River Bridge. But this assault, he said, and motioned to the debouched Union troops advancing on the Confederate works, this is sheer Yankee folly. In fact, it was Jim Richardson's considered opinion that Pemberton had lured Grant here and would keep him occupied until Johnson arrived from the rear with reinforcements. Vicksburg, of course, was impregnable. Why, the whole town can just burrow into the hillsides and allow the Federals to spend their ordnance. Miss Twyla said that perhaps Mr. Jim Richardson would honor their class by joining them for lunch. "We haven't much, I'm afraid. Cornbread, collards, gravy, some hominy." Then she seemed to go real dreamy, Peregrine noticed, like a cat when you scratch behind its ears, and said, "An egg, Mr. Jim Richardson, is a rare and precious thing."

Jim Richardson thanked Miss Twyla copiously, thanked Peregrine, who had said nothing, who had wanted to cry, in fact, at the prospect of sharing Miss Twyla's attentions with a man who knew the names of generals, thanked them, but said that he needed to hasten to the Confederate lines.

Miss Twyla looked at her toes and then at a spot on Jim Richardson's lapel. "You're a for-real writer, are you, Mr. Jim Richardson?"

"Yes, I am, Miss Twyla." Jim Richardson excused himself, lifted his hat, nodded, and took his leave. Miss Twyla gazed after him. "Swanny," she said, "a writer, and so close he could hear my heart beat. Now, Mr. Fontana, would you kindly spread the picnic blanket? And take the larder down from the wagon, would you? The children and I will pray for victory while you get us ready."

Peregrine had smelled the cornbread all the way out on the morning's journey, since before light, and now, in midafternoon, he was famished. He hadn't eaten now in two days, partly because he was so excited with his good fortune, but mostly because he had bartered three squirrels for the day's use of the horse and cart. He wanted cornbread real bad and thought he'd sneak some while the others weren't looking.

Miss Twyla stood in the bed of the wagon, tootled into her pitch pipe, and the children on the grass below sang "The Bonnie Blue Flag." Peregrine cupped a morsel in his hands. He straightened up as nonchalantly as he could and turned to see if Miss Twyla or the choir had spied him. Then it happened.

Dr. Tyson Bordelon, from the Memphis City Hospital, summoned to Richmond to care for Twyla Whatley, wrote the whole thing up in the *Journal of Southern Medicine* (Vol. XX, No. 2, Fall, 1864): A soft lead fragment from a chance bullet fired from a 15-shot Henry repeating rifle, discharged by a Union soldier, caused a tibial fracture in Mr. Fontana's left leg and then carried away his left testicle, carried it away from his groin and toward the abdomen of Miss Twyla W., where it penetrated the skin, the muscle, the membrane of her womb. In other words, Dr. Bordelon explained, and improbable as it might sound, spermatozoa gained access to the uterus via the bullet. More peculiar still, the spent projectile was removed from the scrotum of the baby by Dr. Bordelon after the birth.

Throughout most of Miss Twyla's troublesome pregnancy and for all of her difficult convalescence, Dr. Bordelon left her in the care of Richmond's apothecary, Mr. Porter Epps. For that ten months, Miss Twyla lay in at his home, Chateau d'Epps on the Sondheimer Road. The chateau was nothing more, really, than a Frenchified dog-trot, but was the largest and most splendid structure in that railroad town.

Porter Epps administered to Miss Twyla the usual restoratives and emetics, including Dr. Feelright's Rheumatic and Parturient Elixir, according to the regimen prescribed by Dr. Bordelon. But, in fact, Porter Epps had much more faith in the curative influence of his curious new machine, the Aesthetico-Neuralgicon. He had ordered the labyrinthine appliance for $34.75 through a medical supply house in Baltimore before the war, and it had taken him nearly three years to receive and to assemble it.

As Porter Epps explained it to Miss Twyla, this device with its twenty-two beakers, its intersecting wires, its maze of tubes, and its two menacing steel catheters, could cure any disorder, infirmity, seizure, eruption, or malaise, including milkleg, the pox, and galloping consumption, by introducing the appropriate medicaments into the afflicted tissues through the nose. Porter Epps reassured Miss Twyla at the first of his daily treatments, and thereafter, that though the procedure may feel peculiar, alarming even, she should relax, breathe through her mouth, and be certain that she would not drown.

During Miss Twyla's ordeal at Chateau d'Epps, Peregrine visited her weekly. She had lost her job, of course, the students' parents choosing not to believe in the ballistic theory of conception—they were not fools. The baby, Henry Whatley Fontana, died, Dr. Bordelon surmised, from acute lead poisoning at ten days of age. Peregrine convinced the depressed and destitute Miss Twyla to come live with his family. As the couple were leaving his chateau, Porter Epps drew Peregrine aside and said, "Perhaps you've noticed, sir, that a woman's ways are different from our own," and he handed Peregrine an amber phial of laudanum and said, "This will settle her nerves, or yours."

For her part, Velma Littlejohn was delighted to have another someone around to help her with the chores, an educated woman at that, someone she could talk with, not like the chuckleheads her boys fiddled with. Although she did not mention it, she was relieved as well that the adulterine issue of Miss Twyla's loins had gone to meet his maker. Not that she was huffish, not exactly anyway, about that mercurial outbreed, but she was, shall we say, covetous of her uxorial privileges. As for Bosco and Mangham, they were shy but attentive to Miss Twyla's needs and smart enough to know to keep their glairy eyes and clumsy paws off their daddy's property. Everything remained copacetic for the Fontanas until the day Peregrine limped off to check his traps along Bayou Maçon and never came back.

Page 160:

In 1871 Clan Fontana made a compact with Our Lady of Immediate Succor Industrial School and Model Farm for Girls in Alexandria by which the family agreed to provide room (broadly defined, of course) and board (likewise) for those girls who had outgrown the school and had decided not to enter the Holy Cross Convent. Perhaps because they lived in the absence of men, the girls at the school came into puberty late, which pleased the Fontanas. The arrangement would be the pipeline for Fontana wives from Reconstruction right up until the Great War when suddenly every young, unattached woman in Louisiana wanted to be a nurse, it seemed. We know that two of Bosco's wives, Randeane, and when Randeane died, Caroline, had both attended Our Lady. His first wife, Peyton (née Merriweather), was one of the half dozen mutilated survivors of the Vicksburg siege who had wandered away from that city which had no use for the armless, footless, and in one case, jawless, reminders of the late, ignominious capitulation. The Fontanas came upon the refugees in a stand of poplars west of Richmond, camped beneath a wheeling flock of turkey vultures. Right away Bosco sat down with Peyton, introduced himself, and told her how he was sure sorry about her fingers and her ear and everything. "I seen worse," she said.

Three other letters of interest archived at the Museum also pertain to the Fontanas:

December 3, 1868, Epps, Louisiana
To the Editor, Louisiana Intelligencer Weekly:
  I write, sir, in response to your headline of October last, "Missouri Outlaws Seek Sanctuary in Swamps." As one of those mentioned in your scandalous article, I must object. We are not criminals like you say, but veterans of the Late Friction, that rich man's war, poor man's fight. We, sir, and men like us, are the victims, not the perpetrators of theft. We have been robbed of our youth, our friends, our homes, our country, and we are bitter, and we are desperate. And the rich then are the rich now, and they are not us. They are the reavers, sir, and they are, Mr. Editor, your friends among the Farmers and Merchants Bank, your friends

*among the officers of the occupying forces. My friends and I, we are
fishermen. We harvest sac-au-lait and catfish in Bayou Maçon as
we try to put our lives together. We trade with the Fontana tribe
who have likewise been maligned in your pages as barbarians and
gypsies. The fish heads and entrails you'll find on your drawing
room floor this evening will attest to our vocation and ambition.
Please, sir, do not malign the working class again, lest you meet,
eye to burning eye, the specter that haunts the Delta.*

Respectfully,
Jesse Woodson James

June 9, 1870, Delhi, Louisiana
Mr. Bing Viafuga,

    *I am so happy that as I am able to write I am likewise able to
thank you in person, sort of, Mr. Viafuga, and testify on behalf of
your terrific patent medicinal tonic. Not only can I write, having
been to industrial school, I can too parse a sentence and cipher
within reason.*

    *I was a long time afflicted with peculiar female complaints
prostrating my system with night sweats and all-overs. Thank the
Lord it were not a catching disease as no one in our camp is so likewise ailish. I have tried extract hemamelis what made me feather-
legged. And too have tried cathartic pills and rochelle salts and
paregoric and willow bark to no effect.*

    *But your medicine has fortified me to a remarkable degree
and relieved me of croup, chills, night sweats, jitters, nervous com-
plaints, derangement of my liver, blockage in my sinus, it has
stimulated my torpid kidneys, relaxed my hamstrung womb. I am
gaining flesh (in all the right places) and am thankful beyond my
poor ability to express it. It has too halted acid bumps from erupt-
ing like they do on my arms and legs. Now that I think on it,
Bing's Viafuga Medicinal Tonic and Emetic has also settled my
fungus quite nicely and I know has eased Twyla's touch of consumption. So I thank you, Bing Viafuga, you and your chemistry.*

Clotille Fontana

March 5, 1863, Vicksburg, Miss., C.S.A.
Dearest Sukey,

Save for the occasional report of a sharpshooter's (ours) rifle, all is quiet. We eat well for now. Slapjacks, hominy. Pea flour a bit musty. Beans shipped from Jackson before the seige are now infested with weevils. Last night a shell tore through the General's tent and interrupted his poker game with Colonels Hayes and Williams. No one hurt.

You will want to know that Zack Harris, Mose Harris's boy with the lazy eye (he ran with the Fontanas up in the Tensas for a while), has been killed, and it could have been me. Zack and I, we were fired upon as we walked, carelessly, I'm afraid, along the bluff by the sulter's tent. We ran like mad and scrambled down the hill to where the daguerreian artist's wagon stood and crawled beneath it. Zack put his hand under his blouse and discovered his inner garments drenched in blood. He looked surprised. He looked at his hand. He asked me what did this mean. That is the way it goes with us. I have seen a child outside the pharmacy look up when she heard the whistle and freeze and be struck and exploded so that it rained flesh for several dark seconds. And yet there are days of tranquillity and repose. Last Sunday I heard a stirring sermon by the Reverend Prosper (of Clinton) on the subject of "There Is a Fountain Filled with Blood."

I have been placed in charge of what is left of our Monroe Zouaves and Cadets, who call themselves now the Ouachita Fenables. The oldest of these boys is not sixteen and all do look properly handsome as soldiers. These boys who were once so frisky when they got hold of some Yankee dead near Pin Hook have lapsed into a state of languidness that is pitiful and ill-boding.

They have taken to sleeping at night in the pews of the Baptist church though it is an easier target for the Federal gunboats. With the help of the Vicksburg Ladies Auxiliary, the Fenables will perform scenes from the Bard's *A Midsummer's Night's Dream* on the courthouse lawn Tuesday week. This, I hope, will rouse the boys from their lethargy. We have taken to shooting dogs, who, having nothing to eat, are grown feisty and dangerous.

It's now four p.m. and the shelling has stopped. I was called this
morning to a cave where a young woman of the town, one Essie
Hardaway, was hit by shrapnel and lost both legs above the knees.
She felt fuzzy, she said, like her bones were all humming, and she
could smell something like copper. I said to her, "Miss Essie, we have
stopped the bleeding. You are going to be all right." She held my
shirt by the collar. She said, "Who's going to marry me now, sir?"

When the Yankees finally leave us, I will post this letter to
you, Sukey, and you will know that I will be arriving at your door
shortly. Until then, our trust is in the Lord and President Davis. I
long to be with you, dear, to smell your neck again, to feel your
breath beneath my ear, to touch your waist with my fingertips. I
know you have blue eyes, but what color blue?

Yours in love, Starkey.

Page 180:

When Earlene did finally learn about Varden's death—read it in
the *News-Star*: "Country Singer Roebuck, at 44"—she sent Boudou
to stay the night at Avondale, opened a bottle of Jack Daniel's (Varden's predictable drink of choice), dimmed the living room lights,
clicked on the CD player, settled in the Morris chair, and listened to
Varden sing. She hoped to cry. *Who can say what's true / When I lie in*
bed with you . . . She'd cry for Varden. For Billy Wayne. For all the
boys who came and went, who promised undying love and disappeared. So what then was love to them? An honorable notion, a
fancy, a desire for pleasure, comfort, reassurance, attention.

Varden sang about *the purity of her indifference.* When Earlene
wrote the song it was, of course, *his* indifference. Here was a man
who died from lack of imagination, who thought he needed to live in
misery in order to sing about it, who reckoned that authenticity
equaled truth. Goddamit, Varden, life isn't tragic because you're a
falsifier or a fraud, because you're drunk again or because your coon
hound won't hunt and your pickup won't crank. Life is tragic
because you die, because all our love ripens to pain. We write songs
so we can live other lives, not repeat our own.

Earlene poured herself three more fingers. She put on George
Jones. She felt like a mended pitcher, serviceable, but no longer
lovely. She felt brittle. She took out the Leonard Cohen, the Willie
Nelson. Yes, she thought, the tears would come. She'd have her
release, her relief. *When we meet again up yonder . . .*

Page 193:

Today's JLC Luncheon Menu

> " *It's good food and not fine words
> that keeps me alive.*"   —*Molière*

Appetizers:

Salted Pigeon Eggs. *A dozen beauties steamed or hardboiled, served on
a bed of collards.*

Bass Sperm Crepes. *Chopped and bound in a bechamel sauce. Rolled,
garnished with Romano and butter. Baked.*

Stewed Veal Chins. *Browned, fried in unsalted butter, and simmered in
Zinfandel.*

Tree Snail Escargot. *In red wine sauce and garlic butter. Served with
our homemade cornbread.*

Caesar Salad. *Yes, the eggs are raw.*

Soups:

Fried Possum Stew. *With potatoes, rice, onions, carrots, and tomatoes.*

Hog Head Soup. *With bacon and a rich, creamy tomato broth. Served
over toast points.*

Watermelon Soup. *With chicken stock, necks, and backs, watermelon rind and vegetables.*

Today's TLC Luncheon Menu

*"Food's so fine makes me want to spit
in my skillet." — Gov. Edwin Edwards*

Entrees:
(All entrees served with mashed sweet potatoes, savory grits, and black-eyed peas.)

Great Lakes Lamprey Casserole. *With leeks and carrots, vermouth and wine.*

Baked Armadillo. *Served in shell, stuffed with potatoes, cabbage, carrots, apple, garlic butter, seasoned and basted with butter.*

Cajun Squirrel Ravioli. *Ground squirrel meat sauteed in bacon fat and garlic, chopped with spinach and watercress and covered with tomato ravioli. Served with Tabasco marinara.*

Deep Fried Hedge Eels. *Sliced, dusted with cayenne-seasoned flour, immersed in boiling lard.*

Grilled Breast of Chipping Sparrows. *Cane River sparrows served with natural huckleberry au jus.*

Desserts:

Drunkard's Pudding. *Opelousas yams, Ouachita pecans, and a splash of Jim Beam.*

Fried Apples. *Macoun's, imported from Massachusetts.*

Mango-Banana Pie. *Topped with fresh whipped cream.*

Page 211:

By *sort of* we mean he snuck a bit of the story into the appendix:

At Joe DeSalvo's Krewe of Snopes Mardi Gras bash, guests arrived costumed as their favorite literary characters. The party spilled out of the Faulkner House Bookstore and into Pirate's Alley, where Ruthanne and Macky (Tinkerbelle and Ignatius J. Reilly) sat at a café table sipping vodka martinis and watching Snow White kiss Stanley Kowalski. Macky wondered where he'd find the courage to say what he needed to say. He looked at his wife sprinkled with glitter, with fairy dust. "Ruthanne, I have something to tell you."

"Don't take your mask off till midnight, darling."

"This isn't easy."

"Have you noticed how the Misfit's been hound-dogging Scarlett O'Hara all evening?"

"It's something about myself that I've known for a long time, since before Zack was born." Why couldn't he say it?

Ruthanne tapped him on the shoulder with her wand. "Poof, you're happy!"

"Didn't you ever suspect?"

"Oh, I forgot to tell you about Martine's husband Billy. You know Billy. He's dead. Listen to this."

"Ruthanne, listen to me."

"He's riding along with Buster Cousy in Buster's old Impala down Tchoupotoulas, and they're talking about the eggs sardou at Commander's when evidently Buster stopped attending to the road and slammed into the back of a Federal Express truck, and Billy, who was wearing a lap belt, got folded forward at sixty miles an hour and just before his forehead bent the dashboard, this little metal magnetic crucifix stabbed into his eye, and then he sprung back up into his seat, and Buster looked over to see Our Savior's feet sticking out of poor Billy's bloody socket."

"I need to talk about us."

"I can't imagine what it must be like for Martine."

"I'm gay, Ruthanne."

"Honey, you're under a lot of stress, I know that. So once in a while you can't perform—"

"I don't want to perform with you, Ruthanne. I mean I would, but—"

"You need some time to yourself. Away from me and the job. Some R&R."

"You know where I was last night?"

"Carrie and Harris Postels love the Grand Canyon. Stayed at that El Tovar. Said the whole park was just crawling with Germans."

"I was with a man I don't even know in Greenwood Cemetery. And I had no trouble 'performing,' as you call it."

"Everyone spoke German, even the rangers and the Japanese tourists. Yes. Little Orientals with cowboy hats talking for all the world like Günter Grass."

"You haven't heard a word I've said."

"You liked that book, didn't you? Brown eyes can never see through blue-eyed types."

"I'm trying to say we're in trouble here, Ruthanne."

"I should call the sitter, see did she get Zack in the sack all right."

Macky took hold of her arm, held her in her seat. "You're going to sit and listen." He let go. "Please."

"Take me home, Macky, would you?"

"Ruthanne—"

"I'm exhausted. We'll talk in the morning when we're fresh."

"I'm gay, and I can't go on pretending I'm not. I won't. It's killing me. This lie. Eating me away."

"Home to Never-never Land."

Page 213:

It so happened that Adlai had been loved by Eileen Irick when they were classmates in high school. Eileen was on the way home from school when her sort-of friend Lisa Delcambre caught up with her outside the Tae-kwon-do Academy. Lisa told Eileen what she'd just found out—that Adlai Birdsong had fallen in love with her, with Eileen, and wanted to ask her out. Eileen, ungainly, plain-looking (even her momma said so), certainly not pep squad material, when she got home went to her room, lay for a long time on the bed, trembling with fear. That night she couldn't sleep. She sat at her window looking out across the cotton field to the back of the houses on Ruston Street. She tried to imagine herself and Adlai sitting together on the glider on the front porch. Then she and Adlai at a football game. She and Adlai parked in his car along Bayou Coup de Foudre. And toward morning she had fallen in love with cute and smart and peculiar Adlai Birdsong. And she knew from that moment on, her lips would fill with laughter, dancing, and hope.

She wore the platinum party dress with the floral print and the empire waist, the silver sandals with the wedge heels. She clipped three star barrettes in her hair, wore a black suede choker. She figured Adlai would approach her in home room. Or later at lunch, depending on how nervous he was. She would sit on the bench near the pecan tree. Pretend to read a book, not look up until his shadow darkened her page. Yes, lunch would be best. When Eileen arrived at school, Lisa was waiting for her by the front door. She apologized. It seemed she'd heard it wrong. Adlai wasn't going to ask her out after all. He was asking Anniece Pate.

Page 219:

Excerpts from *The Vindicator* interview.

DH: Our readers want to know about Radley Smallpiece, the man. Tell us who you are.

RS: Well, there's the me flopped here in the chair. Chemicals, minerals, electricity; the me that's answering the question; the me full of passions and desires, fears and obsessions. Then there's the me inside—not the me you see, the me I let you see, the me that folks can pretend to know. There's the younger me in my memory who lives in many places and times, who is young and old, legged and amputated, svelte and dumpy, furious and flaggy, happy, sad, and puzzled all at once. And there's the me that connects all these little—

DH: The Uber Radley.

RS: I'm one me with you, another with Homer, and a different me with the pair of you. I'm a different me when I read than when I talk, different when I watch TV than when I think.

DH: How did you lose your legs?

RS: They were taken from me by the sugar. First the feet, then the legs. Bitch of it is I still feel them, the pain, the itch, the cramps—all of it. Right now I'm kicking you in the cojones.
It's like my brain has this idea of what I am and won't give it up, won't believe my lying eyes.

DH: Excuse me for asking, but how does a convicted felon like yourself acquire a weapon?

RS: Cheese and crust, Dolphus, this is America. You can get whatever you want in America.

DH: Why did you kill the Chameleon?

RS: If I did—and I'm not saying I did—I followed the word of the Good Book: "Thou shalt give life eye for eye, tooth for tooth, hand for hand, foot for foot. Burning for burning, wound for wound, stripe for stripe."

DH: "Be not overcome of evil, but overcome evil with good."

RS: "As thou hast done, it shall be done unto thee."

DH: "See that none render evil for evil unto any man."

RS: We through with Dueling Scripture?

DH: Tell us about life in prison.

RH: I pretty much kept to myself, didn't buy alcohol or drugs from the guards or get involved in prisoners' industries. Just punched out auto tags and watched TV in the lounge. I didn't have that pain under my ribs all the time. You cannot be a derelict without you're a drunk, I found out. You got too much time on your hands; you get too much thinking done; you've got all this energy undissipated by demon rum. It becomes impossible to sit in one spot for eight or nine hours, so you start planning your day at first, and then your life, and then you make lists, and then you do things and consider the consequences of your behavior. Well, once the future enters your life in any guise other than where's the next drink coming from, you're finished as a bum. Soon, you're trying to improve yourself, which, at first, is so easy that you develop a false sense of confidence. Disaster follows.

Page 278:

> *In our boathouse*
> *We'll sleep all night,*
> *My sweetheart dear,*
> *You know I love you,*
> *So hold me near.*
> *My love's as wide as the swamp is wide.*
> *For your love I would*
> *Crawl through Tohu Bohu*
> *For your love I would*
> *Wrestle the Loup Garoup.*
>
> *In our boathouse*
> *We'll dream all night*
> *My sweetheart true*
> *You know I love you*
> *So love me too.*
> *My love's a bottomless lake.*
> *For your love I would*
> *Drink Fontana Bayou*
> *And come home drunk, love*
> *To sleep and dream by you.*
>
> *In our boathouse*
> *"We'll sleep all night*
> *My sweetheart dear,*
> *My sweetheart dear.*

In Our Boathouse

Page 303:

After which Varden listened to the swelling thunder of the approaching semi, grimaced, waited for the thud and silence, saw his momma's face, just her face, inches from his own, opened his eyes, realized it hadn't been too late a half second ago, that that was his momma's message to him, but now it was, and his skull popped open like a melon when the tire rolled over it.

Page 317:

Page 320:

Rance left Bastrop for New York City, where he now lives with the ex-wife of a very famous television chef and makes his living acting. His big break came in a James Bond (yes, really) directed production of *The Merry Wives of Windsor,* and is now in rehearsal for something called *What Part of Us Am I?* that Wayne Maugans is doing off-off Broadway. He plays a hard-drinking, sometimes nasty trailer-park denizen named Bromo. The kind of guy he used to defend in court. He hasn't heard from Emma in years, knows she stopped seeing the Bleeker guy whose wife never died. He thinks about her every day, misses her, longs to talk with her, but is happy to be away.

Page 321:

Not as surprised, though, as our author was to see Miranda outside of Lafayette. Her job had been to characterize Grisham, and nothing else. But when that refrigerator light washed over her naked body and then she made soup on the rocks, well, our author thought one more visit won't hurt. Plus he'd never been to Carencro except to drive through it. And then when she held those fistfuls of chickens and longed for escape, he knew she was not going away. Some characters refuse to be dismissed. Thank God for them.

Page 324:

With the help of Royce's old Confederate half dollar—one of only four such coins minted, and the only one uncirculated—which she sold for $750,000.

Page 325:

The fact that the carnage was insensitively described by some anti-gun activists as "deliciously ironic" did not lessen the tragedy. Seventeen dead, thirty-three injured. The Democratic-Republicans* in Congress debated gun-control legislation for weeks in and out of committee, held hearing after endless hearing, awaited the FBI report, which dismissed allegations of a left-wing conspiracy to embarrass the NRA, and labeled the killer, Randall Crandall, "a mal-adjusted adult acting alone." And in the end they did the expected, they did nothing. Too much money and mythology invested in firearms to turn back now. The NRA's official response to "Heston's Last Stand" was this: "We're talking about an iconic bedrock here. The right to bear arms is the basis of the American democracy which is widely regarded as the first true democracy in the world, and arguably the best."

Page 363:

The Democratic and Republican parties had, a year earlier, stopped their smirking and admitted finally what everyone already knew, that they were indeed one party, and they officially merged, thereby saving the taxpayers hundreds of millions of dollars in campaign spending.

Also by JOHN DUFRESNE

"An extraordinarily generous and lyrical storyteller."
—San Francisco Chronicle

Love Warps the Mind a Little

"Dufresne manages to meld comedy and tragedy in the story of a maniacally humorous, willfully unenlightened fellow from Worcester who must learn the hard way where to find love."
—The Boston Globe

Louisiana Power & Light

"The miraculous beauty of his tale-telling surprises and delights."
—The New York Times Book Review

AVAILABLE WHEREVER PAPERBACKS ARE SOLD

Reading Group Guides Available at
www.penguinputnam.com/guides

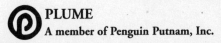 **PLUME**
A member of Penguin Putnam, Inc.